THE ZOO

Annie,
Be Brave!
Patrick McLaughlin

PATRICK MCLAUGHLIN

ISBN: 069293393X
ISBN 13: 9780692933930

A VERY SPECIAL THANKS!

Carol McLaughlin (Editor)
Jason Platt (Book cover artwork)
Kate Duffus (Web Design)
Jerry J. Davis (Photography)
Molly McLaughlin (Encouragement)
Robert McLaughlin (Patience)
Dr. David Birdsell (Photo location)
Jodie Toohey (Wordsywoman)

CHAPTER 1

The Earth circled the Sun in its rightful place in the universe as it has for over four billion years. In the heart of the Midwest, the hot summer was coming to an end, and the days were starting to get shorter. A peaceful community of family and friends went about their daily lives without the feeling of any threat from the outside world. The moon and the stars were cast across the sky as people enjoyed the festivities that summer brings every year. For eight people of the community, this was the night that would forever change their lives.

Laura Redgrave turned off all the lights in the house. She didn't want to be visible from the outside. She wanted to remain invisible to all the people in the night watching her who really weren't there. But her mind told her they were out there just the same. The night time and isolation of the country had a way of doing that. People can see into a lighted house, but the people inside can't see back at them. They are blocked by a solid wall of night. Laura had always been spooked by it. That feeling of eyes on her every move made her skin crawl. Ever since she had been a young girl it made her feel uncomfortable. She came out to her parents' house that night, or any night, to get away from the uncomfortable feeling she had about her life back in Moline. It was the job that she had, the never-ending flow of bills that seemed to stack up in her mailbox, and the perspective that her life was like running in quicksand. She was a waitress at the Bachelor Pad. It was a busy restaurant where every man's eyes stared her up and down more and more as the alcohol flowed.

The money was good but she had taken the job out of necessity. She was twenty-eight years old and after graduating from college she couldn't find employment in her field, and she needed to work somewhere. Her student loan payments were around the corner and they were expensive. But she knew that's the price you pay to get a better job for a better future.

Laura knew that she was worth more than the wishful love bunny to a bunch of men with beer goggles on. She couldn't stand how closing time was the time these men decided that they were lonely and might actually have a chance with her. Laura called it "liquid courage."

Her parents had gone into town for dinner and perhaps a movie. This was an adventure for them because they were homebodies. They stayed away from the city as much as they could and worked on their lawn and gardens. She appreciated their letting her come out for the night although she was always welcomed to visit.

Laura moved into the kitchen and opened the refrigerator. The refrigerator light cast a white square onto the floor of the dark kitchen. The cold air drifted out and felt good on her face. She surveyed the products and grabbed a beer from behind the orange juice.

"I'll keep the tip," she said and tossed the bottle cap into the sink.

Laura walked out on the front porch. She wore jeans and a thin blue T-shirt. Laura thought she might need her sweater later that night.

It was sometime after ten o'clock and the night was beautiful. The moon was out and so were a few clouds that were spread about like patches in the sky. She stood for a minute looking at the road in front of the house. The road led away in opposite directions. The one direction on the left led into the city. She didn't want to look back there.

She decided to look to the right and look to the future. Where will it lead? Like the road leading over the horizon. Where will the road of life take her?

Laura sat her tall slender frame down in the rocking chair. The moonlight cast some light on her pretty face, shapely figure, and long legs. A strong breeze blew her brown hair around and then laid it back down neatly on her shoulders.

She crossed her legs, started rocking, and sipped her beer. The rhythmic creak of the wooden rocker had a hypnotizing affect. Back and forth as if Laura was working together with the crickets to create a symphony of night music.

Laura's thoughts wandered away and her mind fell into a state of passiveness. She relaxed. And as she did so, Laura was letting go of the question of where her life was going. Where will it lead her? That kind of stress built up inside her over time and it scared her. It was like spinning around a merry-go-round, with your legs flying out, and white knuckle hands holding on for dear life. The constant struggle not to let go or risk falling away. But she was starting to let that go. Almost gone was the fear from uncertainty and the unknown. Laura thought that rules and laws existed to be able to predict the future. It was man and womankind's way to know what lies ahead without any surprises. However, that didn't help comfort her insecurities because she still didn't know what surprises waited around the corner for her. But this was a time for no surprises. This was a time not to be vulnerable. She was safe. She was out of the city and at the house she grew up in. Another swig of beer and she put her head back on the chair. Laura was feeling good.

The lids above her eyes started to sink and they were almost closed when something to the west caught her attention. She leaned up in her chair, the wood creaked underneath her, but on a second look dismissed it as her imagination. There was nothing but stars out there.

Again, Laura started to think about her life. She couldn't help it. Her brain was wired that way. She didn't have a boyfriend. Just jerks that she used to date. Her family was good. Both of her parents were healthy and enjoyed the good life.

She looked at the trees across the road. The leaves rustled as soft breezes sifted through them. *They look so beautiful*, she thought. Silent giants that stood tall and proud, reaching up to the sky.

A cloud covered the moon and it was a little darker out. The temperature was perfect for a summer night.

Laura looked up and gazed at the stars. There were so many to see away from the city's glare. It was so beautiful out. A peaceful ambience had covered the land.

Laura followed the stars to her right where the road narrowed and vanished in the west. Her eyes moved from star to star.

One moved.

Laura blinked. It moved again. She leaned forward curiously. One star was growing bigger and moving towards her. It changed direction. Now this star was moving downwards. A boding silence crawled up around her and blocked everything out. Laura stayed still, her eyes so wide open they felt dry. This object certainly didn't move like a star. It kept dropping in the sky.

Laura studied it. She thought the star was jittery like the moonlight was reflecting off it. She had seen that effect on airplanes before. For a moment, she became alarmed and thought it was a crashing airplane. However, she knew it couldn't be. This was moving straight down in a controlled way. It wasn't falling out of the sky.

The star disappeared in the distant horizon behind the trees.

Laura sat back and started to rock in her chair. She sipped her beer and contemplated for a moment what it might have been. She knew it was strange because most things don't move like that. All her life she hadn't seen a shooting star but she knew this wasn't one of those. It couldn't be an airplane. Perhaps it was a giant balloon? A lot of people do that out in the country during the summer. But this wasn't moving like an airplane or a balloon. Again, she couldn't get over that the direction it was traveling was down. Maybe it was crashing? She shook that off immediately and reasoned it couldn't have been a crash and was probably a meteorite heading straight down to Earth.

After a minute, Laura looked back at the trees and around the yard and drank more of her beer. Her attention came back to her surroundings. The crickets were louder now and mosquitoes were starting to buzz around more. She slapped one off her arm and flicked another one from her leg. She hated those vampiric little insects.

Laura didn't want to have her night ruined by everyday frets so she tapped into her inner chi, her energy of life, that she was learning to harness in her Tai Chi classes she'd been attending. She found chi was a useful shield to fend off worries. Laura began to focus on positive thoughts and block out negativity. Laura didn't want to miss her yoga classes next week either. The meditation helped soothe her anxieties. Both disciplines helped her daily life. They relaxed her soul.

And so did her beer. She sipped again.

Laura looked down at the porch floor. There was some strange bug with lots of legs crawling by her foot. She brushed it away without crushing it. Her cell phone beeped in her pocket to tell her she had a message waiting to be read. She pulled her phone out of her pocket and turned it on casting light on her pretty face. It was a message from her parents. She began to read. As she did the phone died. Laura clicked again but the phone stayed blank. Her cell phone had always been frustrating out in the country. She put her beer down, stood up, and held her phone out to catch a signal. Her phone came back to life. Laura decided to call her mom and sat back down in the chair. She started to rock again while the phone rang.

The phone went silent and blacked out. Laura stopped rocking. Something didn't feel right. The crickets were silent. The warm summer breeze was still. Her chair squeaked as she leaned forward for a better listen. The country had become deathly quiet. She looked around. Nothing moved but something was there. The hairs on her arm began to prickle and a chill went up her spine.

Something rose up and hovered above the trees across the street. In the glancing moonlight a massive shape hung level to the horizon. The top of it reflected the moonlight that curved underneath its metallic underside. It was noiseless and didn't disturb the night air.

Her blood froze. Laura's muscles clamped down on her and she couldn't move. Her body was like a statue. She watched it.

The shape started moving towards the house.

Laura sprang out of the chair and ran into the house. She threw the light switch without breaking stride but there was no electricity and the lights didn't come on. She yelled as she tripped over a footrest and went sprawling onto the living room floor. The cell phone flew out of her hand and bounced around somewhere. Cursing, she looked around the room. It was very dark and quiet. The only sound was her heavy breathing. She looked to the windows from where she lay but couldn't see anything through the blinds.

What was out there?

She crawled over to the front window. Leaning against the wall, heart pounding, breath withheld, she slowly peeked outside and saw nothing but the road. Her eyes darted back and forth. Her breath came back to her and she ducked down again. She looked around the room. She looked at the doorways leading to the kitchen and dining room. Laura didn't know what to do so she listened. There was no noise. She crawled over to the window on the side of the house and looked out but only saw an empty yard. She sat in a crouched position and waited. *It's gone*, she thought.

And then she felt it. A presence. Something had come into the house. And now it was in the room. Laura touched the floor. Her fingers felt a slight vibration on the floor but she didn't trust her instincts right now. It might be her frightened body shaking. She could only feel it's presence radiating throughout the room. It was looking. Searching the house to probe for her. Desperately, Laura's mind started to scramble. What did it want? And why?

Then it moved into the dining room. Her mind seemed to shut down. She didn't know what to do except to stay still and hide. The presence passed through the room and moved upstairs. The stairs vibrated in the center of the house. Laura felt the probing in the walls. The ceiling seemed alive. It continued to move throughout the upstairs.

Laura didn't move. She couldn't. She didn't think it had found her yet. A faint glimmer of hope started to grow in her head that she would survive. That she would make it out of this alive and everything would return to life as normal. But that faded when she felt it come downstairs again. It moved into her room. It stopped.

Laura felt paralyzed. Her muscles clenched hard to keep her body from flinching and she held her breath. It was waiting. Under her feet she felt its vibration in the floor boards. She felt it move through her body and echo inside her head.

And then it was gone. It moved out frighteningly as suddenly as it had arrived. Laura sat motionless. She waited listening to the silence. Time in the room slowed down. Nothing moved. She watched. Trying to feel for its presence but there was none. She touched the floor but it was still. Laura sat in the darkness. It was her only companion now. An unwanted companion. The only sound was her breathing. Yet, she couldn't get that feeling away from her that something would come up behind her.

Laura slid across the floor and looked around. Still nothing. After another hard listen to the emptiness of the house, she stood up and cautiously went into the kitchen. The steady hum of the refrigerator was missing and replaced by the metallic tap of a few drops of water leaking from the faucet into the sink.

Laura looked at the dark kitchen. It was like the end of a cliff and she stood on the edge. With one step and she would free fall endlessly. She stepped forward but didn't fall. She was standing in the kitchen. The floor was real. This was real. Slowly, she moved to the sink. Her hands gripped the counter and she looked out the window. Outside there was nothing except the yard that she had grown up playing in.

Laura went back into the living room. She saw the front door had shut from when she had thrown it open. It was too dark to see the furniture, so she took one step at a time, with her arms held out in front to catch herself in case she fell. Relying on her memory of the room, she slowly walked through it to the front door, and peeked out from behind the shade. It was pitch black outside. There were no cars driving on the road. She didn't see the massive shape. Laura grasped the doorknob. For a long moment, she squeezed it and held her breath. Then she turned the knob, cracked open the door a little and listened. It was very quiet. She opened the door and began to go outside. The floor creaked. It echoed throughout the house. She froze. Nothing happened. The only sound she heard was her breath escaping from within when her body relaxed. She felt more confident now and stepped onto the porch.

The silence was eerie. Laura got the shivers. There wasn't even a nightly breeze. On her left the rocking chair was in its place. The beer sat on the porch. Laura held on to the doorframe as she looked around. The darkness was creeping around everywhere. It crawled up her legs. Then she stepped forward to the top of the porch stairs, looked up at the sky, but there were only stars to see. And it was all quiet.

The earlier feelings of panic and fear had turned into bravery. It was gone. Everything was all right and she was safe. Laura walked down the front steps and out into the yard.

From above a beam of light surrounded Laura and her body was thrown back rigid. She was scared again! Her body was held in an invisible grip. She couldn't close her eyes. Yet, they didn't burn. A humming sound radiated down and surrounded her.

The hovering shape moved out from over the house with the beam shooting out of the center underneath. It stopped directly over Laura. The shape was a metallic craft wider than a house. Laura focused above her. Three lights shined red and blue around the center beam of bluish-white light. The humming had a life of its own and she was surrounded by some sort of power.

Laura felt her feet lift off the ground. She screamed but nothing came out. Tears swelled in her eyes. Laura felt herself rise upwards. She was moving up into the craft. Laura went into helpless panic. Her thoughts were disbelief and fear. She screamed again, but without knowing if her mouth got her cry out. "Oh, my God! No! No! Not me! Take someone else! Please!"

The beam vanished. The lights disappeared into the center and the shape shot off without a sound.

The only sound left was from the porch where the chair rocked back and forth.

CHAPTER 2

Robert Stein drove along in the country staring ahead at the headlights as they disappeared into the darkness of the night. Robert couldn't help but think of his sports car as a cross-eyed monster screaming down the road. A metallic hellion in which he was the master and in control.

He turned up the volume on the radio and started to play the imaginary strings of a guitar on the stick shift. Robert was feeling festive. It was Friday night and he was coming from closing an advertising deal. The commission would be a good one. Money. Money. Money. That's what he liked! Robert realized that the long drive outside of town was worth it. The world of radio sales was hard. Many people had warned him beforehand that it was the toughest sale around. On top of that was the large margin of turnover in the business. It was like a revolving door of people coming and going. Secretly, Robert thought that might be the reason he was still around. Enough sales people above him had either quit or been fired for him to inherit some of the good accounts. It was so much easier to make a monthly sales quota that way. However, even with some consistent accounts he was struggling. Robert didn't think he was cut out for sales. His friends told him that he didn't have the discipline for it. Robert was a smart-ass, if that was a required skill. However, he kept trying and to this day he had still made it. The deal he had just closed would help. All he had heard this week was that their ratings were down. *To hell with the ratings*, he thought. It's time to celebrate.

The dashboard lights illuminated up at him and he felt a little better. He was only a few miles out of town but the darkness of the night surrounded him. He looked out the windows and the rearview mirror and it made him feel alone. A feeling of isolation came over him. There was something about being away from civilization and the control of man-made environments that can do that to people. Right now, Robert was one of those people.

The road flew by underneath him and the music rocked from the speakers. The windows were down and the wind was whipping around inside. It felt good. Robert started to amuse himself by turning the car's brights on and off. Maybe he would see the reflection of an animal's eyes staring blindly back at him. Just not on the road. Anywhere but there.

The DJ cut in over the radio: *We're approaching eleven o'clock, so let's kick off a set of maniac rock-n-roll, with a classic "Lights out."*

The song burst over the airwaves and Robert rocked.

Robert's mind turned to women. Maybe I'll find one tonight. Maybe I'll meet one with the same weird interests as myself. Movies, science fiction, heavy metal music, beer, money, shooting pool, sports, and especially football are all desirable interests he told himself. Football and women? Sure! Women like football more than people think. At least on Superbowl Sunday they do. *The rest of himself,* he thought, *will just have to stand behind who he is.*

Robert kept his eyes on the road.

The song blared through the speakers. Robert strummed his air guitar and pressed down on the gas pedal. The car got louder as he sped through the night. Take me home one-lane road.

The radio cackled and static filled the air.

"Ahh, come on," Robert said as he pushed the dials.

"Where's my rock-n-roll?"

Static was on all the stations.

"What's up with that?"

Robert frowned because that was strange. The aerial that broadcasts his stations' signals must be out. But it wasn't just his stations because all the stations in the area were out. One broadcasting aerial knocked out isn't out of the ordinary and he understood that. It happens. But all the signals over town being down? That was strange. Rob knew it could be from a lightning strike but he looked around and didn't see a storm. It could be heat lightning but he hadn't seen any flashes in the sky. Lightning could have struck one aerial. However, lightning striking all the aerials in the area seemed impossible and he knew that the odds for that must be astronomical.

Robert fumbled for his cell phone but kept his eyes on the road. There was still no sign of lightning. He clicked on his cell phone. More static. His phone was tossed on the seat in disgust. A hundred-dollar phone bill and for what? Hundred-dollar static.

Robert continued to eye the sky around him as the road went on endlessly. He felt like he was driving on a conveyor belt. It didn't seem like he was getting anywhere, much like he felt about his life at times, and to make it worse he had no music and his phone wasn't working.

There was still no lightning and the moon was out. It looked like a big cookie that was pasted to the sky. Stars decorated the night. The static sounded like a hundred snakes in a bad mood. Robert bit his lip as he imagined all of them inside his dashboard, upset, and ready to get out.

The road rolled by and he switched on the air conditioning. Between the wind from the windows and the cool air blowing on his face he felt very comfortable. He loosened his tie and checked the stations again. The radio continued to hiss.

Robert sighed and continued to stare at the headlights ahead. They pulled the car along through the night. No matter how fast the car went he would never catch them.

The static from the radio began to take over. Robert stared ahead as the hissing surrounded him and spread out through the car. It moved over the dash, up the seats, and around the sides of the car. The sound reverberated inside his head, bounced between his ears, and he went under a spell. His eyes blinked more slowly as his mind started to rest. His focus was just on the road ahead. The tires thumped on the cratered road like a heartbeat. Air cooled his skin and his breathing got slower and heavier. It felt good. He gripped the steering wheel as his sense of hearing and touch felt fulfilled. His mind stopped thinking but his instinct to drive didn't. The ambient hissing comforted Robert like a friend. The friend sang to him in a language his conscious didn't understand but his subconscious did. The friend's song said to him that everything was safe, he should pull over and stop the car. The friend assured him that everything was wonderful and that he would like to stop. All so slightly, the friend praised Robert as a super human being, and great rewards waited for him when he stopped the car and got out.

Pull over. Pull over.

Robert snapped to attention as a grinding roar of tires and gravel erupted underneath him. His body jerked as he rolled the steering wheel to the left. The seatbelt held him tight. Rocks shot out the back as the car veered back onto the road. Clouds of dust were left behind. Robert steadied the car and blinked hard. He looked back through the rearview mirror but saw only darkness. Pay attention! He was angry at himself.

The car was steady again. Robert let out a big exhale as he gathered his thoughts. He was thinking in overdrive and had to regain control. Robert questioned himself as to what was he doing and scolded himself for how clumsy and stupid he'd been.

Robert looked around him. He was still driving east into town. The moon was high in the sky and the headlights continued to pull him through the night. The radio was blaring static so Robert turned it off and pressed on the gas. The clock was blinking twelve o'clock. Great. Now it'll have to be set again.

A minute or two went by and he was still feeling shaken. Alertness wasn't a problem for him now. He opened his eyes as wide as he could to bring back a full awareness of consciousness. Nothing around him seemed to have changed. The road was still bumpy, and aside from an occasional cornfield, trees surrounded the road like walls. Robert thought they probably hated the road. It prevented them from formally meeting their brothers and sisters on the other side. They were dark. Robert couldn't see anything through them. They were like an army standing in line. There wasn't any sign of animals either. Robert thought that he might have seen a few earlier but there wasn't any sign of them now.

Robert pressed on down the road as his headlights led the way. Robert saw a road up ahead that branched off to the right. He couldn't see where it went before the trees swallowed it up. He started to slow down. The car calmed as it obeyed the driver. He decided to turn here as he came up to the road. But he questioned himself why? He knew this road didn't take him back to the city and there certainly wasn't anything out here to see. Who knows where it leads to? Yet, Robert felt this was the thing to do.

Turn here. Turn here.

Without stopping Robert hit the blinker and turned right. For some reason, he had to go this way. He even wondered for an instant why he used his turn signal. There wasn't anyone out here. But that was habit. However, it wasn't habit for him to do something so spontaneous like this. Robert liked plans. Things were always premeditated. They didn't always get followed in order or done to the minute. And he didn't like to waste time driving. When there was a place to go, he wanted to get there in a hurry. Turning off the main road didn't help him get to his destination, back to civilization, but still he had turned off. There was some driving force, some reason, motivating him to do this. It was something he had to do. He didn't care. This was the way to go.

Robert started to feel as if he was being watched.

The car was shifted into fifth gear and dust kicked up as it gathered speed down the one-lane road. The army of trees aligned on both sides of the road. They were taller now and closer to the road making the road look smaller. To his peripheral vision, they were marching along in formation with his car, but he kept his eyes on the road ahead that stretched forth and didn't have an end. He was looking at the same picture of road, trees, and the darkness intertwined about. The headlights gave no clues but they continued to pull him along. Something kept driving him on. He knew this was the way to go.

Robert eyed the clock. The flashing was replaced by a fast rotating pattern, moving left to right, and repeating every second. Robert's eyes darted between the road and the clock. He knew this was strange. His clock was alive and was behaving hysterically. The pattern was systematic but he didn't recognize it. The clock continued left to right. It was as if the car's mind was being read.

Robert stared at the clock. It was drawing him in and hijacking his vision. He knew he couldn't let this happen again. He tore himself away and saw something up ahead. There was a shoulder on the right of the road coming into view.

Turn off. Turn off.

He slowed the car down.

Pull over. Pull over.

He turned the blinker on.

Turn here. Turn here.

Robert arrived at the clearing and turned into it. The car bounced him around before he steadied it. The sound of the dirt road was an echo replaced by the soft grassland. He put the car in neutral and rolled to a stop.

The headlights lit up the trees standing twenty feet in front of the car. A fence was holding them back. The red brake light cast the same picture in the rearview mirror. The only sounds were the car motor and the air blowing on his face. His eyes felt dry. He blinked.

Over his shoulder crept up that feeling of being watched. The creeping perched on his shoulder like a bird. It moved up the neck and ran like fingers through his hair. It crept and drifted throughout the car. Robert began to feel a connection between this and out there behind the trees. Something there in the woods was watching. He stared through the window and waited.

Get out. Get out.

The clock was blinking twelve o'clock again.

Come here. Come here.

He pulled the emergency brake and got out of the car. The night was perfect. The moon and stars were out. High up were a few clouds that added to the picture. They were outlined by the moonlight. A slight breeze passed over the land. It was warm out without much humidity.

However, there was something amiss that he couldn't put a finger on. Standing next to his car door, he looked around, but nothing was out of place other than his being there. The question lingered on his mind: What had compelled him to come this way? And then it was gone. Remaining was the feeling that this had been the way to go, that everything was safe, and there was nothing to fear.

The moon moved behind some clouds.

Leaving the car door open, Robert walked in front of the car and stopped on the other side. He stared into the woods. The woods stared back.

He moved toward the fence and stopped. The country night was dead silent. Robert knew that was weird. He listened harder. Still there was nothing. No insects. No frogs. There was only silence other than the soft hum of his car behind him.

Robert continued to the fence. He watched and waited but it was only dark and remained quiet.

Now Robert wondered why he had gotten out of the car. He would never do something like this. Turning off the main road was bizarre enough but getting out of the car too? Again, his thoughts were overridden and told him this was what to do.

Robert stared at the trees and out beyond them. They filed in formation back into the night. They stood like soldiers, some with perfect posture, others leaning to the side, waiting for the call to battle. His eyes moved up and down the trees, and he could see the darkness creeping around, intertwining with the army. The blackness formed a web, a solid bond, that prevented any penetration by his eyes to see any further. However, it wasn't only his eyes that disturbed him. It was the feeling of eyes being on him now. The feeling of being watched was growing stronger. With that the silence was increasingly ominous and he began to feel as if he was waiting for something.

Then something slowly rose from behind the trees in front of him. Red and blue lights glowed underneath it. Robert's mouth dropped open and his eyes widened in awe and he saw a massive shape. A flying saucer? Robert watched in disbelief but he knew this was happening. It was real. The shape hung at tree level. There was a pulsing sound like an electrical heartbeat emanating from it. The object hovered in the air. Robert waited.

It moved forward towards Robert but he didn't move. He knew he should run but couldn't get his legs to move. His mind kept telling him that standing there was the correct thing to do. However, Robert didn't think it was his mind telling him this, and it was coming from someplace else. The shape floated and stopped directly over him. Rob saw that the shape was a spacecraft. The pulsing radiated all around him and was rooted in the ground. His feet felt it vibrating underneath him. Robert stood staring up at it and saw the red and blue lights glowing around a bluish-white light in the middle. He couldn't look away. It was mesmerizing. The craft blocked out most of the night sky. The pulsing grew stronger each second. Robert's feet stuck hard to the ground while he studied the bottom of the craft. He could see that it was smooth and there weren't any visible markings or symbols. His eyes stared. The lights glowed down on him.

Then Robert's mind started to stir and he remembered stories about people being abducted by aliens and taken aboard spaceships and never seen again. There were stories about strange tests being performed on them. Stories about alien babies with human mothers. Stories about medical procedures from hell. Stories that people are ridiculed for. Stories that scare people. Now he was scared.

Robert turned and ran to the car. He ran as fast as he could despite slipping a few times in his dress shoes. Air sucked down into his lungs and burst out each time he got up. He rounded the car, almost lost his balance again, his torso way out in front of his legs, jumped in the car and slammed the door behind him.

Robert looked up and saw that the craft was over the car. It had followed him. The pulsing now vibrated throughout the car. Looking up he began to feel horror-struck.

He slammed down the emergency brake and floored the car in reverse. His mind was racing in a mad scramble. Robert was acting on instinct to get away.

The tires screamed and grass and dirt flew from underneath. The car drove back away from the craft. He was leaving it behind. The craft now hovered in front of him. He floored the gas pedal.

The car jerked violently to a stop. Robert snapped back and was thrown forward. His head slammed against the steering wheel and he felt pain. Something warm rolled down into his eye. In the rearview mirror, he saw a gash on his forehead. He was bleeding.

There was a metallic crunching sound and the car started to move forward. Robert panicked. It was still in reverse so he pressed the accelerator. The car still rolled toward the craft as if a magnetic force was pulling it. He threw the stick in neutral and slammed his foot down on the brake. The car continued forward as if it had a mind of its own. Robert swore! He didn't know what to do. He pulled up the emergency brake but that didn't help. The car rolled forward anyway. Through the windshield he looked up at the craft. He was moving closer to it. Robert freaked. It was as if he was a puppet at the end of the strings. He was powerless to get away. His mind was confused and he couldn't think.

Closer and closer the car was pulled back to the craft. The lights glowed down over the car. The craft hovered perfectly.

The car went dead. Headlights, interior lights, and air conditioning stopped. The sound of the engine was gone. Its vibration throughout the car was still. Robert sat inside the car which was dark and quiet. He stopped his emotions from grouping together into hysteria and resigned himself to the thought that he was going to die. Death was pulling him in. However, he wouldn't go quietly. Robert would fight if he could. The car was a cage that he was trapped inside of and he didn't dare to step out yet. In the back of his mind questions rattled around that wouldn't go away. Why had he come this way? What had compelled him to do this? Why me?

A calming feeling came down and took possession of him. Robert's body relaxed. His soul put to ease. As before, reassuring feelings flowed into his thoughts. All is good. Everything is marvelous. This is what to do.

The invisible force pulled the car underneath the craft. At first nothing happened. Robert looked up through the windshield. It was the same as before. Red, blue, and the bluish-white light in the middle shined down on him. He opened the door and got out. Robert stood there, looking up at it and felt closure. He was completely serene. Whatever was going to happen should happen now. The answers to all his thoughts, emotions, feelings of being watched, and overall strangeness to the evening would be revealed.

Do not be afraid.

The only sound was the pulsating hum. The lights glowed. Robert stared without blinking.

The bluish-white light in the center flashed and he was momentarily blinded. It surrounded him. It grabbed him. Robert felt his feet lift off the ground. He tried to move but couldn't. That was impossible. He was paralyzed. He was going to die. At least it wasn't painful. He was floating up into the ship. At that moment Robert asked God for forgiveness.

The beam of light vanished and the shape went dark and moved silently to the east.

The moon broke from the clouds. The car came back to life and coughed silent.

CHAPTER 3

Travis Rhodes tightened the tripod on which the camcorder sat.

"Got it. All set. I just hope the batteries were charged," Travis said as he straightened up. He looked over to his right.

Katie Dawson swung the backpack off her shoulder and walked his way. She was petite with blond hair down to her shoulder blades.

"Hey dude, we're charged like Marge," she answered.

They were at a spot on a hill they knew well because during the two years they had dated, they liked to come out into the country and watch the stars at night. They always dressed in black to keep in the spirit of their adventures. Travis had a good telescope. They liked to look at the constellations like Orion, Cygnus, and Scorpius and to look for the now rumored Sagittarius X that scientists thought existed somewhere in the Sagittarius constellation.

Katie dropped her backpack on the ground and it landed with a thud. Travis bent over and unzipped the top. He reached in, fumbled around, and pulled out the camcorder. He turned it on and looked through the eyepiece.

"We're gonna get proof tonight," he said moving the camcorder around. "The tabloids will want us. The media, too. They'll pay big money for this stuff."

"Evidence, Travis," said Katie. "Evidence. Proof is the end result. You need evidence to build a case." Katie spoke to him like she was smarter than he was. That was fair play though. He did that to her too. It was a game. "That's right though. They're out there. We're gonna get a UFO sometime and one of these days, one of these days, we're gonna get one."

"When you said sometime was it with one word or two?" Travis slowly smiled as if he had dealt the final blow in a debate. He usually found grammatical error in her papers for school. For him it was enjoyable to point out errors and watch a scowl come over her face. It was a signal that he'd won. Each time was a victory in their little games. But mostly he did it because he loved her and wanted her attention in any way that he could get it.

Katie, on the other hand, had the better grade point average. They were both students at the local community college. Katie was really good on tests. She had enough discipline within herself to buckle down, block out the world, and study the information that people learn for tests and is forgotten within weeks. She had managed an A average so far and was very proud of that. So were her parents.

Travis wasn't the greatest student. He had a C average but didn't think it was his fault. He was a smart person just like Katie. However, textbooks and subjects that didn't interest him were a waste of time. Most of all they didn't stimulate him to learn. Travis viewed a college degree basically as evidence that he'd paid a lot of money for the right to get a leg up on the ones that didn't for the job. Or at least that's the way it used to be.

What they both had in common was a fascination for UFOs. Both believed that life exists in the universe. They considered it ignorant to think that it didn't. There was just too much out there for the universe to be vacant. They had seen the television shows with videos of flying objects, witnesses who have seen spacecraft and beings from outer space, and people taken aboard the crafts. The government wouldn't admit it. There seemed to be an endless number of skeptics. But despite all of that it hadn't convinced everyone. Especially Travis and Katie. They believed something was happening all over the world. There was no credible evidence. Travis and Katie were looking to get some.

Travis aimed the camera at the moon and focused the lens. Then he panned left and right. Feeling satisfied he walked over and sat down next to Katie. She had a notebook and a pen out. Two binoculars lay on the ground next to them. Together they both looked up to the sky and began to wait.

CHAPTER 4

Carol Anderson always drove the speed limit even when out in the boonies. While in town the speedometer hardly went over thirty miles an hour. On Interstate 80 it didn't break the speed limit either. On the few times that it did the speed of the car drifted upward just because her foot got heavy on the pedal. That was easy to do while she drove along in comfort. It didn't make good sense to Carol to risk getting a ticket and all the hassle that came along with it. First there was having to pay out money for something that wouldn't have happened if she'd exercised more patience. That was such a waste of money. There was the embarrassment as people drove by feeling good that it wasn't happening to them. Then lying underneath all that was that you don't get to your destination any faster by being pulled over by a cop. She was so careful to watch her speed that she was driving forty where there probably wasn't a cop within miles outside of town. But then again there might be one parked on the side just waiting for someone to tempt fate. That was easy to do living out in the sticks.

She drove along singing to the music on the radio. The mile markers passed by as she counted them. Being out this late was extremely rare for her. However, she needed milk for the milk shakes that she was going to make for the kids and their slumber party the next day. Carol frowned every time she thought about how she had spaced off buying milk the last time she was at the store. Carol chalked it up to a momentary lapse into stupidity.

She was divorced from her husband Jack for five years. He had decided that it was fun to behave single again. Carol had been devastated for a good year afterwards but had now recovered very well. She still festered some anger towards him for leaving her with two kids and not being too bothered by the split. He had taken her for granted. He also thought he was going to get the house too. It didn't happen. That was a victory for her.

Her kids were Kenny and Ashley. Kenny was eleven and an underachieving student. He was an overachiever with his video games though. He loved soccer and was an excellent defender. While dominating the defense, he felt on top of the world. He resented the fact that his dad didn't come to many of his games. It was a fire burning deep down inside him.

Ashley was seven and already a bookworm. She didn't harvest too much resentment towards her dad yet. Carol worried every day that anger would start to boil. In fact, she thought it was already there lying in wait and that Ashley was hiding it. If that was the case, Ashley was hiding it well so far because she was doing well in school and had many friends. She was also happiest when she played with her doll Molly. Carol smiled as she thought of Ashley, sitting in the living room, hair pulled back into a knot, with Molly on her lap, and reading a book.

The kids behaved well. That made life easier to handle whenever a crisis in her life developed. She thanked God for children who did what she asked when she was dealing with the stressful times. Another smile pierced her face when she thought of her children.

Most of the stressful times were brought on by her job. It wasn't even the job so much as the environment she had to work in. Carol had worked at a country club for the past nine years. At first her duties were to answer the phones, take messages, and do the "shit work" that the other women in the office didn't want to do. That also meant she was dumped on by every person ranging from the complaining members to the lazy staff. That was the first week.

Then came the newsletter. This was a pain in the ass. Carol had to take all the written articles from the general manager, the board members, the golf pro, her own boss, the chef, the head maintenance man, and the groundskeeper and edit them and make them fit on the pages. It would have gone a lot smoother if she didn't have to change everything every day. Carol thought the big shots at the club were illiterate. She had to constantly correct their spelling and rewrite their incomplete sentences. The President of the Board would change his column five to six times right up until deadline. She thought about how this guy who was making millions had to rely on small-time Carol to make him look good.

After a while more job duties were thrown onto her lap and she tried to look at it as making her more of an asset. However, as the responsibilities continued to mount for her, the pay didn't. She was already thinking of taking her skills and getting a better job somewhere else. A friend had a lead on another job and would get back to her after a few phone calls. Carol would know within a week.

Along with the work she had to deal with were the office politics. Cynthia was the office manager. She was generally kind to Carol but had her times when she made snide comments whenever Carol made a mistake, or the everyday stresses of life grew too much to handle. Carol didn't get too hurt by them because she had learned a lot from Cynthia. More than anybody else at the club, Carol considered her a mild friend.

However, it wasn't Cynthia that hurt Carol. It was Margarette. She was a virus in the office. Margarette gossiped about people, was rude on the phone, and picked on Carol every time she could about no matter what. She had called Carol stupid, illiterate, and a bitch. The abuse Carol had taken from her over the years was about to boil over.

Carol hated her job. Her children again. She smiled.

CHAPTER 5

Travis and Katie sat silently and waited. In the last hour, they had seen five airplanes, two pairs of headlights east to their left, and a headlight west to their right that seemed to bob up and down. Probably some three-wheeler out enjoying the dirt and a few wheelies under a beautiful summer night. They hoped it wasn't somebody who would discover them and kick them off their land.

CHAPTER 6

Carol rolled the car into the driveway and pulled the emergency brake. She grabbed the bag of groceries and stepped out of the car. As soon as the car door shut she had an uneasy feeling. The lights were on downstairs. She looked through the living room windows as she walked by and didn't see her children. She pressed the key into the front door and went in.

Nobody.

"Kenny! Ashley! I'm back from the store! I've got milk!"

No one answered. In the center of the house were the steps leading upstairs. It was quiet. She went through the dining room and put the groceries down in the kitchen.

"Hey kids, I'm back!"

No one came.

"Time for ice cream shakes!" Carol thought that would do it.

She didn't hear a sound or movement of any kind. Usually, they came running to get to the goodies before the other could. Possession of ice cream, cookies, or chips meant power between the two of them.

"Ashley! Kenny! Hello! Where are you?"

She waited but no reply. Nothing like this had happened since their father picked them up for a week last year. He arrived three hours early and she had only been at the neighbors for ten minutes. Carol was frantic when she got home and they weren't there. They had simply disappeared. She was livid with Jack when she got hold of him on his cell phone but at least she had found out that they were all right. It still took a while before relief eventually set in. Those fifteen minutes of panic remained with her this day.

"Kids! Answer me! I've got snacks! If you don't answer me right now I'll remember this at Christmas!"

The sound of her voice didn't get an answer in return. Something moved through the hairs on the back of her neck and crept down to her spine. Carol's motherly instinct took over and she was starting to worry. She went down the hallway and looked in the laundry room and into the den but nobody was there. She was getting really concerned. Carol turned around and opened the door leading down to the basement.

"Kids! You down there? Come out, come out, wherever you are."

No one answered. Now she was getting angry.

She closed the door and went into the living room. The television over on the left was off. Blankets were spread out on the sofa. There were compact discs on the table and movies lay around the floor. Even the family cat Dinky was nowhere to be seen. The silence began to get louder inside her head.

Carol walked over to the bottom of the stairs and listened. There was no noise from upstairs. Next she would check the bedrooms. They were probably hiding in them playing a game. Carol began to climb the stairs. She took each step quietly for the stairs were carpeted. At the top, she stopped to listen. Nothing.

"Anyone here?"

Still no answer.

Carol peered into her bedroom on the left. She flicked on the light but didn't see anyone. Then she went down the hall to the right and came to Ashley's room. Carol opened the door.

"Ashley, honey. You there?"

The only sound was from the ticking of the clock. Carol turned on the light and walked around inside. The room was the same as it always was. Her dolls lay about on her perfectly made bed. Posters of children's movies and television shows decorated the walls. Only a day-old cup of orange juice on the table by the bed was out of place.

She moved down the hall to Kenny's room and pushed open the door. Darkness greeted her. Her eyes adjusted. Some light from a passing car sneaked around the edges of the drawn window shades to pierce the dark. Carol turned on the light. She could see that the room was empty. She stepped inside and listened. Carol's worry turned to fear. What happened to my children? Carol started to leave the room. Then she heard a whimper.

Carol stopped. She heard it again. Her motherly instinct beat down her reaction to scold and she whipped around with her arms held out. Kenny burst out of the closet and into her arms. He buried himself into her shoulder. He was sobbing and she held him tight. Tears rolled down his face and her hair soaked them up.

"What's the matter? Doll baby, what's wrong?" She spoke with a low soothing voice. "It's okay, honey. Everything is okay."

She stroked his hair and he calmed down.

"Why didn't you answer? Why were you hiding in the closet?"

"I was scared," crept from his mouth.

"Scared of what?"

"The flying light."

"Flying light. What light?"

"The light that flies around in the backyard."

"Kenny." Her voice now firm. She held him out with her arms and looked straight into his eyes.

"Where's your sister?"

"She went out with the light."

Carol had no idea what that meant. She needed to keep her thoughts rational.

"What do you mean out with the light? What light?"

"The flying light in the backyard."

Carol stared at him. He looked at her blankly. She didn't know what he was talking about but she knew it wasn't good.

"I don't think it's there right now but it scared me," he continued. "It'll come back."

Carol was cemented where she knelt and unable to move. Her entire focus was on the eyes of her son. She didn't think this was her boy's wild imagination anymore. For her children's sake, she feared whatever this light was.

"The light? What light? What do you mean? Where's your sister?" Reality of the situation was starting to come back to her now. "What do you mean that it scared you?"

Kenny was more calm now. He sniffled and looked at his mom.

"The light that came into the backyard, Mom."

"What do you mean that it came into the backyard?" Carol was starting to get frustrated.

"The light's been here before, Mom." He waited for her response. She continued to look at him. "It's come and asked questions about us. It says that it knows us and wants to be friends. It tells us not to be afraid … but I am anyway. I think it's bad, Mom."

"Who was it?" Carol's anger reflected in her voice. "Was it a man or a woman? Where did they come from? Did they threaten you?" Her grip tightened around Kenny's arms. He winced.

"No, Mom. I told you. It was a light. The light flies here from behind the backyard. It just comes sometimes and talks to us."

"The light is a flashlight," Carol said as a matter of fact.

"No. It's not, Mom. It floats around and asks us questions."

Carol was at a dead end. Nothing floats around. She didn't know where to go with it. And time was going fast and she didn't know where her daughter was.

"It scares me," he added.

She gripped him harder. "Where's your sister? Why aren't you with her?"

Kenny started to cry again. "I told you, Mom. She went with the light out in the backyard. I hid so they didn't take me."

She took him by the hand and led him downstairs. She marched him through the dining room and right up to the glass doors in the kitchen that led to the patio. Carol took notice that the door was unlatched before she opened it. They stepped onto the patio and looked around. Light from the house cast white squares down on the grass. The white squares were decorated with little crosses from the framework of the windows. The swing set was motionless waiting to be played upon. In the back, it was the black of night. A pleasant breeze passed around them and through the trees behind the yard. Clouds hung in sporadic places in the sky and the moon watched over the land. There was no sign of Ashley.

CHAPTER 7

Katie's eyes grew wide with excitement. "Look. Look." Her voice rose as she smacked Travis in the arm.

His head jerked up and he saw it immediately. Down the hill from them, there was a cone-shaped light shooting down to the ground about a half mile away to the west. Something hovered over it. The moonlight reflected off the top to reveal a massive shape in the air. The cone-shape light beamed out from underneath. It was beautiful! There seemed to be someone on a three-wheeler driving around it.

"The video!" Travis yelled. His legs kicked out and he jumped up behind the camera. He immediately panned it over. Travis looked through the lens and started recording. Katie was on her feet and focused her cell phone camera. Their bodies surged with adrenaline as if they were hunting for game.

Katie bobbed up and down and snapped photographs continuously.

"Are you getting this?" yelled Katie, looking back at Travis. She was very excited and breathing hard.

"Yeah, I'm getting it. Oh, man. We're getting it." Travis stood in a trance watching calmly through the eyepiece.

Katie took some more pictures. Travis focused the lens more closely. Then simultaneously they both stood up and stared in awe. The light from the three-wheeler rose, flew towards the shape, and up into the light. They looked at each other with dropped chins.

"Did you see that?" Travis asked, but he didn't expect an answer. Katie didn't give one.

The object with its cone-shaped light was hypnotic. In the moonlight, they watched it hover. There was a humming noise with a pulse radiating from it.

"This is awesome!" said Katie.

"A spaceship!" said Travis.

"Our very own flying saucer."

"Yeah, it is babe. A UFO."

"What's it...." Katie didn't finish.

Something walked into the light. It was a person.

"What is that?" Katie's voice had a sharp edge. "Who is it?"

"I don't know," Travis answered.

They watched the figure in the light. It was shorter than an adult. It was a child.

"Oh, my God," Katie said as realization set in.

"Oh, no." Worry emanated from Travis's voice. He knew this was turning into something more than a Friday night excursion. "What's going on? This is too weird."

Judging by the child's long hair Katie thought it was a girl. "It's a girl. What's she doing?"

As best they could tell, the child was looking upwards into the light, and was waiting for something. She clutched what looked like a doll in her hands. Then the girl's arms raised and began waving. The girl rose off the ground and floated upward into the spacecraft. The beam of light vanished. It was replaced by a slow revolving pattern of dim green lights on the dark ground. The craft remained.

"Holy...." Travis never thought in a million years that he would be witness to something like this. Neither did Katie.

"We better get over there," Katie said as adrenaline, mixed with a touch of fear, coursed through her to create an incredible surge of excitement.

Travis felt it too. "Yeah, you're like so right," he answered. Travis dug into his backpack.

"Hurry," Katie said, impatience overflowing her from within.

Travis grabbed a hunting knife that his dad gave him as a kid and left the backpack on the ground. It would only slow him down.

"Keep the recorder on the saucer!" Katie shouted.

"I am!" Travis yelled back. What did she think, that he was just going to turn it off?

Travis burst down the hill in front of her. Katie ran behind with her camera phone in hand.

They ran toward the lights and their fate.

CHAPTER 8

"Ashley!" Carol stood at the edge of the patio slab. "Honey baby! Come home. Mommy wants you!" She felt as if her voice didn't travel out any farther than the backyard. Her daughter didn't answer back.

Carol cupped her hands around her mouth. "Ashley! Where are you?"

Mother and son waited for what seemed like an eternity. It was only seconds, but they were seconds that sucked out the hope of a quick resolution, and lost that hope out in the night air. Carol knew what she had to do.

She kneeled, took Kenny by the arms, and looked him right in the eyes. "Kenny, now you go inside, lock all the doors, and stay there." She paused. "You do what I say, hear me?"

"Uh-huh," he replied, his head nodding up and down.

Carol stood and walked through the yard and down into the ravine.

Kenny watched her disappear into the darkness beyond. Then he hustled back into the kitchen and locked the patio doors. He quietly stood at them looking out and waited for his mom to return.

She never did.

CHAPTER 9

Travis and Katie rushed through the woods. They dodged trees, swatted away low branches, and leaped over sinkholes. Their vision saw trees rushing past them and hills growing and descending in front of them as they ran. They couldn't see the craft anymore, for they had been on higher ground before and had run down the hills that slanted westward. Their legs felt exhilarated from the sprint. They felt electric up to their waists. Air pumped through their lungs and burst out their mouths in exhaled exhilaration. They were Olympic. They also didn't stop to think through what they were doing. Even if they had, it wouldn't matter, they were going.

A minute or two raced by and Travis braked himself against a tree. Katie was with him in a second. Both breathing heavily.

"Do you see it?" Katie asked in between breaths.

"No." His chest rose up and down. There was nothing like a good run to get the blood flowing. Both were feeling energized.

"How far have we come?" Katie whispered. "We didn't pass it, did we?"

"No. No. We couldn't have," Travis answered. He was looking around, scanning the area.

Then they saw the light flash again. It was just ahead of them, plainly visible, between the trees. They were close.

"Get your camera phone ready," Travis whispered, but he didn't have to tell her. It was in her hand ready to shoot. But Katie wasn't fast enough. There was a flash and the light was gone.

They dashed forward through the trees in a crouching run and zig-zagged along some brush and stopped. Everywhere was quiet. Not an owl. No insects. Nothing. Travis crept forward a few feet and Katie ducked down behind a tree. She watched Travis. He stopped, waited, and signaled for her. She moved up slowly and stopped. They were at the edge of a clearing. It was the size of a small backyard with waist high grass ringed around it. But the center was mowed down. They stared at it for seconds. Why would the center be mowed?

Travis took a step forward and waited. Katie stayed like a statue behind him. They listened carefully. Silence inhabited the area. It lived there. Nothing moved. Not a sound was made but of their own breathing. The silence of the dark woods crept along the ground, up beneath every tree, and circled around every blade of grass. Travis hesitated a few seconds more whenever his intuition told him to go. The woods remained still. He deemed it safe and moved out into the tall grass. Katie swallowed. Then she stepped forward. Travis led her out into the open one step at a time. He stopped. She came up over his back and peered forward. The ground that was mowed down was burned. The moonlight cast enough light to reveal a black circle about twelve feet in diameter.

Travis knelt and felt the burnt vegetation. It was dried black like charcoal and felt like it hadn't received rain in months. The whole area was cooked. Heat emanated up from below. Travis passed his hand over it and felt the warmth. He looked back over his shoulder at Katie and thoughts passed between them. What power could have done this?

Katie was looking around for a sign of anything. It was deathly quiet. No insects buzzed around or anything else called out in the night. There didn't seem to be a sign of anything living. Only she and Travis. Alone....

And where was the child? Or the spacecraft thing in the air? What happened to the ground? Travis looked back at Katie again and one thought passed between them. What are they doing there?

On their right a light circled them. It looked as big as a basketball and it moved fast through the trees. Travis and Katie saw it was the light they had mistaken for a three-wheeler earlier. It circled them. The light was erratic. It went up and down like an electrical signal of a heartbeat. Their eyes followed it. Then it leveled out and flew in a steady motion staying beyond the edge of the clearing. The light was observing them. It flirted with Travis and Katie. They didn't feel flattered. They felt like getting away.

Quickly like rabbits, they dashed back the way they came. They cut in between the trees and crashed through the foliage. There was no need to be quiet anymore as they had to get away. Back to their car. Back to the city. They stumbled a lot, often going down on all fours, scuffing their arms and knees on the foliage but never stopped moving. Immediately, they were up and running again. Katie followed the sound of Travis bursting through the underbrush ahead of her. Travis wished that he had brought a flashlight. Even with the moon out it was difficult to see more than a few feet in front of him. He slapped branches away from his face like he was swatting at flies. His legs hurt from a tree he had slammed into. That slowed him up a bit and now Katie was keeping up with him. She tripped again but scrambled and kept going. Branches slapped and chopped at her in Travis's wake. They stung all over her. Her breathing got faster now. The wind was starting to go out of her sails. But that didn't matter now. She had to keep her will to get away strong. However, she slowed again and glanced around her. The light was darting around in the trees almost parallel to them. Katie sucked in air and dashed forward with a renewed burst of energy. She felt a blinding jolt.

Travis pulled the knife out of his back pocket. He wasn't going without a fight. Just keep running and they will be all right. He and Katie will be back in town again. And with proof. No, it will be evidence, as Katie would say. He looked back over his shoulder but couldn't see her. Travis couldn't lose her out here so he had to stop. He braced against a tree to help stop his momentum. Blood coursed through his body in unison with his breathing. His vision adjusted. It was so dark.

Where's Katie? He couldn't see or hear her. Did she fall? Maybe she ran another direction in panic? Time inside the woods ticked past him slowly. He hugged the tree not to be seen. His eyes grabbed at everything he could hoping to see Katie lying on the ground or running in another direction but he didn't see her. His ears listened but didn't hear her either. There were no cries for help. He was really scared now. She was out here somewhere. Tonight was turning into a disaster for them. He felt as if the whole night had been a trip through the feelings of the soul. He had felt excitement, elation, mystery, panic, and worry that had now grown into fear. That fear was turning into dread that someone very close to him might be hurt. That Katie might not be within his reach anymore. In the moonlight, Travis saw a tree not far from him, and he looked at it for a moment too long. The branches appeared to coil into a configuration of the Grim Reaper's hood and extend out like a scythe. Travis's consciousness dug deep down to his subconscious and shook him free of reality. He shook his head to clear his mind. Travis was a believer, and if the hood and scythe were a dangerous sign, death was here in the woods. And so were he and Katie.

Travis broke free of its grip and refocused. He wasn't going to lose and wasn't going anywhere without Katie. He moved forward, taking each step cautiously and moving up behind tree after tree. Travis was scanning the area for her. He debated for a second to call out for her but decided against it because it might alert the hovering craft to their location if it didn't already know.

He moved up behind a few more trees and stopped. Something glinted in the moonlight. It was small and lay on the ground about ten feet away. After a careful glance around, feeling like a mouse being drawn to an ounce of cheese, Travis dashed to it. He picked it up and saw it was Katie's cell phone. She must have dropped it. But he noticed that it looked broken. He wondered if she had thrown it. Travis stepped over to a tree a few feet away. Using the moonlight, Travis squinted hard, and looked real closely. The cell phone was scarred. He knew she must have thrown it. Travis wondered, *why?* He knew this was a bad thing to find. Where was Katie?

Just then the moon around him was blacked out and the night got even darker. Travis looked straight up at the massive shape as it hung directly over him. The shape began to glow. He was mesmerized by the lights. For an instant, he felt his feet cemented to the earth. Then he flinched.

The light shot down upon him as if from the heavens. Travis dropped Katie's cell phone and stabbed the tree with his knife. It didn't brace him.

Travis felt the light's grip on him tighten and he didn't feel the ground anymore under his feet and he was airborne. Drifting up and away. Helpless. Arms outstretched to nothing. His mind was mystified. The light shielded him from the blackness of the night around him. Where's reality? Where's Katie? Where's he going?

The light vanished. So had Katie and Travis.

CHAPTER 10

Laura Redgrave's peeking eyes opened into a warm, grayish, boring room with a lot of light. In fact, so much light that at first it was hard to open her eyes. Her vision was cloudy on the ends and she couldn't match everything she saw with an answer. Looking around she saw that she was in a metallic room with three tables separated a couple feet apart. There were five distinct lights hanging over each table. She didn't know what the tables were used for.

She looked to her left and saw three naked people sitting on a bench like the one she was on. A man with dark hair, around his mid-twenties, sat on the left. Next to him sat a woman in her forties with brown hair down past her shoulders. A young girl was next to her. The girl also had brown hair and looked old enough to be in first or second grade. Laura's mind was hazy but there seemed to be some resemblance between the girl and the woman around the cheekbone area. The hair color was the same too. They must be mother and daughter. That made Laura question what are they doing here? More importantly, what is she doing here? Where is here?

Laura's mind began to unscramble and focus more. Her eyes scanned the room back over to the right where she saw another man sitting up against the wall. He was also naked and sitting on a bench. Then she realized he was looking back at her.

CHAPTER 11

Shawn Lasky didn't know how long he had been awake. That was if awake was the correct word to describe it. He was alert but not sure if this was real or not and thought it like a strange dream. An all too realistic dream. The room was very well lighted with what looked like autopsy tables positioned in a line in front of him. The little green people that were walking around had been using them. They actually looked more greyish-green. Shawn wasn't sure how many there were. What he did know is how ugly they were. They had these big oversized heads on these little skinny bodies. They were gross. The most frightening thing was their great big black eyes. They were like huge bug eyes and when they looked at you they bore a hole right into your brain. It set his soul on fire. It hurt when they did that. He hoped that one grey guy didn't do that again.

That didn't last as long as the feeling echoing inside his head. This calming feeling kept resonating inside of him and told him to relax and not to worry. It reassured him that he was safe. This feeling made Shawn realize that everything was going to be fine although he didn't know why. Shawn wondered if this were just a dream then why wouldn't things be all right? The feeling was constant like a leaky bucket of water dripping onto his head. Shawn knew that he wouldn't wake up for a while. This dream still had some story to play out.

Shawn looked around the room and his eyes locked onto a pretty, young, brown-haired woman on his left. She was nude and sitting on a bench attached to the wall like he was on. Then he looked down at himself for the first time and realized he was naked too. Shocked from being exposed, he examined himself to make sure he looked all right, but he looked the same. It wasn't cold in the room. He felt quite warm. Shawn tried to tuck his legs together anyway. That was hard enough because his body was mostly paralyzed and he couldn't make any extreme movements. Shawn had tried to get up and walk around but couldn't move and that feeling in his head talked him into staying where he was. He wasn't sure which had held him back more.

Shawn stared at the young woman for a while longer. Again, he thought she was pretty. Then he wondered what's she doing here and how'd she get here? Then his thoughts broke free a little and his consciousness came back to himself. What is he doing here? What happened to him? Shawn remembered that he was fishing and a boat came up to him with a real bright light. Then he was in the light. He remembered a floating sensation. That could have been the beer he had drunk but he was sure that it wasn't. In fact, he wasn't sure what it was. That's about all he could remember other than when he woke up here in this metal room. Shawn was now convinced there wasn't a boat. But for some reason a boat kept popping into his mind, almost like someone or something was putting it there, like placing a book back on a shelf. Deep down he knew that hadn't been a boat. It had been something entirely different.

Shawn kept staring at this woman. His thoughts turned to her safety. What are the little grey dudes going to do to her? They had left him alone so far as he knew. But what he saw them do to the others had been horrifying. The dark-haired guy, the mom, and her daughter. Oh, my God. The little girl. They performed tests on her. You can't do that to a little girl.

But they did.

She screamed like the rest of them. Then she cried until the end. She didn't stop crying until they took her over to the far side of the room with the others. The mother and the dark-haired guy were over there too. At least that's where the grey people put them after it was over.

Shawn realized there were two possibilities and both scared him down to his bones. He was powerless to stop either one. That's just how he felt. Powerless. The first was that the grey people had already done tests on him. At least they seemed like tests. That bothered him because they could do anything they wanted to him. They could just take him like he was a pet, or a lab rat, and do whatever they pleased. He had no choice in the matter. What he wanted didn't mean anything. They didn't care how he felt about it. If they wanted a blood sample from him they could get it in the blink of an eye. If they wanted a piece of his brain, they could take it from him. If they wanted his....

He shuddered at the vulnerability. The feeling of helplessness took away a person's feeling of control, free will, and most importantly their feeling of owning their own inner self.

The other possibility was even worse. Maybe his tests by the grey people weren't done yet. If so, that meant his nightmare was yet to come. With that he more than shuddered. That made him horrified. Shawn hoped they had done whatever it is they do to him while he was unconscious. Shawn thought he was sleeping anyway. This can't be real. Even though he knew it was otherwise. Shawn wondered what God might have to do with this. He knew the answer was nothing. Otherwise, he wouldn't be here. However, if tests were done on him while awake or not, like the ones he had observed done to the others, both were a losing position for him. Again, it's only a dream. Shawn continued to look at the pretty brown-haired woman.

CHAPTER 12

Laura felt shocked. He was looking at her with the same confused look the other three had on their faces. The same look on her face that she must reflect back to him. Laura studied him for a minute. He had brown hair, mixed with some gray, and a bit of a belly on him. His legs were tucked together. Then she felt exposed. Laura looked at herself. She was naked too! Her breasts were in full sight for that man to see. It was no wonder he was looking at her. She tried to cover up but her arms wouldn't move. They seemed glued to her sides. She couldn't move her legs either. Only her head could move. Laura tried even harder to get up but her mind told her now to sit still and relax. *I want to get up*, she thought, but she couldn't move. Every time she thought about moving, another thought came into her mind that covered over it and calmed her into submission. Just stay where you are and everything will be as it should be.

Laura looked back over at the man. He was still staring at her with that confused look. She realized that he must be in a daze just like she was. He wasn't looking at her because she's naked. He was trying to figure things out just like she was.

How did I get here? wondered Laura. The memories in her mind started to swirl around and take shape. Laura remembered being at her parents' house and it was night outside. She remembered being on the porch, looking at the sky, a star moving towards her, and then being chased and absolute fear....

A mental block stopped her memory in motion. She went blank for a split second and then remembered feeling tired and going to bed. The beer she had drunk made her sleepy so she went to the guestroom, pulled the covers over her, laid her head down on the pillow, and slept in the next morning until lunch time. But that didn't make sense. *No! That's not what happened*, she thought. *I was taken....*

Laura's mind stopped and shifted down into neutral. Then a passive feeling of calmness rushed through her mind and down into her body. Laura felt relaxed again like she was sleeping in her parents' guestroom bed. In fact, she was in it right now. This was the place to be. Everything was fine.

The room's temperature set in around her. It was comfortable. The warmth from the floor under her feet channeled up her body and seemed to shoot out her head like she was a conduit between the bottom and the top of the room. She felt so relaxed that sleep was an option now.

Laura looked to her left again. The three visitors sat in the same positions as before but with a scared look painted across their faces. How could they be afraid of something? *It's so nice here*, she thought. They were looking across the room to her right in the direction of the potbellied man. Laura looked back over to her right. The man wasn't staring at her anymore. He was looking the other way. His eyes were wide open. It appeared as if he tried to stand up but couldn't do so. His body raised above the bench but eased itself down again. It was as if someone had directed him to sit and behave.

Laura saw them! Two grey-colored beings walked in front of him. They stood upright, had arms hanging down like humans, and weren't wearing any clothing at all. Their skin was smooth, almost glazed, and their fingers were the length of her hand. They appeared to have a mouth but it was hard to tell. They were only about four feet tall. They were strange looking. They looked like ... like ... those grey people from outer space that you see on television. What are they called? She remembered they're called Greys.

They stood in front of the potbellied man. He looked up at them and stood up like a puppet. *What are they going to do?* she thought.

He turned and walked behind the table to the other side of the room from Laura. The two Greys turned and followed him. She saw his head bob up and down moving from right to left. Then the man crossed the aisle in front of her and stopped at the end of that table. He stood straight without moving. The Greys crossed the aisle too. She saw the tiny back of one standing behind him. It seemed to be waiting. But waiting for what?

Laura looked back over to her left at the three people sitting on the side. They stared with eyes of stone at the man and his escorts. Laura read fear in their eyes. She shifted her focus back in front of her. The man was lifting himself onto the table. Both Greys walked next to the table. The man slid onto the table and lay there motionless. The Greys stood on both sides seemingly at attention.

Laura's eyes shifted to her left. The three against the wall just stared. She shifted to her right with a need for a cry for help. No one was there.

She looked back and now a taller Grey was walking up the aisle to her left and stopped next to the man. It was different from the other two. This Grey was taller and had a longer neck and bigger black eyes. There was a thin mane of green hair that started near the back of the head and went down its back. She sensed this Grey was a male. It also wore a single piece yellow-colored uniform that went down to just above his knees. There was a silver-colored symbol on the front of it that looked like the star symbol that you see on a phone. It walked up next to the man with a gracefulness reserved for a god. Every movement like waves on the ocean. It looked at both Greys and they bowed their heads in obedience. It lifted its long skinny arms in the air as if calling to the heavens.

Something happened above. A giant piece of machinery disconnected and came down from the ceiling. There was a slight reverberating noise as it slowly moved down and positioned itself a few feet above the man. It stationed itself almost like an arm holding out its hand above him. He lay there motionless. At first to Laura, he seemed not to realize what was going on physically, but as she looked harder at his face she saw that he was scared. No, he was more than that. He was petrified stiff!

The Grey stood tall like a flagpole looking at him. Its head tilted downwards on its long neck and scanned over the man from head to foot. This Grey's neck was a sight to see. It reminded Laura of a giraffe's neck. The Grey looked him up and down and its mouth seemed to extend straight outwards almost in a smile.

At that moment Laura felt horrified. The Grey enjoyed what was lying in front of it like the man was a science project. The kind of science project you had back in junior high school where you would cut open the frog's guts to see the eggs. It watched over him like a proud conqueror and would command obedience of its subject on its next step. And yes, it did.

The yellow-dressed Grey nodded to the smaller Grey across the table and then to the Grey standing to its left. They stared back in a complete obedient trance.

Laura looked over to the people on her left. They were watching the table. In the wide eyes and pale faces the inevitable reflected back to her off their faces. *Hell* lies in front of this man.

The mechanical arm extended its fingers out and prods descended and attached themselves to the man's arms, torso, and legs. He yelled out a roaring scream simultaneously as the tentacles connected to his body. Then the prods turned red and a pulsing sound started to emanate. His body seemed to inflate with air and lift off the table for a moment. The yellow-dressed Grey spread his hand out over the table and performed some hand signals.

The metal arm answered.

An electrical surge jolted his body for a second and then a sharp object came down from the mechanical hand above him. It dove quickly down and cut into his gut and sliced without any blood dispersing out. The device cut up and downward and then retracted as another prod descended. This prod positioned itself above and extended small rods that went down into his body and attached something to him.

He screamed and his body shook!

The Greys watched him as the prod ascended back up into the arm.

Laura cried.

The three people over on the left stared stone faced but their eyes gave away their feelings inside. They were suffering too.

The Grey doctor looked over the man in admiration of their work. It was eerie how he moved. His arms waved out in an articulate motion over the table. The Grey had a reptilian movement about him by moving with purpose but without emotion. Yet a sense of pride and arrogance came forth and rushed over Laura as she watched it. The two smaller Greys continued to stare in obedience.

At the end of the table a helmet structure lifted and attached itself to the man. The helmet clamped down and Laura saw he was breathing in and out of his mouth at an accelerated pace. His skin pulled tightly around his muscles as they contracted but he couldn't move. An electrical surge burst down the cord into the helmet and his body wrapped around the table in agony. His head tipped back and his mouth opened and a faint scream leaked out but something too great was happening. His scream died before it could fulfill its frightful life. The man's eyelids closed and Laura could see the eyes darting around underneath. Something was happening to his brain! His toes and fingers flexed sporadically as if suffering from seizures. The three Greys watched without any emotion. It was like ice ran through their veins.

But not for this man.

The surge stopped and the man's body relaxed flat on the table. Laura thought he wasn't even conscious now. Perhaps he wasn't alive. She watched his chest and saw that he was breathing. The Grey doctor signaled to the smaller Greys and they started touching the ends of the tables in front of them. It looked like they were pushing buttons. Then the doctor Grey lifted his head above and there was movement from the ceiling. A large dome-shaped light lowered down and positioned itself a few inches above the man's midsection. The light hesitated for a moment before it moved closer and covered his pelvic area. Lights blinked on and off and a surging sound came down through the instrument.

The man's eyes popped open and his bones seemed to extend outside his body's own limits. Something terrible was being done to him again and he was in shock. From her angle, she could see his face was in a trance gripped with pain. The dome light continued to blink and a white liquidly substance, surrounded in water, shot up through a tube and into the ceiling. The Greys watched. They didn't move. Laura looked again at the three people on her left but this time they were staring back at her. This made her nerves quiver. They turned back to watching the man on the table again.

The dome light lifted off the man and up to where it fit perfectly back into the ceiling. A white-colored tarp covered over it and melted into the ceiling. Laura thought about what kind of technology could do that? Then she quit thinking about it right away because she knew the answer. Only people not of Earth could do that. She shuddered.

And so did the man on the table.

Afterwards, his body seemed to just relax and spill out on the table. His penis was erect but quickly went limp and sent out a discharge. Laura looked away. *They messed with his penis and must have taken his sperm,* she figured. How horrible! *What a violation of human rights,* she screamed inside her head! But she quickly realized that these weren't humans, or anything alive, that could value human rights. These were entities that intruded when they wanted and didn't care about a person's feelings. There was no regard for a person's well-being. They were incapable of understanding the human psyche. These aliens couldn't acknowledge humans. They didn't even realize what people were. These beings were monsters.

The man lay unconscious. The smaller Grey on the left moved around the table and stood with its partner across from the doctor Grey. He looked at them and they reflected back acknowledgement. Laura had no idea what had corresponded between them but the doctor Grey made a signal with his right hand, another probe appeared, and descended from the ceiling. It moved down silently and positioned itself above his stomach. Next a rotating sound like a saw emanated from it and a small blade spun outward and down to his stomach. The blade hummed as it cut into his skin with very sharp precision. Blood quickly shot out and rolled down the sides of his body. The blade cut deeper and more blood spilled but not by splashing all over. The surgical procedure bled in an organized pattern down the sides of his body and into the table where it vanished. The blade stopped rotating, shifted 180 degrees, and then cut down into him again. More blood spurted out and streamed away. He lay unconscious. Judging by the directions the blade had used, Laura figured his stomach was cut in a plus sign pattern. The Greys watched him. Laura felt the doctor Grey approved of what they had done. The skin was flapped up but Laura couldn't see anything more. For this she was grateful. The blade stopped rotating and ascended to the ceiling where it disappeared.

Two small mechanisms that looked like antennas descended from the ceiling and quickly plummeted into the open area. They jerked around in circular patterns and performed whatever task they were meant to do. Laura thought their motions looked like two hands in a sink washing dishes. The bleeding down the sides of the body slowed. Something was happening. The antenna-like arms kept moving. The bleeding came to a stop. The arms stopped as well. They lifted back up into the ceiling and two different thin arms descended and hovered over the open stomach area. Both arms looked like miniature laser guns. The one on the left shot out a white-colored laser that pulled the skin layers back over the open wound. The right gun exploded a blue-colored laser that fused the skin together. A small patch of smoke rose and the smell of burning flesh drifted throughout the room. The laser continued until his skin was repaired. Then simultaneously both rose back up into the ceiling. The man lay motionless.

The doctor Grey looked across at the smaller Greys and they moved to each end of the table. Another surge moved up the table and into the man. He became conscious. Laura thought it was weird how it seemed to carry upwards and out through him. It was technology beyond what she had ever seen. Then his eyes opened. He was conscious again. Without any instruction, he leaned up and over the side of the table and stood. The Grey doctor and the smaller Greys watched him. The man acknowledged another unseen command and walked around the end of the table and back to his original seat. The man stopped, turned rigidly, and sat down where he was when Laura first saw him. The smaller Greys followed him to his seat and stopped. After a moment, they turned and walked to the far end of the room. So did the doctor Grey. They disappeared from Laura's view.

The man sat there motionless physically but emotionally his face reflected pain.

Laura's attention was pulled back to the front of the room. The smaller Greys walked up and stood in front of her. They were so ugly. Their eyes were terrifying. Their fingers even looked longer being closer to them. She was scared. Then she stood up without trying to. Now Laura was terrified because she knew what was next. Across the room the Grey doctor was waiting for her.

CHAPTER 13

Laura's eyes opened and light filled the room with a silent bang and drifted down from above like the spray of an air freshener as it settles upon a living room rug. She felt the comforting ambiance of being at home pass over her. Laura lay backside on the ground, looking up, and her eyes adjusted to the scene. At first, she thought she was home on the floor after falling asleep from watching television the night before. However, as the scene revealed itself she saw a ceiling of light above her. She couldn't see anything solid. It was more like a blanket of light expanding across the sky. Laura sat up while her senses adjusted to the surroundings and took in where she was. Or as it came to her, what she was inside of?

Laura's hands propped her up into a sitting position and it was time for her mind to calculate her new surroundings. The numbers started at zero but slowly added up. It was a room big enough for a football field. A wall stood in front of her that looked transparent although she couldn't see through it. From where she was sitting, the wall looked like a mirror but gave off no reflections. Laura couldn't see herself in it or anything beyond. She stared at it a little more and saw it was moving. The wall flowed together in blue and white colors that reminded her of the ocean. It was as pretty as it was strange.

Laura felt grass between her fingers. She squeezed it a little and her fingers felt it bend. It felt a little different from the grass in Illinois. Laura picked a blade and looked at it closely. The grass seemed artificial in a way. It felt unnatural and its greenish color was weird. She looked around and saw the land was filled with green grass all around her. It even spanned right up to the bright wall in front of her. Laura was sitting in an everyday front yard that you'd see driving along in the country. There were trees spread about the landscape. Over her shoulder, she saw a fountain with a dragon spitting water into the air that rained down into a small surrounding pool enclosed with stone blocks. The splashing of the water was tranquil and had a lazy effect on her. Laura didn't want to get up. Her legs were heavy and her butt felt flat. She'd rather just lie there and vegetate. Laura fought back the lazy spell and wrestled to her feet. She stood unbalanced for a minute, hands outstretched like wings, while her legs adjusted and held tight from buckling under. Something was different. Laura just didn't feel right. She didn't feel at home. She didn't even feel this was the same planet.

Laura sensed something big behind her. She turned around and saw a big white house. In front, there was a porch, a bright blue front door behind a screen door, and four windows with bright blue shutters. The roof was a matching blue and pointed upwards with a chimney of bright-red bricks sticking up in the center. Facing the house, Laura saw a line of trees that formed the boundary of the yard on the left side of the house. There was a group of trees that did the same on the other side of the house. She couldn't see where they ended. In the back behind the house, there were more trees that cast shade in the yard.

Laura took a step forward and stopped. There was something lying on the ground across the yard. Something large. Carefully, she stepped towards it and quickly realized that it was a man.

She ran over to him and knelt down. He was young, probably in his twenties, and had brown hair. There was a cut on his forehead. He was unconscious but breathing.

"Hey, you alive?" she said. "Hey, wake up." She shook him. He didn't move. "Hey, get up. You've got to get up. You have no idea where you're even at." Laura looked around. "Neither do I for that matter."

She looked at his clothes and he was wearing casual business pants, nice shoes, a button-down collar shirt, and his tie was stuffed in the pocket. Everything was wrinkled. She thought he was a good-looking guy. He had short clean-cut hair, albeit messy. No wedding ring. She thought he must be the business type.

Laura started to shake him again. "Get up. Get up!" She shook him some more.

The man started to move.

She continued to shake.

He burst out with a shout and sat up. Laura fell back and pushed herself away a few feet. The man stared forward for a few seconds, getting cobwebs out of his mind, looked around and his gaze landed on her. Laura thought he looked like a deer caught in headlights. The man stared at her. He spoke.

"Who are you and where am I?"

"My name is Laura and I don't know where we are."

"What do you mean you don't know where we are?" He was annoyed. "You're there staring at me while I was out of it."

"I wasn't staring at you." Laura was starting to think he was a jerk. "I woke up myself and started to look around. I haven't got an inkling of where we are. I started to walk around and then I saw you lying here. But I can tell you what ... I don't think we're home."

"What do you mean by that?"

"I mean I don't think this is the Quad-Cities. Or Illinois for that matter. That is if you're from there."

"Yeah, I'm from the Quads. Moline." He looked around. "What do you mean you don't think we're home? Of course, we're home. We're just in someone's yard where we shouldn't be. And how'd I get here anyway!" He started to get upset.

"Whoa, relax tiger. Don't get pissed at me. I can't help it if you don't believe me, but I'm telling you again, I don't think we're anywhere familiar."

"Of course we aren't if we're lost in somebody else's yard."

"I'm not saying we're in somebody else's yard." Laura needed to make him understand. "I'm saying we're someplace else entirely."

The man looked at her for moment like she was insane.

"Are you a tripper chick or something? What are you on anyway?"

Laura was starting to get frustrated with his mouth. "I'm not on anything, asshole! Listen to me and quit being such a jerk!"

The man was stunned by the rise in her voice. "What? Are you serious? You're telling me that we're in wonderland or something? Come on, don't give me that shit." He continued to look around and his face changed to a concerned expression. He focused on the bluish watery-flowing wall. Next he looked up at the bright shining ceiling, got very perplexed, and stared back at her.

"This is weird," he said.

"Yeah, I know. And don't call me chick."

"So what you've managed to tally so far is that we're not in the United States anymore?" The man was more rational now.

"I'm not sure but I get the feeling we're not even on the same planet anymore."

"Huh?"

Laura looked around the yard and her mind drifted off. "I seem to remember seeing a falling star...."

The man looked at her. "You are a tripper chick, aren't you?"

Laura was still spaced off. Her mind was having trouble remembering. "Don't you remember anything that happened to you before this?"

The man hesitated in thought.

"I don't really remember anything but I do get a weird feeling about yesterday. I don't know why, though."

"What about that cut on your forehead?"

The man touched his forehead. "Huh, I don't even feel it or remember how I got it."

Laura sat back with her legs crossed and looked convinced that he was being honest. "It's foggy on my end too, but I remember being at my parents' house." She hesitated some more. "And being afraid...."

The man stared at her some more. "Yeah, I think I was outside of town," he agreed. "Can't remember anything else right now."

Laura came back. "I think it will more and more as we wake up."

"What's up with the ceiling?" He nodded upwards. "It's all bright and I can't see the sky. And this weird wall in front. I can't see through it."

"I don't know. I just got here the same as you did."

"This is messed up. I want to know what's going on."

"So do I, but we won't find out right away, or by sitting here. Let's look around. I was just noticing the house when I saw you."

"That's fine." The man looked over at the house. "Who lives there anyway?"

Laura rolled her eyes. "I don't know."

"Cool dragon."

"Yes, I'd say so."

They both stood up and brushed themselves off.

"What's your name?" Laura asked.

"Robert Stein. You can call me Rob. And you are?"

"Laura Redgrave."

Together they looked around surveying the land.

"So where do you want to look first?" Laura asked. "I was about to go into the house before I saw you."

"I don't know. Why don't we look around outside first before going inside a closed area? Especially, before we really know where we are and what we are doing here." Rob looked around. "Maybe we'll figure something out first."

They started to walk around the right side of the house. They gazed at the trees that stood in a single file pattern off into the distance. It was bright out like a sunny day and the trees stood like tall giants basking in their prominence. The side of the house was a perfect shade of white that gave off a smell of fresh paint mixed with an aroma of mixed flowers. It smelled wonderful. Laura and Rob sniffed in the pleasant scent. They both slowed their walks as they inhaled the pretty pleasure and became enthralled with its magic. It cast a spell on them and they stopped and stared at each other. Their eyes met and wonderment filled their faces. It was so good! Their noses breathed in the pageantry, and their senses became overrun with pleasure, like a river flowing over the rocks beneath. They stood motionless basking in its beauty. It was like the dawning of a new day … a new life.

And a new memory from Laura. "Hey, don't you remember anything weird happening like bright lights, a spaceship, and being sucked up into it?" she asked. "Don't you remember being in a bright doctor's room with weird grey-looking people walking around in it?"

Rob thought about it. "Yeah, I remember some stuff like that. I was driving along after closing a big business deal. I pulled off the road and went another way for some reason. There was a thing in the air with lights and then a feeling of being suspended in air and then...." He trailed off and looked directly back into her eyes. "Then the emergency room where they did something to me. Almost like tests but I know I wasn't injured."

"Good. It's starting to come back to us."

There was movement in front of them.

They both snapped back to reality and froze into defensive positions. Something had moved swiftly behind the back of the house. Laura and Rob exchanged glances and focused back on the yard. Whatever it was looked to be about the size of a person but had moved too fast for a good enough look. Laura's heart began to pound like a hammer throughout her body. Rob's palms began to sweat and he suddenly felt hot. Adrenaline was pumping though their veins. There was a possible threat behind the back of the house. It must be waiting for them. He looked back at Laura. She was staring straight ahead and didn't notice that he was there anymore. For an instant, he thought about how pretty she was and about how her face was now covered with a growing sense of fear. Rob thought it was a waste of pretty looks and how it wasn't right for her to be in danger. He realized that he'd have to be the protector and save them both. He wondered if he was up to it. Or more importantly, what was that in the backyard?

Rob shot a look back over his shoulder to make sure nothing had come up behind them and their back was clear. He looked at Laura. She returned the look. She seemed a little better now. Rob took the lead and together they slowly walked towards the back. Laura thought they must look like the people do in horror movies as they are baited into a trap just before a maniac axes them. She checked behind them but nothing was there. There was a window on the side in the back but they couldn't see inside the house. The leaves in the trees chattered as a breeze blew through them. It was the first wind either had felt so far.

The backyard was a step away. Rob primed himself for something to jump out at them when they rounded the corner of the house. He hesitated for a second and pulled his internal courage up from within. Bracing his hand against the side of the house, Rob stepped forward, and peered around into the backyard. There was nothing. He didn't see anything except for a backyard that could be found at any regular house.

On the back of the house there were four windows. Two were on the bottom and two more above on the second story of the house. There was a small red deck in the back connected to the house. It had steps leading up to it. The yard had some trees that lined the back like a wall to provide some shade and privacy. Rob didn't move. He wasn't going to get out into the open just yet. Maybe something was hiding?

Laura put her hand on his back and took her turn to look around. The house blocked her view of the left side of the yard. She struggled to get a better look but Rob held up his hand to wait. Together they listened but didn't hear anything. There weren't any sounds in this place. It was strangely quiet. Just the two of them.

Rob gently elbowed Laura, pointed to his eye, and gestured to look around and he focused on the back of the house. Laura watched the trees that stood in rows off into the distance and didn't see anything that moved. She thought the grass was prettier now. It was almost too green to be real grass. That struck her as odd and not natural. She didn't see anything trying to sneak up behind them either and that was a relief.

Rob continued to watch for any movement in the backyard but didn't see any. He reached back, never breaking his concentration, and squeezed Laura on the arm. Rob stepped into the back. She followed him. They kept their backs up against the house, ducked below the window, and moved up to the deck. Slowly, Rob knelt on his hands and knees and looked beneath it. The deck rested a foot above the ground. It was dark but he could see grass underneath. Laura was crouched over and watching for anything that might come out at them. Rob couldn't see anything hiding under the deck.

"Do you see anything?" Laura said in a loud whisper.

Rob raised up and cracked his head on the deck. "Shit," he cursed, grabbing the back of his head. "What are you doing? No, not yet."

"Sorry," whispered Laura. She continued to look around.

Rob rubbed his head, took a glance around the yard, and looked back under the deck but this time avoided its edge. The grass was landscaped like the rest of the area. It was as if the land had been mowed just before he woke up. Or arrived here. However, there weren't any cut shavings of grass anywhere. Laura was looking at the trees in the back of the yard. There was more land behind them that rose up on a hill. Then something flashed like a glint of sunlight at her. It was behind the trees at the bottom of the hill. She looked harder at it and began to realize....

"Hey!"

Laura and Rob whipped around to their left.

A man in his forties stood at the corner of the house. His face was mixed with panic and confusion. He had thin graying-brown hair above his receding hairline and was wearing a gray T-shirt that read Lasky's Liquor with a pair of baseballs on it, that stuck out over his potbelly. For some reason, Laura felt she'd seen him before. The man rounded out with brown shorts and white sneakers. His mouth hung open as he stared at them before he spoke again.

"What are you two doing?"

Laura and Rob both tried to answer but it sounded like gibberish between them. There was much astonishment and surprise in their voices.

Another person was here with them. They both felt relief as the sudden alarm that his voice had stirred dissipated.

Both relaxed.

"We're looking around," said Laura. "What are you doing?"

"I'm lost I think," burst out of the man. He seemed to be stressed out. His fingers were twitching. "I'm looking for people. Or help. Or something."

"This is all we've found so far," said Rob.

"My name is Laura--"

"Do you know where we are?" the man cut her off.

"Not yet. We're just figuring that out now," she answered.

Rob spoke again. "This house and this yard. And the land that goes back there with those trees. Did you go back there? Where did you come from?"

The man looked around from side to side. He looked like he was going to make a break for it. He was breathing deeply.

"Uh, I came from over there," he said. The man pointed to the trees behind them. "Not far. I just woke up and…." His voice trailed off. He looked more confused than before.

"My name is Laura Redgrave. What's yours?"

"Uh, I'm Shawn." The man took a few short steps towards them. "Shawn Lasky. I live in Bettendorf. I own Lasky's Liquors in Rock Island."

"Oh, I know the place," said Rob.

Laura and Rob leaned back and smiles broke on their faces. They walked around the deck.

"Aw, I'm from Moline," she answered.

"I'm Rob Stein and I'm also from Moline." Rob was trying to assert himself in this. "We don't know how we got here so we're looking around. You see anything yet that might help?" Rob didn't expect much from this man considering he looked like he was about to have a panic attack at any moment.

"No. Just this house." Shawn was staring blankly at the two of them. "And the trees here." He stepped back to look at the rows of trees that stood all around them. To Shawn, the trees stood at attention, as if waiting for orders. They didn't seem normal. He was bewildered. What happened? One moment he was enjoying himself while fishing and having a beer. The next he doesn't know other than that he's here.

Rob walked over and peered into his eyes.

"Hey, you all right?"

Shawn looked at him.

"Dude, you gotta chill man. We're here with you. We'll find out what's going on and everything will be cool, man."

"Yeah, everything is going to be okay," Laura said as she walked over. "It's gonna be all right."

Shawn looked back at her too.

"It's gonna be good, man," said Rob. Shawn's head swung back to him.

All three stood in silence.

"Shawn," Laura spoke up. "Do you remember anything about home before waking up here…."

A rustling cool breeze swam through the trees and circled down around their legs and seemed to flow into the ground beneath them. The leaves rustled above them and sounded like beautiful musical notes being played to perfection by a concert musician. They rustled and harmonized. Leaves among leaves. Rolling and singing.

Laura and Rob looked up and lost their eyes in the giants that now swayed back and forth together in perfect teamwork. This place wasn't natural but this was the first kind of general activity in this new home of theirs. A *home* yet to be determined but definitely not of their choosing. It was the first time this new place seemed to have any kind of pulse. Something that was reminiscent of home. Their real home. Like Earth.

Yet, now all Laura could remember about home was a falling star.

CHAPTER 14

"What's that?" said Shawn, who snapped back to the present. A flash from behind the house caught Shawn's eyes. Laura and Rob both turned around. It flashed again.

"Oh yeah, I saw that right before you spoke to us," Laura said.

"What is that?" said Rob, very curiously.

There was another small flash from below the hills. They started to walk towards it. The trees continued to sway around them. Back and forth they went. The breeze felt good on Laura's skin. It was refreshing as it covered her in an invisible cool blanket of air. The wind blew through Rob's hair and his body felt a nice chill down his spine. Shawn breathed the gusts deep into his lungs and it made his chest feel exhilarated. This was the best they felt since they woke up here.

Suspicion was replaced by a feeling of comfort. But only momentarily. As careful as they had been before, they were now feeling more safe. Momentarily. As the wind subsided the comfort zone for all three of them whisked away as well. They had no answers so far. Now they were about to find out what was glinting from behind the backyard.

Slowly, they walked to the trees which were spaced apart by a few feet, and Rob stepped forward. His eyebrows rose. It was a man!

He lay unconscious flat on the ground with his arms and legs spread eagle. Then he moved a little and there was another flash. It was a reflection off his belt buckle from the light above. Laura looked up again but it was still a sky of bright yellow. Rob stepped forward through the trees and Laura and Shawn followed him. Rob kneeled next to the man, who was breathing slowly and didn't appear to be hurt. He looked to be in his fifties, had short whitish-gray hair, was wearing a short-sleeved black T-shirt that said Pegasus on it, blue jeans, and sneakers. Laura glanced around and everything looked safe so far. Shawn stood there staring at their new discovery.

Rob touched the man on his arm and he flinched. Rob tapped him a few times. This time he rolled over onto his left side. Rob gave Laura a look. She looked at Shawn. He just looked at the man. Rob walked around and pushed him back over with his foot. His eyes opened wide like golf balls.

"Hey! What are you doing?" He said directly to Rob as he pried himself upright.

"Nothing. Just getting you up. Relax," said Rob.

"It's okay," Laura said quickly. "We aren't going to hurt you."

The man looked over at her, then at Shawn, and back at Rob again.

"Who are you?" He said with squinting eyes. The man looked down at himself, then the ground, and then all around. "Where am I?"

"Don't know." Rob shook his head. "The three of us just met before we found you here. We're trying to figure things out. Like where this is." He looked around.

"Why am I on the ground?" he asked.

"This is where we found you."

"What's your name?" Laura asked.

"Harold Sanders," he said as he got up. "You can call me Harry."

"Okay, I'm Laura Redgrave." She nodded towards Rob.

"I'm Rob Stein." They shook hands. "That's Shawn Lasky."

Harry turned to Shawn and extended his hand. Shawn still looked dazed about everything but he managed to shake hands. "Well, it's good to meet people otherwise I would have started to worry."

"Let's not get too comfortable," said Rob. "There still might be more worrying to come."

Harry started to look around. "Nice place but I don't recognize it. I've never been here before."

"None of us have," said Laura. "Rob and I woke up on the other side of the house. We started walking around. Found Shawn. Or more like he found us. He said he woke up over by those trees." Harry followed her directions as she pointed out everywhere that she was talking about. "We might not have noticed you if not for your belt that kept reflecting in the sunlight. I mean light." She looked above. Harry did too.

"That's weird. Where's the sun?" He paused and gestured above. "It's almost like a super ceiling covered with light bulbs. But you can't see any light bulbs."

"Yeah, it's strange," said Rob.

Harry looked at Shawn who just stared back at him. He felt a little concerned for the guy. He didn't seem to be quite with it.

"Anyway, let's call for a ride and get out of here. My wife is going to kill me." Harry reached down into his pocket and stopped. Then he patted both his pockets and felt around. Slapped his thighs and hips as if he had lost something. Harry realized something really big.

"I don't have my cell phone."

Then like a cold blast of air the others realized it too. Since the moment they woke here, everything that had happened before was pretty much a blur. Nobody remembered. They just knew today and who they were. And they'd been engrossed with this place. However, Harry's recognition made them realize they didn't have their cell phones either. Laura, Rob and Shawn all patted their pants, dug in their pockets, and searched the ground for what wasn't there. A key part of everyday life for millions of people which is taken for granted was gone. A saving grace that could help a person in an emergency, or more importantly save a person's life, was gone. All four of them were empty-handed. Where were their phones now? They all must have had them before here. And how or why were they gone? Each one of them started to remember just a little. Laura was back at her parents' house. Rob was in his car. Even Shawn realized he was on the lakeshore with his fishing gear. And Harry had his before....

CHAPTER 15

In a flash the memory bank inside Harry's mind clicked and churned and he remembered. As a teacher at the Pegasus School he was working late on a Friday night. Much later than he usually did. Harry had been finalizing a report for his boss and was trying to get it finished by that weekend. The school was on the outskirts of town. There was a train that ran through town every hour a couple blocks away. It was literally the last stopping ground for anyone on the way out to the highway.

Harry left that night through the front doors. He locked them, turned towards his car and stepped out into a gorgeous summer night. There were a few clouds scattered about but the stars were out and shone brightly on what seemed like a blanket of blackness covering the Earth. Harry carried his papers under his arm. They were neatly separated into their appropriate folders. He got to the parking lot across the street when one of his folders fell forward. He reached to catch it but he was too late and the papers spilled out onto the pavement. Harry, feeling stupid, gathered them up and that's when he heard something. He froze and strained to listen. There it was again. Harry stood up and looked around. A third time and it came from his left. It sounded like a child. It sounded like.... There it went again. It sounded like a cry for help. To the left of the parking lot was a big field. It may have been farmed at one time but it hadn't been during the time Harry was teaching at the school. The field belonged to the owner of a house about a block down to the right. This house always stood out when you left the school because it had a tractor collection in the backyard. There was another house with lots of kid toys all about the yard just to the left of the parking lot as well. In the back, behind the field were trees. That was the end of the town and where the country started. Every March Harry could hear someone shooting off a gun back there. He didn't know if they were hunting or just practicing their aim.

"Help." Faintly the word drifted across the field to Harry's ears. Someone needed him. He knew it was coming from back behind the field in those trees.

"Help!" Harry heard it more distinctly now. Somebody needed his help.

"Help me." It was a child.

Then he saw a light! Yes, a light behind the trees. There must have been an accident.

Harry ran to his truck, jiggled his keys out of his pocket, opened the door, threw his folders and his cell phone onto the passenger seat, started his truck and drove it in reverse out into the street. There was a gravel dirt country road a few blocks down, behind the tractor collection, that led back to the trees. He whipped around a right turn and then turned left down the road. Dust kicked up behind him as he drove to the trees with his truck brights on. He saw the light distantly back within the trees.

"Help." Harry heard it again.

"Help." He thought it was a little girl.

The trunks of the trees lit up in the bright headlights of Harry's truck. He braked to a stop. The tires made a sliding sound on the gravel below. Some rocks rolled away and made a falling rock sound. The rest of the field was very quiet.

Harry got out and stared into the trees but couldn't see anything.

"Hey! You need help?"

Nobody answered.

"I'm right here! Where are you?"

All quiet. No light.

Harry got his flashlight out of the glove compartment and turned it on.

He turned back to the trees and listened some more. Still nothing.

"Hey!" Harry started waving his flashlight around. "Where are you? Need help? You there?"

This is strange, he thought. Now he didn't hear the child and the light was gone? Harry walked around to the front of his truck, and using the headlights, peered into the trees. He didn't see anything. Was he just hallucinating and hearing things?

"Hello!" He yelled again desperate for a reply.

Harry dropped his arms to his side and turned around to get back in the truck.

"Help me." He turned around. It was the little girl. She was there somewhere. It was faint but resonated to him for what seemed like an eternity. Then he saw the light for just a brief second back in the darkness of the trees.

Harry ran to the trees and climbed through them into the underbrush.

"I'm coming! Sound out where you are!" Leg up over leg he stepped and then he was on more level ground.

He listened again but heard nothing. Harry flashed his light in all directions but he only saw trees. He looked above him and the night was as beautiful as it had been all year. A few clouds and the moon shining bright.

Harry's flashlight went out. "No. No." He said. Harry hit and smacked it but it didn't come back on. He thought he'd put new batteries in it a few months ago and it was hardly used.

"Hurry!"

Harry's head shot up. The little girl needed his help. Her voice had come from off in the distance ahead of him. He continued to slowly pick his way through the woods in that direction. He heard her again. However, she didn't sound any closer to him than she did before. Was she moving away from him? Harry realized that he better move faster if he was going to help her.

Then Harry thought what is this little girl doing out here in the first place? Did she get lost? Does she live around here?

He looked back to his truck but by now he was farther into the woods than he realized. The headlights highlighted the brush he'd walked and climbed through so far.

Harry turned back and stepped into a hole and stumbled to the ground. The flashlight flew out of his hand and bounced away. Harry rolled onto his side and began to get up. Then a feeling drifted down upon him like a command from out of the darkness.

Now don't be scared.

Then there was a flash of light.

CHAPTER 16

Donald Tabor sat on his back porch with all the lights turned off in his house. He sipped some whiskey and watched the moonlight glisten on his tractors. When he looked beyond he saw nothing but the great outdoors. *Ah, this is living*, he thought. It was time to relax for the night. He took another sip and the ice cubes jiggled around in his glass. Then he heard a motor, and headlights quickly drove down the road past his backyard, sending a dust cloud up in the air seen though the rear lights. This was interesting to Donald but he hoped it wouldn't ruin his night. He took another sip. The cold sharpness of whiskey went down his throat and warmed his stomach. It was a beautiful night outside. Not too hot, quiet, and had been undisturbed. Donald saw the red brake lights as the truck stopped at the end of the road. He got up and walked to the kitchen. Donald filled up his glass and dropped some more ice into it. Nice and chilled. He opened the refrigerator and scanned the contents inside. Donald couldn't make up his mind what to eat yet tonight. He closed the door and walked back to his porch.

Just then he saw out in the trees a giant beam of light, coming from something he'd never seen before, shooting straight down to the ground. From the moonlight's reflection, it looked like a metal object. Then the light disappeared and the object shot off to the east without making a sound.

Donald slammed his whiskey down, went to his phone, and called 911.

CHAPTER 17

"Oh Jesus," said Harry. He remembered. The experience shook him to the bone. He had heard a little girl from the trees. He went to help. He fell. Then a great big flash. He couldn't remember what happened next. He just woke up here. What had happened to him? Was it real?

The others stared at him as Harry changed from calm and collected to seemingly lost. Harry just stared at the ground. He didn't talk or move. He just blinked.

"Harry," said Rob. "You okay?"

He didn't say anything. Laura waved her hand in front of his eyes. They responded. He looked at her. Then at Shawn. Harry now thought that he might understand why Shawn is in the condition that he was. Shawn was looking at him too. Harry thought that he and Shawn might have something in common. In fact, they all might.

CHAPTER 18

His eyelids folded back and Travis looked at the ceiling above him. It was white and looked very smooth. Travis raised up on his elbows but felt groggy, like he just came out of a deep sleep, and his eyes adjusted while he looked around. He was inside a house but it wasn't any house that he'd been inside before. Travis was lying on a couch. He leaned back and touched the wall. It was smooth. He swung his legs around and began to stand up but fell back immediately. The sofa cushions were thin and he bounced up and down. The springs underneath stabbed at his rear. He settled himself and saw the room was white with a brownish carpeted floor. His legs didn't feel strong yet and there was a slight painful feeling in his stomach area. There was a small plastic coffee table in front of his couch. The wall on the other side of the room had a fireplace and two entrances at both sides that led into another room. It was too dark to see what was in the room. Next to him was a window the length of half the room. Another large window spanned the front wall of the room. It was light outside. To the left of the window was what must be the front door. Travis figured he was in the living room. But whose living room? Next to him on his left, up against the back wall, there was another couch and immediately he recognized the most beautiful blonde hair that he'd ever seen. It was Katie. Travis quickly stood up, this time without any problem with his balance, and moved around the table and sat down on her couch beside her. Travis looked her over and she didn't seem hurt. She was resting peacefully. He brushed her hair back with his hand. He tickled her earlobe.

"Hey, wake up." He gently shook her. "Katie, wake up."

She stirred.

"Yeah, wake up. It's Travis," he said shaking her softly.

She moaned a little. He nicely shook her some more. She rolled onto her back, opened her eyes, and looked up at Travis. They both smiled together.

"Hey," she said softly.

"Hi, babe," he answered.

"Uh, where are we?" she asked. Her eyes darted around the room.

"I don't know. I just woke up over on that couch." He gestured over his shoulder. "I feel like I've slept for a month."

"Hmm, were we out partying?"

"I don't know. Don't think so. I can't remember." He looked around the room and then back to her. "I have this weird hangover feeling but I don't think it's from beer."

"I've got a weird feeling, too. Not sure. How about something to drink?" She sat up.

"Good idea," said Travis. "I have a little pain in my stomach area."

"Me too. Maybe it's something we ate," she said. "Could be too much beer."

"Yeah, but I don't think it was brewskies."

They kissed and stood up.

Other than the two sofas, fireplace, and the table there wasn't anything in the room. Behind them was a hallway leading to the back of the house. It was all quiet.

Katie felt around her pockets. "Where's my cell phone?"

"Oh yeah," said Travis. He had completely forgotten. Travis grabbed his pockets but nothing was in them.

"I don't have my cell phone," Katie said. "You see my purse anywhere?"

"No," Travis said as he looked under the table and around the sofa. "I don't have my phone either." He noticed he also didn't have his wallet or keys.

"Well, I need my cell."

"I know but I don't have it," he answered. "Or mine."

They both continued to look around and even checked behind the seat cushions.

"It would help if we could remember where we were last night," Katie said.

"It sure would, but I don't have mine, you don't have yours, and we can't remember last night. Hate to think we left them somewhere."

"I don't think we'd do that. I can't live without my cell phone. It's like my life's blood."

"I know," said Travis and he smiled at her.

"If we just had our cells we could call out of here."

"Shit, we don't even know where we are yet," Travis said.

Katie looked at Travis. "Have you heard anyone? Actually, called out to see if anyone is here?"

"Uh, no," he said embarrassingly. "I was kinda laying low because this is so weird and we don't know where we are." Now he felt stupid. He cupped his hands and yelled, "Hello! Is anyone…?"

"Shhhh," Katie said and pulled his arms down. "Better idea. I just thought what if they're all psycho? Maybe we should just look around first and make sure everything is okay."

Travis nodded. "Good idea. That's what I was thinking in the first place."

Katie slowly stepped over to the hallway. First she took a quick look through the entrance into the next room, deemed it safe, and then peered down the hallway. It was dark. No light from the windows made it this far inwards. Katie took a step into the hallway and the ceiling lit up with light. She screamed for a startled second. Travis rushed over and put his arms on hers and they stared up at the ceiling.

"Wow! This is strange. How's it doing that?" she said.

"I don't know. There aren't any light bulbs. It's solid ceiling," he answered.

They looked back down the hallway and saw doors on each side.

"More rooms," she said. "Hello." Nobody answered.

"Look," said Travis. "I want to check to see if there is a kitchen."

"Of course there is." She chuckled and looked back at him. "It's a house."

"I know it is but you never know. This house has light without any lights."

"Yeah, that is freaky," she said. "Maybe it's one of those new government houses made for life on the moon or Mars or something."

"Made by the military," he answered. "It's all advanced shit. New technologies. Area 51 stuff. Maybe it's everywhere."

"Cool…." She trailed off. For some reason, she thought of the old films seen on TV of houses with test dummies inside them being disintegrated back in the fifties during nuclear bomb testing. "Oh no. You don't think we're in a testing site, do you? For bombs."

"Hope not," said Travis. He stepped back into the room. "Like in New Mexico? Nah, we're in Illinois anyway."

She stepped back. The light went out. She stepped in. The light came on again.

"Like I said, I want to find the kitchen. I'm thirsty," Travis said. He looked in the left opening and saw the outline of a kitchen, but he wanted to check out the front of the place, so he started walking cautiously to the front door.

"Okay," Katie agreed. She followed him through the living room to the front of the house. They turned and on their left was a stairwell leading upstairs. The steps looked like brown wood and so did the handrail which climbed on the right side. The handrail posts underneath were very skinny and white like the walls. Travis didn't know what kind of wood made up the stairway but thought it looked cool and newly made. Katie thought the steps looked pretty. It was dark at the top.

In front of them was the kitchen. It had a green counter that lined the back two walls. A big sink sat in the middle of the counter on the left and there were brown cabinets above and below. There was a big black machine that looked like a microwave in the corner on the counter. The front of the room had two big windows. Standing against the far wall next to the counter was a red refrigerator. That's what Travis wanted to see. He started towards it but stopped when he saw something through the window. He saw people.

CHAPTER 19

Harry was freaked about his memory. He saw the others were looking freaked out with him. He better break out of it. Harry calmed himself and came together.

"I'm okay. Just remembered something. Pretty bad," he said.

"Yeah? You looked bad for a moment," said Laura in a questioning way. She thought it was weird to disappear mentally like he did. She had no idea that for her it was only a few seconds but it had felt like an eternity for him.

Rob asked, "What was it?"

Harry turned slightly enough to look at Rob. "Oh, I don't know yet," he said. "I've gotta think about it for a while."

"You don't strike me as the 'I don't know' type," Rob said. "You seem too smart to not know. It's like you became unwound for a few seconds and then came back." Rob was suspicious of it. The guy was calm and then became lost and scared. What made him do that? Did it have to do with them? That scared Rob to think that it did. Especially, the way he had behaved. "What kind of a thing was it related to?" he asked further.

"I'll let you know," said Harry. He wanted to move on. "I promise. I'm not sure if it was my imagination or not. I need to put it all together first." Harry looked at Shawn. As usual Shawn just stared back.

"Please do," Laura said. She was looking at him sideways now. Harry seemed to be a smart and organized guy who for a moment had become white as a ghost. It unnerved her. Now he was back with them again but she wanted to know what had happened. What made him trip out? She was afraid it had to do with their predicament and it didn't look good. It added to her ever-growing fear that they would learn the truth eventually and it scared her more that it might be an awful truth. They had to find out what was going on and for that matter what were they going to do now?

"Well," said Harry. He slapped his hands on his legs. "Where were we?" He cocked a smile.

"If I remember correctly we were looking for our cell phones," said Rob.

Laura was still watching Harry. Still unnerved but he seemed okay now. "Yeah, and none of us has one at last count." The four of them looked around and the realization set in. They didn't have a way to call anyone.

"Does anyone remember the last time they had their cell?" Harry asked.

All three said no.

"No wallets either," said Rob. "Nothing."

"And my purse isn't here," Laura said. "Unless it's in the front yard but I doubt it."

"Does anyone have a watch?" asked Rob. Everyone shook their heads no.

"I don't have my wedding ring," Harry said.

Shawn touched his hand. "Neither do I," he said.

"Well, we'll sure be in trouble with the wives," said Harry. He smiled at Shawn trying to put a little humor into a deteriorating situation.

"I think it's safe to assume that they were taken from us," Laura said. "And for a reason."

"That's the scary part," Rob said. "What's the reason?"

"And by who?" said Laura.

They heard something that sounded like a yell but it was only for a second. They all faced the house. Each of them listened intently but there was nothing more. The wind continued to blow through the perfect trees and they made a nice rustle in return. Perhaps the wind was drowning out the sound? Maybe what they heard was actually the wind? By now it was possible their feelings of uncertainty, frustration, and growing anxiety, mixed together were starting to play tricks on them.

Now they heard a scream! From a woman. She sounded young. This came from the house.

"There are people here," said Rob. "After all, thank God." He started forward.

Harry wasn't moving. "This is great news but why'd she scream?" Harry said. "Might want to be careful." Rob walked right by him. Shawn followed Rob. Laura forgot about the scream and the house for a moment and stared at Harry. She knew they had to be careful.

"She probably needs help. Hurry!" Rob said and he started to run.

Laura agreed with Harry. "Wait. Stop!" Then she lowered her voice. Both Rob and Shawn stopped and looked back at her. "Don't be in a hurry." Rob started to back talk because this woman could be in danger. "Harry is right," she continued. "You gotta be careful. You don't know what's going on in there. We don't even know where this place is."

"You don't know who is in there." Harry cut in. "Or what?"

Shawn didn't know what to think. He looked back and forth between Rob and them.

"Listen," Laura said. "I don't hear anything."

Rob was annoyed but he calmed down and started to think rationally. Harry and Laura waited. Then Rob spoke. "Yeah, I gotcha. Good idea. Let's go but be cool about it." His eyes squinted. He had acted dumb.

Together they walked around the side of the house. The trees were on their left and the wind blew over their faces. Harry's mind went to ease. What had alarmed him minutes ago seemed to have blown away. The last thing he remembered was leaving his school on a Friday night.

As they passed each window, no one could be seen inside. They came to the porch. Rob peered around the front. It was all clear. Rob, Shawn, Harry and Laura came around the side and walked toward the stairs of the front porch.

CHAPTER 20

The front door opened and Travis walked out on the porch smiling with his arms outstretched. "Hi! Do you live here?"

"We heard screams. Was that you?" asked Laura.

"Oh yeah, that was us," answered Travis. "Hey, we're sorry. We didn't mean to trespass. We didn't break in or anything."

"No. That's fine," Rob said shaking his head. He put his foot on a step, leaned forward, and looked directly into Travis's eyes. "Do you live here?"

Travis stood back a step. Apparently, this guy hadn't heard what he had said. "No."

"Who does?" asked Rob.

"I don't know."

Katie walked out the door. Rob's first thought was that she was hot. She looked happy just to see people. He looked back at Travis. The others came up behind Rob. They looked happy to see people too.

"What are you doing here?" Rob asked.

"I don't know," Travis answered.

"We just woke up, if I dare to say, inside here," Katie said. "We don't know anything."

The faces of the four new people told Travis and Katie a lot. They've already gone through the same questions without answers among themselves as the two of them had. And neither group had answers for the other.

"Do any of you have a cell phone?" asked Katie.

Everyone shook their heads no.

"We don't know what happened to them," said Laura.

"Neither do we," Katie answered. "I never leave without it. We had them last night."

"Yeah, same on this end, too," said Laura. "Everyone remembers having cell phones last night but they're gone now."

"Same here," Katie said.

"What's going on? I thought I remembered something earlier but now I can't. None of us can remember anything about how we got here," said Rob. He looked back at Harry who smirked right back at him. Harry didn't like feeling like he was a suspect in something.

"We can't remember either," said Travis. "This sucks, man. We gotta figure out what is going on."

"What's inside?" Harry asked. "Anything we can use?"

"No," said Travis. "At least not that we found yet. There's a kitchen--"

"We just started to look around," Katie interjected. She noticed the overweight guy was just kind of staring. He seemed a little spacey or something. She thought he might need some help.

"What's your names?" asked Rob.

"I'm Katie Dawson. This is my boyfriend Travis Rhodes. We're from the Quad-Cities."

"Aw cool, so are we. What city?" asked Rob. He was looking at her pretty blonde hair.

"Moline," Travis answered.

Rob looked back to him. Somehow it wasn't as much fun getting an answer from him as it was from her.

"I'm Laura Redgrave." She stepped up onto the porch and shook their hands.

"Hi," said Katie.

"I'm Harry Sanders." He shook their hands. "I'm a teacher out at Pegasus."

They both nodded up and down like they knew the school even though they didn't.

"And this," said Harry as he turned and pointed. "Is Shawn Lasky."

Shawn waved and said hi. They returned the greeting. Katie thought he seemed better now.

"Shawn does...." Harry hesitated. "What do you do, Shawn?"

"Fish."

"Looks like Shawn coaches baseball too," Rob added.

Shawn nodded.

"What's your name?" asked Travis.

"Oh yeah, I'm Rob Stein."

"How's it going, bro?" Travis and Rob slapped hands and Travis did a handshake that Rob didn't understand.

"So what now?" said Katie.

"I guess we need to look around and start to figure out what is going on here," Harry answered.

"Let's go inside," said Travis. Everyone followed his gesture to the door.

Slowly they all walked into the house and filed out into the kitchen. Glances were given to the living room but overall the house didn't create a lot of interest. It was an ordinary house.

"Well, looks like it has the bare necessities," Harry said. He pointed to the sink and the refrigerator. Harry noticed the black machine in the corner. It had a few buttons on a panel next to its door. "A microwave, I guess," he said.

That ugly feeling surged in Travis's stomach again. His thirst returned and he opened the fridge. The only thing inside was a giant glass globe that was full of what appeared to be water. In the door, there were eight clear glasses. Travis wondered why there were eight of them. He grabbed one. It was made of plastic. He grabbed the nozzle at the bottom of the globe and turned it. A clear liquid flowed down into his cup. He turned it off and took a sip. Water. It flowed down his throat. He could feel it circle around his stomach. Its refreshing feeling sent strong chills through his body and Travis felt stronger than he did before. He finished and poured some more.

"Hey, good idea," said Rob as he came over and poured a glass.

Laura and Katie remained near the front door giving a thorough look over of the kitchen. There wasn't a kitchen table or chairs. "Hmm, nowhere to sit and eat."

"I see that," answered Katie.

Laura pointed to the cabinets.

"What else is there?" asked Laura.

Harry turned around and opened some of them. Shawn did too. There was nothing in them. They opened them all. Still nothing. Harry opened a few drawers and there were some eating utensils. He turned and looked back to everyone.

"At least they use forks and knives," he said holding up a fork. "Spoons. Napkins, too."

"Yeah, but how weird. They don't have any food," said Katie. "And who has a fridge like that?"

"I don't know but the water sure tastes good," Rob said as he downed a glass of water. "I didn't realize how parched I was."

Travis had already drunk two glasses. He looked at Katie. "Want some?"

"No, hon. I'm okay for right now," she answered.

"I have a friend in Peoria that when I visited him all he had in his fridge were sports drinks," said Rob. "He said he didn't like the sugar in juice. That could be it," he shrugged.

"Why don't they have anything a kitchen needs?" Laura asked. "Is this some sort of living within our means thing?"

Harry was squinting in concentration about something, lines darting out around his eyes. Everyone else looked at each other.

Shawn spoke, "Maybe they don't like buying a lot."

"Maybe they just went to the store and that's why nobody is here right now," said Katie.

Laura was looking at the fridge. "That must be one of those water filter things that gets advertised on TV all the time," she said.

Rob was pouring himself another glass. "Nah, there's no filter on this. Man, this is good," he said before drinking some more.

"Yeah, some of you should try this," Travis said. He finished off another glass.

"Be careful," Katie said. "They might not like it that we're drinking their water." Travis smiled and Rob simply looked at her.

"Good point," Laura said getting uncomfortable. "Maybe you shouldn't drink anymore. In fact, aren't we breaking and entering? We should get out."

"Relax," Rob answered. "We'll just explain."

"Heck, when are they coming back? That'd be nice to know," Shawn said.

"Did it occur to anyone that it's not for *they* but for *us* to use or drink?" Harry asked.

They all stopped and stared at him. Then they all started talking at the same time.

"What do you mean?" asked Rob.

"Yeah. What's up?" Katie asked.

"Hold on. Hold on," Harry said. "Since we've been here we haven't seen anyone. Not even a car. Did you notice there is no driveway? And what about that weird wall out in front?"

Everyone was quiet.

"I don't think there's anyone here," he continued. "That's the feeling I'm getting."

There was still more silence before anyone spoke. Harry's words seemed to be sinking in with the group.

"It's pretty weird so far," Laura spoke. "We're still looking. There's got to be someone around."

"I agree," said Katie. She stepped forward. "Has to be."

"Maybe that someone is us," Harry said back.

"Yeah, man. There's somebody around," said Travis. "This is a house."

"I'm thinking there's not," answered Harry.

Nobody liked what Harry was saying. Although, nobody was exactly sure where he was going with it but they were starting to catch on.

"Harry," said Laura. "Are you implying that this is our new home?"

He looked at her for a moment. "Yes," he said.

"That's crazy," Rob said among the stirring of the group. He shut the refrigerator door, put his glass on the counter, and put his hands on his hips. "Dude, we don't live here. How are we supposed to live here? And who said so?"

Harry just looked at him.

"Hey, wait a second now," said Shawn. "What you're saying is … not cool. That can't be. I can't be here." Shawn was sounding panicked. "I have a family and a liquor store to run."

Harry looked at Shawn.

"Why would we be here?" asked Rob. "Who'd want us?"

Katie flipped her hair over her shoulder and looked at Harry with a glare. "What for?" she asked.

"I don't know," said Harry. "But some way. Somehow. We're here." They didn't seem convinced yet.

"Look," Harry continued. "You've all seen for your own eyes so far. We've woken up here." He pointed to Laura, Rob and Shawn. "I'm sure the both of you did, too." He pointed to Katie and Travis who nodded in return. "We don't have any of our possessions. They must have taken our stuff."

Katie touched her ears where her earrings would have been.

"Who's they?" Rob asked, sounding alarmed.

"Anyway," Harry continued. "We certainly don't have our cell phones." Harry was using his hands while talking. "Obviously, we're not supposed to call out or be able to communicate with anyone. Whoever…." He looked around the group for emphasis. "Didn't want that."

"Harry, who in the world…?" Laura didn't finish because she knew there was no point even asking because they didn't know yet.

He looked at her solidly. Then looked around the room again. They looked more convinced now. Harry thought it was important for everyone to understand what kind of situation they were in.

"Think it's the government?" asked Travis. That was just along the lines of his kind of thinking. Nothing would excite him, or his girlfriend, more than being in the middle of a government conspiracy. Katie was ready to hear Harry's answer as well.

"Don't know yet," Harry answered.

They were both disappointed.

"Harry, I don't have time for this," said Rob. "Man, I've got some contracts to close back in the real world."

"Yeah, we have school," Katie said.

"Harry, I have work," said Laura.

"But they don't care." Harry came back with.

That stopped the conversation. Everyone got his point now. No matter what they thought or had to do in their lives there wasn't anyone to reason with right now. At least not yet. All they knew was that they were now in this house and hadn't seen anyone else other than the six people right here in this room. Harry thought the potential enormity of the situation still wasn't understood by the group yet. He wasn't completely sure of it yet himself. What really worried him was what they still didn't know. The unknown.

"Speaking of earlier. The TV. Where is it? That might help," asked Shawn. He seemed to come to life a little bit more.

Katie shook her head. "I don't know," she said. "There isn't one in the living room. There's probably one somewhere else in the house. We haven't seen the rest of the house yet."

Shawn walked between Laura and Katie and went into the living room. Nobody else seemed interested in the television right now. However, for Shawn, he might find some answers on TV. Like what city they were in. Or it might just help him feel normal again and that everything was okay with his life.

"Harry," said Laura. "Since the moment I've been awake here there's been like this feeling of memories on the top of my head, almost like hovering there, but I can't quite reach up and grab them yet. That's how I feel. Earlier today I thought I could remember some, but now I can't."

"Yeah, me too," Rob agreed.

Harry stared back. His memory was now blank. He couldn't remember. Harry knew he could a few minutes ago but what it was about he didn't know. It was something to do with what happened to him before he got here. And a little girl lost in the woods.

"When I can finally remember them," said Laura. "I think it will help shed light on what's going on."

Everyone agreed and started to converse. They all had memories that couldn't be recollected yet. It was as if they were on the brink of understanding what was happening, what had already happened, how and why, but couldn't quite reach it yet inside the depths of their memories.

"I'm sure it's only a matter of time," said Harry.

"Well," Laura started. "I think...." She stopped. Her eyes looked up and peered to the left. Her head turned upwards following where her eyes were leading her. Then they spread wide and she was startled for a moment with a quick jolt of astonishment. Her wits recovered as she came to the realization of what she saw at the top of the stairs. The other five in the room followed her gaze upwards. Together they stared in silence. There was a little girl at the top of the stairs and a woman standing behind with her arm on the girl's shoulder. The girl was cuddling a doll.

The group was dumbfounded. How long had they been standing there? The girl and the woman had expressionless looks on their faces. For a moment, nobody spoke.

Then the woman said, "Hi." Everyone waited. "We've heard everything you've said." She had a mature, non-threatening, voice that carried down nicely from above. She was neatly dressed in a white blouse and khaki pants.

"Hi there," Laura answered with a smile. She wanted them to feel welcomed. "You did, huh. What's your name?"

"I'm Carol Anderson and this is my daughter, Ashley." She patted Ashley on the shoulder. The girl wore a flowery shirt, and her blue jeans were decorated with sequins in the shape of a butterfly.

"I'm seven," said Ashley holding out her fingers.

"Oh, I can see that now," Laura answered with a big comforting smile.

"How many of you are there?" asked Carol. Just at that moment Shawn stepped back into the kitchen. He was astonished like everyone else.

"There are six of us," said Laura. "Now there are eight." She turned and looked at Rob. "And they are…." Her voice trailed off as she signaled for the rest of them to speak. Everyone introduced themselves.

"Have you been up there the whole time?" Rob asked. "Have you been around the house or outside?"

"No," Carol answered. Ashley shook her head. "We just woke up and heard you all. I'm sorry that we listened for a while but we weren't sure."

"Got that straight," Rob said. "We're not sure what is going on yet."

"Do you remember anything?" Laura asked.

"Not really." She kept her arm on her daughter who was starting to relax more. "We just remember waking up here. Not much before. Can't remember right now. I think it will come back to us in a little bit."

"Yeah, that's what we've been discussing," Laura said. "None of us can quite remember yet either." She thought back to seeing a falling star while at her parents' house. The rest was a blur.

Everyone in the room thought back as far as they could but to no avail, other than blurry memories of where they were just before a big flash of light and waking up here. It was a mystery.

"What's up there?" Harry asked. "Is there a phone?"

"No. Not that we saw," Carol answered. "Just some beds."

That was an immediate let down. It was always the same thing. No easy answers.

Then the little girl spoke. "Is there ice cream?" she asked and pointed to the refrigerator.

"No, I'm sorry. There isn't," Laura answered.

Carol leaned over her daughter. "Don't get your hopes up, honey. I don't think there is much of anything here."

"At least we haven't found anything," said Rob. "Except this tasty water." He turned and got another drink. Then he looked back up at the Carol and Ashley. "Want some?"

"We will in a little bit," Carol answered. "Thanks, though."

Ashley looked up at her mom. "My tummy hurts."

"Mine too," said Carol. "It'll go away."

Everyone stood silent for a moment. Nobody knew what to say next. Then Carol and Ashley started to come down the stairs. They walked slowly going step by step at a time. Both clung to the railing as if that was their only means of security. Their grips on the railing were like their only way to hold onto any mental stability and to fall down the stairs would be to lose oneself. Carol knew that she and Ashley were putting on a good front of being calm but deep down they were very scared of the new events that had transpired in their lives.

"Okay," said Harry and clapped his hands. "Let's form a plan." It sounded good to Harry but everyone seemed to be looking back at him for the plan. Or everyone was starting to get mentally fatigued a bit. They had been wandering around, had met each other, but hadn't moved forward very much with assessing their situation.

"C'mon now," Harry said. "Let's see. What do we need to do?"

Still everyone else was quiet as if afraid to be the first to speak.

Then Rob spoke. "Get the hell outta here." Everybody nodded in agreement.

"Okay, that we can all agree on but that's not where I was going with that," Harry said. "I meant what are our goals and options?"

"Get some information," said Laura.

"Find out where we are," Travis said next.

"Has anyone really checked around outside much?" asked Carol. The group looked at her. Travis and Katie shook their heads no but the others simply shrugged their shoulders.

"Well, I mean," Carol continued. "If we look around outside there have to be some clues. Some other people. Another house or farm. Something." Her calm voice seemed to take an edge off the emotions that ranged from immense concern to growing fear and danger. It had a refreshing effect on the group.

"No. Well, we looked around some in back," Laura answered. "That's when we found Harry just lying there." Her head tilted in his direction.

Harry's eyes darted around to the rest of the group. He felt a little silly at the mention of being found. It was like being a lost kitty that was rescued by firefighters. Harry didn't want the group to pause on that thought for another moment.

"We've got this house," Harry said. "The trees to the side of the house. The backyard with more land behind it. Did anyone notice anything on that side of the house?" He pointed to the living room.

"No," said Travis.

"We hadn't checked yet," Katie said.

Others nodded no.

"Heck, I'm not sure I even remember," said Rob. "I think there are some trees."

"Yeah, and it slumps down a little bit," added Laura. "And then rolls up into a big hill, I think."

"Then let's divide up," Harry said. "Two of us check the rows of trees. Two check behind the house. Two more check out the house. And two check the other side of the house. Okay?"

Everyone was fine with that.

"Ashley and I will check downstairs," said Carol. Although, deep down she wanted to get outside and explore. She figured there wouldn't be much to see downstairs, just like upstairs, and they'd be done quickly and she and Ashley could move outside.

Rob looked at Laura and gestured to her. "Why don't we take the row of trees?"

"That's fine," she answered.

Harry looked at Shawn. "Want to go out back?"

Shawn just looked back at him with his typical glazed look and agreed. Harry figured nothing more needed to be said from him.

"Travis and I will take the other side with the hill," said Katie. Travis was cool with that.

They all split up and went in their own direction.

CHAPTER 21

Laura and Rob stepped off the front porch and walked toward the trees. The footsteps of the others leaving the porch reverberated from behind. They came to the edge of where the trees started and stopped. Harry and Shawn walked past behind them. Harry was talking about strategy and Shawn was basically agreeing with him all along the way. Their voices disappeared as they moved into the backyard. Laura and Rob continued to look around out at the rows of green giants. For both of them the trees were like the first stop of a long journey. The trees were the first thing they had seen when they started to explore outside around the house. Now it was back to square one again.

"Any particular row that you want to start on?" Laura turned and asked Rob. "It all looks the same," she added.

"Nope. Not really," he answered simply.

"Okay. Let's go," she said and started forward.

"That's fine." Rob followed her one step behind.

As they walked Laura was thinking that Rob was acting a little strange. He now seemed a little disconnected with his short answers and wasn't being abrupt like he'd been during the short time that she'd known him. She looked over at him to try to catch his eyes. In response, his eyes shifted and looked back at her.

"What?" He said sharply with a trace of annoyance in his voice.

"Nothing," she answered. "Just you seemed a little different. That's all."

"Nah," he said. "I'm just tired of this place already and I want to get out of here." Laura nodded in agreement and they continued to walk on.

The trees stood tall above them. They were covered with brown rugged bark and long limbs that stretched out like umbrellas and would shield someone during a rain storm. The leaves were dark green with jagged edges. Every few seconds a peaceful breeze soared around them and through the trees causing the leaves to rustle and tingle as the branches swayed back and forth. It gave Laura and Rob a heaven-sent feeling as it flowed smoothly over their skin, through their hair, and calmed the anxieties building inside each of them.

The rows of trees went on and on in front of them. They couldn't see anything at the end. As they walked it was tree after tree with no stop in sight. Every tree was perfectly positioned in a row, almost like it was an orchard. They looked landscaped by design rather than randomly like a forest.

Laura and Rob looked up into the trees to see anything of interest. It was shady and dark under the canopy. Light from the strange ceiling above broke down through the foliage in various areas to touch the ground and cast what seemed like white shadows around them.

Laura tilted her head back and breathed air into her nostrils and deep down into her lungs. It felt so good. Her lungs expanded underneath her chest. The oxygen rushed through her body and up to her head and it made her feel very alive. That's when she realized that something wasn't right. In truth, it was just another thing on a long list that wasn't right. From the moment she woke up here everything had been either wrong, unexplained, or out of touch with what is normal. Nothing added up to make sense and they hadn't discovered any answers yet. However, this was so obvious and should have been noticed earlier, that Laura couldn't believe she didn't think of it until now. It was almost like not seeing a cow standing in the middle of the road and hitting it when driving on a bright sunny day. She looked around some more and examined the bases of the trees around her, the grass beneath her feet, and the branches and leaves above and settled on a reality. What was undeniably noticed by her was the absence of birds and insects. Where were the birds? No birds flew from branch to branch. No birds called out into the sky with the expected "caw caw!" No birds swooped above their heads on their way to get food and bring it back to the nest. No insects either. There wasn't anything buzzing around her face or biting her arms. No flies or gnats shooting into her mouth. No mosquitoes flying onto her arms and sucking blood. Where was all the life?

"There are no birds or insects," said Laura. "Or wildlife for that matter. That is really weird."

Rob was looking around. "You know, I was starting to notice something was really weird like that, too." He continued to look. "Just makes this place worse. God, I hate this place."

"But how can there be no wilderness?" Laura said. "Did everything get killed off?"

"Nah, I don't think so," Rob answered. Now he looked at her. "I guess something could have, but the way this is going, I don't think it's a very natural place."

"What do you mean?" she answered, even though she knew the answer.

"We wake up, hardly remember anything, have a ceiling that's like a giant light, and find other people around and inside the house. We haven't seen anyone else. There are no phones of any sort. And there are no common everyday regular birds, animals, or bugs. That's pretty fucked up," said Rob.

"That's for sure," Laura answered. She looked back in the trees. There was something else she was trying to remember. It just wasn't there yet. She was squinting her eyes and seeing bark, roots, dirt, and grass. Laura couldn't quite grasp it. What was it? No birds. No bugs. Or....

"That's it! There are no plants." She turned to Rob. "Where are the plants? No flowers either. The land is flat with grass." Laura pointed around. "No wonder it's been boring to look at. And we've been so confused that we've been missing the obvious."

Rob nodded in agreement. "Yeah, that's weird too. This place is so messed up. It's not natural."

"Why is that, do you suppose?" she asked.

"I don't know," Rob shrugged. "How should I know? How should any of us know?"

They both looked around some more. Rob walked to a tree and stared up into it. Laura looked back the way they had come. She could see a window of the house in the distance. She wondered what the others had discovered if they had found anything at all.

Rob went over to her. "Let's go on, check some more, and then get back. I don't want to be caught out here too far and get lost. I don't trust this place."

"It's simple," Laura answered. She pointed behind her. "We just go back that way."

"I know that but in this place...." Rob let his voice trail off to make his point and his hands extended out.

Laura didn't speak but she got it. Nothing was normal here.

They continued on. Beams of light broke through the trees in various places around them. The breeze blew every minute. There was no sign of any other people. There were no houses or roads. They didn't hear any cars or trucks.

They kept walking and something changed. There was a wall ahead of them. The same kind of wall in front of the house. It too looked transparent but they couldn't see anything through it. They walked faster. The trees around remained the same. The wall was closer. Together they glided into a run. They ran right up to the edge of the trees and stopped. The wall was in front of them.

They looked at each other and walked up to it. Many questions came to their minds. How can a wall be there? What's on the other side? Doesn't having a wall here make their predicament even worse? Maybe it's a way out?

Laura and Rob looked at each other again. Neither one was sure if they should touch it or not. They wanted to but were afraid of what would happen. Maybe it was dangerous? Maybe they would die? Perhaps it was like dry ice? That would be a horrible way to go! They looked more closely. It looked like open space stretching out ahead of them, mixed with a watery look, and flowing patterns of swirls. They didn't see their reflections or the trees behind them on the wall either. The wall was just like the one in front of the house.

Laura reached out with her hand. As did Rob. Slowly, their hands got closer and closer. They inched forward until finally their fingers touched it. Nothing happened to them. It was smooth and felt cool. They didn't change. The wall didn't change. There was no pain. No electricity shot through their arms. No burning sensation on their fingers. There was no disintegration like what is seen in the movies. It was a strange wall.

To Laura this raised a new question. She mulled over it for a second. Rob was still touching it in different places both high and low. He might have been testing it. Laura pulled her hand back. She had enough of the wall by now.

"Rob, I was thinking," she said.

"Yeah?" he said. Now he was squatting near the ground looking for holes.

"What is the wall for?" she asked. "And does that mean we can't leave? Are we trapped here?" she added.

Rob stood up and looked at her with concern. What Laura said made sense. For him it was starting to come together more. Obviously, it was for Laura too. They woke up at a house with a wall in front of it and now they've discovered a wall in another direction. It was plausible that there were two more walls in the other directions they hadn't been to yet. Rob looked at Laura and they stared at each other for a long moment to further comprehend what their new developments were.

"It seems we're not supposed to leave," Rob said. "That's two down and two to go. If there are walls surrounding in the other directions," Rob stopped momentarily. "The others will find out."

Laura knew what this meant. They were trapped.

CHAPTER 22

Harry and Shawn walked to the edge of the backyard. They stepped through the trees and stopped. For a minute, they stood with an unwillingness to move beyond. They fought through it and took another step forward. Then stopped again. This is the farthest anybody had been behind their new home. The mystery of what was out there quietly called them. Everywhere was green. Beautiful grass covered the land. It ran from beneath their feet out into the open as if it was trying to share itself with every part of nature. A breeze came along and brushed them both. It seemed to be welcoming Harry and Shawn to come and join its world. To come and see what wonders were waiting for them. It was such a pleasant feeling they both staggered a little to keep their balance. The breeze moved along the grass and up into the trees. The sound of ruffling leaves floated over them. Before them was the hill with its beautiful green grass waving over it. Behind the hill there were treetops in the distance. By a trick of the eye the trees appeared to be sitting on the hill. There were rows of trees on the left and right that filed back over the hill.

Then Harry looked down at his feet. A creepy feeling climbed up his legs and over him. This was the spot where he had awakened. Where he had been found. A feeling of defenselessness clamped onto his back. He had to shake it off. The moment of pure contentment with nature was gone. One quick moment of floating among the clouds and another of crashing down to earth into the dirt. *Maybe that's the way it is here, that a person gets the extremes of both sides of things*, he thought. Right now, Harry was on that free fall. One of the worse feelings in the world is of vulnerability. Of that you can't protect yourself. Of powerlessness. And that is what he felt now staring down at his spot. And so far, for all of them, there was no help in sight.

"Hey, are you okay?" asked Shawn.

That snapped Harry out of it and he looked at Shawn. There was an alarmed look on his face. Harry realized that Shawn was very concerned. That took him back a bit and made Shawn more human to Harry. Not that he wasn't a human before but until now Shawn had been the weakest of them. He seemed very distracted and unable to comprehend anything they'd been through. Now Harry thought of Shawn as a person, and not so much as a guy that mumbled and walked around like a zombie. He mattered more to Harry now.

"Yes, I'm fine," Harry answered. "I just realized … never mind." He shook his head. Harry thought there was no point in threading all his thoughts together from the last minute. They needed to move on.

Harry took a step and stopped. He looked up at the strange ceiling, sky, or whatever it was that shined light down on them. It was the strangest thing. No sky, no clouds, no moon. When you looked up, it was obviously a giant ceiling high above that was powered by something. Yet, when you didn't look up there was nothing evident that there was no sun lighting the way.

Harry took another step and stopped. This time he looked all around. Shawn looked at him wondering what is he waiting for? Nothing changed. Nothing moved. The hill was still there. The trees stood tall all around them. The grass was pretty. The plants and flowers were….

"Wait. There are no flowers. Or plants," Harry said.

Shawn looked around. It was true. A fact of life which barely is noticed during our regular routines of daily life was missing and he hadn't realized until now when Harry pointed it out. Where are the plants, flowers, or bees and insects for that matter?

"You're not kidding," Shawn said. "There's nothing here. No bees or bugs."

"Or birds," added Harry.

Shawn bent over and looked down on the ground. Harry crouched down and looked in between the blades of grass. Looked for any bugs. Looked for ants. Looked for a worm. Looked for creepy crawlers. Looked at the dirt. He picked up some of it but it didn't seem like dirt. It felt more like a synthetic material but of what he didn't know. But what he did know was that it felt fake.

"No bugs," Harry said. "No life." He ran his hand through the grass. Harry scooped up some more dirt, shook it in his hand, and let it sift back down through his fingers. It all felt pleasant enough but didn't feel earthly. Harry looked around. "Even the grass and dirt seem unnatural."

"Oh...." Shawn's voice trailed off. He touched the ground. It felt different to him but not to the extent that Harry felt it. Harry continued to rub his hand through the grass much in the way he would run his hand through his hair. This place kept getting stranger and stranger. Another refreshing breeze carried over them and whisked their fears away over the hill and through the trees.

They stood up and stepped forward. The hill had a moderate incline but neither of them had any trouble walking up it. A breeze soared above them again and seemed to carry them along. They reached the top of the hill. Grass flowed all around. The hill was clear in front of them before another grouping of trees started. On both sides of them, more rows of trees stood off into the distance.

"Well, not much here," Harry said. Shawn nodded in agreement. "It's nice but I think it's safe to say that we still have no idea where we are." Shawn nodded again.

They moved forward into the clearing. As they walked nothing changed or moved except when the breeze flowed along with them and rattled through the leaves. The ground wasn't hilly or bumpy. There were no other signs of life. Also, very prevalent was that there was no danger. None at all. They both felt this way. All the apprehension was suddenly gone. Harry felt completely comfortable. It was as if he was back home in the safety of his own yard. For Shawn, it was the same. He felt as if he trusted his surroundings now like a kid does with his mother or father.

Harry and Shawn walked together to the other side. Their steps started to feel long. Maybe it was that their feet were getting smaller? Maybe the trees were moving away from them? That couldn't be. How could that happen? Harry thought that it couldn't. Shawn thought that it shouldn't. It was probably just a trick of the mind. Everything had been a mystery so far without any real answers to speak of. They kept on. It was a short distance but step after step, left after right, and eyes focused forward, they eventually reached the trees. Harry looked behind them. There wasn't anything behind them except for the back top of the house over the hill, the row of trees behind the house, and the trees that aligned both sides of the house. Shawn examined the new patch of forest. It looked safe enough. They looked at each other and slowly entered.

As they moved along the trees stood tall all around them. They were evenly spaced between themselves. Harry and Shawn were dwarfed by them with their size. They dwarfed them with the branches that hung over their heads. The tough bark looked intimidating. The light from the mysterious ceiling shined down through the breaks in the foliage above them. It left spots of light on the ground. The green of the leaves touched memories of lush forests seen in faraway places on television. Was this such a place? Another breeze blew by and rustled beautifully throughout. It was so pleasant that neither Harry nor Shawn now cared that no other life had been found yet. It was an important fact but pushed to the back of their minds for now. They continued to walk, eyes darting around at everything they saw, trying to take in every bit of detail to not miss anything. However, it was all the same. The grass did seem to grow greener on every side. One tree after another. No plants. No flowers. Then Harry stopped. Shawn looked at him.

"What?" Shawn asked. Harry's eyes narrowed and Shawn's widened. He followed Harry's gaze straight forward and saw it too. There was a wall ahead of them.

Harry's intrigue was written all over his face. Why is there a wall here? Shawn's surprise was plastered all over his face too. They'd been walking around for a while, nothing else in sight, and they've finally found something and it's a wall.

"What's it for?" asked Shawn.

Harry shrugged and moved forward. Shawn followed. The last couple of trees were the same as all the ones they'd seen before them. One indisputable detail about this place was everything was the same. The trees, their branches, their leaves, and the grass were like the one before and after them. They were all duplicates. There was a vacancy of color in the land. No movement or sounds of life. No diversity of plant life. The strange light came down from above and never changed.

Harry walked right up to the wall without any hesitation. His curiosity overtaking any kind of caution or prudence. He stared right at it. He tried to stare through it. The wall looked transparent, seemed to be made of flowing water, but he couldn't see what was on the other side. Nothing was reflected back. Not him. Not Shawn. Or the forest around them. Harry was reminded of the same wall that was in front of the house. It stood from the ground all the way up to the ceiling. There was no way to see or climb over it. The wall ran from left to right until his sight was blocked by trees. It appeared there was no way around it either.

He stuck his hand out to touch but didn't. He held it there in the air. His elbow was bent, his hand flat, and ready to go but something stopped him. What if....

"Are you going to actually touch it?" said Shawn, alarmed. Harry didn't answer. He didn't move. "Dude," Shawn's voice was rising. "What if it's dangerous?"

Harry reached out and touched. Nothing happened. In fact, it felt good. The wall was cool to the touch. It had a soothing feeling to it. Almost like running water inside of it. He enjoyed touching it.

Shawn saw Harry smile and knew it was okay. He exhaled in relief.

"What's it like?" asked Shawn.

"Go ahead, feel it." Harry waved him forward. He was staring up at the wall and the light ceiling.

Shawn stepped up, touched it for a long moment, then took a couple steps back content with what he had done. Shawn didn't feel the need to touch it for too long as he felt he was getting along fine now with his new environment. He decided it wouldn't take any turns for the worse. He was happy with the way it was for now.

"Yeah, it's nice," said Shawn. Harry turned to him and cracked a grin. Now Shawn seemed a little silly to him. He was way too uptight in Harry's view. Things were weird right now but this was a nice and friendly wall. *Shawn should relax a bit and settle down*, he thought. It's just a wall.

"Did you feel the water-like motion inside it?" Harry asked. He stopped touching the wall.

"Yes, kinda," Shawn answered.

"You didn't touch it for very long. You sure?"

"Yeah, I got it. It's weird though. How could it do that?" asked Shawn.

"I don't know. Could be there's water on the other side."

"It's not like any other wall that I've touched before."

"Nope. And this entire place is turning out to be that way."

"The ceiling is weird, too."

"Yes, it is." Harry looked back at the wall. He touched it a few more times but it was solid. It had a plastic and glass feeling to it and not like brick or cement.

"So we have a wall in front of our new house and behind us as well," Harry said. "Wanna bet we're surrounded?"

Shawn didn't answer. He looked around them again. Shawn looked at the trees, and the path they'd come, but didn't see anything new other than this wall.

"Yeah, if there's a wall back here," Shawn spoke. "I wonder how long it is."

"Hard to tell," Harry answered. "It could go on for miles."

That thought sounded depressing to Shawn. How the heck could someone get out of there with miles of wall keeping them inside?

"Maybe the wall is to keep things out?" said Harry.

Shawn felt better. When Harry touched the wall, he was very scared of this place. However, nothing had happened to him. His arms didn't fly off. His head hadn't exploded. No ray beams had incinerated either of them. Now it seemed more docile and friendly. He was starting to relax a bit. He no longer thought that something was going to jump out of nowhere and attack them.

Harry turned to Shawn.

"Let's go back and report what we found and find out what the others found as well," he said.

Shawn nodded. Together they started back. It was good too because Shawn thought that he had started to notice a smell. And it wasn't a nice one.

CHAPTER 23

Katie thought it was a nice day for a stroll. Too bad it was in this place. She and Travis had left the house, passed through a small group of trees, and were now in a clearing of grass. On their right was a new group of trees. Where it went, nobody knew. Until Harry and Shawn find out. They went in *that* direction. On their left was that mysterious wall. They had no idea what to make of it. Why was it there and what's on the other side? How come you couldn't see anything through it? It looked like glass after all. Rising in front of them was a hill with some trees on top. They pondered the question of what was on the other side. They couldn't see over the hill. It had an easy incline and didn't look like keeping your footing on it would be a problem.

Travis looked at Katie next to him. She looked so pretty. Her blonde hair was magnetic when she turned. Travis was very proud of her. And here she was with him in the greatest adventure of their lives. Or the greatest mystery. It depended on how you looked at it. However, at the moment they hadn't found much to know what they were in the middle of and didn't know what they were going to do about it. The six others were investigating their areas and he and Katie had theirs to check out. This included finding out what was on the other side of the hill.

"Kinda makes ya think about what comes over the hill doesn't it?" Katie asked.

"Yeah, like something out of a movie or something," Travis answered. "The big troll comes over the hill from its lair looking for people to eat."

They both busted up laughing. It was a good feeling too. Everything had been so confusing since being there.

"Maybe it's a dragon?" said Katie.

"A hogzilla?"

"Oh no, it's a Bigfoot, Loch Ness, combo."

"Yeah, it's athlete's Footloch!" Travis answered.

They laughed again.

A nice breeze blew along and settled them down. Katie's hair blew kisses in the wind to Travis. He was enamored with her. She was being more serious than he was right now. He was thinking about her and she was thinking about exploring their new world. He had to snap out of it. Then it occurred to him that they were being very careless in this strange place since they left the house and their new friends. They were walking along freely, laughing, and didn't know what was out there yet. And now they were right in the middle of it.

"You know what we have to do, don't you?" Katie asked. She liked the way his hair was ruffled and uncombed. It made him look a little rough to her. Especially for a skinny guy. That made the stress of their predicament easier to bear. Albeit only for a few seconds.

"Yeah," he answered and looked at the hill. "Cross into the great wide yonder over there."

"I'm afraid we do," she answered.

"Over the hills and far away."

"We gotta find out what is going on."

"And then get out of here."

"Sounds good." She looked around a little more. "Ya know, I'm starting to wonder if we're going to find anything at all."

"Too early to tell. Heck, we just started." Travis stopped to listen. "It's really quiet here."

"What'd you say babe? I can't hear you from all the noise." Katie laughed. Then her eyebrows narrowed.

"There's nothing here," Travis added. "No noise other than the wind in the trees."

Katie stared at him. She listened. "But how can there be no noise. I mean…." Katie walked around in a circle and looked at the trees, the hill, and back toward the house. "How can't there be any noises other than…."

"Us." Travis finished her thought.

"Is anything even alive here?"

"I haven't seen anything. No birds flying. No squirrels. No rabbits. No insects. It was starting to bug me for a while and now I know. It's so obvious now."

"Yeah, it's stuff we take for granted. Although I don't mind the no insect part. But what is this? Like a never-never land or something?"

"I don't know. But now I don't like it even more."

"Me neither." Katie flipped her hair back. "Let's check out that hill and then we can get back to the others. Maybe they found something."

"Like people."

"Exactly."

Together they started walking toward the hill.

"Or a phone," Travis continued.

"Exactly."

"Ah, I miss my cell phone."

"Exactly. Dude, I totally miss mine. Not to leave out how boring this place will be without it."

"Just hope we don't have to stay here long."

"That would be awful. Hopefully, this is some sort of sick practical joke. Or a parallel reality or something."

They walked at a moderate pace.

"Or a dream," he said.

"I'll take dream right now."

"Babe, I don't think it's a dream."

"Hey now, don't crush my dreams," she laughed.

"Yeah, I won't." Travis smiled back.

They were getting close to the hill.

"Shhh," hushed Travis. "We've been way too loud, I think."

"Okay," Katie answered and put her finger to her lips. "Loose lips sink ships," she said softly.

"Cool," he hushed back.

"What if something comes running at us like a bear?"

"Then we run."

"Bears can run fast."

"Then we run faster."

"What if it catches us?"

"We'll yell."

"And if that's not good enough as it eats us?"

"Then we're screwed."

"And chewed."

"Yep. And you know what?" He looked at her.

"What?"

"You're beautiful," he said with a wink.

"And so are you my dawwwwlynn...." She imitated a southern accent. They laughed.

"Although, at this point, I don't think there are gonna be any bears," Travis said.

"Or lions or tigers," she answered.

"Nope. Or tin men."

They kept walking. They were almost at the hill.

"What about snakes?" she asked. "I don't do snakes."

"I know." Now Travis was starting to feel she was asking just to have something to ask.

"Mermaids?"

"We haven't seen water yet."

"Or a snow monster?"

He laughed. Now he knew she was messing around. She was so funny.

"Nope. Not even a snow monster. No Yeti ... yet."

Katie was smiling at him. She loved joking around with him and not letting up. "A Yeti?"

He laughed again. "That requires snow. Yetis don't use sun block."

She laughed. It was easy to forget their current troubles when the two of them were together. But now they were at the hill and stopped. They looked up at it and then at each other. Now it looked steeper than before so footing might be a problem. Otherwise it looked okay.

"We have to go," Katie said.

"Yep. We do. The sooner we check it out the sooner we can get back with the others." Travis looked back at the house which was behind that thin line of trees and beyond the grassy land they had just walked through. The house had a nice old-style profile from the side with its pointy blue roof sticking up over the trees like a hat, blue shutters on the side, and red chimney on top. The sound of the water shooting up in the air from the fountain could faintly be heard. He turned back to Katie.

"After you, my lady." He bowed with his arm extended out leading the way up the hill.

"Why thank you, kind sir," she said with an imitated English accent. "You are a gentleman and a scholar." She curtsied back.

She started up the hill and Travis followed her. Walking up it was a little harder than expected. They both had sneakers on and couldn't always keep their footing on the grass. What strange grass it was. It was a pretty green but didn't feel right when he picked at it.

"This grass is weird," he said. "Kind of like artificial turf or something."

"Like fake lettuce," Katie answered. She was still in that mood.

"Yeah, something like that."

"In other words, don't eat it or smoke it."

More laughter.

"That's for sure." He watched her butt shift back and forth and started feeling a different kind of mood.

They were almost at the top and they felt it in their legs. Walking up that steep angle had been much harder than it looked. They both had sore thighs and calves. Going up wasn't something the two of them were used to. To them, didn't graduation from high school mean no more mandatory physical activity? Didn't it mean permission to be lazy if one wanted to for the rest of their life?

They got to the top. Immediately, they enjoyed being on higher ground.

"Maybe we should join a gym when we get back," Travis said.

"If we get back," Katie answered. Her mood was gone. It was replaced by a different mood. A more serious one.

"Hey, now babe, we will," he said. It was contagious because now he wasn't feeling relaxed as he looked around. This was serious.

Katie saw that the hill went on a slight decline down in front of them. There were trees in rows going down the hill as well. Most of the ground was blanketed in dark because of the tree canopy above except for some light that shined down where there was some breakage in the trees.

Travis looked around. He saw trees, grass, the strange light ceiling above them, and that strange watery wall which seemed to serve as their front yard. Or as the substitute neighbors across the street. He kept looking. More trees. More grass.

"What is this place anyway?" Katie asked. She meant it more as a rhetorical statement. They'd been through this already and still didn't have any new answers other than more trees.

"Still no birds or animals," Travis noted.

"No flowers. No plants. No bees buzzing around. No flies," Katie said. "Whoever thought they'd be glad to have a fly land on them?"

"Not I," Travis said. He hadn't thought of it that way yet. This place was so weird and unnatural that a few of the annoyances of everyday life would be welcomed now. Even appreciated.

"There just isn't any action if you know what I mean," Katie continued.

"Yeah, I know what you mean. It's boring," Travis said.

"Have you noticed any smells really?" She inhaled deeply, held it, and let out a long exhale. "I guess there's that tree smell."

Travis breathed deeply too. The tree smell she was talking about was definitely a tree smell. What kind he had no idea. But it reminded him of when he was a kid playing in the yard and using trees to hide or duck behind for cover. It was a smell reminiscent of his childhood.

"Yeah," agreed Travis while looking around. "That's about all I recognize."

"I'm not liking this even more. I mean we haven't seen anything yet that can hurt us but we haven't seen anything yet to make things better."

On instinct, she reached for her cell phone, and so did he, but they were empty-handed. They squeezed their pockets but no cell phones were in them. They slowly looked up at each other

"Oh, I forgot," said Katie.

"So did I," answered Travis.

They shared a look of anxiety on their faces. They felt defenseless almost. How easy it was to forget that they didn't have their most prized possessions, other than each other, anymore. The cell phone was something that came hand in foot with any person as if it was a fifth limb on the human body. Theirs weren't here. Their best way to get in touch with the outside world, or at least away from here, was gone. Their best weapon, one might say, gone.

"You know, I think something took our cell phones," Katie said with a stern look on her face.

"Me too," Travis said. He returned her a strict look of his own. "Something else is out here somewhere. Has control."

"I can't live without my cell," Katie said again.

"But you're going to have to," said Travis. "Someone, or something, made sure of that."

"Yeah, no kidding. And I don't think it's a joke."

Then a nice calm breeze blew over them, down the hill, and into the trees below. The leaves fluttered and the branches swayed a bit. Instantly, they felt better. It softened their skin and their tensions. No need to worry or get upset. Everything was fine.

"Let's move on," Travis said. "We have to be able to go back and tell them we found nothing and mean it."

"Unless we find SOMETHING."

They walked down the hillside. It wasn't too steep a decline so they didn't have much trouble walking down it. Trees were in rows all around them. All seemed to be evenly spaced apart. Katie thought the leaves looked sharp and jagged as if they'd been cut into shape by a cookie cutter. No plants, flowers, or weeds grew at their bases. They didn't grow anywhere else that they could see. After a while the hill leveled out. Nothing else changed. The silence lived everywhere. No bird calls crying out over them. No squirrels jumping around or vaulting from tree to tree. Just them.

After a nice walk, their eyes widened and their brows rose. They saw a wall.

CHAPTER 24

Carol and Ashley stood on the front porch. The steel dragon shot its flames in the disguised form of water up into the air. It rained its havoc onto nothing other than the pool of water around it. The splashing sound was comforting to the ear. Behind it was the strangest thing Carol could imagine right now. It was that wall. A bluish watery-looking one at that. What was it and what was it for?

"What's on the other side?" Ashley asked her.

"Hopefully, good things," she answered but feelings inside let her down that it wasn't true.

Light shined down from the ceiling sky. Otherwise to look around one would think it's just another beautiful summer day. It wasn't that hot outside and was quite comfortable like a pleasant afternoon. Carol figured that she and Ashley had only been up in the new home, their new world, or call it a place of existence for about an hour. She couldn't know for sure because they had no clocks. She assumed they had electricity because their weird refrigerator worked. Of course, it could be some other power source, but what did that matter as long as they had power. Then again if the power ran out, and they didn't know how to get that power back, they were screwed. She decided to forget about that. Her motherly ways already had enough to worry about.

"Mom, are they coming back today?"

"Yes, hon. They will," Carol answered. Nobody had returned yet and they were anxious to find out what others had found. "They're just checking out the new farm, to sorta say." She thought that sounded good. Carol didn't have an exact pinpoint hold on what this was, where this was, or what all was transpiring yet.

"Farm? I don't see any animals. I don't see any cows or pigs."

"We don't know if we have any yet. That's what our new friends have gone to look for."

"If they find horses can I ride them?"

"Sure you can, sweetie. If they're not wild." Learning to ride horses. Now that's one more thing she might have to worry about.

The two of them had already done their part. They had systematically gone through the house, room by room, and didn't find anything very useful. The only items that ran on power were the fridge, the assumed microwave machine, electric razors found in the bathroom, and the ceilings that lit up when you walked into a room. She had found switches on the walls so the automatic lights could be deactivated and only turned on when needed. That was a positive development. No more "let there be light" moments. Otherwise, it was a bland and boring house. However, the structure made it a good-looking house. The wood was nice. It seemed sturdy. The windows were shut tight and wouldn't open. The fireplace wasn't real and its chimney was sealed. The house had no phones. No landlines. She couldn't find her own cell phone either and her watch and jewelry were gone. Carol also noticed there were no air conditioning, furnace, washer, dryer, or dishwasher machines either. The basic inventions that make modern life easier and bearable on a daily basis were missing.

Carol watched Ashley playing with her hair. Her daughter was okay and that was the most important thing right now. She and Ashley were unharmed. Although, several times earlier she had felt a small pain in her stomach and Ashley had complained of one too. She didn't know what was causing it. Perhaps it was from hunger pains. However, it wasn't a growling stomach but more like a quick stabbing feeling. They had felt better after drinking some water and got hydrated. Carol hadn't figured this one out yet but for now they both felt fine. For the moment, that was more comforting than dreading that this was going to be a more severe problem that would have to be dealt with in the future.

They found the house had a simple layout. On the first floor, there were five rooms. The kitchen and living room were in front with three rooms in back. Those three rooms were two big ones in the corners and a smaller one in between that was a bathroom. That was an important find! It was complete with a shower in a tub, toilet, and sink. It had personal items for men and women. It had other necessities such as towels, toothpaste, deodorant, and shaving supplies but was missing toilet paper, soap, and shampoo. She wasn't sure of why on that one. Maybe they'll find some later? It's either that or if they're stuck here for any real amount of time, they'll all be very smelly, and nobody would be happy with that. The two rooms in the corners were bedrooms, each equipped with a bed, and a big two-door closet. Each room had two windows, one on the side, and the other window faced out the back of the house. Long blue curtains hung down in front of them. There was no basement.

The upstairs was more of the same. Four bedrooms were in the corners and a bathroom separated the two rooms in the back. The stairs led up in front of the bathroom door. All the rooms had the same interior design and accessories as the bedrooms on the first floor.

Carol stared up at the lighted ceiling for a minute. She didn't need her sunglasses here. She didn't even have them if they were needed.

Carol had thought a lot about their predicament in the last hour and had made some sense of the current events. However, she was having trouble remembering what happened leading up to them. She remembered a bright light and a flying sensation. That's where it pretty much stopped. Now a new memory was starting to creep into her head. It was of her running around outside in the dark but she was having trouble grasping it entirely. She thought with a little more time she could further understand the meaning of it. She hoped it would give her a few answers as to how they got there.

Ashley sat down on the front steps and rested her head in her hands. Carol could tell she was bored. There wasn't anything around for her to play with. There were no games, television, or computers to take up her attention. She thought about how amazing it was that in the time of her forty years of being alive, life had gone from board games, basic video games, phones with cords attached to the wall, three major television channels, and Beta and VHS to incredible video games, smart phones, over 1,000 channels of television, Blue Ray and Blue Tooth, High Definition TV, and reality television shows. Not to leave out they had none of that here. Now it was going to be even harder to keep Ashley entertained. She would have to think of something fast.

While she looked at Ashley, something she had said earlier inside the house, grabbed her interest now. It was something about flying glow balls. She didn't know what that meant and hadn't picked up on it before. Ashley had said it when they were inspecting the rooms upstairs, but Carol was so focused on the house that it went unnoticed. Until now.

"Ashley, honey," she said.

"Yeah, Mom."

"Do you remember what you said earlier inside? Something about flying glow balls?"

"Yeah, Mom."

"Well," she hesitated. "What did you mean?"

"I remember them. Don't you?"

"No, I don't. Tell me about them."

"Like want? That they fly around?"

"Yeah, stuff like that. What else? How do you remember them?"

"I don't really know, Mom." Ashley shrugged. "I just do. It was back home. They were round lights that flew around. And they glowed. Like flying glow balls," she said playfully.

"Back home?" her mother questioned. She was having trouble even remembering home. "Where'd they come from?"

"They just came to the back door."

That alarmed Carol! They came right up to the back door?

"There were three of them," Ashley continued. "One was right there glowing at the back door. The other two were flying around in the backyard."

Carol was trying to process all of this. Trying to make sense of it.

"It wanted me and Kenny to come out and play."

Oh, god! Her other doll baby…. Where was he and was he okay?

"But Kenny was too afraid and ran and hid. He didn't like it. Said it was bad." Ashley was balancing herself on one leg in front of the porch stairs. "Some tough big brother he is."

For some reason, Carol couldn't remember much of anything before being here at this place. Slowly a bit and a piece here would jab at her memory but there wouldn't be anything more to put together as a whole. It was difficult to put together her past. Something was blocking it all from her. And what about her other child Kenny? How could she have forgotten about him? She felt guilty and unworthy of being a mother. But it wasn't her fault. Something, or someone, was stopping her. It was preventing her from knowing her life up until she woke an hour ago. In truth, she hadn't had the time or brain power yet to even concentrate on life outside of here. It had been a big ball of confusion without any time to reflect. She hadn't seen Kenny yet so he might be okay. Where was he? Someplace else other than here. Frustration was growing within her. Carol had to remember. It was her natural born instinct and God given right as a mother to know where her son was and if he was okay. She needed more jagged edges to stab at her brain. To cut her if necessary so she could remember. At least so she could know where Kenny was. Now her daughter was telling her about these bizarre glow balls which may or may not be real. Could they be part of her brainy girl's imagination? Are they imaginary friends? Carol had one when she was a child. Kenny had one when he was little too. Ashley had an imaginary pet dog named Tog when she was in kindergarten but she was too old for imaginary playmates or pets now.

"Where is Kenny?" Carol asked.

"He didn't come, Mommy. Remember?"

"No, I don't remember. What do you mean he didn't come?"

"He didn't come outside. He never did."

Carol was confused. She was here in a place with complete strangers, albeit seemingly nice people, with no apparent sky other than a great big light bulb. In front of her was a strange-looking wall, which obviously was to keep them there, but she didn't know what was on the other side and that didn't settle well with her. She was having trouble remembering her life before this, even though she knew it was in her head somewhere, but she couldn't quite reach it yet. Her precious little girl was here with her playing on the porch. She was safe but where was her little boy? Why wasn't he here with her where he belonged? Then again why were they here in this new home where they didn't belong? A home which didn't seem real but was real. To mix in with that confusion was the frustration that she didn't know how they got here.

"I don't know why he's so scared of them," Ashley continued. "They've been there before."

Carol's eyes widened. "Before.... When?"

"Oh, a few times, Mom."

"How come you never told me?"

"They didn't want us to. It's a secret."

Carol felt anger swell up upon hearing this.

"It's okay, Mom. They don't hurt us." Now Ashley was swinging her body outward and holding onto the front stairs railing.

"Be careful, sweetie. Don't fall off." Her motherly instinct to protect broke in.

"They aren't bad," said Ashley.

Carol wasn't so sure of that.

"They ask us questions?"

"They do?" More surprise. She still didn't know what these glow balls were. She believed and trusted her daughter but couldn't completely buy into her daughter's story. Carol figured it was more a figment of a seven-year-old's imagination concocted to fill in place for what really happened and didn't want to remember. There weren't any flying glow balls in the world. Let alone any that ask questions. She would have to ask more questions to get to the root of it. "What do they ask you?"

"Oh, questions … like our names, how old we are, and what we like to do." Ashley jumped down into the front yard. "They ask about you too, Mom."

"They do huh...." Carol was intrigued. "Like what?"

"Where you are and when you'll be back."

A feeling of alarm signified to Carol that Ashley's flying friends only come around when she wasn't home like when she has made a quick trip to the store. It also meant they didn't want her around. Their mother! Their protector! They want her out of the way. But just when she started to be sucked in and believe the story she remembered that these things aren't real. Could her little girl be harvesting some deep-rooted feeling of resentment about when she isn't around to be with her? That would be the perfect time for her little girl's imagination to run wild and receive visits from *supposed glow balls*.

"Usually you aren't gone for very long, Mommy, so they don't stay for very long."

"I see." *That's convenient,* Carol thought. When she gets back home there is no need for her glow friends anymore. Mommy's back and her little girl's imagination is interrupted and they just go away. She would gently press her daughter for more. "Did they ask anything else?"

"Like what, Mommy?" Ashley had skipped over to the fountain. Water was shooting up from the dragon and clamoring down with a splash.

"Anything."

"Hmm, like they wanted to know why Kenny won't play. Where Daddy is."

Carol thought those seemed like typical questions a little girl would ask. Perhaps she was imagining these glow balls from basic questions or things that were bothering her? She was becoming more convinced of this. Of course, what little girl wouldn't wonder where her dad is, the lying cheating jerk, when her parents divorced so early in her life.

"Is there anything else they asked you?" Carol asked.

"Yeah, Mom. They asked if it's true that you can no longer have babies."

Carol was stunned! How did Ashley know that? She never told any of her children this. Never mentioned it on the phone when they were home or anywhere around her. She hadn't told her sleazeball ex-husband either. How did she know about this? It didn't come from any of her friends. They knew Carol didn't want her children to know this.

"Uh, Ash, how do you know that?" Carol said, still taken back a little. She felt exposed in a way. "Who told you that I can't have any more babies?"

"The light!" Ashley said smiling from ear to ear. "Betcha didn't know I knew that did ya?" Now she was having fun with her mom almost like a guessing game.

"You mean the glow balls told you this?" Carol asked sternly.

"Yeah, they're very smart. They know lots of things." She hopped back to the porch and stood in front of her mom. "They know Kenny goes and hides in the closet whenever they come but they don't want me to tell him because it will hurt his feelings."

"Who is *they*, Ash?"

"Oh Mom, I told you. The glowing lights. You know that. You aren't paying attention." She started spinning around like a ballerina. "They also told me that old man Mr. Johansson is a peeping Tom and that you caught him in the yard one night when I was at Daddy's."

Carol just blinked. And blinked again. No words came to her lips. She caught Mr. Johansson sneaking around their yard one night last spring but never told Ashley or Kenny about it. She didn't want to scare them and make them paranoid of the night. Kenny was already having enough trouble sleeping as it was. There was no need to make matters worse. It was a problem that had puzzled Carol ever since it started a few months ago. Until that point she had never had any problems like that with either of her children. But Kenny had started. He seemed to think that something was lurking under his bed. Mr. Johansson had given some excuse about seeing something in her yard and coming over to investigate it. Carol didn't report him, only told a few of her girlfriends, and let it go. She figured he was embarrassed enough and that would keep him away. Again, how did Ashley know that?

"Ash, how many times have you seen or talked to your glow ball friends?"

"A couple."

"How often? Every week?"

"No. Just a couple times ever since spring." She looked up at the house. "They don't like the cold, Mommy. Don't like winter."

That makes two of them, Carol thought.

"Do you think they have winter here?" Ashley continued. "Maybe they'll come here?"

"I hope not, Ashley. What makes you so sure they're your friends?"

"Cuz they are. They talk to me and they're nice. They don't like the cold from where they're from. They don't have cold."

Once again Carol's interest was snagged in this story. That was a surprise to hear. First these glow balls are mind readers and now they have a home which they come from.

"They told you that?"

"Yep. The first time I met them." She squinted and got a real serious look of concentration on her face. "It was just after winter. That is how I know they don't like it." Ashley laughed.

"Yes, I understand what they mean," Carol answered. She wasn't fond of winter either, like most people weren't, so it was easy to see where Ashley got this from. The glow balls shared the same thoughts as most people about winter. But what took Carol aback was that Ashley knew things that only Carol knew, and that it supposedly came from them. Once again, how could she know this? Unless these glow balls, that is supposed glow balls, had told her. Immediately, she put that idea to the side because that was impossible. It was stupid. There are no glow balls flying around talking to children. Maybe in their imaginations but not in the real world.

However, Carol was getting more confused. She knew the idea of lights that fly around and talk to children was preposterous but her daughter was completely convinced that the story she was telling was true. Ashley told it without a hint of making things up. But what really packed a punch was that she knew about Carol not having more babies and the peeping neighbor. Those two facts started to make her wonder if this was true. Carol knew that sometimes if people make up an outlandish story that the crazier it is the more people will believe it. However, she didn't think this was one of those circumstances. Certainly, not from her daughter. Every minute that went by now was starting to chip away at Carol's belief that this was just a child's imaginary friend, or playful fantasy, and sculpt a little bit more the possibility of it being true. The more it built inside her mind the more it connected to where they were now. What in the world was this place? All this didn't make sense. Her reality was starting to settle right down in between what was pretend and what was real.

"Did they say why they don't have the cold?" Carol thought she would press on. "Are they from Arizona?"

"No, Mom. Don't be silly," Ashley said with a hint of disbelief. Her voice gave away that she didn't believe her mother's question was even serious. "They aren't from Arizona. They're from another place."

"Where is that?" Carol shifted her stance.

"Not there." Ashley jumped backwards off the porch stairs. "Someplace else where it's a lot hotter."

"Mexico?"

Ashley tilted her head and stared at her mom. "No, Mom. From far away."

Carol crossed her arms and leaned against the porch support beam. "Like another planet?" she asked.

"Yeah, Mom. Like that." Ashley began to jump up and land in a baseball player's crouching stance. "I'm bored. Can we go, Mom?"

Carol wasn't sure of anything yet. What she wanted was to wake up and be at home in the safety of her own kitchen cooking up a nice healthy dinner for her and her children. And where was Kenny? Oh God, where was Kenny? She looked around but the only thing to see was the porch and this strange yard.

"What planet?" Carol continued. Maybe her daughter would say something that would reveal she was making all this up. Although, it wasn't looking like she was making it up. Or that she was aware that she was making it up.

"I don't remember." She continued to jump up but now would walk like a sumo wrestler after each jump. "They like their planet, Mommy. Not as cold, they said."

"Well, how hot is it there?" Carol was beginning to be surprised that there was more and more to this story.

"I don't know, Mom. But hotter. Like a desert. No ice cream can grow there." Ashley laughed.

Carol smiled. That was a nice feeling. The last hour hadn't been funny. "So why are they here? What do they want?"

"They like to visit." She was staring to the right in the direction that Travis and Katie had gone. "They like our planet."

"Okay, but...." Carol stepped down off the porch. "Why do they come visit you?"

"They like us, Mommy."

"I know that, but do they want to play?" Carol asked.

"Yeah, they want us to come out and play. Only I do, though."

Surprise streaked across Carol's face. Her little girl went outside with a stranger? With these things? That couldn't be. She knew better than to do that.

"They want me and Kenny to run around and chase them. I didn't though cuz you said not to leave the yard."

Relief washed over Carol's body. Her daughter didn't follow the strange lights.

"Where do they want you to chase them to?"

"Wherever they go." Ashley was swinging her arms around in circles.

"Which is?" Carol's voice narrowed.

"The yard. The trees. The woods. No place that's cold."

Carol thought that was good. There was nothing about running away. She still felt there was something that hadn't been revealed yet.

"What do they say when you don't play?"

"That it's okay and safe. They don't want to hurt us."

Carol thought that sounds just like what child predators might say to young children. Then a cool refreshing breeze blew by and she was content again. All was good. *This is a nice house*, she thought. A nice house in which her daughter's imagination could run wild. A nice house where she could listen to her daughter tell stories all day long. Just then Rob and Laura walked around the end of the porch talking between themselves. Ashley was still looking at her mom.

"You do believe me, don't you Mommy?"

CHAPTER 25

Rob and Laura appeared to be arguing but weren't. However, something was obviously bothering them. They walked up to the front steps heavily into their discussion.

"What'd you find?" Carol asked when they stopped.

"We're trapped," said Rob. He was angry. His cheeks had a reddish glare to them.

"There's a wall," Laura said. "It's like the wall in front here. Watery." She pointed over her shoulder.

"There's no place to go," Rob continued. "The wall goes up to the ceiling. And you know how the ceiling is." Rob was glad nobody answered that. It wasn't meant for an answer. It was just meant to show how upset he was now. At first it was discovery. Now it's entrapment.

"Do you mean that if we walk that way we come to a giant wall? Like enclosed confinements?" Carol asked. She pretty much understood what they were saying but just wanted to clarify so she could picture it in her head. "A wall in front and to the side?"

"Yep, nowhere to run and nowhere to hide," Rob said.

Carol was bothered by his tone. She didn't feel this was the time for smart-ass comments. The truth is that Rob's brain was in overload.

"Yes, that's it," said Laura. She wasn't feeling too optimistic anymore. When they set out to look around she figured they'd find something or someone to help. Now she knew different. As far as she had seen it was just them. There weren't any roads out of here.

"Did you see any glow balls?" little Ashley asked. They all looked at her expressionless. Or perhaps is was confusion masked by blank faces. Her voice was far too sweet and innocent to be locked inside here. "Did you see any flying around?" Ashley asked again.

"Huh?" Rob mumbled.

"No, they didn't, honey. Those are just for fun and games back home." Carol knew that Rob and Laura didn't know anything about what they had been discussing. That was just between mother and daughter. She didn't want to have to get into it and try to explain that. Especially to Rob. He was quite agitated right now and there was no telling what he might think.

"Any of the others back yet?" asked Laura. She figured there weren't but asked anyway.

"Nope. You're the first," said Carol. "I wonder what they found."

"If it's like what we found it's more of the same. And I'm thinking it's a good bet they did." Laura said. She looked around. "And if that's the case then we're...."

"Trapped," said Rob. He sounded resigned to it.

Ashley started doing cartwheels around the yard. Water was splashing out of the dragon's mouth. Nothing else moved. Not the trees. Nothing flew around them. No bugs buzzed in their faces or their ears. The earlier breezes had gone quiet. The air seemed stagnant like it was being held in place but the temperature was comfortable. It felt around the mid-seventies. That was a good thing.

"Did you find anything?" Laura asked Carol.

"Bathrooms." Carol smiled. "Thank God for that at least."

"That's for sure!" said Rob. "Hey, hey, something positive."

"Some bedrooms upstairs," Carol continued. "Really nothing else, though. No phones."

"Why am I not surprised at that?" Laura said. Her sarcasm bounced off the front windows.

"Oh, and I did find switches to turn off the ceiling lights that turn on automatically," Carol continued. "The only other things that use power seem to be in the kitchen and bathrooms."

"We don't know where the power is from but I guess that doesn't matter right now anyway," said Laura. Then something caught her eye.

From the left two shapes emerged from the small grouping of trees just at the end of the yard. Everyone turned. Travis and Katie were coming back.

"Whew, we know they're okay," said Carol. "What about Harry and Shawn?"

"Don't know yet," Laura answered.

"We can probably go looking around back," Rob said shaking his head. He didn't think there was too much reason to wait for them. Most of them were back now and depending on what Travis and Katie had discovered, which Rob didn't think was anything much at all, they needed to work on a plan of what they were going to do.

"Oh, but no toilet paper." Carol wasn't finished yet.

"What!" Rob yelled. That brought him right back to where he had been just a minute ago. His newly found seriousness a thing of the not so distant past. "That's not cool at all!"

"Hold on. Hold on," Laura said. "There's got to be some TP somewhere. Did you check the bathroom closets?"

"Yeah, I did." Carol shrugged. "Didn't see any. Unless I missed it but I don't think so."

"Shit, that's inhumane!" Rob said.

"We'll find some," said Laura.

Ashley tumbled and rolled right up next to Rob's leg. She smiled at him. It took him a moment but a smile broke out on his face too. It seemed to break him of his foul mood.

Travis and Katie approached the porch and stopped.

"Well...." Travis said opening his hands.

"What'd you find?" asked Laura.

Travis and Katie looked them over reading their faces. What they saw wasn't inspiring. They looked at each other and shrugged.

"Not too much," said Travis. "We went over the hill, walked among a lot of trees, and really just wandered til we came to a real weird wall like we have here." He gestured to the front wall.

"Yeah," Katie cut in. "It's trippy to look at. Sorta like it's made of water and it goes right up to the ceiling." She pointed upwards.

"We couldn't get out," Travis added.

"Doesn't look like we can get out, period," Rob said. "That's what we found our way too."

"We don't know what Harry and Shawn found yet," Laura said.

"They aren't back yet?" Katie said with a touch of alarm in her voice.

"No, not yet," Laura answered. "We're about to go look for them."

"Did you hear anything from back there? Like yelling?" Travis asked.

"No. We really just got back ourselves," Laura said. She could tell they were getting too worried too soon. "We'll go look in a minute but chances are they found the same thing we did."

"Which is nothing except that we're stuck here," Rob said. He was getting frustrated again.

Travis looked at Carol and checked out the house. It had a Midwest country look to it.

"How about you? Did you find anything useful inside?" he asked Carol.

"Not too much. A few rooms. The upstairs is the same as the downstairs pretty much without a kitchen. We have two bathrooms."

"That's good," said Travis. He and Katie smiled.

"But no toilet paper," Rob said disbelievingly.

"That's not good," Travis answered. Their smiles went away.

"We'll find some," said Laura again.

"Watch!" Ashley's sweet little voice rose up from below. She did a cartwheel.

"Wow!" said Katie. "You're really good!"

"Thanks," said Ashley. "Wanna see another?"

"Sure," Katie answered. She really liked Ashley. She seemed like a nice little girl. While Ashley did a few more cartwheels Katie thought about how she reminded her of herself when she was that young. It was a nice moment for all of them as it broke up the seriousness of what they had been discussing.

"Do you want to go around back and look for them?" Travis suggested.

"I wanna go!" Ashley said hopping up and down.

"Sweetie, we'll stay here," Carol said.

"Ah, no fun," said Ashley. She sat down and made a sad face.

"I'll go," said Travis. He nudged Katie in the arm.

"Oh, I'm going," Katie said. "Gotta keep a watch on Travis so he doesn't get himself hurt." She smiled at Travis.

"Ha!" Travis laughed. "So far I haven't seen anything worth getting hurt over yet."

That reminded everyone about one of the strangest things about this place that they had no answer for yet which was the absence of any other life. The only activity was the metal dragon spilling out its water into its pool.

"Hey, did you see any wildlife or bugs or anything?" Rob asked. It seemed like such an obvious question now that neither of them had asked yet.

"No." Travis and Katie both answered.

Together all of them knew that there was something very weird about this place.

"Never in my life did I ever think I would actually want to see an insect or something," Laura said. "A fly. A mosquito. Or even a mouse." She couldn't believe she was saying it as the words left her mouth.

"I know what you mean," Carol said.

Just then they all heard voices coming from the side of the house. The voices were getting louder. All of them turned and waited as Harry and Shawn came around the side and into the front yard. They were talking about which was the better sport. Was it football or baseball?

"Baseball has tradition. Football is too violent," Shawn said.

"That's what people want to see. Some dude flattening out another. Action," answered Harry.

"I like football, too, but it's more brutal. Baseball is cerebral," Shawn countered. "Baseball has bases loaded and the bottom of the ninth inning."

"And I like baseball, but I'm saying football is action packed, and every play is exciting. Touchdown!" Harry wasn't willing to give an inch. "Baseball is too slow. It's pedestrian."

They stopped. Shawn grimaced for a second. He couldn't stand it when people said that about the game he loved. The game he coached.

"So uh," Rob started in. "Must not have found anything too significant if you're talking sports radio."

They looked at Rob. Shawn didn't say anything. Harry was annoyed but quickly blew it off. They're in too much of a strange situation to start quarreling among themselves.

"I guess not," Harry answered. "Other than we walked back there, through a clearing, through trees, and found we couldn't go any further when we came upon a wall like the one in front here."

"Yeah, we all did," said Rob. "Laura and I found one. And the kids found one on the other side. They're all like this wall here in front."

"It would appear that way," said Harry. "What about the house?"

Carol shook her head. "Just a few bedrooms, a pair of bathrooms, and the upstairs is about the same as the downstairs."

"And both don't have toilet paper," Rob added. "Tsss, can you believe that?"

"What are we going to do with no toilet paper?" Shawn said with sudden alarm.

"It's okay. We'll find some," Laura said again. She was starting to feel like the toilet paper police. If toilet paper could start a panic, there is no telling what else they might discover that would really break things down among them. They had to stay calm and focused. They had to stay together. "Okay! So what do we do next? Let's figure out a game plan."

"We don't have any phones. No cars obviously. No other people," Harry said. His educated mind was starting to dive right back into their predicament. No more fun talk about sports. It had been a nice diversion on their walk back but now he had to focus on what they were going to do next. "We've got no food apparently. Although, we do have a weird looking microwave." His eyes rolled in the direction of the front windows of the kitchen.

"And that water that tastes good," Rob said. "And some forks."

"Yes," Harry said. "And we've most likely established that nobody lives here so they won't be coming home for dinner and a movie and finding us here." He was being a little sarcastic at the end.

"There is some furniture," Carol added.

"Okay," said Harry. That didn't leave them with much.

"No other animals or plants or flowers," Katie said.

"Okay," Harry said again. That left them with even less.

Ashley bounced up to the porch and gave her mom a hug. She didn't seem too worried about things. She was enjoying their new home.

"I guess that's about where we're at," Harry said. "Unless it gets any weirder."

Just then a wave of light shimmered down the front yard wall. The light separated in the middle and peeled back to the sides. The waterish wall that was constantly in front of them was open. The other side of the wall was revealed to them. They all stared. They gasped.

"Mommy," Ashley said. "Glow balls…."

CHAPTER 26

The pitch black inverted eyes pierced their hearts at first sight. The light was gone and what before had been their front yard wall was now a room of some sort. In the room stood six grey creatures so shocking that the people were frozen down to their inner cores. The two in the middle were taller. They stood the height of a tall man. They had long necks that their huge heads rested upon. Both had thin manes of green hair that started at the back of their heads and ran down their backs. The one on the left wore yellow clothing that looked like a dress that cut off at the knees. The one on the right wore the same but it was red. Both had a golden star-like symbol on the front. There was no other visible clothing. Not even shoes. The other four were smaller. They were about four feet tall. They didn't have any clothing on. Just their skinny little grey bodies. Their heads were very big in proportion to the rest of the bodies. Their eyes looked like upside down drops of water patched on a head that was stuck on top of a neck like a lollypop stick. They looked like stickmen. Long arms and legs. Tiny little torsos. No mouth, nose, hair, or ears were visible. And those eyes....

They were staring at them. Watching them.

"We're not in Illinois anymore," said Rob.

Seven of the eight didn't move. They stood transfixed and stared back. Nobody flinched a muscle except Ashley.

"Mom. Mom," said Ashley in a whisper. She was tugging on her mother's leg looking up at her trying to get her attention. She was kicking her leg back. "Mom."

The seven of them stood like statues looking at the new visitors. It was as if an invisible shockwave had torn through and paralyzed them. Paralyzed their nerve endings. Their muscles. Their thoughts. Nobody was thinking. They didn't know what to think if they did. Emotions vanished too. There was no friendship from Laura. No camaraderie from Rob. No educational guessing from Harry. No gamesmanship from Shawn. No excitement from Travis. No enjoyment from Katie. And no nurturing motherly instincts from Carol. But for some reason Ashley seemed more at ease. It was as if she was in a state of awareness about these grey people while the other seven, the adults, were trailing far behind and needed to catch up. She was trying to get her mom's attention. However, her mother's attention wasn't to be gotten right now. Her mother, as was the rest of the group, was focused on them. The stickmen with the big black eyes.

The yellow Grey raised an arm and pointed at them. He kept pointing at them. Both tall ones were male. There were no recognizable male attributes yet everyone knew. They could feel him pointing at them. The two smaller Greys at his side also stared at them. Nobody knew what sex they were. However, they could feel them staring at them too. It was a scary feeling. A penetrating one. It crawled down to their bones. Next the red Grey pointed at them. They could feel the two Greys next to him stare as well. It surged down to their souls. The yellow Grey stopped pointing. The red dropped his arm too. Then all four of the smaller Greys pointed at them. And they kept pointing at them.

None of the group did anything. Nobody moved. Even Ashley was still now. Resting up against her mom's leg she watched them back. The smaller Greys stopped pointing. They turned their bodies in unison and looked up at the taller Greys. There seemed to be some sort of communication going on between them. The taller ones didn't move. The smaller ones looked back at the eight of them. The taller Greys pointed again. The smaller ones all nodded in agreement. The group felt it all as it happened like darts aiming for their chests. The taller ones stopped pointing and the smaller ones would point. The smaller would stop and the taller would point again. Back and forth it went. It was clear that the taller Greys were in charge. They were either the adults, possibly parents, or at least in some sort of position of authority or genuine status. In any case, it appeared that a teaching moment was going on. The smaller Greys were either students or Grey children. And the eight knew they were the subject of the lesson.

After their immobility from the shock of what they were witnessing their brains started processing. Their minds started to have thoughts again. Thoughts that started to trip over themselves and roll around in circles. A few of them had thoughts that started to spin out of control. Others' thoughts would catch onto something and hold steady. No matter where their thoughts were they all thought the same. Alarm! Emotions woke up too. They were no longer restrained and broke free inside their immobile bodies. They flowed down from the mind, out from the heart, and spilled into their arms and legs. Emotions tingled in their fingers and their toes. Pins pricked their backs. Their new emotions mixed with their surging thoughts and together turned the sense of alarm they were feeling and produced another feeling. Fear! It was fear of helplessness. Fear of not knowing what will happen to them. Fear of not being in control. Powerlessness.

Still nobody moved. Now the only Grey doing any pointing was the tall one in the yellow. He seemed to be in charge. The Yellow seemed to be *educating* in their alien kind of way. However, the eight didn't have any idea what he could be communicating about. They didn't see a mouth moving. Didn't see any facial feature movement at all. This was true with all of them. True with all the stickmen. The alien eyes didn't blink. They just watched. Their stare causing pain. Whether this was true physical pain or emotional pain nobody was sure of yet. The eight knew that it was real. That it cut.

"Jesus Christ," said Rob. The words slowly escaped his mouth.

"I wish," Laura said.

"What are they?" Rob said.

"They're ugly. That's what," said Carol.

"And not our friends," Katie said. She looked at Travis next to her. Now she could make her body respond. No longer paralyzed with shock. Only fear was filling in for that now. Travis looked back at her. Together they realized that their childhood dreams of little green men, alien spaceships, Roswell, and making contact wasn't the enlightening sensational experience they had dreamed it would be. They realized it's easy to sit in your living room, drive in your car, or stare at the open sky on a moonlit night and wish to meet beings from another planet. It's easy to want to make contact, see it with your own eyes, and be one of only a few in the history of mankind to see and talk to an alien. It's easy to want this all your life. However, after years of believing this, now on this day, at this moment that science fiction kid dream took a dark turn. Realization set in that this wasn't the miracle experience both had expected. So set in their beliefs they had been, that a different reality had never occurred to them. The reality was that it could be a bad experience. A dangerous experience. An evil experience. Katie and Travis knew it now.

"What do they want?" Shawn said. He took a few steps backwards.

"I'm afraid it's us," Harry said.

"I'm afraid too," said Carol. She gripped Ashley's shoulders so hard her fingertips turned white. Ashley's mouth flinched with pain. Carol caught herself and stopped immediately.

"We're the prize," Harry said dispiritedly.

"Or the main course," said Rob.

"I don't think it's an eating thing," Harry countered. "I don't think we're livestock in that way." He was sure of this much and he didn't want the rest of the group to panic. Especially not the little girl or the women. He didn't care so much about comforting the other guys. They still had no answers to what or why they were here.

"In what way do you mean then, Harry?" asked Laura. She was right in front which made her very uncomfortable. If these Grey things did anything she'd be the first to get it.

"Yeah, what do you mean, Harry!" Carol shouted at him. She immediately felt the attention of the yellow Grey pass over her body. It was spooky. She looked at the Yellow. She could feel the Yellow look back. With a shiver, she looked back at Harry. "Don't say those things, Harry, unless you have a good reason for it." Carol lowered her voice this time but she wasn't playing around anymore. Carol had her daughter's life in her hands. What bothered her more was that her little girl's life might be in the hands of the freaks staring and pointing at them. The freaks with the big black eyes.

"Calm down, Carol. Let's keep it cool," Harry answered very softly. He didn't want to alarm the Greys. He didn't want them to see any signs of aggression from them. There was no idea as to what the Greys might do then. Harry was waving his hand at her in a settling way. "I'll explain later."

"Later! What do you mean? Harry, you don't have any children here--" Carol stopped abruptly because now she felt the attention of the red Grey slide over her body. She looked at the Red out of the corner of her eyes. She was very scared now. Her heart pounded in her chest. Did she let her emotions get away from her? Did she just put her life and her daughter's life in jeopardy? She kept looking but didn't move. She wouldn't move her head. She didn't want them to know she knew she was being watched. Her heart was beating faster and she was afraid that would give her away. Carol could still feel their alien gaze on her. She didn't move a muscle.

"Carol, just chill out," Harry whispered. "We'll all talk later."

He could feel their gaze on her too. They all did.

"Yeah, Carol, it's okay," said Laura as she slowly turned her head around and looked at Carol. When their eyes met, she nodded to her. It was a small nod meant to make her feel calmer and to convey that they were all in this together.

Travis and Katie were quiet. They didn't move. Both were completely focused on their visitors. On their spectators. Or more accurately, they themselves were the visitors, and now they knew who their hosts were. And what they looked like.

The Yellow and Red stopped. Their vision could be felt by everyone. Now they felt it shift. The small Greys seemed to be communicating with the Yellow and the Red. Talking without speech. No sound at all. It was some sort of invisible language. A conversation could be felt but not understood.

Carol was very shaken. What had just happened scared her. In an instant, she thought she had put her life in danger. Had been put in the crosshairs. That she had been examined for death. Examined by them. Her breathing was stressed. Her self-control very rattled.

The discussion among the Greys continued. Harry started to think the Greys were inquisitive students. It was like some of the students he had in his classes. Harry thought the Yellow and Red were teachers. He was even more sure of it now as he watched them. Katie and Travis were more relaxed now but didn't speak. They didn't want to bring attention to themselves. Both kept thinking over and over that they didn't want to be here. Shawn didn't speak. Shawn didn't move. He was just breathing and he still had that dazed look on his face. However, his face was peppered with traces of fear. He looked like a Halloween mask.

The Yellow pointed right at Laura. She shivered as if covered with hypothermia. *Oh, no, they're looking at **me** now*, she thought. Laura wanted them to point the other way. To look at something or someone else. It pained her to feel that way. A person should never want someone else to be injured, or even worse than injured, instead of themselves. That works in theory. But that's not how it works most of the time. Certainly, not inside the inner workings of the mind. People did it all the time. People can't help doing so. It's a natural human characteristic. No normal person wants pain or grief set upon themselves or anyone they care about. Laura was one of those people. However, at this very moment when set upon by the stare from those big black eyes. When that penetrating feeling passed through the body like an x-ray. When you realize that you are in the sight of the stickmen. That's when she shut off all moral thinking and felt instinct. That was "not me" but somebody else. She couldn't help it. The same as most people couldn't.

Then the Yellow pointed at Ashley. Carol covered her little girl with her body. *No, not my baby you wretched monster,* she thought. Then she felt the stare. The Yellow's attention was back on her again. Carol thought that it must have read her thoughts. She didn't mean it. *I'm sorry,* she thought. She didn't think that the Yellow was a wretched monster. But yes, she did think that. The truth crept back into her mind. It crept to the forefront of her thoughts. And she knew it was true. And if she knew this then the Yellow knew this too. Carol wanted to change her thoughts. She wanted to think of something else. Think of something that wouldn't get herself or her little girl killed. She thought of how nice the Yellow and its friends were. But that wasn't true. From the other side of her mind came that truth. It slammed into her pleasant lie of a thought. It pushed it right out of her thoughts and over the edge of her mind. The truth was that they were scary, ugly, weird-looking things. They were like stickmen with frightening eyes. She hated the eyes. Carol tried to bring back pleasant thoughts. She wanted to conjure up more nice things. More happy things about them. About her new friends. About how wonderful they were. How handsome and pretty they looked. But that didn't work either. The truth would not allow it. The truth knocked it out of her mind. It swept in and said "you're evil!" Carol got the feeling that the Yellow didn't care what she thought.

Then Carol felt the Yellow leave her. It left her body and her mind. Ashley looked up at her mom.

"Mommy," Ashley turned around and said. "I don't think I like the lollipop men anymore."

CHAPTER 27

All the Greys pointed again. It was as if they were pointing the fingers of death at them. It felt ghostly. The entire eight felt it. Everyone wished they would stop.

Then there was a great flash and a wave of light peeled in from the sides and met in the middle. The light carried back up the frontal wall. The window to the aliens was replaced by a surge of water that was locked into place. The water wall was whole in their front yard again, flowing together in perfect harmony with colors of blue and white intertwined. Yet it was a pretty reminder of a reality that was very ugly. A reality that was defeating to the mind. The kind that can destroy hope. They didn't know where they were yet. However, they knew the reality was that they were meant to be here and they weren't leaving anytime soon.

"Oh my God," said Laura.

"What's happened to us?" said Carol.

"That was awful," said Rob.

"What are they?" asked Carol.

"They're called the Greys," Laura said. She had a gross look on her face. "But what they are, nobody knows."

"Yeah, those bastards," said Travis. "Katie and I have seen them on TV shows about UFOs"

Katie nodded in agreement. "For years they were little green men. Maybe it's alien political correctness," she added sarcastically.

Carol tried to relax. She looked down at Ashley who was staring back up at her. Carol ran her hand through her daughter's hair. *At least my little girl is safe at the moment,* she thought.

"We're screwed," Travis chimed in. "We're prisoners. We're not going anywhere."

"Relax, relax," Harry said. "Let's not panic." He walked out in front of them.

"Are you kidding?" said Travis. "Did you not see that? Didn't you get those weird feelings?"

"It's not gonna do us any good to get hysterical," Harry spoke sternly.

"I'm not hysterical. You haven't seen hysterical yet. But I'm saying we're fucked."

Laura turned and looked at Travis. Until this moment he had been a cool character. Especially for his age. But now he was starting to crack a little bit. Katie was still looking at the front wall and not saying anything. Laura didn't know if she was that calm or the opposite of that and silently freaking out. She understood Travis's feelings but she agreed with Harry. They needed to keep everything rational. That would be the best way to proceed. By not doing so they could fall into chaos.

"Look," Harry continued. "What I'm saying is we need to chill and think this out. Think things over. We don't wanna make any mistakes or miss anything."

"I'm kinda in agreement with Travis," Rob turned and said. "We're fucked. And it's not cool."

"Relax." Harry turned to Rob and said, "Let's keep it together."

"Relax?" Rob answered. There was a lot of attitude in his response. To him the scout leader mentality of Harry wasn't realistic. They were in a bad situation and it was starting to look like there was no way out of it. Rob thought they needed some sort of action now. At least that, or the best-case scenario of getting rescued, and he knew that wasn't likely.

"Yes, let's figure this out." Harry started counting things off with his fingers. "We're here. Nobody around to help. We've seen our kidnappers. We have no weapons. No cell phones, that's for sure. And seemingly no way out."

"Yeah, in other words we're fucked," Rob broke in.

"There's gotta be a way out," said Laura.

"If we had gotten in here we could get out. Problem is we didn't put ourselves here," Harry continued. He knew all the education and college degrees in the world couldn't necessarily get them out of this. They were going to have to literally find a way out by doing it themselves.

"And what are those things, the Greys?" Laura asked again. She meant it more as a rhetorical question and didn't expect any real answers. How were any of them supposed to know? If they knew what they were dealing with it would make it helpful. She remembered a lesson from reading *The Art of War* by Sun Tzu while back in college: Know the enemy!

"The lollipop men." Ashley's sweet little voice rose above them all. Everyone turned towards her. Laura's Sun Tzu philosophy halted. Rob's defeatism stopped. Harry quit analyzing. Travis didn't crack anymore. Katie stayed the same and Shawn came to life a little. The experience of the Greys ripped into the souls of the seven adults. Feeling that way having never seen anything like them before was completely natural. Conventional wisdom would be the adults would be more in control of their emotions and would hold things together more. Yet it was Ashley who had been affected the least. She hadn't panicked. Instead of her body freezing she was responsive. Instead of her mind numbing she was alert. The alarm of seeing their apparent keepers hadn't sounded inside of her or shut her down. She had an awareness. It was like a familiarity. The visitors with the big eyes didn't seem foreign. They didn't seem alien to her. Ashley even had a name for them.

"What'd you call them?" Rob asked.

"They're the lollipop men," Ashley answered. "They came to my house. In the backyard." She started to play with her hair. "They look like lollipops."

Carol put her hands on Ashley's shoulders in a protective position.

"They would send glow balls to play with me," Ashley continued. "And my brother. But he wouldn't play. Right, Mommy?" She looked up at her mom.

Carol felt everyone's eyes switch to her and she felt uncomfortable. She scanned their faces. Some of them looked confused. Other faces were blank. She thought their eyes were accusing. Projecting suspicion onto her. As if she knew something they didn't. As if she was holding it back from them. However, maybe they didn't think this. Perhaps it was all in her imagination. Just a natural effect of the ordeal they've been going through. But they still looked at her. And she was aware that she knew something. That the something was just told to her by Ashley, while she waited for them to return to the house, after exploring their new home. Could they know that? Was it written on her face? Does that make her a bad person? *Of course not!* she thought. She had only found out about it before the stickmen had revealed themselves. They still stared at her. Carol thought they were waiting for an answer.

"What?" Carol cleared her throat. "You think I know something?"

"What's she talking about?" Rob asked.

"Yes, what's she mean?" asked Travis. He had a touch of anger in his voice.

"How would I know something?" asked Carol.

"C'mon, Carol. You can tell us," Laura said. "Why'd she say that?"

Carol thought she should come clean. But what did she have to come clean about? She hadn't done anything wrong. Her daughter just told her the story. Carol didn't even believe the story at first. At least she didn't believe it until now. She didn't have any power to control it or stop it. Carol was afraid they might blame her. Or worse blame her daughter. It was not her or Ashley's fault that they were here in this place. They didn't put them here. The stickmen did. Carol felt she better hurry up and answer. She felt honesty is usually the best policy.

"Before you all got back from checking around," Carol began slowly. "Ashley told me a story."

"It's not a story, Mommy." Ashley turned and looked up at her mom. "It's real. Didn't you believe me, Mommy?"

"I didn't know what to believe, doll baby." Carol scanned around at the others. "I thought it might have been part of your incredible imagination. Like when you thought the slime monster was living under your bed."

"That was Kenny, Mom. A giant spider was living under my bed."

"Right, doll baby." She patted Ashley on the shoulder.

"Remember? And Kenny killed it with his anti-spider laser gun."

"Yes, dear. I remember now." Carol smiled down at her. Ashley smiled back. Then she hopped up and turned back to the group. In return the group just stared at her. The looks on their faces told how they felt. *How could you be having a playful time when we're stuck in this place?* *Because she's a seven-year-old girl … that's why*, Carol thought. She watched them all a little longer. Nobody said anything yet but it was coming. She thought she better break the silence before any trouble got started. Before they got the wrong idea.

"As I was saying," Carol said. "Right before you all got back Ashley told me a story." She caught herself, looked down at Ashley again and continued. "Told me that she was seeing these lights flying around in the backyard--"

"Glow balls," Ashley interrupted.

"Yes, glow balls." Carol nodded.

"What's a glow ball?" Rob asked.

"It's what she saw flying around in the backyard," Carol said.

"How many?" asked Rob.

"I'm not sure," Carol answered. "I really don't know."

"What'd they do?" Laura asked.

"Uh," escaped from Carol's lips.

"How big are they?" Rob asked.

"I don't know. Like basketballs probably," Carol answered. Frustration was starting to swell up inside her. If they'd just let her finish she could tell them.

"But you saw them," said Travis with a sharp edge.

"No, I didn't. Ashley did." Carol stopped. She didn't want to put the focus on her. Did she just get her daughter in trouble? What's wrong with these people? Why are they drilling her with questions? "This is what she told me. Right, hon?" Carol looked down at her.

"Yes, Mom," Ashley answered.

"How many times did you see them?" Harry asked, sounding very interested.

This made Carol feel more at ease. Harry was a rational guy who was also a teacher. His honest interest seemed to deflate any threat she might be starting to feel from the group. If he was interested, then she might be able to make the rest of the group understand too.

"Ash, why don't you tell them what you told me?" said Carol.

"They would come to visit me when my mom wasn't there," Ashley addressed the rest of the group. "They came to the back door from behind in the woods. They were bright and shiny and moved like this." She made circular motions with her hands. "They were really fast. They were glow balls."

"How often did they come?" Harry asked. He leaned forward towards her and his eyes squinted.

"Oh, I don't know. Probably once a month since winter ended."

"What'd they want?" Laura asked. She made Ashley feel good in a big sister kind of way.

"They wanted me and my brother to come out and play, but he wouldn't. He was scared of them. But I wasn't. At least back then I wasn't. I thought they were nice. Now I don't."

"Why not?" asked Harry. He looked back over his shoulder at the front wall. He didn't want to let their new watchers out of his eyes even though he knew the situation was more the opposite. It was the eight of them being in sight of their eyes. Those disgusting alien eyes. The black hollow things.

"Cuz they're friends with the lollipop man," Ashley answered.

"Who's that?" asked Harry.

"Yeah, who's the lollipop man?" Laura asked.

"He would come to the house and ask us to come out and play with his friends. He is one of them."

Carol was alarmed but that made her speechless.

"How often did he come?" Laura asked. "Like all the time?"

"Not always. Mostly the glow balls did. But he would come to the back door sometimes, too."

"The lollipop man came to your back door?" Harry said, almost in disbelief.

"Yep," said Ashley. "I saw the other lollipop men behind in the woods. Then they would go hide."

"So this one lollipop man acted like your friend?" Harry asked.

Carol's face was red with anger.

"Yep," said Ashley. "I don't think I like him anymore, either. He was nice but he's friends with the rest of the lollipop men." She pointed towards the wall that flowed like water behind glass. "They don't seem friendly."

"Easy to see why," Laura said. She shook her head. *This is so strange,* she thought.

"You didn't think to tell us this?" Travis said accusingly.

"She's a little girl. Leave her alone!" Carol snapped. She pulled Ashley close to her. "Don't say that to her! It's not her fault. What do you think she can do about it?"

Katie poked Travis in the chest. "Chill, Trav. Be cool."

"We're all in this together," said Laura. "We need to stay together."

"You mean we're all stuck here together," Rob said. His tone was so negative it could flatten a truck.

"She's right," Harry said. "We've got to stay calm and figure this out." Rob's snide comments were starting to annoy him by now. They were completely in a situation without any control on their end and he was not making it any better. Each time he made a wise crack like that it made him sound separate from the rest of them. Granted, this wasn't a good situation, but they would need him if they're going to get through this together.

"Look, we've been saying that since the moment we all met," Rob said. "And now it got worse. Did you see those things?" Rob pointed in the direction of the wall.

"Yes, I know," Harry answered. "I was here, too. We all were. I'm just saying let's not lose our cool."

"All right. Hey, at least I'm not the one yelling at the girl."

Travis shot a look at Rob, his face red.

"Stop it!" yelled Laura. "Knock it off."

Everyone froze. Then Katie rubbed her hand on Travis's chest. He relaxed. His awesome girlfriend had the magic touch when it came to him.

Laura gave him a quick stare and directed her attention back to Ashley.

"Ashley," Laura continued. "What did the lollipop man, or men, say to you?"

"It was just one lollipop man. He wanted me to come out and play. Wanted to show me his airplane. But it was a different kind of airplane. That's what he called it but I knew what he meant. It was a UFO. It could go places. He said I could go, too."

Carol gripped her daughter's shoulders. The thought of someone taking her girl away terrified her.

"Did the lollipop man ever take you to it? Or try to make you go with him?" Laura asked. She saw Carol's firm grip on Ashley's shoulders.

"Nope." Ashley shook her head and her hair tossed around. "But he kept asking every time he came to play."

"Did you ever see it? The UFO. The spaceship," Harry asked, curiosity written all over his face.

"Not til the last time. I knew it was there before."

"So where did it want to take you?" Harry got down on one knee in front of her. He completely wanted her calm which she was. Harry was impressed that during this experience the little girl had remained quite composed. In fact, she never came close to breaking down in the slightest way.

"Away." She pointed up. "To its home. Another planet."

"Wait, let's back up," Laura leaned forward and put her hands on her knees. "What did you mean by the last time?"

Everyone's eyes focused narrowly on the little girl. Carol rubbed her daughter's shoulders.

"You know," Ashley answered. Her voice was bouncy and playful. "The last time. That's how we all got here."

"Last time what?" Rob asked.

Ashley gave him a silly look. "The last time they came to see me I saw the ship. That's because I went with them and it pulled me up into it. But now I think he tricked me. I don't like him or any of them anymore. They're fakers."

"You did go with them?" Carol questioned, even though she knew her daughter's earlier story was true. She'd seen it with her own eyes now, as unbelievable as it sounded, just minutes ago. But on a personal motherly note, now Carol was taken aback. Her earlier feelings of relief that her daughter wouldn't go with strangers, or whatever kind of strangers you would call the Greys, disappeared. Ashley had left the house when she was gone and disobeyed her mother's house rules. She was disappointed and scared at the same time. It may have been the only time. Just once. But that one time was enough to get Ashley and her mother here as prisoners in a jail, or house, or whatever this was they were inside now. And to make it worse they still hadn't determined where they were yet. Although they were getting closer.

"Yes, Mommy. I'm sorry." She looked up at Carol. "Like I said. They tricked me."

"How'd they do that?" Laura asked. She shifted her weight from side to side. Everyone's attention was completely focused on what Ashley was saying.

"Mommy, they told me you were hurt and that they knew where you were. That they were helping you. So I went. I followed the glow ball back into the woods." Ashley was making flying motions with her arms now and her hands were the flying objects. "Then I got back into the woods and the UFO rose up and over me. Then poof! A light flashed down on me and then I was here with you."

Nobody said anything. Everyone was watching her to see what she would say next. To see if there was any more to what she was saying. They were all processing what she was telling them. Inside everyone's head, their brains ran through the story she told them, how it related to each person individually, and to how each of them had gotten there. All their memories were dark right now. Everyone was having trouble remembering what they had been doing before waking up in this weird place.

"Don't you remember?" Ashley asked. "It happened to all of you. Didn't it?"

After wandering around, being confused, and not finding any answers, the other seven of them came to the realization of what happened and how they got here. Unless this was some elaborate hoax or experiment, and after witnessing the stickmen behind the wall, they had come to one conclusion albeit as impossible as it may seem.

"Shit! We've been abducted by aliens," Katie said.

"I thought you always wanted that," Travis said.

"Yeah, if you're living in the QC!" She gave Travis a harsh look. "It's easy to say it then. Don't think I really want to go through that, do you?"

Travis didn't answer. He knew he better keep his mouth shut. This was the first time he'd ever seen that look on her. At least directed towards him.

"How do you remember this but we don't?" Laura broke that mood up. "I've been struggling since the moment I woke up over here on the front lawn to remember. It's a blur. I do remember some sort of bright light though."

Harry was looking at Laura. He remembered again. There was more than a little girl lost in the woods. When he woke up here on the ground the memory sprung up from his subconscious. He didn't know why or how but it did. If he had been meant not to remember, like the rest of the group, then his memory had sprung a leak, and it flowed out on the ground into his consciousness. Harry hadn't told anyone at the time because they'd think he was crazy. In fact, Harry thought he might be crazy. The idea that he left his school, was lured into the nearby backwoods, and then abducted by aliens was insane. It also made him sound stupid and not at all educated. Having seen it in his mind he thought it must have been a dream. The memory had drifted away, but now he remembered it clearly. Now it was an awakening. It was true.

"I don't know why I remember." Ashley shrugged. "I just do."

"Well…." Laura stopped. She shook her head again in disbelief. How could this happen? She still couldn't remember much before here. Before this place. She stood on the edge of her memory trying to look into it, but a foggy mist kept blocking her view. There would be holes that poked through and she saw quick glimpses of her memory only to be covered up again by the flowing mist in her mind.

"Jeez," Katie said. "We're freaks. If we get outta here I'll never be able to show my face outside again. I'll be scorned from society. We all will."

"Hey, Katie babe," Travis said. Now things had reversed. He was trying to comfort her. "Remember what we always said. We'll get rich."

"Right now I don't wanna get rich." She turned to him. "I wanna get outta here."

"We will. I promise," Travis said. "We're going to have a heck of a story to tell people."

"How do you know?" Katie was gesturing angrily. "How're we gonna get out of here? How're we gonna live? Are we trapped here forever? Right now, we're screwed."

"It's like something out of the movies," said Shawn. Everyone turned to look at him. They were surprised to hear him speak. In the brief time of knowing Shawn he hadn't said much. It was especially surprising because he had been quiet since they had returned to the house. Maybe it shouldn't be that way to them but it was. A time like this should bring out the best of everyone. They would need the best of everyone now. Maybe instead of being a silent observer he would become a doer and start to contribute to their situation. "Getting taken away by little green men. It's crazy. Yet, we can't remember what we did before here. I can't. All I remember is fishing and a big flash of light. Then some pain. I wake up here with all of you. None of you I've ever met before. This place is strange. There's nobody around. Now despite how stupid and crazy it all seems, we're all coming together here and figuring out that it's true. My god, we just saw aliens."

The group didn't say anything. What Shawn had said made sense. Heck, they'd just seen aliens. They'd seen little grey people, or things, or whatever they might be. They'd felt them too. Not physically but in their minds and bodies. It was an eerie feeling that had coursed through their bodies. The Greys had an ability to project their minds onto them. To search and look around inside them. Especially when the Yellow and Red were looking at Carol and Laura. The entire group had felt it. They had projected an angry hostility towards them. Projecting it inside them. Letting all of them know how the Greys felt. Letting the group know that they were in charge. The projecting had a maliciousness to it. It wasn't soft in the sense of a whisper either. It was hard down to their cores. And clearly they didn't like Carol. When she had panicked and raised her voice at Harry her aggressiveness was perceived as a threat. Like she was trouble waiting to happen. Together they all would have to get past this. This past "visit" ended up serving as a cautionary warning to the eight of them. But more importantly they knew what put them here.

"Well said," Harry said. He nodded approval to Shawn. "We seem to know more now about what we're dealing with. Even though it sounds crazy, or more like a dream, it seems true."

"They were watching us like people watch animals at the zoo," Shawn said. Everyone looked back at him. "It was like when I was a kid and my parents took me to the zoo. We stood there and pointed at the animals. Now I know how they felt."

Nobody said anything as Shawn's observation settled down and took root within them all. Just like animals in a zoo....

CHAPTER 28

The cool breeze returned through the trees and passed right through the group. The leaves chattered with its arrival. The flowing air circled their bodies and made them feel relaxed. The swelling of their fears lessened for a minute. They took time for some deep breaths and looked at one another. In a very short time they had all been through a lot. They would need to stick together to get through this. They all knew this. But whether they could stay together as a team was not clear yet. It was a tricky question. Upon seeing who their *hosts* were, some cracks were already forming within their group. Mostly there was anger from a few, directed toward Carol and her daughter, as if they had been hiding something. Sweet little Ashley had some prior knowledge of the Greys and had communication with them over a period of months before. The Greys seem to like her. Her mother knew about this too. Although, she said she just learned about it. There was fear about what was going to happen to all of them. The anger that came with that must be directed at someone. That someone was starting to be Carol. However, the cool gusts calmed the growing negativity. At least for the moment.

Shawn's last words had bounced between them like a pinball game. Now it echoed in their consciousness. They all knew it. They were living it.

"I don't know what else we can do right now," Harry said. "We don't seem to have any tools or resources to help us out either."

"This sucks!" Katie declared. "I wish I had my phone."

Travis rubbed her shoulder. He wanted to keep her in a good mood. Carol switched from rubbing Ashley's shoulders to tying ponytails. Laura was looking around. Harry and Shawn had been looking at each other ever since Shawn last spoke. And Rob thought of his stomach.

"Anyone hungry?" he asked.

Seven heads slowly turned towards him. The question surprised everyone. The overall feeling was how could he think of food now?

"I know. I know," Rob said seeing their faces. "It's a strange thing to say but hunger pains just hit me all of a sudden. I want to double check for food. There's got to be something."

Laura didn't know what to make of Rob now. He'd been cocky, reasonable, a little angry, and now hungry. His range of personality traits seem to jump all over the place.

"You know," Travis spoke slowly. "Now that you mention it. I think I am, too."

"You sure it isn't that same pain you were feeling back in the house?" Katie asked.

"No, hon. It's not. But I think I'm hungry now." Travis was shaking his head.

Now Shawn touched his stomach. "Hey, me too."

Good Lord! What is with these guys? Laura thought. One guy says it so they all start feeling the same way. Were men subject to the power of suggestion more than women?

Harry looked around. "I don't think we're doing any good just standing out here. Doesn't appear to be anything else here but us."

"'Appear' being the key word there, Harry," Katie said. She was giving him a dubious look.

Harry looked straight at her and thought that Katie was one sharp girl. She'd be able to help them. "'Appear,' right," he answered. Harry wasn't going to say anymore on that.

"There wasn't any food before, remember?" Carol said. "What makes you think there would be some now?"

"Yes, that's true," Harry answered. "Maybe we should look again. If we are, uh, hostages here, then they've got to supply us with something. We're here for a reason so they wouldn't starve us or let us die."

"Ya never know," said Katie. "Perhaps they're incompetent aliens."

"They don't look very incompetent so far," Travis said. His voice sounded disappointed at his own words.

"That is true," Katie turned and said. "Which is probably for the best for us then. We wouldn't want a bunch of screw-ups holding us prisoner."

"Good," said Rob. "Then this time there might be some food. Maybe the ugly things put some there now."

Laura gave up. The men had decided their stomachs were empty and needed to be filled. Although, she had to admit that she was starting to feel hungry herself. She followed Rob as he led them through the front door and into the kitchen. This led to their next problem.

As everyone filed into the kitchen Rob looked around in the cabinets. He still found nothing. The cabinets looked vast and starving as the cabinet doors were flipped open and closed. The group's stomachs felt very empty. He stepped back from the sink and raised his arms into the air with fingers stretched out. From behind he looked like a preacher speaking to his flock. Everyone backed away and gave him space.

"What the hell!" said Rob angrily. "Where's the food?" He turned around to everyone. "Do they plan to starve us?"

"Not likely," said Harry. "I don't think they'd bring us here and keep us here just to starve us."

"Unless they want to see what we look like when we turn to skeletons," Katie said.

"Or maybe it's a test or game to see what we'll do," Travis said. "To see if we'll start killing each other off for their own entertainment. Or pleasure."

"Terrific," Laura said. She didn't believe this was the case but she could tell this had gotten more complicated without food at their hand.

Also, judging by the last few things said the overall mood was getting more pessimistic.

"Relax," said Harry. "Look, we don't know what their intentions are yet. Don't get ahead of ourselves and freak out."

"I think we know enough already, man," Travis said. "We all saw it. We're here, they're there, and there's nothing we can do about it."

"Don't they know we need to eat?" Rob continued. "Don't they know anything?"

"Who knows?" said Katie shaking her head in frustration now.

"For all their smarts," said Rob. He was starting to pace around. "For their magical water walls, dropping in and watching us, UFOs, and stuff, I tell ya they sure seemed to miss the boat on a couple things."

"That makes sense," Laura said. "They look at things through alien eyes. And what disgusting eyes they are." She grimaced. "No human factor with them. It's just the Grey factor."

"Food. Toilet paper ... remember?" Rob stopped pacing and looked at Laura. His eyes got wider and he pointed at her. "We don't even have toilet paper. That's nice, isn't it? What are we gonna do about that?" He leaned back up against the counter in front of the sink and crossed his arms.

"We'll think of something," Laura said in a pleading gesture. She didn't want Rob to become an angry problem for them to deal with. They already had the Greys and that was bad enough. "We'll figure something out."

"You know," said Harry. "We could...." He was waiting to see how everyone was going to react. "They are intelligent. More than us obviously. We could try to communicate with them. Talk to them."

"Eh, not me," Katie said sounding dismayed.

"I won't," Carol said. She was still shaken by the invading feeling felt from the Grey's mental examination of her. It was going to take a while to wash the fear away from her body.

"They don't seem too interested in talking with *us*." Travis spoke with a heavy emphasis on the last word.

"You can talk to them, Harry," said Katie. "I'm staying out of this one."

"We could try," insisted Harry. "Hell, I'll do it. Why not? Maybe they'll listen. Strike an understanding. Get more personalized with them. Like what hostages can do sometimes with their captors. Supposedly, if the captor looks at its hostage, victim, or whatever you want to call them, as a person rather than just as a number or thing, then it makes it harder for them to do any harm or kill them."

Nobody seemed to be buying it. The consensus was the Greys were hostile and not in the friend-making business. At least not with them.

"They just want to keep us here like pets," Shawn spoke up. "I mean really, do the animals in zoos ever get to go home? Hardly."

Everyone was quiet as they contemplated what he'd said. It was a strong point. Shawn was the quietest of the group but his last statements made them all think hard.

"What will you say to them?" Laura asked. She wanted to get everyone back on the subject on hand. Laura didn't want to fall down that empty hole of being prisoners and helpless to do anything about it.

"I don't know yet." Harry's answer wasn't very reassuring. "Probably ask them who they are, what they want, and what we're doing here."

"How about 'take me to your leader?'" Rob said. "Or tell them 'we come in peace.'" Rob was smirking. To him this was all starting to sound ridiculous and he was losing faith that they could get any help, from whatever or wherever it may be, at all.

"Don't be a smart-ass, Rob," Laura said with an edge. "We need all the help we can get and need to stay focused together. Snide comments don't help."

"Oh, please." Rob rolled his eyes.

"How do you plan to do it?" Laura looked back at Harry and asked. "I mean really do you plan to just go up to the wall and wait to see if they answer? Wait and see if they grant you an audience?" Now Laura was coming off a little sarcastic but she didn't mean to. She just wanted to make a point about what he was suggesting. If it's something that would help, then she was all for it. But if it wasn't a good idea and a waste of time and potentially dangerous, then it shouldn't even be attempted. This needed to be carefully thought out.

"Now you're sounding like him," said Harry. He gestured at Rob.

"I'm sorry. I don't mean to but I'm just trying to make a point. Is this a good idea or just a waste of time?"

Harry stared back at her. "Doesn't anyone think we should do this?" His question was meant for the entire group. "Heck, I'm willing to do it. None of you have to."

"You can tell them we need food. We need to eat," Rob said. "And that we need toilet paper."

"Yeah, but will they give any of that to us?" Carol asked. "Or will they just point back with their little stick fingers, on their stickman bodies, and mentally violate our bodies by reading our minds and thoughts?"

Based on that, the group was starting to worry that Carol's experience outside had started to make her a little unhinged. Ashley turned around and hugged her mom. Laura wanted to say something to keep them on track but nothing worthwhile came to mind. She decided that if Harry had decided to do this then let it be and they'd see what would happen.

"Don't forget to tell them that we need to get outta here," said Rob frowning. He didn't actually believe they would just decide to let them go.

"I'm afraid that's not what they have planned for us," Travis said. He immediately regretted it. The sound of his words was like doom. No escape was a scary proposition. It lingered for a few moments.

"I wasn't gonna wager too much on it, Travis," Rob said shaking it off.

"C'mon now, we need to keep positive," said Laura. "We've got enough of a situation as it is without turning negative." She could see on a few of their faces that she was becoming the annoying one. The one that was always upbeat even when nobody else could even sense anything to be positive about. Laura did not want to become that person but she didn't think drifting into the shadow of despair would be helpful at all. Certainly, not mentally.

"Yeah, stay positive." Ashley's little voice drifted up and smoothed some of the rough edges they may have been starting to feel. Her hair was now covering her eyes as they looked up at Harry and Rob. It was cute to see. Her childlike nature made Harry more resolved to try to speak to the Greys. It made Rob's growing anxiousness recede a little bit. Maybe this seven-year-old innocent girl would be their beacon of hope if things didn't get better. Perhaps they could look to her if they felt despair. Maybe her child's perspective, untainted with morbid endings, could ease their minds whenever theirs turned gloomy. As adults with years of experience under their belts, it was easy to judge where they were without any real answers to their questions, and look ahead to the future, and if they would even survive or not. However, Ashley's young mind was still growing and wasn't filled with predictions of doom yet, so they might be served to rely on her youthful naivety, to stay together, focused, and to find hope and not give up if it came to that.

"Hey, there's that water that you guys thought was so tasty in the fridge," said Shawn.

Again, it was surprising when Shawn spoke. Everyone looked at him. This time he returned a surprised look back at them. Shawn had been more like a walking statue in the group and they weren't accustomed to him making contributions. It was a good feeling because it made the group feel he would be more of an asset in getting out of here. It was evident they would need all the help they could get and would need to put their collective efforts together.

"Yeah, there is," Travis said excitedly. "It was good. I almost forgot." He walked over to the fridge, grabbed his glass, opened it up and started pouring. "You want some?" He turned to Rob.

"Yeah, I think I will have some," Rob answered. "It's all we got right now. That is until Harry talks to them and gets us some pizza."

Harry's eyes squinted. He didn't like that comment. It was a sarcastic zing at him and all he was trying to do is help them all.

Rob was now pouring himself some water. It flowed out of the globe and circled down into his cup. He had been thinking about Harry's idea and it still didn't sound any better to him. Clearly they were here for a reason and having a dialogue with the Grey beings wasn't part of it. A dialogue in which the Greys would dictate after all. He didn't turn around and look at anybody. Rob stood there at the refrigerator pouring and drinking more. He felt a little like a jerk now. The first one to not be a team player even if it had been for just a moment. He felt like they were all staring holes into his back but in truth they weren't. But he felt it anyway. Travis was to his left leaning up against the counter. He handed Rob his glass, which Rob filled up, and gave it back to Travis who gulped it down and suffocated a belch afterwards.

The group was waiting around for something to be said or for someone to do something. To do anything. An idea or an action that would make things better. That would make them feel good. There was no food. No entertainment. Seemingly no way out. And the only plan they'd come up with so far is Harry talking with the Greys. The more they thought about it as a collective whole it didn't seem like an idea that was hopeful.

"Honestly, if you want my opinion, I don't think it will work," Laura said slowly. She was trying to read their faces to see how they felt. Everyone looked the same which was undecided and hopeless. "But what alternatives do we have?"

"None," said Katie. "We don't have much of anything."

"So we have to give it a try."

"Why not give some of this water a try?" Rob said. He leaned against the counter next to Travis. "It might make everyone feel better. It did me. And Travis." He looked at Travis who smiled in agreement.

"That doesn't sound too bad," said Shawn reaching for a glass in the door. "I'm thirsty."

"Go ahead," Rob said pleased with himself. "There's a glass for everyone right there." He pointed at the door.

Shawn poured himself a glass, downed it, and got another one before stepping away. Then Harry got some water too. Immediately, the slight stomach ache he'd been feeling was gone and he felt better.

Katie was next. She winked at Travis as she took her first sip. Her eyes got wide with approval. "Pretty good," she said nodding up and down. Immediately, her attitude was better. Katie had gotten pessimistic which was easy to do after their "visitation." She hopped over and leaned against Travis. Together they were happy again.

"Isn't it weird that they had eight glasses set up and there are eight of us?" Laura said.

"We were expected," said Rob, smiling at her.

"Doesn't that bother you?" said Laura. She wasn't getting this relaxed happy feeling that Rob had now. Just a while ago he was sarcastic and getting angry, but now he was cheery. Even Travis looked that way. He was smiling at Katie and she was smiling back at him. "I mean, eight glasses. Eight of us." She fluctuated her voice because she didn't think anyone was getting her point.

"What? That it was all planned out for us to be here?" Katie said. "I think we know that already after the Greys performed their little theatrical play outside."

"Yeah, I think we know that already," Rob said. "And I guess we could say we know there won't be anybody else joining us then either."

"Well, okay...." Laura's voice trailed off. She thought there was a deeper meaning to it such that they were going to be there for a long time. That it had been planned that way in advance. Eight cups for eight prisoners, eight animals, or eight whatever they were supposed to be. However, nobody was picking up on that. Laura wasn't going to push that point anymore for now. It seemed like a waste of breath if she did.

Carol held Ashley back from the water. They were going to wait and see how the others acted after drinking it. So far it seemed okay and not poisoned. Rob and Travis had some about an hour earlier and nothing bad happened to them. They were alive. No sickness. No nausea. It was also evident that their moods had improved now. They were happier.

Rob had smiled at Laura and was no longer angry. Travis and Katie were flirting again. Harry looked relaxed. And Shawn was smiling. No more did he look spaced out of his mind. All this after they drank water from the globe in the refrigerator. Could there be a connection or was it just a coincidence?

Laura had been watching and noticed the change too. She and Carol shared a glance with each other. The two women silently agreed. Especially, because both of them, and Ashley, hadn't had any so they could be objective about it. For some reason the rest of the group got a morale boost from drinking the water. The only source of food they had discovered so far. Of course, it could be a lot simpler than that. They could have just been dehydrated, and they had stopped that condition by drinking the water. Laura's stomach had a little pain and she was thinking she might feel better by having a drink of God's liquid.

"Okay, is everyone good now?" Harry said. He had remained quiet thinking everyone had forgotten his plan to try to communicate with the aliens. Now he wanted to press on with that. "If everyone is good after their water binge," he smiled trying to make a joke. Nobody laughed. However, the mood wasn't dire as it had been before. Rob, Travis, and Katie looked at him pleasantly enough. Laura, Carol, and Ashley were watching him waiting for what he had to say next. Shawn was looking out the front window. Harry wanted to get back to business. "As you were saying, Laura, you don't think it will work?"

Laura had momentarily forgotten what they had been discussing but it came back to her in a flash. "Oh yeah," she answered. "I'm sorry but I just don't know if it'll work." She didn't want to make him feel bad because it was his idea, he was willing to do it, and she wanted to remain positive. Then she remembered her complete thought and what she had been getting at. "But I don't see us having any other choice right now. What other alternatives do we have? Should we just wait and see? Or should Harry try to talk with them?"

"I think Harry should try to chat with them," Rob said. "Who knows? Maybe something good will happen. Like get some toilet paper." He was back on that again.

"I don't think it will do any good but what the hell," Travis said. "What else do we have to lose?"

"I'm not so sure about this," Katie said.

"We need to do something," said Shawn.

"Yeah, but what if they don't like it and do something to him," Carol broke the mood with that one. "They felt through us with their minds. Remember?"

Everyone was worried that Carol would break down but she didn't. She seemed stronger now. And she raised a good point. Could Harry afford to do this and maybe put his life at risk? Could they afford Harry to do this? If the stickmen can look inside their minds what else could they do? Was it better to lay low and see what happens, than to engage them, and run the risk of inviting them even more into their lives than they had been so far?

"I'm willing to take that risk," Harry said.

"What if they zap you?" said Katie. There wasn't a hint of sarcasm in that question.

"I don't think they will," said Harry.

"Why not?" Travis asked.

"Because, I don't think they'll do that. Too advanced."

"You sure about that? Like, how do you really know?"

"It's just what I think. I think they're beyond killing us."

"Yeah but," Laura said extending her arms. "Based on what?"

"I just think they're beyond killing us like we're bugs and have bigger things on their minds to do. If they wanted to kill us off, they probably have an easy way to do it with technology far greater than ours."

"Like bug spray," said Katie. "But it's human spray."

"Better than that I'm sure." Harry raised his arms and looked around. "Heck, look at where we're at."

"How advanced do you think they are?" Katie asked.

"Not enough to get us toilet paper," Rob cut in.

"I'd say pretty far," Harry ignored Rob. "You've seen it. They were outside that wall and peeked in when they wanted."

"It was awful," Carol said.

"That's for sure," Laura said. "But I'm not sure we've seen enough yet. Other than them, what we know is this house, trees, a weird ceiling, and that we're surrounded by a strange wall made of water."

"I'd say that's pretty good," Harry said.

"But what else? Where are we?"

"Iowa, Illinois, Nebraska?" Rob said.

"I know we're not," Ashley said shaking her head playfully. Everyone looked at her. "I don't know where but I know we aren't there."

As a collective group, it was amazing that a seven-year-old had so much credibility when she spoke among the adults. She had seen the Greys before. She had seen the UFO, the glow balls, the lollipop men as she called them, and seemed the least affected at times by everything that had happened so far. Ashley didn't even seem scared.

"Then where are we?" asked Katie.

"Not home."

"Let me guess. You don't mean as in the Quad-Cities home? You mean as in Earth home?"

Ashley nodded up and down.

"Great," Rob said. "Like that helps us out. We need to get outta here. Find a way."

"Please be a dream," Katie said looking up at the ceiling. "If it is, wake me up."

"Let me talk to them." Harry was back onto that again. "I don't see anything else we can do right now. I think it's worth a try." Now Harry was starting to plead a little like he felt he needed their permission.

"Or we could find a way to break through that wall somehow and get out of here," said Travis.

"Right," Rob said sarcastically.

"And go where?" Laura said. "We don't even know what's on the other side."

"Not to leave out they wouldn't like that too much," Carol said. "They'd probably zap us." She looked at Katie who agreed.

"Okay, okay," Travis said putting his hands up defensively. "I wasn't that serious. I was just saying. But a way out of here isn't a bad idea."

"We need to do something," said Katie. "So we need to have a plan then."

"Things will get better once we get started," Laura said.

"Okay, cheerleader!" Rob said. That was twice he'd slung a verbal slam.

"Don't be an ass!" Laura shot back. Her eyes looked on fire.

"We don't need that right now," Carol said. "We're trying to work together here."

"Yeah, let's chill out," Shawn said. "A bunch of bickering won't help us much." He had remained quiet staring out the window but he'd been listening. Shawn had no idea what they should do.

"And infighting is what people that fail do," said Harry. "There's no teamwork."

Rob rolled his eyes, crossed his arms, and looked at the floor. He was frustrated and getting angry. He wasn't angry with any of them. It was everything else. Being trapped in a jail against his will would make most people upset.

Laura's feelings were hurt. All she had tried to do is remain positive, keep everybody focused and upbeat, and do her best to help. And this jerk was shooting off his mouth at her! All her life she'd been a nice girl. Always the sweetheart. She didn't deserve to be spoken to that way when she was trying to help. It must have been her bad luck that he was the first person she knew here. She didn't have much choice either because she had woken up on the front yard next to him.

A few seconds went by without a word. Everyone was waiting for someone else to speak up.

"Okay, so what are we gonna do?" Katie tossed it out there.

"Harry." Rob walked across the kitchen next to Shawn and looked out the window at the wall. He stared at it a little. It seemed to flow around in an endless number of circles. It reminded him of how a hurricane looks on a radar screen. "Why don't you try that. You go talk to them."

"I think I should," Harry said although he wasn't convinced that Rob meant what he said. He wasn't completely sure it would work but he was more convinced than anyone else and felt he should try. It was a typical move for him. Always the teacher looking out for everyone and trying to lead. Right now, they didn't have many options, so communication with the Greys seemed to be their best bet, hoping to get an understanding of what they were doing here. And perhaps an understanding between them and the Greys.

"You should," Rob said. He was picking at the window with his finger.

"Do you know what you're gonna say?" asked Laura. She was still offended but trying to move on. Seeing Harry talking to the Greys certainly would help do that.

"Yeah, what's your plan?" Katie asked, playing off what she had said a moment before.

"I don't exactly have one yet."

CHAPTER 29

Harry stood watching the wall from about fifteen feet away. It swirled in hypnotic motion in front of him and he thought it would be easy for someone to come under its spell if one looked at it for too long. Walking up to it had been hard. Harry had to will his legs to make each step he'd taken. First it was out the front door, down the porch, and then across the yard until he stood where he was now. He felt he was walking on sacred ground. Trespassing with each step and being watched while he did it. Closer he had gotten until he was close enough. If they were watching him they knew he was there. Harry's imagination skipped ahead and he foresaw himself being shot by armed guards at a border crossing, reminiscent of the days during the Cold War. None of them had been this close to the front wall yet. The front wall in which the Greys had made their appearance. The front wall that was a divider between their group of eight and them. Between the good guys and the bad guys. It possibly was their shield. Maybe it would be best to leave it alone and not try to speak with them? That would invite the Greys back into their lives. Back into their current home. As of now they were on the other side and they didn't have to see them.

But they should try.

Harry would try. He had volunteered. It was Harry's idea, and he thought if he didn't try, by no means had they made any advancement in their situation any better. Everyone fell into agreement as well. Nothing ventured. Nothing gained.

Harry hesitated before he made his grand appeal to the Greys because he had to get everything straightened out and situated in his mind. He needed to get his mind focused on what he wanted to say and how he was going to do it. Questions to ask like where are they? Why are they here? What is going to happen to them? Who are the Greys? These kept knocking around inside his head. Another question was what were they going to do about food? His plan was to try and find out answers to what he thought were the basic questions first. Then depending on how the Greys responded, to go on from there, and see about establishing a relationship with them. But first thing was first.

He turned and looked back at the house. Everyone stayed back inside and was watching from the front windows. To Harry they looked like a scared bunch with their faces plastered up against the windows. Then the front door opened and Laura walked out on the porch and so did Rob. They went to opposite sides of the porch. Laura was on the left and Rob was on the right. He appreciated that they wanted to show support. Other than his seven companions, it didn't look like there'd be any support coming from anyone or anything else.

Harry looked around. The light seemed dimmer now. Earlier you couldn't miss a thing in the open space the way the ceiling blasted down its light from above. Now it looked a little like when the sun fades at dusk. Personally, Harry's body told him that it was probably about seven o'clock in the evening. That probably didn't mean anything though. At least not here. He had gotten used to the lack of animals, insects, or birds that people are accustomed to having around. He'd been so involved in the discussion with the group that he hadn't had time to notice lately. It was strange and unworldly at first, but now after what they had witnessed, it must be a normality for this place. The trees stood tall and motionless all around. Their unorthodox color of dark green was nice to look at. However, there was no breeze to feel right now. The air seemed to be at a standstill. The silver dragon was spouting its breath of water in a splashing arc down into the pool. It felt good on the ears to hear.

With one final look back at the house he turned again to face the wall. He held his hands out in a way that made him look like he was praying to the sky for rain. Harry lifted his head, opened his mouth, and the words stuck on the end of his tongue. He couldn't speak yet. A good dose of fear shot through his body and it stopped him. His mind scrambled the words he was going to say and he couldn't remember them. Then his thoughts settled down on one fear: What if this was a big mistake? There he was in plain sight of the wall with his arms outstretched like eagle's wings. Then Harry mentally beat down his fear and got over it. This was his idea and he was going through with it.

"Hello!" The word sprang from his tongue. "Can you hear me?"

Both Rob and Laura crouched down on the porch. Everyone inside ducked and peeked out the windows.

"Is anyone there? My name is Harry. We just want to talk." That sounded a bit silly to Harry but he couldn't think of anything else to say. "Will you come out and talk?" That sounded worse. Harry thought he better go back to basics. "Hello. Hello."

Nothing happened. The wall remained the same in its watery mixture. To Carol watching from back in the house he looked like Jesus. Travis and Katie were expecting the wall to open and a big alien laser gun to reach out and zap him. Shawn felt helpless. Laura felt frustrated and the whole scene started to look stupid to Rob. *We are probably a big joke to the stickmen*, he thought.

"Hello, Aliens," Harry continued. "Grey Aliens." He thought he better try again. "Greys, are you listening?" He dropped his hands to his side and waited. The wall continued in its way of flowing over itself. Harry wondered if he should speak louder but quickly dropped that idea. The Greys might interpret it wrong. A loud voice or yelling is usually a sign of extreme aggression or alarm. He didn't want that! They were trying to make friends with their captors after all. Or at least negotiate with them. He decided to progress with his talk.

"If you are listening we need food." Harry was calm. "We also need toilet paper. That's the stuff...." He made a wiping motion behind his butt.

Everyone back at the house knew exactly what he was talking about. Especially Rob. Then they saw him making a motion like he was eating a sandwich. Next a drinking motion. After that he was scooping food into his mouth with imaginary cutlery. Then back to the rear-wiping motion again.

Harry stopped and they waited.

Still nothing.

To the people back at the house, Harry standing out there alone, looked very far away. But he was just in their front yard. Although he did look alone. Carol absently twirled Ashley's hair and Ashley twirled her doll Molly's hair. Everyone else exchanged glances with one another. However, the Greys didn't appear. There were no bright lights or the peeling back of the water wall. A ray gun didn't pop out and laser Harry, to the relief of Travis and Katie. If that had happened, they figured all of them would get it next. After a little longer, Rob and Laura leaned over their sides of the porch, and looked around. Each thought it smart to check and make sure nothing was coming up behind them. Of course, there didn't seem to be anything alive in their new "neighborhood" other than the eight of them. To a careful person a touch of paranoia is a virtue.

The Greys didn't appear. They didn't answer him. The group back at the house saw Harry's shoulders slump a little. Their first attempt to communicate had failed. However, perhaps that was a good thing because nobody knew what might have happened.

Harry's arms felt like long rubber hoses hanging down to the ground. Disappointment was like a heavy weight on his shoulders. He told himself that at least he tried and that he would try again soon. He turned and started to walk back to the house.

For a second Harry felt a tingling feeling trace up and down his body. Then it was gone. But Harry thought they might have listened.

CHAPTER 30

Harry walked through the front door looking rejected. Laura and Rob came in behind him. The screen door swung closed with a metallic bang and caught Rob in his back. They all filed back into the kitchen. The light outside was fading fast like at dusk so it was dark in the room. Laura punched the light button they had found on the wall and the room brightened. Harry took the center position in the room. The rest gathered around.

Harry felt foolish. He didn't know what to say to them. At first he had felt stupid out there. It was his idea, his great all-knowing idea, to try and talk with the Greys. He did. They didn't listen. It failed. His vocabulary sunk to the bottom of his stomach. What was he going to say? Everyone was listening. Except he hadn't said anything yet.

"Well…." he started. Or maybe it didn't fail. A half-smile broke on Harry's face. The tingling sense he experienced when he walked away felt distinctly *alien*. The more he thought about it the more he was convinced it was them. But how does he tell the group this? How can he prove it? The wheels turned inside Harry's head and he decided just to tell them bluntly.

"Despite what you saw I think it worked," he said.

Everyone sighed and exhaled in a combination of disagreement and disbelief.

"What?" Rob said. "It didn't do shit."

"Why do you say that?" Laura asked.

"Yeah, dude," Katie said. "No offense but what are you talking about?"

"Yeah, man," said Travis. "How do you know? All I saw was you stand there and nothing else." Travis spoke with annoyance. He thought Harry was a nice guy, but that he was too into his educational self, and trying to know things that others didn't. For Travis, this was clouding Harry's judgment. Especially, because Harry was a smart guy.

Harry held his hands out. "Relax, relax. Let me explain."

"Please do cuz I don't get it," said Rob.

"When I turned to leave out there I had a feeling come over me."

Carol sucked in her breath.

"No, no, it wasn't a bad feeling this time. Not invasive. More like a tingling sensation."

"Did you imagine it?" Katie asked.

"No, I didn't. It was real."

"Well, so what? A tingling sensation. Big deal," Travis said.

"Yeah, but it was distinctly an alien feeling. I think they read me."

That caught everyone's attention. Eyes shared quick glances with other eyes.

"Do you know what I mean?" Harry asked.

"How?" Laura asked. "Like a book?"

"Yes. Up and down."

"Oh great, they're like alien stalkers or something," Travis said.

Katie laughed and elbowed him in the stomach. "That's not what he means, honey."

"I know that," Travis said leaning over her. "I meant alien peepers. This whole thing gets crazier as we're here."

"Okay, so you felt like they probed you, or something, up and down your body," Rob said loudly wanting to get back to seriousness. "But this time not in a bad way like we felt before. Right?"

"Yes," Harry answered. "I'm pretty sure of it."

"What do you mean by up and down? Your brain?" Laura said.

"I mean my body. My legs. Upper body. Torso. Up to my head."

"And you think they were listening when this happened?" said Carol. She tried to disguise the nervousness in her voice with a calm skepticism.

"Yes. That's the feeling I got."

"If they did, what good did that do us?" said Rob. "Still no food."

"We'll have to wait and see."

"We can't go too long without food," Katie said.

"I know that. Look, at least we know they were aware of us. That we had their attention. Maybe it'll get through. I mean they have to know we need food to survive, and they put us here for a reason, so they would have to sustain us."

"I don't like 'em," Carol said sharply.

"None of us do," Shawn said. He walked to the kitchen window to look out. The light outside had continued to fade and now it was almost dark out.

"And for what reason are we here?" Carol said.

"We don't know yet," said Harry.

"I'm sure we'll find out," said Laura. Those words crawled across her back.

CHAPTER 31

The light outside was gone. Faded into dark obscurity. So had the hopes of the group for a quick resolution. They had already been through a lot during their short stay, but at the end of their kitchen conversation, two big questions were left looming over them all. What was yet to come and why were they here?

Everyone became tired and they divided up the living arrangements. Carol and Ashley took the upstairs bedroom in the back left. Laura took the one in the back right. The upstairs front left bedroom was taken by Travis and Katie. Harry took the other bedroom in front. On the first floor, Rob took the right bedroom in back, and Shawn took the one across to the left.

The night was dark and quiet. Laura stared at the ceiling for hours before falling asleep. Carol held Ashley all night. Travis and Katie re-sisted their desire to fool around for about an hour before succumbing to each other. It was the first time they felt normal since they'd been here. Both Rob and Shawn, even though in different rooms, stayed awake for a good part of the night, each man listening for any disturbance or sign of danger. None came.

CHAPTER 32

Light crept in around the window curtains to stretch out and shine morning onto Laura's face. Her left eye opened and then her right eye. The plain white ceiling of her room hovered over her. It was very boring. That was quite a contrast to the day before which had been anything but dull. She rolled onto her right side and stared at her bedroom. She had slept on top of the bedspread. There had been no need for cover because it hadn't been cold overnight. That at least was one good thing about her new house. There was a lock on the door so that made her feel a little better. Her eyes looked around the room. It looked the same as the day before. Just boring.

Laura felt good albeit she was hungry. The night before she had managed to fall asleep after a few hours and slept well. The pillow was soft. The mattress comfortable enough. And nothing had happened during the night. No boogey man or creature of the night had come in to take her away. She didn't hear anyone else in the house. No talking. No sounds of anyone moving around. Her mind replayed the events of the day before. All the mystery, unanswered questions, feelings of loneliness, and the Greys were too much to bear this morning. Her mind thought perhaps all of that was just a dream, and she had woken up from it, but she didn't believe that. This wasn't even her home bedroom.

She sat up and stretched by doing some yoga poses. A good stretch did the body good, she always said, when she went to the gym to work out. It made her body get in harmony with itself. Laura stood and went to the window. She slowly pulled the curtain back half expecting to see something she didn't want to see. However, all she saw was the side yard and rows of trees stretching away. She went to the closet and opened it. It was empty. The same as the night before. Laura didn't know why she expected anything different. Just hope, she supposed. But if all the closets were the same they would need more clothing. It was apparent they were here for a reason. For how long they didn't know yet, but if that reason was a long time, then they couldn't get by on only one day's clothing per person.

Laura went to her bedroom door and unlocked it. Slowly she opened the door a little and peeked out into the hallway. Nobody was there. She opened the door and walked out. Everyone's doors were closed and nobody appeared to be up yet. Laura stood at the top of the stairs and looked down it. Did she dare? Yes, she had no choice. Better go down and see what's down there. She was confident enough that it would be the same as yesterday, but if something bad was waiting for her downstairs, she couldn't do anything about it anyway. A sharp pain cut through her stomach for an instant. Laura grabbed the railing to steady herself. She didn't know what might have caused it but quickly blew it off as fast as it had come. *This place is strange enough*, she thought.

Laura started down the stairs and heard a click over her shoulder. She stopped. Then there was a squeaking noise. Laura looked over to her right and saw the bedroom door open and out popped Ashley's cute little face.

"Hi, Laura," said Ashley with an innocence to her voice.

Laura turned and smiled. "Good morning," she said. "What are you doing?"

Carol came to the door. "Be careful, honey. Don't go out without me yet til we know more about this place." She looked at Laura and smiled. "Hi Laura. She's okay. How are you?"

"Good morning. And yeah, I'm not so bad. How was your night?"

"Pretty good. We slept well. Although, our stomachs hurt." Carol put her hand on Ashley's head.

"Molly slept good, too," said Ashley. Her doll was in her hand.

"Is anyone else up?" Carol asked.

"I don't think so. I'm going down." Laura put her finger to her lips. "I don't want to disturb anyone."

"Okay," Carol answered. "We'll follow you after we use the bathroom."

"Sounds good," Laura said. She turned and continued down the stairs.

A few steps creaked as she reached the bottom. Upon looking around downstairs Laura concluded that nothing had changed overnight. The kitchen looked the same. Some of the strange light came through the windows from outside. Their living room was the same. However, no television in the room stood out. Somehow a living room doesn't seem right without a television even though some people would benefit by not having one. Laura thought they might benefit too, but without any sort of entertainment, the eight of them might go nuts. To make it worse, they would start to get on each other's nerves, and then the infighting would start. That was another thing they didn't need right now. Not to leave out Rob had already shown signs of being chippy.

Laura walked into the kitchen. She looked out the windows but it all was the same. Nothing moved except the dragon was still shooting its water up into the air and the strange wall was still in front holding them in.

"Hey."

Laura jumped and turned. It was Rob standing in the entrance way under the stairs.

"Oh, hey," she answered trying to get her heartbeat down again. "Don't sneak up on anyone here."

"Oh, sorry," Rob said at the end of a yawn. He leaned against the wall and looked at her. "Anything new?"

"I don't know yet. Doesn't appear to be." Laura felt a little annoyed that Rob didn't seem to take her request seriously enough but they needed to get along. "Did you sleep okay? Notice anything weird during the night?"

"No. Slept like a baby eventually." He scratched his shoulder. "You?"

"Good. That's kind of a surprise considering...."

"Yeah, I agree."

"I think you, me, Carol, and Ashley are the only ones up."

"Okay." Rob rubbed his stomach. "I'm starving. My stomach hurts. Don't suppose there's anything to eat."

"I was just going to check," Laura said. "I'm hungry too."

That thought was interrupted as Ashley came bouncing down the stairs one step at a time. A wooden plank sound echoed every step she took.

"Careful, don't fall," Carol said following behind her.

To Laura they both looked very happy. Ashley sprang from the bottom steps and landed in a crouch. She smiled at Laura. Carol got to the bottom and shared her grin.

"It's good to see the two of you having fun," said Laura.

"We went to the bathroom," Ashley said.

"Okay," Laura said wondering why that was a big deal.

"Whatever floats your boat," said Rob between more yawns.

"And there was toilet paper," Carol said giving them both a thumbs up.

That seemed to wake Rob up. "Cool!" he said. "Maybe there's food."

Laura opened a cabinet and smiled. Then she opened all of them. The rest moved closer. Now everyone smiled. To their joy there were boxes of what appeared to be food in all the cabinets. Laura grabbed one. It was white and the size of a regular microwavable meal. She held it up for the others to see.

Ashley skipped over to the counter. "Mommy, Mommy. We can eat now." She was jumping up and down.

"Yes, hon," Carol said. She was looking over Laura's shoulder.

Rob started to pick through another cabinet. "What's in here?" he asked. "Do you see any coffee?"

Laura rummaged around in the cabinets a little more. "No, I don't."

"Man, that sucks," said Rob. "Like how are we supposed to go without coffee?"

"At least we have food."

"Yeah, at least. What's in the boxes?"

"I don't know but let's find out," said Laura. She dug her fingers into the side of the box, which seemed to be made of a thin cardboard, tore it off and pulled out another plastic box in the shape of a small food tray. The top was sealed with a plastic wrap. Through it she could see what looked like chicken.

"What do you think?" She held it up to the others. "Chicken?"

Everyone nodded in agreement. Laura put it down and grabbed a yellow one from the cabinet next to the refrigerator. She opened it and out slid a sealed tray. Inside it looked like scrambled eggs. Rob tore a brown cover off his box and it looked like beef inside.

"I want one," Ashley said. Her mother picked a box from the cabinet next to the refrigerator. It was gray with a light brown stripe down the middle. Carol opened it and Ashley grabbed onto it to take a look. There was a big white circle surrounded by a grayish ring inside. "Mom, what is that?"

"I don't know, Ash," said Carol as she examined it more.

"There is only one way to find out," Rob said. "The microwave." He walked around and opened it.

"Is it safe you think?" Laura asked.

"Do we have a choice?" He put his meal inside the microwave and closed the door.

"I guess not," Laura said unconvinced. "We don't even know if it's a microwave for sure."

"It looks like one." Rob was studying the buttons on the front. "What else could it be?"

"I don't know. That's just it."

"But once again," Rob turned around to them. "What choice do we have?"

Laura, Carol, and Ashley shared looks with each other and shrugged.

"You don't think the ugly stickmen would starve us, do you?" asked Rob.

They just stared back at him. Rob knew they weren't convinced.

"Okay, give it a whirl," Laura said.

"But first I think everybody better step back," Carol said inching back to the front window. Ashley came with her.

"Oh sure, so I get zapped," Rob said smiling. "Some of you might like that. Ha!"

"You're the one willing to try it," said Laura. "And you don't have to tell us there's no other choice. We gotcha on that."

"Funny," Rob said sarcastically. He examined what must be buttons on the front. There were three of them. Blue on top, red in the middle, and green at the bottom. They were square-shaped and the size of a playing card. Rob reasoned that because green means go that might be the on-button. Red is the color of blood and usually a warning color, and used on stop signs, so that must mean stop. Blue must be something else. Blue is a good color, and it's the sky and ocean back home. He pushed it and the door popped open. *That was easy*, he thought, put his box tray inside, and pushed the door closed. Rob's confidence in his examination grew stronger. He'd try the green button next. His finger went up to it, he counted down from five to one and pushed.

The machine came to life. It whirred with a steady hum, some lights came on, and instantly the smell of cooked beef floated throughout the room. Rob rubbed his hands and stepped back until he almost walked into Carol and Ashley. Through the glass door his meal circled around inside. Rob's mouth was starting to water in anticipation. The hot beef smell started to drift out of the kitchen. Laura's stomach growled. Ashley jumped up and down as her mom scanned the cabinets for what she would choose to eat. The machine dinged, lights went off, and it fell silent.

"Oh, yeah," said a very happy Rob. He walked over to the counter and opened a drawer, pulled out a fork, knife, and napkin. "Woo-hoo! Time to chow."

Carefully, he touched the microwave and it seemed cold. He pushed the blue button and the door opened. Inside sat his breakfast with the sealed wrap inflated like a balloon. Using his napkin to protect his hand he pulled it out and slid it along the counter. The balloon wrap deflated. Rob turned, opened the fridge, poured himself a glass of water, and prepared to eat.

Laura stood next to him. "I wonder how it tastes," she said.

"Only one way to find out," Rob said. He tore the wrap off and a puff of steam exploded in his face. Rob blinked but wasn't burned. It just filtered through his sinuses. Then he stabbed his meal with his fork, held it up for examination, looked sideways at Laura, and took a bite. Rich moist flavor of roast beef melted through his mouth and caressed his taste buds. Rob tilted his head back and smiled in delight. He chewed some more and swallowed. The euphoria inside his mouth flowed down into his stomach. Rob had been hungry for a day now. He wasn't anymore.

"Good, huh?" Laura said slightly amused at the look on his face.

"Uh-huh," Rob answered. He cut some more and stuffed it into his mouth.

"I see," said Laura. "That's nice to know."

"My turn, my turn," Ashley said. Carol took her daughter's meal, put it in the machine, and pressed the green button. Instantly, the smell of gravy leaked out from it and started to overtake the beef smell from Rob's food. The machine hummed and flashed until finally it dinged silent. Carol used a napkin for protection and grabbed the meal out and put it on the counter. She turned and looked around and frowned.

"We're still missing a kitchen table," Carol said as she reached for utensils.

Rob mumbled something and kept eating.

"Oh yeah, noticed that yesterday," Laura agreed, looking around. "We'll have to have Harry ask for one."

Rob nodded up and down while chomping on his food.

After the plastic wrap deflated, Carol pulled the plastic seal off the meal with a couple tugs and set it down in front of Ashley. The white circle was bigger now and it was surrounded by a thick grayish liquid. Ashley scooped some of it up with a spoon and tasted it.

"Do we have any orange juice, Mommy?" asked Ashley.

"I'm afraid not, doll baby," Carol answered.

Ashley chewed a little bit. She smiled and looked up at her mom. "Biscuits and gravy," she said.

"Yummers," her mom answered.

CHAPTER 33

Laura and Carol heated up some meals for themselves. Laura's was scrambled eggs and Carol found one with waffles and syrup. None of them were sure if they were in fact eating what it tasted like. Their meals resembled what they were supposed to be. The beef resembled beef. Biscuits and gravy looked kind of like biscuits and gravy. The eggs were egglike. What saved them was the food tasted great. Even the water. There wasn't anything else to drink so they drank the water from the fridge. It had a soothing feeling to it with a taste that neither of them knew how to describe. They seemed to want more of it as they drank. It was like the taste fed on itself.

The aromas of delicious food spread quickly throughout the house. It wasn't long and everyone came into the kitchen starving for breakfast. First it was Shawn, Harry was next, and then Travis and Katie came down from upstairs wearing giddy smiles on their faces. There was disappointment that there wasn't any coffee but they were happy just to have food. They all ate and drank the water until the globe in the refrigerator was half empty.

The morning's breakfast served as a morale boost. It was the first good thing that had happened for them since waking up here. They weren't hungry anymore. The problem of how to get food was solved. They weren't thirsty. The mysterious water tasted good and was fulfilling. Their stomach pains had gone away. However, the lack of a kitchen table was evident. This would have to be addressed in some way because everyone had used the kitchen counter top to eat. Some kitchen chairs were needed too.

Underneath the sink Carol found a trash can of some kind. They disposed of the meal boxes that way. The trash can sucked the garbage down a small tunnel that led to somewhere they didn't know. It had a small hatch that could be tightened over the garbage hole. The kitchen sink worked well. The water wasn't quite the same as their drinking water but it was clean. It tasted different so they reasoned their drinking water had special additives in it. The sink water was good at cleaning off their eating utensils and drinking glasses. Afterward they all gathered in the living room. Laura and Rob stood in front. Carol and Ashley sat on the couch in back and Rob and Shawn sat in the couch on the side. Travis and Katie parked it on the stone inglenook by the fireplace.

"How'd they do that?" asked Katie.

"Do what?" Rob answered. He was holding his stomach and holding back from belching.

"Fill up the kitchen with food," she said. "What'd they do, come in overnight?"

"Must have," Travis said rubbing Katie's shoulders.

"It's like they came in overnight with boxes, filled everything up, and just walked out."

"Yeah, and we didn't even hear them," Shawn said.

"Not over your snoring, dude," said Rob.

"You could use a mouth plug too, dude," Shawn said back.

"Just kidding, man." They both laughed.

"They gave us what we needed," said Laura.

"Some of what we needed," said Travis. "We still need a lot more."

"True," Laura agreed.

"Like to get outta here," Travis continued. "And fast. I'm not gonna be able to stand another day here."

"Don't think we have a choice, Trav," said Katie.

"Yes, I agree," Laura continued. "But for now we have food and water."

"And thank God, toilet paper," Rob said. Everyone smiled a little on that.

"You know what that proves?" Laura said.

"What?" Travis spoke while the rest of the group asked with their eyes.

"That Harry was right. The Grey things listened to him."

Harry psyched up a lot and out popped his chest. His plan had worked. He had communicated with aliens! He had gotten them what they needed and now they knew it. This was a testament to Harry's brilliant mind. He was the one that taught and educated the youth at his school. It was by no accident that he would guide and help these people in this crisis. A feeling of jubilated satisfaction ran through his body. Harry smiled.

"Thanks," Harry said. "Now we know we can talk to them."

"We'll see," said Katie. "They helped us this time but we don't know if they will the next time."

"If you consider giving us food help," said Shawn. "I call it necessity."

"I do," Laura said. She didn't want Shawn or anyone to take them down the negative path again. Especially right now. They needed to stay upbeat.

"I don't trust them," said Carol. "Not at all."

"I know we can't trust them," said Laura. "But maybe they'll help us more if we ask them again, or as we go along here."

"Yeah, right," Katie said sarcastically. "We'll see."

"I don't want to go along with them anymore," Travis said.

"My mom's right," said Ashley. Everyone stopped and looked at her. "They were so nice before. They wanted to play. Now they're the bad guys. Big fakers."

"Right, right," Harry said trying to move on. "Look, I will try to speak to them again. Let's figure out what we need to say to them. What else we still need." Everyone agreed. "Think about it throughout the day and I'll try it again this evening."

"Think you can score up a TV or something and some football?" Rob said.

"Funny, I'll try," Harry answered.

"How about some cell phones?" Katie asked with a half-smile.

"Yeah, sure. I'll try."

Laura was pleased. That was a positive moment for the group. They all had come together on their next course of action. She hoped they would stay united.

"Okay, so what do we do now?" Katie asked.

"What can we do except sit around here?" Rob said with a negative tone back in his voice. His hand was still on his stomach like he was palming a basketball.

"We can go outside and look around," Harry said. "Let's see what's out there today."

CHAPTER 34

The group went out onto the porch but immediately their spirits were disappointed. Nothing had changed. The wall was still in front of them spinning its watery web. The weird ceiling light was turned on. The dragon fountain spouted water. They heard no sound outside other than themselves and the fountain. Still no other life that they could tell. No birds crying, no insects buzzing, and no animals running around or jumping from tree to tree. The breeze did blow its comforting ambiance that made them feel better. They still were alone here. Nothing else. Just them.

They formed into their groups again and explored around. Only this time Rob and Laura searched the back area. Travis and Katie searched the right side which Rob and Laura had looked at last time. Harry and Shawn went over the hill on the left side which Travis and Katie had explored the day before. Again, Carol and Ashley stayed home but got some exercise by walking around the house. By the middle of the day everyone was back with nothing new to report. Although, both Rob and Laura mentioned something about a faintly rancid smell in the back somewhere. Otherwise, their surroundings hadn't changed.

They all ate lunch and cleaned up afterwards. The need for a kitchen table was palpable again. The strange garbage can, or garbage disposal, sucked the garbage out and away. Afterward they all dispersed onto the porch or into the living room. They had no real means of entertainment so they spent the rest of the day waiting around and discussing a variety of topics. The discussions ranged from being trapped here to their lives back home. However, they weren't able to remember much about their daily lives from before they got here other than in small bits and pieces. Add to that, it was also frustrating that they couldn't remember much about their abductions either. Mostly that experience still stayed out of reach of their memories. So they focused and discussed what they could remember. Laura remembered playing music and volleyball in school. She also relaxed by doing yoga and Tai Chi. However, she never thought about her home life since being here. Rob was a business major and played football growing up. He knew he liked to party and shoot pool because that's what he thought about a lot. Travis and Katie were smart college kids who didn't know what they wanted to do yet. But they were excited that the whole world was out there for them to explore and conquer. Travis remembered his dad but not his mom, but Katie couldn't even remember her parents. Carol told them about her hardships like taking care of her mother who had fallen ill, her miserable job, and her divorce. Yet, she struggled to remember her son Kenny. Ashley was the star of the afternoon. She asked everyone cute questions that burst with curiosity. At one time, she asked Rob if he learned to be a jerk in college or did it just come natural. Everyone laughed including Rob. They needed more laughter to help heal their worries and fears here. Ashley didn't have any kind of abduction amnesia at all and remembered everything. Ashley's dreams ranged from being a dancer to a doctor. Harry was married, had a son and daughter, but couldn't recall their names. His mind did know he had been a teacher at his school Pegasus for over twenty years. Shawn was married and had two sons. Unlike some of the others, he could remember their names and some memories of family time. He knew he owned a liquor store in Rock Island named Lasky's Liquors. One thing they all had in common was everyone had grown up in the Quad-Cities.

As the afternoon passed on their discussions switched to Harry and what his message was going to be to the Greys. They decided he would thank them for the food. This counted on the Greys understanding the concept of thankfulness. Laura mentioned they needed a kitchen table and Harry noted it. Rob and Shawn suggested a TV. Harry told them he would inquire about the lack of wildlife. It was all too strange to be outside and feel like you're the only people alive in the universe. They decided against asking if they could go home. They even decided against asking questions about where they were and why they were here. Everyone was afraid to anger them or bring any kind of punishment down on themselves. Especially, when they had made some forward progress overnight. One thing they didn't want to do was to anger the Greys. They had all the power.

Later that evening Harry went out to the same area in the front yard that he had the night before. They had all eaten dinner and everyone else settled down in the kitchen or on the front porch to watch. Harry's ritual was like a family gathering together to watch TV after dinner. Harry stood in front of the shifting wall and held out his arms again. He'd decided if it worked the day before then not to depart from it. To Laura it looked like it was going to become a ritual. Harry spoke with a deferential voice. Back at the house his words couldn't be heard very well except for bits and pieces. The house was too far away to hear clearly. Carol went into the living room and started to pace back and forth. This scared her. She didn't trust the aliens, and felt that reaching out to them of any kind risked an opportunity for the Greys to hurt them. Especially her daughter. Harry didn't speak as long this time. He stood there after he was finished in case the Greys would make an appearance. In Harry's mind, it was meant as an invitation to communicate. After a minute, he walked back to the house. The light from the ceiling above began to fade. Everyone retired for the night to their bedrooms.

The Greys never showed themselves.

CHAPTER 35

Something moved in the night.

It sifted between trees. Nothing was around to pose a threat. With impunity, it noiselessly traveled its course towards the house. The night remained undisturbed. It blended with the night. Peace covered the land like a blanket. For this was brother to silence. Its path came from behind the house. Upon seeing the vastness of the backyard, it moved around in a semicircle to the side of the house but stayed back hidden in the forest. It came to the edge of the trees and stopped. It waited.

Watching.

Time became inconsequential. Neither slow nor fast. Then with utmost stealth it crossed the yard and moved around to the front of the house. Like a shadow moving within a bigger shadow it crept up to the front door. Again, it stopped. Nothing moved anywhere. Nothing made a sound. It slipped under the front door.

Inside the house was pitch black. Everyone slept. It knew this. Jagged breathing came from the back of the house in a whistling sound. The living was back there. But it was also upstairs. It climbed the stairs. Slowly it went. Step by step. Silently. Until it reached the top. Quiet. It waited some more. Still quiet. A calm seemed to have passed over the house in an almost deadly way.

It crept across the floor boards to a closed door on the right. Inside breathed a female. It hesitated. The darkness of the night drifting around seemed to wait as well. Then it started to go under the crack at the bottom of the door.

There was a loud crashing sound followed by smaller clanging sounds in the adjacent room.

In an instant, it retreated down the stairs and out of the house.

It slipped away unbeknownst into the night.

CHAPTER 36

Ashley opened her bedroom door yawning, rubbing her eye, and holding an empty water glass in her other hand. She was mad at herself for spilling her water all over the floor. At least her mom didn't wake up completely. Just tossed and turned. She had to get a towel to clean up the mess.

Her nostrils flinched and she stepped back. Ashley's face twisted a little.

"Ugh." There was a repugnant smell in the hallway. She looked back at her mom but she was sound asleep. Ashley pinched her nose. She held her breath, went into the bathroom, grabbed a towel, and hurried back into her bedroom and closed the door.

CHAPTER 37

The next day started the same as the first. Laura woke from her slumber and stretched out to all four corners of the bed and exhaled. The plain white ceiling still hovered over her. It looked even more boring today. She missed her family, her friends, yoga class, working out at the gym, going to the movies, but not her job. Although, she would take that any day opposed to being trapped here.

Laura got out of bed and looked out the window and saw that everything was the same. Next she did a few yoga poses to stretch. Then she strolled over to the closet and opened the doors. There was still nothing inside. No clothes. No bathrobe. Nothing. Laura didn't know why she even checked it other than probably more out of habit than anything else. A little bit of home still resided inside her. That was good. However, she had been wearing the same clothes now for two days, as had the rest of them, and they needed fresh clothing. Something had to be done about that. Then it dawned on her that Harry hadn't asked the Greys for new clothing. Perhaps that was why they didn't have any yet? She would bring this to everyone's attention today.

Laura unlocked her bedroom door and opened it. There was a sharp pain in her stomach and she flinched a moment. Carefully she checked the hallway, saw that everything was clear, and softly went down the stairway. Upon reaching the kitchen she immediately smiled. There was a small round table up against the front wall underneath the windows. They finally had a kitchen table.

"Hey again."

Laura turned around startled. It was Rob.

"You did it again," she said. "Stop it."

"Sorry, I didn't mean to. I don't know what else to say."

He looked sincere enough to Laura. "Okay, I guess so." She pointed to the table. "Look. We have a table now."

"Cool," Rob said nodding. "That's progress."

Laura walked over and put her hand on the table. "It looks like wood but it's some sort of hard plastic just like the coffee table."

"Alien plastic, huh? Like I said, it's progress." Rob kept staring at it. "But still, you know what we don't have?"

Laura looked at him and then back at the table. She knew. "You're right. No chairs." She sighed. "I just figured kitchen chairs would come with the kitchen table. Looks like we're going to have to ask for everything. These superior beings still need some mentoring."

"I'd say. Maybe they don't need things like tables? Or toilet paper?"

"Maybe not," said Laura. She got a glass of water from the globe and started to drink. "Maybe they just think it and it happens. But I'm sure they need to eat, too."

Rob walked over, picked out a breakfast meal, and put it in the microwave. He drank some water while it cooked. Within a minute the downstairs started to flow with the smell of pancakes and syrup. Laura heated up a meal of waffles and syrup too. Because they had nothing to sit on they ate standing at the kitchen counter. At least everything they ate was close to what they thought they were eating. So far it tasted good and they were alive.

It wasn't before long and everyone was awake and coming to the kitchen. Shawn walked into the kitchen and stopped. He was staring at Laura and Rob through starving eyes. There was a loud rumble in his stomach that signaled his hunger.

"Man, I must be hungrier than usual because my stomach sure hurts," said Shawn. He touched his stomach and grimaced a little.

Both Laura and Rob moved their breakfasts over to the kitchen table to get out of Shawn's way. Like a bull in a stampede, Shawn bulled his way to the microwave, chose any meal out of the cupboard, and started to cook it. The smell of eggs and bacon floated about. While his food cooked, he slammed a few glasses of water from the globe. The cooker dinged that it was finished and Shawn proceeded to chow. Laura and Rob shared a few glances and chuckled together. They knew Shawn was the type of man that could eat.

Soon everyone was in the kitchen. The first thing everyone did was drink water from the globe. There was something about the globe that caught Harry's attention.

"Hey," he said. "Has anyone noticed that the globe is filled back up with water every morning?"

"Nope," said Rob. "Too thirsty to notice."

"Yeah, I guess," said Laura. "How do you think that happens?"

"I'm not sure," replied Harry. "I can't see anything but they might have a hose or pipe that comes up from underneath and pumps it in overnight."

"That's good to know," said Travis with sarcasm.

"Yeah," Katie chimed in. "It's good to know we won't turn to dust around here."

"I sure wish we had some coffee though," said Laura. "That seems to be one thing they won't give us."

"Yeah," said Katie. "I don't know if I can live without my cup of joe."

"No kidding," Travis added. "I need my caffeine rush."

"Yeah, the stickmen suck," said Rob.

Breakfast continued. Harry was next to warm up food. Travis and Katie were leaning back against the stairs talking together. Carol and Ashley were in the middle of the room. Laura made it a point to show everyone that she and Rob were eating while standing over their new addition to the house. She also pointed out they had no chairs. Harry noted it and said he would ask the Greys for chairs later in the day. This was becoming a ritual for him.

Carol and Ashley started whispering between themselves. After a few quiet exchanges, it became obvious to all that something was on their minds. Carol noticed everyone looking at them with curious faces. She kneeled next to Ashley.

"Everyone, Ashley has a question," Carol said putting her arm around her. "Go ahead honey, ask 'em."

Ashley looked up at everyone and made a funny little face with her nose. "Did anyone smell anything last night?"

"Like what?" asked Rob wiping his face.

"What kind of smell?" Laura said.

"A nasty one," Ashley said. "I had to hold my nose."

"What? Like the dead animal kind?" Harry asked in between bites.

"Like the stinky kind."

"Where'd you smell it?" Katie asked.

"Upstairs. In the hallway."

"She told me she got up in the middle of the night to get water after she spilled her cup," Carol cut in. "That she smelled something really rotten in the hallway above the stairs."

"Yeah, rotten," Ashley said looking up at her mom.

"I didn't use your bathroom if that's what you mean," said Rob. "We have our own bathroom." He nodded over at Shawn who agreed with him.

Carol patted Ashley on the shoulder. "Okay. Well, she thought she smelled something so we're just checking."

"Okay. Thanks," Laura said. She couldn't quite remember if she had or not. The last two nights she had slept like a log. That was at least one small good thing about this place.

"Laura, you're across the hall from us," said Carol. "Maybe we'll smell it again."

"I hope not." Laura smiled. "No problem. I'll keep an eye open. Or nose." Something was tinkering around in the back of her mind. There was something in the backyard of her memory.

Rob looked up from across the table at her with a concentrated look on his face. "Hey, do you remember yesterday...."

Laura blinked. She was hunched over staring out the window. Blinked again. She looked closer through the window but didn't say a word. She knew everyone was looking at her.

"What is it?" Rob asked.

"Yeah, what is it?" asked Katie. She was hesitant to move away from the stairway and look herself out of a little bit of fear of something bad being outside. They had enough problems as it was. The whole group seemed to emanate this.

Now her face was up against the window. She squinted forward. A small black shape quickly crossed over the yard.

"Oh, my God, there's something moving outside," Laura said. Her voice trailed off into surprise that rose above everyone in the room.

Rob followed her gaze to the window and outside. Nothing looked different to him. The same porch, dragon fountain, and the circulating water wall behind that. Then another black shape graced the grass and was gone. It was a shadow of something. "Hey, she's right." Rob was astounded. Then another shot across from left to right. "There's something flying around out there."

Everyone rushed over behind them to peer out the window. Shoulders rubbed against others as everyone jockeyed for space to look outside. Carol put Ashley up on the table. At first there was nothing new to see. The yard in front seemed to be asleep. Heads bobbed up and down, side to side, trying to catch first sight of their new arrival. Then quickly a shape zoomed around in a circle and flew off. There was a collective wonder in the group as they shared the same thought of what could it be?

Laura turned to the group. "We have life."

"It would appear," said Harry. "But what?"

"Should we go outside?" Carol asked. "Is it safe, you think?"

"There's only one way to find out," Rob said. He backed away from the table politely, squeezed out between everyone, and opened the front door.

"I'm with you Rob but I'd advise caution," Harry said following him. "We don't know what's out there."

"That's all good, Teach." Rob smiled back at him as he opened the screen door and stepped out onto the front porch. The rest filed out onto the porch after him. What they walked out into was a delightful sight for the eyes and the ears to hear. Birds were flying from tree to tree. They were circling around and dive bombing the ground in search of food. To the left of the house a robin ripped a stringy thing from the ground and flew off with it dangling in its mouth. There was rhythmic chirping from the trees. Black birds flew about echoing their famous "caw" back and forth from afar. When they weren't sounding off, cries of "birdy" would fill in the ambient gaps of silence, and then be answered from elsewhere in their bird dialect. Over to their left a few squirrels dashed and darted around the trees, and then ran up them in a race to the top. A rabbit nibbled on the strange grass. It looked at them and wiggled its nose. Then it hopped around and continued to eat again. The group of eight spread out on the porch and relished it. The familiarity of home provided great relief for them. Each feared this would last temporarily but it was very welcomed. For a while they would feel a small bit of peace of what it's like to be home again. Even though they knew this certainly wasn't home.

"The Greys. They put them here," Katie said. "Even worms for the birds to eat."

"It appears so," Harry said. He walked from end to end of the porch. Nobody was talking. People were leaning against or sitting on the porch rails watching and listening. Ashley and Carol sat down on the front steps. Harry was thinking now about his last two meetings with the Greys. They weren't exactly meetings as the aliens didn't show. But Harry knew that they had listened to what he had asked for. That in a way was a meeting between them. He could communicate with them.

"What's up, Harry?" asked Laura.

He stopped and looked at her.

"We've noticed you started walking back and forth," said Katie. "Is something bothering you?"

"Yeah, despite all the other things here," Travis said.

Harry knew that everyone was looking at him. He rubbed his chin. "They understand what I'm saying to them. I don't mean that they understand the English language. But I can communicate with them."

"That seems to be true," said Rob smiling. "You ask. We receive."

"I'm pretty sure they're reading my thoughts," Harry continued. "The ability to read feelings, or literally words in the brain, is just phenomenal. It's amazing. But then again these are aliens so it shouldn't be that much of a surprise. They are way more evolved than us. Just look at their heads. Those ugly, upside down, heads. They help prove the point."

"How's that?" Carol said. "I hate their heads."

"However, and wherever, in the universe that they evolved, it was cerebral, and that's why the size of their heads is so big. I think it's to store all that knowledge they have learned. Hence, the size of their bodies is so small. They don't need their bodies in the same way as we humans do. They haven't evolved needing strength and bulk to survive. Or if they had it must have been thousands upon thousands of years ago that they did. However, then they did evolve more on intelligence and developed into the way they are now."

Harry saw that he still had everyone's attention.

"I think that humans are starting along that path now too." He started to shake his hand up and down as if he was teaching a class. "The days of needing to survive by brute strength are over for humankind. We have spent the past thousands of years developing our lives and societies by making discoveries and evolving in nature and creating and evolving our own technology as we lived. It was very slow at first from walking on all fours and then learning to walk and run upright. Then we learned to use tools and slowly upgraded from the rock to the spear to the gun. We made discoveries of fire and electricity and learned to utilize them. Now we have exploded in development. In the last hundred years, we have gone from the invention of the telephone, exploring outer space, to genetic reproduction. And the last twenty to thirty years alone have seen great advancements at an accelerated pace in technology ranging from the internet, global positioning systems, to people basically living much of their lives through a small handheld device called the cell phone."

Harry was on a roll. "I think as we evolve, we too would become like these aliens. Like the beings in science fiction mythology. We will become smarter with bigger brains. This as intelligence and reasoning have paved our course of evolution and will continue to do so. And if we didn't grow bigger brains then we would learn to use the rest of our brains. They say we only use about five to ten percent of our brains as we are now. I don't know if that's true or not but if we could tap into the other ninety percent, the possibilities are endless. I think we might be looking at the future of the human race in the form of little grey men."

"That's some pretty wicked stuff, Harry," Travis said.

"That's the kind of stuff we've talked about before, Trav," said Katie excitedly. She punched him in the arm. "What the heck the little grey men are and what we'll evolve into."

Travis grinned at her for a moment. "Yeah, but that's before we got up close and personal with them."

Rob shook his head and laughed slowly. "Harry, dude. My friend. Take a chill pill. Let's not get all crazy."

Harry shot Rob a cold look. "I'm not joking." He was offended that Rob wouldn't take him seriously. But then what could he expect from a young cocky twentysomething.

"Hey wait," Laura said. "There's some good logic in what he said. It's an interesting thought."

"Yeah," Rob said dismissingly. "I don't have the patience to worry about thousands of years from now. We're screwed now. Here!"

Everyone felt a little squeamish by Rob's anger. Sometimes he seemed like a ticking time bomb ready to go off.

"What are we doing here anyway?" Rob asked in a more subdued tone. "We still don't know."

"It's like we're a stage show," said Shawn. Again, everyone was surprised to hear him. "We're here to be observed. Like I said earlier." He spoke with a ring of sadness in his voice. "It's like we're the animals."

"We're in a zoo?" Rob said. His eyebrows raised.

"And we're the main attraction," said Laura. "Holy...." Her voice trailed off as Laura's mind raced off into thoughts that she didn't want to go into but she couldn't help it. They were all going to die.

"Let's face it," Shawn said. Desperation from their situation was dwelling inside of him. He turned and looked out at the trees. They were the only view he had now other than the watery wall. By looking at them he could remember the trees around the lakes and rivers back home where he would fish. This was the only bit of peace in his mind now. His memories.

"You know it, Rob," said Carol. "You've seen them come. Come and look at us. They stared at us. It was so creepy." The tone in her voice sounded slightly unhinged again.

"I know, I know." Rob was irritated. "I just haven't seen any other animals in jail cells, or whatever we keep things locked up inside here yet. So, I don't know what this is."

"But back to my original point," Harry busted back into the conversation. He didn't want to get off point and was afraid there was going to be an argument. "They are listening to us. Or me. But they're listening. We can talk to them."

"Right, Harry. We've got that established," said Rob. Going back to that again was just retread for him.

"And now we have some wildlife here with us," Harry said. "Just like home. But not really."

"Maybe we'll get a cat like my cat Dinky back home," Ashley said. "Or a dog?"

Katie smiled at her. "That'd be cool, Ash. We'll name it Pillows or Spot or something." Ashley smiled back at her.

"Okay, so we have squirrels and birds and the like." Harry's mind was trying to organize their situation again. "Next time we'll ask for chairs." He looked at Laura who was staring at the porch floor. "Laura, are you okay?" She looked up at him and he saw that the optimism she normally displayed was gone from her face. Laura shook her head and looked out into the yard. Harry didn't press it and let it go.

"Then maybe we can continue on with them and ask to go home?" Harry said. His voice was painted with hope but failed to inspire much of it within the group. Everyone was feeling confined inside this human cage. Nobody had any premature false hope of getting out of there soon.

Then a flash exploded from the front wall and cut down the middle of it. The sides of the watery wall opened to reveal six standing aliens. There were three tall skinny Greys and three small skinny ones. At first they watched.... Then they started pointing.

CHAPTER 38

Twelve black eyes stared at the porch. Three tall adult Greys stood in the back. Their large heads on stick-thin necks loomed over the three shorter Greys. On the left was the one that wore yellow and on the right was the one that wore red. But this time there was a female amid them. She was in the middle and wore a light green tunic that also had a golden star-like symbol on it. This Grey had a distinguishing female attribute: long golden hair from the top of her head and down her back!

Eight sets of eyes returned the stares from the porch. Especially onto her. At first glance she was a shock and caused them to gasp. The combination of the oversized head, big inverted eyes, ugliness, with golden tresses was bizarre. None of the other Greys which they had seen were even close to human. Yet, this female had a human, or Earthly, characteristic. It was the first common feature between the two of them.

The pointing continued from the Yellow, the Red, and the smaller Greys. The Female didn't. She just watched until the small Grey in front of her turned to face her. Then her arm went up to point and direct her Grey towards them. As if on cue the Grey turned and followed along. For about a minute they would stop, perceivably discuss something within their minds, and then continue on.

To everyone on the porch it was a distressing experience. The first time this happened had been a shock, and they were still organizing among themselves, and coming to their earliest conclusions. Now two days later, with each of them aware of their powerless predicament, and after steps in a positive direction, the aliens' return served as a humiliating reminder of what they were. The pointing belittled them more.

The looks cast forth onto them from the aliens felt very strong from across the yard and had the same unnerving feeling as two days before. The Greys' stare made their skin crawl. Everyone was careful, especially Carol, not to think aggressive thoughts back at them. Nobody wanted to bring any anger on themselves or the group. This and the pointing were a harsh wound on their psyche. Even though they were humans, they were the subjects.

"So now we get it," Laura said. Her voice was very down. "They get to see us in our habitat. Complete with animals. Like on a farm or something. We Earthlings."

"It's like they're partnered up," Rob said. "Each alien with a kid or something."

"Great," Travis said sarcastically. "Just when it seems to be getting a little bit better this happens. Again."

"I don't know how much more of this I can take," Shawn said. "If this gets worse I tell you...." His voice trailed off as if he had given up.

"Hold on, everyone. Let's relax for a minute," Harry said very quietly. "You remember last time. Let's just hang here til they go away."

"Yeah, Harry. We don't have any place else to go," said Travis.

The aliens dropped their arms and their penetrating stare faded away. There was another flash and the sides of the wall folded together and sealed up the middle. They were gone. Left was the ever-watery wall again to shift and swirl.

Nobody spoke for about a minute until Katie did.

"Do you think they sell stuffed teddy bears of us to their alien kids?"

CHAPTER 39

Katie's sardonic question never got an answer. It hung in the air for a while until it floated away and was forgotten. The aliens' observation of them had brought morale down very low. Everyone was quiet and waited to see what would happen next. Nothing did. Other than blinking eyelashes and confused thoughts rolling around, nobody did anything. Nobody spoke. It was evident to all that they were going to be here for a while. How long remained to be lived out.

A light wind from the left blew along the ground, brushed over the porch, and sifted through them on its way to the other side. It calmed their nerves and their fears. Some of their anxieties that were spinning around and threatened to overtake their emotional states settled down and stopped. Another breeze swiftly followed along from the left and calmed the eight survivalists. It swept away the invisible wall of despair that had been standing between all of them since the visitation they had all experienced. Now a little bit of normalcy took root again in the group.

"Did you see that?" Carol was the first to speak. "Now there's a female alien?"

"That was freaky," said Laura.

"I know," Rob said. "Hope she's the nice one."

"This gets weirder and weirder," Travis said. "I mean, she had hair." Disbelief filled his voice.

"I know but we all saw it," Laura said. "Like a blonde alien. Goldilocks." She was in a little bit of disbelief too. However, she had seen it with her own eyes. Perhaps talking about it would convince herself that she was real.

"But if you think about it," Katie said as she walked around the porch. "You wouldn't expect them not to have women in their species, in their society, would you?" Everyone mumbled no in a variety of ways. "Then what's the big deal? So what, you know?"

"I think it's the way she looked," Shawn said. He stepped into the middle of the porch next to Harry. "I almost swallowed my tongue when I saw her."

"Yeah, no kidding. She's a freak," Rob said. "Those eyes, with that round shaped head, and then blonde hair. I'm not even sure it was blonde. More like golden or yellow."

"Maybe she's nice, Mommy." Ashley looked up at Carol.

"Maybe, honey," she answered unconvincingly with a frown.

"Well, there's nothing we can do about it now," Harry said. He'd been listening to everyone's comments and collecting his own thoughts. They were obviously in an observatory of some sort. These grey aliens put them there. There were tall ones that appeared to be in charge. There were smaller ones also. Some that appeared to be children. And now they knew there were female Greys too. Plus, their place of confinement had been adapted little by little to exhibit a normal living atmosphere for them: the subjects. And done with his help. Technically, it was their help, but Harry was the communicator among them, and it had been his idea to reach out and establish a dialogue with them. He wanted credit for that and felt just in thinking so. "But we need to discuss what I'm gonna say to them tonight. I want to ask for a little bit more."

"Chairs. New clothes," said Laura as she stretched out her legs.

"Got it," answered Harry.

"Harry, what do you mean by a little bit more?" Carol asked. The thought of dealing with these skinny beings scared her. She didn't want any of them to push the Greys in any way that might make them retaliate.

Harry's mouth got crooked and he looked up at the porch ceiling before answering. "I mean asking about the weather. Asking if we can have some weather."

"What's the matter, Harry? Don't you like sunny and no chance of clouds?" Rob said. There was a soft laugh among everyone.

"Very funny," Harry said smiling. He could appreciate a good joke and it was good for the group. "Yes, I do mean asking if we can have some weather. Otherwise, I think it will drive us nuts with the same thing over and over. We've got nothing else to do."

"Just how long do you think we're planning on being here?" asked Shawn.

"You know what I mean. I think we all know that we don't know the answer to that but unfortunately it might be a while. And remember, it's not our plan, it's their plan."

"If it's a while, at least we're still alive," Laura said looking back over at the wall. "Not that it's any big-time comfort to be here for a while."

"We'll get out," added Harry. "Little by little."

"Do you mean piece by piece, body part by body part?" asked Travis.

"No!" Harry said quickly. "I mean slowly we'll find a way."

"So what's up with you?" Rob looked at Laura. "You're always the positive attitude girl."

"I know." That's all Laura said.

The rest of the day went the same as the previous two days. The birds that flew about and the squirrels that jumped helped reduce the isolated feeling the group had felt. Everyone mostly hung around at the house, either on the porch or inside, but there wasn't much to do. Ashley did somersaults in the front yard and Carol coached her. Travis and Katie joked and giggled between themselves. Harry and Rob discussed and argued various topics from back on Earth that were easier to remember now, that ranged from politics to sports. None of which existed here that they knew of. Shawn had retreated within himself by sitting on the porch and staring at the swaying trees. Laura did the same, all the while trying to keep her spirits up and not get too despaired.

In the afternoon, they divided into their groups and went walking around the compound. The disturbing feeling of being watched by the aliens had worn off a little by then. It was obvious they had the freedom to move around inside. There wasn't anything new to see in the surrounding land. At least they would get some exercise and it helped relax them. They ate their meals and drank their water like they usually did.

Harry went up in the evening and did his ritual in front of the wall. It was beginning to be a little like asking Santa Claus for gifts and waking up the next morning to find them.

The ceiling light faded and everyone retired for the night and went to their bedrooms. Sleep settled down over them and each fell asleep quickly. All but Ashley. Motionless, she stared at her bedroom door.

CHAPTER 40

Laura's eyes stared up at the white light methodically positioning itself above her. It moved slowly from side to side with blinking lights before lowering to a close distance above her head. The brightness of the light blinded her down to her peripheral vision. There she saw a giant head of a Grey alien walk up next to her. Then another one appeared on her other side. Their faces were like emotionless masks. They seemed not alive to her. Like scarecrows. The alien eyes were holes of blackness to look into. Laura tried to move but she couldn't. Frustration started to build. Not even her fingers would obey her wishes. She tried to cry out but her mouth stayed silent. Her back was cold. Then her shoulders. And her breasts. She was naked. Frustration became fright. Her eyes darted from side to side. She knew this wasn't her bed anymore. It was a metallic table of some kind. The alien heads looked at her still. From behind them another walked up to the table. It was taller and wore yellow clothing. Then she heard something. A noise. An automatic one. From somewhere above the light there was movement. Coming down. She tried to see what but couldn't. The intense light blocked her view. But she could hear it. The noise continued. It hummed and from out of the light came down an image like an arm extending at the elbow. A white colored object about two feet long, and shaped like a tube, shifted down from behind the light and over her torso. Laura's eyes went white. She tried to scream again but it was caught in her throat. The tube detached from something above and moved very close over her body. She watched, waiting for what was next. The ugly Grey faces looked upon her. The shades of eyes burrowed into her brain. From one of the Greys she heard a feeling. It was a communication. She understood the words: *It'll be okay. You won't be hurt.* Laura didn't know what that meant or why that had been sent to her. Then the Greys turned and looked at the tube and it started to pulsate. The bottom of it opened and turned a reddish color. The pulse turned to a hum and she felt something all over her waist. She couldn't see anything but it was an invading feeling. It was inside her body. Poking around.

Laura sat up in bed with a shriek. She was wet with sweat and gripping her bed covers. Her breathing was rapidly coming in big gasps. Laura looked around the room but didn't see anything. No aliens. After a few large exhales her breath returned to normal. Her mind was foggy from sleep. It seemed so real. After a few minutes her mind was cleared again. It was just a bad dream. But it seemed more real than that.

Across the hall Ashley heard the shriek. She knew she should go check on Laura or wake her mom who still slept. But she was too scared to do either. Ashley didn't want to go into the hallway again at night.

CHAPTER 41

Early the next morning there was a soft knock on Laura's door that woke her from a deep sleep. Her eyes opened but she didn't move as she wasn't quite sure if the knock had been dreamed or not. Laura also felt a little unsettled although she didn't know why. Then it rapped again and she knew it couldn't be ignored. The bed sheet was flung to the side and she quickly shuffled to the door and unlocked it.

"Hello," Laura said before she opened it.

"Laura," came back pleasantly from the other side.

Laura smiled and opened the door. It was Ashley. "Good morning, young girl."

"Good morning. Are you okay?"

That question surprised her from the touch of concern in the girl's voice. Just then Laura knew why. The nightmarish dream she'd had. Ashley must have heard her cry out when she awoke from it. And that was also why she felt nervy this morning. There was something about this place that made people forgetful. "Yes, I'm fine. Just a little sleepy. That's all." Laura smiled. She wanted to move past the nightmare with Ashley as quickly as possible. "Is your mom up?"

As if on cue the bathroom door opened and out walked Carol. They looked at each other.

"Morning, Carol," said Laura.

"Hi, how are you?"

"Good," Laura answered. "Looks like I'm no longer the first one up every time. The champion is dethroned."

"Yeah, for today at least. Ready to go down and have some of that breakfast of champions that we have every day?"

"Sure am." Laura sniffed her clothes. "It's been days with the same clothes on. I stink."

"I know." Carol laughed. "Sorry, I didn't mean to imply that you stink or anything."

Laura laughed with her. "Oh, I know." She was leaning against the door frame and having fun now. Her nerves were settling.

"But me too," Carol tugged on her blouse. "And nobody's been courageous enough to use the shower here yet. No offense to the guys but they're starting to rank a little bit now."

"They call that man stink, Carol," Laura laughed.

"Mom, I stink too. I have man stink." Ashley looked up at her mom.

"Yes, you do, honey. Big time stink," Carol teased. They all laughed. "But yours is little girl stink which means you smell like sugar."

"Yea!" Ashley cried with jubilation and stuck her hands up in the air. Everything seemed to be better with Carol as long as her daughter was happy.

Carol looked at Laura. "I just thought of something. Did you check your closet yet? I didn't think of it until now. You had Harry ask for clothing. It was your idea. I hope he did. I hope." Carol's voice held on to that last word in optimism.

"Oh, good point. It was my idea, wasn't it?" Laura turned and went to her closet and opened it. She dropped her arms as relief filled her body. From left to right it was full of clothing. Everything was on hangers. Laura picked through the wardrobe sliding the hangers which made a little squeaking sound on the bar that supported them. Everything was mostly the same. There were about thirty outfits of shirts and pants. The shirts were green short-sleeved shirts, loose fitting, and like what nurses or dental hygienists wear. The pants were blue and loose like sweatpants. Packed on the shelf above was woman's underwear. On the floor lay a couple pairs of white running shoes and about thirty pairs of white socks. Carol and Ashley came in and stood next to Laura.

"I'm impressed," Laura said with a slant of the eyes in Carol's way. Carol returned the look.

"Hey, Mommy, maybe we have new clothes, too." She rushed to the hallway and into their room. Both women knew there was new clothing when they heard Ashley holler in excitement. Carol went over to see for herself.

The next thing Laura thought was that she was going to shower up and get a change of clothes after breakfast. Her stomach growled. Then there was a sharp pain for a second. She bent over and it eased a little. Every morning this happened but she didn't know why. What she knew was that it wouldn't return until the next morning. Laura went to the top of the stairs and waited. Ashley trotted out of the room dragging her doll and Carol followed her.

"You know what I just thought of?" Laura asked Carol.

"Not sure. What?"

"Like how'd that stuff get in our closets? Without us noticing."

"Do you mean when we're asleep?" Carol thought about it. "Yeah, you're right. It's one thing when they're putting things in the house downstairs but...."

"This time it was in our rooms. When we were in them."

"They're creepy. I hate them."

"But like, how are they doing it? I haven't seen them or noticed them yet. I've been asleep." Laura hesitated as she remembered her dream last night. Then she continued. "I don't think anybody else has seen them either. I mean, what do they do? Do they come in like movers or just materialize? It's like they just show up. Do you know what I mean?"

"Yeah, I sure do. We'll have to ask everyone today."

They agreed and went down the stairs. Immediately, Laura noticed three chairs around the kitchen table and five more stacked in the corner next to the refrigerator. They were made of the same hard plastic as the kitchen table. She pulled out a chair for Ashley to jump into and then sat down herself. Carol remained standing. There were two full glasses of water and two meal boxes on the table and the smell of bacon and eggs floated gently up into their nostrils. Carol's lips were dry from dehydration so she got everyone glasses filled with the strange water from the globe. Laura took a big drink and set her glass down on the table. Her eyes caught a movement reflected in the glass. From outside. She looked out the window and saw Rob and Shawn in the front yard. They were pointing in the air above and discussing something.

"What are they doing?" Laura said in surprise.

"What do you mean?" Carol said. She bent over the table and looked out. "Oh gosh, who knows with those guys."

"Yeah, I know what you mean, but they do look like they're looking at something. Something high above."

"Maybe it's glow balls, Mom," said Ashley.

"Let's hope not, Ash," Carol said. She brushed her hair. "But I don't think that's it."

"Nah, I don't either. Let's go see," Laura said. She pushed herself away from the table and led them all out onto the porch. Both Rob and Shawn barely acknowledged them.

"What are you looking at?" Laura asked. Rob and Shawn keep muttering between themselves. This annoyed her. "Excuse me?"

The tone of her voice worked as they both stopped and looked at her.

"Would you men of the world please tell us what you are doing? What are you looking at?"

Rob made a face at Shawn and then back at her. "Why don't you come out here and we'll show you. Nope, better yet. First, do you notice anything different about our paradise here?"

Laura ignored his smart-ass tone of voice and stepped down onto the porch stairs. Carol leaned on the porch railing. Both looked up. The light from the ceiling was bright. By the standards for this place of confinement it was a typical morning. But immediately they could see the difference. The light was coming from the left side of the compound. Laura walked down into the yard and turned around to get the big picture. It looked like the sun was rising in the east just like back home. Her head turned as her eyes followed the sun's rays. She followed them as they gradually faded across the interior of the compound to the other side on her left. It was dark there. To Laura it looked pre-dawn. Darkness hung among the trees there. It looked slightly ominous and made her glad to be standing right where she was.

Carol moved about to stare above, but the porch roof blocked a good view. She abandoned the porch and joined Laura down in the yard. At first Ashley wasn't interested. However, upon seeing her mom's interest she became so, and with a hop and a skip she sprung into the yard and next to her mom. "Cool, Mommy," Ashley said. "It's like the Sun."

"Yes, it is," Carol answered and turned to Laura. "How do they do that? They change things overnight. Food. Clothing. Now the sky."

"They've given us a fake sun." Laura nodded, still enamored with their new horizon. "I guess you can when you've got superior technology."

"Yeah, sure," Rob butt in. "It's like we're in their own little playground. They make changes as we go. Or as Harry asks."

Laura turned to him out of annoyance. "Are you complaining? Some of the changes we needed to make things better for us."

"Yeah, I know. You've got me there. But my point is that we're like toys to them. And that we're helpless."

"Did you check your closets this morning?"

"No. Why would we?"

"Ours are full of clothes. We can change now."

"Thank God!" Rob smacked the sides of his legs. "I'm tired of wearing these threads. They're gross with three days of being worn on them. Heck, they're for closing sales deals. Not playing adventure games."

Shawn pointed to the east of the house. "If you watch closely enough it does seem like it's moving," he said and stopped pointing. "Well, sorta," Shawn retracted his words a bit. "It's just like at home. Or on Earth. Or wherever. You don't see the Sun move, but then after a short time, you can tell it has moved across the sky. You know."

Laura watched the morning show a little longer. It was a pretty sight to her. It seemed more natural, unlike the ceiling of light that had lit up their compound before. The light had the resemblance of a circle. The trees on that side looked nice and awakened. However, something was missing.

"Something's different," she said. "Has anyone noticed?" She waited for a response but all she got were shrugged shoulders in return.

"Noticed what?" Rob finally asked.

It wasn't from the rising sunlight or the trees. Rather it was missing from the whole interior. An absence of some kind. Laura looked at the ground. Her eyes traced her steps up to the house. She looked to both sides of the house and around the yard. Then she knew.

"What we just got yesterday," she said looking around at them all. "Is gone."

Everyone started to look around and at each other. Nobody said anything, but after a few seconds their bodies quit twisting, and there was a collective understanding on all their faces.

"No birds or animals," said Carol.

Missing from their eyes and ears were the sights and sounds of common everyday nature. There weren't any birds flying from tree to tree. No birds breached the horizon. There was no movement on the ground either. The squirrels and rabbits that the day before had seen scurrying about weren't there anymore. The first two days of their existence in an environment without creatures had been an absence felt by all. It was a psychosomatic effect that put even more distance between home and the confines in the minds of the group. However, that absence was replaced by the presence of animals the instant they appeared the day before. The effect filled in a hole of insecurity among the group that never would have been opened if they had not been taken away from their normal lives on Earth. It was a hole that had desperation and helplessness growing deep inside. The partial return of the natural world inside their domain here had rooted out some of those feelings. Now that hole was slowly opening again.

"It's like they just came and took 'em," Shawn said. "Here yesterday, gone today."

"Did you get that from a song dude?" Rob said. He glanced over his shoulder at Shawn with a sneer mouth covered with a bit of disgust. For

Rob, everything was starting to wear and tear on him by now. Especially on his mind and his patience.

"Mommy, what happened to the animals and the birds?" Ashley grabbed her mother's pant leg. "The lollipop men didn't take them, did they?"

"I don't know, honey. But they seem to be gone somewhere."

"That is so strange," Laura said sounding a bit rapt. She rubbed her lower lip with her finger. Her thinking changed. It tipped over from her positive persona and fell down into her negative side. Foreshadowing thoughts started to flow inside her mind and washed around the seeds of doubt that were already planted. "This can't be a good thing."

"Nothing here is good," Rob barked.

Just then the front door burst open and Harry walked out onto the porch.

"What's going on?" he said. "Did I miss something? Why didn't you wake me?" His face was a three-way mix of excitement, curiosity, and annoyance.

"What do you make of this, Harry?" asked Rob.

"Make of what?" Harry shrugged. If they'd just tell him he could quit asking.

"They've disappeared," Shawn said.

"Who?"

"The animals," said Carol.

"The animals?"

"And the birds," Ashley chimed in.

"The birds?"

"Yeah, overnight it seems," Carol said.

"Do you mean they're utterly gone?" Harry was confused. What are they talking about?

"Yeah, that's what she means, Professor," Rob said as impatiently as he was frustrated with this place.

"How could that happen?"

"And the sun is out," Ashley said. She pointed east. "See!"

Harry was even more confused now. He stepped off the porch and looked around. The strange round light in the ceiling displaced the missing animals for the moment. There it was, bright and overhead. He glanced over to the other side and saw it was dark there. The light emanating from this new sun was only starting to reach the far side of their compound.

"Ah, I see what you mean," Harry put his hands on his hips. "It's like a giant light bulb in the sky."

"Fake sun! Fake sun!" Ashley yelled, jumping up and down, as for her this was a fun thing. A new development in their days here. In fact, any new discovery for her was exciting as long as it didn't involve the lollipop men.

"This is another good thing." Harry's chest pumped out again as he was on a roll. For the third time, he'd asked their grey hosts for some changes and they had done as he requested. He was getting them things. If this would persist, he would begin to ask questions to the Greys, and slowly dig for information about their state of being. And if that went well then he would ask for their release back home.

Those thoughts of Harry's plan made his view of this compound take a new direction too. That he would ask for their release made it seem like a jail cell. Their compound was their new home. But it was a cell. They already knew they were prisoners taken and locked away against their will. To this point nobody had been willing to call it this. Perhaps it might change the way they mentally viewed their predicament and make it worse? They didn't need any more morale deflation.

"Okay, I'll bite," Rob said cynically. He pursed his lips. "Why is that?"

"Because they listen to me when I go up there and communicate," Harry answered.

"Oh, yeah. Your little ritual. Just between you and them," Rob started to laugh. "They're your new friends. I'm sure you can trust them. Maybe they can scrounge up a pick-up game of football while you're at it. I'd sure like to clothesline them."

"What do you think of the missing animals?" Carol asked as she was tired already of the bickering that was about to start.

Harry looked at her with surprise on his face. Then his mind recovered. He shook his head for a second. "I was so busy with our new fake sun," he nodded to Ashley, "...that I forgot and hadn't had a chance to think about that yet. So, they're gone?" He stopped and looked around. "How do you know they're gone?"

"We haven't seen anything yet and we've been out here for about a half hour," Shawn said with a dour voice. His outlook on this wasn't positive at all and it was sinking each day. The anxiety he felt each day because he missed his wife and kids was feeding on itself and threatening to eat up his soul. They were stuck here. The grey aliens popped in and viewed them like they were animals, not human beings, whenever they wanted. Now the domestic animals inside with them had vanished. Shawn knew his own personal truth was that he had given up.

Harry noticed Laura had been silent the whole time he was out there. From his view, she looked like her mind was somewhere else. She was distant. Her finger was just rubbing her chin. "Laura, are you okay?"

Her eyes looked at him but she remained still. "The animals are gone. I doubt this is good."

"Hold on. We don't know if they're gone yet for sure," Harry said quickly as he didn't want anyone to panic or for things to get out of control.

"Are you kidding?" Rob said. "There's zip out here except for us."

"They vanished Harry," Laura said through tightened lips. Her eyebrows raised up as if half asking a question and half making a statement. "I'm watching, and I don't see anything." Her eyebrows lowered and her eyes shifted towards Shawn. Ordinarily, she wouldn't look at him too much, but had noticed him grimace a little in pain, and touch his stomach.

"We haven't even looked around yet," Harry said. He ignored Rob and directed his reply to Laura, with whom he was surprised, because she was always the positive one among them. She didn't seem to be staying optimistic anymore. "Look, I believe you. I agree that I haven't seen anything yet either. I just don't want us to jump ahead yet."

"There's nothing to jump ahead to, my man," Rob said as he went back to checking out their new sun. "This new light bulb sun doesn't burn our eyes though. Just something else that's fake around here."

Laura was about to remark but her attention was caught by the swaying curtain in the window of Travis and Katie's room. She didn't see either of them in the window but deduced they were probably now on the way downstairs.

"You see, Harry?" Carol said. "Nothing. Not a peep in the sky."

Harry was standing in front of the porch with his hands on his hips. To Ashley he looked like a scarecrow. Except his head was looking around from side to side. He stopped and turned to them. "I do declare they seem to be gone."

"Oh, brother," Rob said. "Dude, we've been telling you that."

The front door opened and through it Travis and Katie walked onto the porch. They stood looking out at the group. Both looked sleepy.

"What's up?" asked Travis.

Harry turned to them. "We seem to be animal-less."

"What do you mean?" Katie asked.

"He means our little nature preserve ran away," said Rob still looking at their sky.

"What? The birds?" Katie frowned. Together they looked out from the porch.

"And the squirrels. And the rabbits. They seem to be gone that we can see," said Harry. He waved to the trees.

"Or can't see is more like it," said Rob.

"Gone?" Travis yawned. "How?"

"We have no idea," said Harry. "Woke up and found this out."

"Maybe the stickmen and their ugly eyes took them," said Carol with a sneer. Her voice radiated hate when it came to the Greys.

"I don't know," said Harry. "We'll need to look around. Maybe we'll find something."

"We have a sun now, look!" said Ashley excitedly. She pointed up above. "A fake sun, but it's like our Sun."

Travis hopped off the porch and looked to his left. Katie walked to the end of the porch and looked out. Both saw the giant light in the ceiling. It did look like a sun. Round and glaring. The ceiling couldn't be seen but each of them knew it should be there. The brightness seemed to hide it away, tucked behind it. Travis looked back to the other side and saw it was dark there. It was a simulated daybreak.

"How about that?" said Travis. "The little grey men seemed to have made it a little more like home for us."

"How nice," said Katie. She looked at the trees in front of her. Dangling and stretching out amid them were the trees' shadows. Some of them were short. Others were long. They cast a visionary black web among the foliage. The trees on the edge of the yard cast the longest shadows. They extended toward the house. Toward them. A brief chill crawled down her back.

"Hey, baby," Travis said.

She turned to Travis, flickered her eyebrows, and then walked to the front of the porch. But mainly she walked away from the trees and their shadows.

Katie stopped on the steps. Everyone watched her to see what she would say or do next. However, she didn't do either. Just stood looking at Travis.

"They made a sun," Travis said.

Katie held her hands out to her sides. "They made dawn!" she said with a bit of a smirk.

Travis laughed. "Makes you think what else they could do," he said. Katie started to laugh along with him. For a few years, they had dreamed and imagined alien life and what technologies they might be capable of. Now they were seeing it together.

"It's like they've given us a recreation of life on Earth," Harry said, hands back on his hips. "At least a little bit, that is."

"It's like we're a construction project," Rob said. "The Earthling Zoo."

"That's all nice and dandy but what about the missing animals?" Laura said.

Harry sighed. "From suns to missing squirrels. We go back and forth. We have all these mysteries inside this ... how do I say ... cell." He was testing them.

"Are we next?" Carol asked.

"What? Do you think we'll go missing?"

"Oh, no," said Shawn, shaking his head. His demeanor was giving up.

Harry held up his hands signaling to relax. "Now don't go freaking out."

"We're already freaked, Harry," Rob said. "This whole place is a freak."

"They're gone. The question is why. And worse yet, by whom?" Laura's pessimistic tone caught everyone with surprise coming from her. In the four days of their being here, she had slowly gone from the positive one to being negative. Gradually, this place had worn down her optimism and flipped it on top of itself. "What should we do now?"

"Yeah, that's a good question?" Shawn said. "Who took them?"

"I bet the evil ones had something to do with it," said Carol. She knew each comment like that might bring the anger of the Greys back on her if they were listening. The invasive mental touching they could do frightened her. Other than protecting her daughter the thing she didn't want the most was them prodding around inside her mind again. Yet at times her festering hatred for them couldn't be contained. It swelled up and had to be released.

Now Harry was starting to think that he was losing them. Slowly their morale was slipping away. He'd have to change the direction of the dialogue. With Laura seeming to have a chink in her mental armor now, he might have to take on the role of cheerleader too. The makeshift sun was a positive thing. The disappearing animals weren't. He needed to set a new course. "Let's divide up into groups again, go out, and search around. Maybe we'll find something."

"You know what, this place is so screwed up, that sounds good to me," said Rob. He started to walk to the house. Shawn followed him. "But first I need to eat. I'm starving and my stomach hurts."

Laura wondered if that was from hunger or something else. She kept watching Rob.

He and Shawn went up the steps, walked past Katie, and through the front door. Almost immediately everyone outside heard the beeping from the microwave as Rob and Shawn reheated their breakfasts. Everyone remained standing out front looking at each other waiting for something to be said. Waiting for something to be done.

A few seconds went by and Katie spoke. "I guess that's that. We have a horizon, no pets, and we're going to get our daily exercise by strolling around the confines again today."

"That's badass, babe," Travis said. He loved her wit. He held out his hand and they bumped fists.

"We're all set then. Breakfast is served and then we go out," Harry said as he smelled bacon.

"Mommy, Mommy, I want pancakes," Ashley said. She rubbed her doll's stomach. "Molly wants some, too."

"Okay, we'll look for some," Carol replied as she followed her inside.

Lastly, Laura walked to the porch but she saw Katie grab her stomach. She stopped next to her. "Are you all right?"

"Yeah, just the cramps."

Laura didn't think so.

CHAPTER 42

After breakfast the group convened on the porch. They decided to go out in different groups than before. Rob and Shawn went east, Travis and Katie went in the back, and Laura and Harry went west which was lit up by the sunlight now. This would be the first time for each person to explore the area they hadn't been in yet. However, they did it differently this time. The overnight disappearance of the creatures had been unforeseen and unnerving. This led to a decision that only one group would go out at a time. The rest would wait in the yard at the house as a lookout. Not only for anything strange that might occur, but more to keep a watch on each group, as it ventured out to look around.

The artificial sun in the ceiling had moved a little closer to the house which signaled around midmorning for the time of day. Everyone was eager to get started. Rob and Shawn went first. They casually walked through the trees as if it was an ordinary afternoon back home. As usual a calming breeze flowed along briskly and the trees waved in unison with it. Still there were no birds flying about, squirrels jumping, or rabbits running. It was as if the flurry of activity from yesterday had never existed. Rob split off a little to the left and walked along a different column of trees. Shawn remained on his same path. The ground hadn't changed either. The artificial grass was strangely green but very pleasing to look at.

They hadn't gotten too far when they stopped. Shawn looked at Rob and he returned the look with his typical cynicism.

"Nothing yet," Shawn said.

"Of course not," answered Rob. "That's the way it seems to go here. They're gone now. God knows where. I wonder if we're next."

Shawn ignored the last comment for his thoughts had already sunk down into glumness and he didn't want any more of his fears to be stoked by what Rob said. Shawn's thoughts had been drifting to think about what the end would be like here, but his conscious mind had put up a wall, and fended them off. Missing his wife and kids was bad enough for him and he kept beating back those sad thoughts, all the while they've been getting visits from the Greys, and getting exhibited in front of what may be their children. Now they had a pleasant but small thread of home, in the form of suburbia wildlife yesterday, and today found out it was probably extinct already. They vanished!

Out of the corner of his eye he saw Rob's back moving away from him. "Don't go too far."

"I think it's okay, Lasky." Rob didn't turn his head and slowly kept on going. "Nothing here but us aliens." His laughter trailed off in between them.

Shawn looked up into the trees. They were majestic in their way. Strong and powerful. The branches extended out like strong muscular arms with dark green cookie-cutter looking leaves. There was all that and yet nothing with a heartbeat. Except for them.

He looked forward and started to walk and his feet stopped. His eyes blinked hard a few times as if to wash away any blurriness that he really didn't have. Up ahead he saw something in the grass. It was dark and spread out like a snake but wasn't moving. To his left he couldn't see Rob anymore. He looked back and started forward again. With each step, he saw that it was a black wavy line about six feet long and an inch thick. The thing was more like a substance. To Shawn it resembled an oil streak, or grease stain, and was quite the contrast to the pretty green grass that surrounded it. Shawn crept forward a little more, watching it closely as he didn't know what it was yet, and he certainly didn't want to risk it jumping up at him. Although, with each step he took, it didn't appear to be alive. It still made no movement or any sound. Shawn went into a crouch position and looked around. He checked in the tree above the black streak but didn't see anything threatening. What he did notice on the tree was a strange zigzagged pattern in its bark going from top to bottom. Shawn chalked that up to a strange luck of nature, or artificial nature for here, that it formed that way contrary to the other trees he'd seen so far. He then looked around at the adjacent trees as well but didn't see anything. Nothing appeared to be waiting to attack. All was quiet. The birds were gone so there wasn't any singing or bird calls. The breeze flew along again and that always felt good on his skin and his nerves calmed. He pressed on.

Shawn was impressed with himself as well. The fact that he was going it alone on this one, investigating the spot on the ground by himself, made him feel strong, and made him learn something positive about himself. A little something but still it was a good feeling. Shawn may be overweight, balding, and not particularly athletic anymore but he was taking control and wasn't scared.

A few feet away he stopped. His nose prickled. Tiny little daggers of stench were jabbing at it. He wriggled his nose. From the black streak on the ground a nauseating odor permeated upwards into his nose. Now it burned. Shawn took a few steps back which made it better. Then he twisted over and threw up his breakfast. He coughed a few times, spit out the rest, and let out a long breath of air. Shawn took a few more steps backwards and was better. The smell had caught him by surprise and had been a lot stronger than he could have guessed. In fact, it seemed to just prick at him at first, and then came on stronger almost like it had tested him.

Feeling recovered enough, he called out for Rob. The acidic taste still in his mouth made his throat burn a little. When Rob came running over he saw Shawn leaning over with his hands on his knees.

"Whoa, big fella, are you okay?" Rob patted him on the back.

"Yeah, now I am. I gotta whiff of that." Shawn gestured toward the black streak with his head. "You know what that is?"

Rob looked ahead and immediately grimaced. "No. It's disgusting. Reminds me of an ex-girlfriend I had."

Shawn cleared his throat.

Rob continued, "Looks like an oil leak gone bad or something. What is it?"

"Heck if I know." Shawn coughed again. "But it stinks like shit."

Rob took a few steps forward and swayed back again. He turned to Shawn with a foul look on his face. "No shit man, that stinks!"

"At least you have to be close to it to smell it. What's it come from, do you think?"

"Who knows around here. This place sucks. That made you puke, huh?"

"Yeah, I wasn't ready for it."

"Who would be? Maybe the professor can ask the aliens for some garden freshener or something."

"Where'd it come from? What did it?"

Rob looked at the black streak a little harder. "It looks like it was discharged or something. Like out of the back of an airplane, or car, or something."

"Except we don't have anything here like that."

"I know that. I'm just saying. Look at it."

"Yeah, I agree. It looks like a trail or that something got leaked. I don't see any more things like that around."

Rob looked around and agreed.

"Where'd you go anyway?" Shawn asked.

"I just went over there a little. Not too far. I didn't see anything. No deer. No grizzlies. No farmer's daughters. And all looked the same. Tree after tree. The closest thing I've seen to a snake is what you found."

"I don't care about looking anymore. This is strange enough. We should go back and tell the others. This place is crazy."

"Okay, sounds good. We certainly didn't find any birds or squirrels."

"I want a beer."

"Yeah, you and me both, buddy. Too bad we don't have any. Even Cheapster Beer Lite would taste good now."

"I agree. We sell those at my store, too."

"No thanks. I've had it before. I'll pass if we get home."

They turned and started to walk back to the house. Each of them looked over their shoulder at some point to check if anything was following them, or to make sure the black streak wasn't moving in any way or form, with their backs to it. However, it didn't seem to be a living organism and then it was reasonable to conclude that it was a harmless, albeit smelly, byproduct of this compound which they were in. It would be interesting to hear what the thoughts were from the rest of the group. The black streak was definitely alien to them. However, what confused Shawn more is that the smell hadn't seemed that foreign to him. It smelled familiar.

CHAPTER 43

When Rob and Shawn arrived back at the house Travis and Katie were already in the back heading out. Impatience had gotten the best of them. Their anticipation of doing something had been held up by the boredom of this place and the two of them waited like runners before a race for the first sign of the guys' return. Rob and Shawn didn't have a chance to tell them about the discovery of the black streak lying on the ground. They only saw their backs and her swinging blonde hair walking away into the backyard.

While they waited Rob and Shawn told the group about their search which had two parts. Rob said they found no animals and Shawn described the smelly black mark. They found this interesting as much as repellant. Nobody wanted to get a whiff of it. Harry was putting a lot of thought into where it must have come from. It fed into Laura's small but growing foreboding. Carol certainly didn't want to go anywhere near it, and to Ashley it sounded like dead animal smell on the side of the road out in the country.

Everyone remained on the porch except Harry who stood watch on the side of the house pondering what their new development might be. After about an hour went by Travis and Katie walked through the last line of trees into the backyard. They held up their hands at Harry to signify they didn't find anything. He hadn't been too hopeful that they would. Together all three came around the corner and back onto the porch. Katie mentioned a foul odor she smelled faintly somewhere in back. Travis told her again that was her imagination and this place was playing tricks on her mind. She insisted that it was real and stared a little miffed at him. They both calmed down after Shawn told of the black streak and Rob backed him up on it. What grossed them out was the description of the nasty smell, and done in a way that made them think it was toxic, and could peel paint off the back of a truck. This also lent credibility to what Katie said about something foul in back. Could the black streak be like what she smelled in back? Travis thought this place was getting weirder and Katie didn't like the endless scenarios that perhaps this might lead to. Most of them didn't feel good to her. The first questions they wanted answers for were what it was and where'd it come from?

From there it was time for Laura and Harry to head out together and do their sweep of the compound. They stepped off the porch, turned to their right, walked through the first row of trees and down the hill into the grassy land. Frankly, Laura was relieved to be with somebody other than Rob. He'd been her partner in a way since the moment they woke up here, and they had teamed up in every search so far. However, Rob's verbal shots at her, along with the anger that she suspected was slowly developing underneath his sarcasm, bothered her and she didn't want to be around him anymore. Besides he and Shawn had gotten to know each other better since they had been occupying the first floor. Shawn had seemed detached from this place many times over the last few days and his personality didn't seem the type that would let Rob's bickering get to him.

A new batch of foliage waited for them in front up the hill. As they walked both scanned the trees for anything flying but there wasn't. Both scanned the grounds for any little creature but none were there. There was no hopping, no bouncing, and no running. Harry hadn't spoken since leaving the house which Laura thought was a little odd. He looked distant and deeply in thought when she looked at him. She thought she'd pick his brain a little.

"So what ya thinking?" she asked.

"Not a whole lot," Harry answered like an airhead. "Then again, I'm thinking a lot."

That didn't do Laura much good. "Okay, what is a lot?"

"Just thinking about everything that's happened today. The fake sun, which is a good thing. The disappearance of animals, which probably isn't. And now this weird black stain on the ground."

They started up the hill.

"Yeah. And?" Laura replied. Her feet dug into the hill as she walked upwards.

"I don't know yet. I'm just wondering what it all means." Harry's foot slipped out from under him but he caught his balance.

"It's a little steep, huh?" said Laura.

"Yeah, more than I thought." He kept climbing.

"I'm using the balls of my feet more," Laura said. She took each step carefully. "I don't want to scruff up or stain my sneakers on this alien grass."

"Ah, I see. This strange grass, with it's strange green color, is on this strange dirt, but it's almost like Astroturf or something. It doesn't seem real or it's just not what we're used to. Especially, if it's from another planet."

"Alien Astroturf." Laura laughed. "Now that would be the next big thing in sports, wouldn't it?"

They were almost at the top.

"I think I will ask them later today what happened to the rabbits." Harry took a deep breath. For fifty-seven years old, he was in good shape but his quadriceps were getting a good workout.

"Good idea. Although, it would be a good thing if you didn't have to ask them for things anymore."

They reached the top.

"Besides." Laura looked at Harry gaining his balance. "I think they're going to kill us."

Harry was stunned!

Just then something caught their attention through the corner of their eyes. Both looked forward. In front of them the grass rolled forth and the trees stood majestic above them. A breeze stirred up from behind, flowed over the hill, whisked around their bodies sending a relaxed feeling throughout the ambient overgrowth. Darting through the wind there was a bird.

"Look!" Laura pointed. "They aren't gone after all."

It landed on a tree. The bird's head bobbed up and down but it didn't chirp or sing. After a few seconds, it flew off in the other direction and disappeared behind some other trees.

The eyes on Harry's crinkled face narrowed as he looked around. There wasn't anything to see except for trees. He looked back at Laura who was smiling for the first time in a while. She looked positive again. And very pretty!

"What do you think?" Laura said, snapping Harry out of his moment of admiration. "I don't see any more of them but let's go."

Harry agreed but she was already ahead of him. Quickly, they walked through the trees following in the direction that the bird had flown. Light from their artificial sun broke through the trees in various spots. They looked like white patches on the grassy floor. They walked a little more before they saw another one. It flew over them and perched on a limb. The bird seemed to be watching them. A few moments went by and it flew off. Laura and Harry continued for a few steps but stopped. Another tree had a pair of black birds standing on a branch. Their heads bobbed and weaved to the sides. The birds took notice of them and flew off in the opposite direction.

"Have you noticed?" Laura said, looking sideways at Harry. "It's very quiet. I don't hear anything. And the birds aren't making any noise." Her voice was in a hushed tone now.

Harry nodded. He wasn't talking either.

They moved on, passing by a few more trees before a squirrel poked his head out from behind a tree. The squirrel looked at them, mouth twitching, and climbed up the side of the tree before springing off and running away. Then to their left two rabbits ran along, one chasing the other in circles. Laura and Harry kept walking and they saw more birds, squirrels, and rabbits. The animals stayed clear of them but here they were all around them. They weren't gone!

Harry shifted his weight uncomfortably. His face showed concern. Caution infected his eyes. "We found them but what are they doing here?"

"What do you…?" Laura gave herself the answer with her own question. Looking around the animals seem to be flourishing. She saw the flowing water wall in the back behind some trees. They were in the corner of the compound.

"Let's check something. C'mon." She broke into a steady jog to their right.

"Hey," said Harry, but it was useless. That wouldn't stop her. He ran after her on his sore legs for a few steps before slowing into a quick walk. Laura ran ahead but not far enough that he couldn't see her. He watched her stop and turn around. She was looking for something. Harry continued to walk toward her. She put her arms up and started back his way. He was relieved he didn't have to follow her anymore but a small part of him, perhaps the teacher inside, wanted to chide her.

"No offense, but that was a little reckless for this place," he said as she walked up to him. "It's way too unpredictable here to go running off."

"Yeah, I know," said Laura, her breathing a little rapid from the run. "But I wanted to check something."

They started walking back to the corner of the compound.

"Like what?" Harry asked.

"There are no animals back there. Not even a bird."

"Uh-huh."

"The animals have gone to this side, in the corner," Laura continued. "They're all over here." She motioned at the birds in the trees in front of them.

"Yeah, I was puzzling over that and then you ran off."

Laura rolled her eyes. "Okay, but why are they all here?"

They stopped. Harry thought for a minute. Some squirrels scurried between the trees and a rabbit nibbled on the grass nearby. It was strangely quiet. No birds were caroling their songs. The two of them stood together among the trees, with the animals, surrounded in silence.

Harry turned to her. "Aren't animals known to run away from danger? Like when there is a coming earthquake or volcano. Didn't the zoo animals run to high ground before the tsunami some years back? The animals know stuff like that."

Laura contemplated a moment. "Yeah, they do. Stories about cats and dogs acting funny before a disaster." However, this posed another question. "But what danger?"

Harry looked around some more. "We don't know yet."

"From us?" Laura asked, a strong tone of disbelief in her voice. She looked up in the trees. "And why are they so quiet? It's like they're hiding."

He looked at Laura. Her eyes held trepidation. There was also a seriousness that delivered her point. Over her shoulder another black bird on a branch watched them.

"Are they afraid?" Laura asked.

"Perhaps, but they aren't running away from us. We aren't a threat to them, and they probably know that. Don't forget, we don't know what they're doing yet. Like I said, this place is unpredictable."

Laura's mouth pursed. She knew this place was bad, and thought they were missing something, and to her Harry's hesitation to recognize a possible threat didn't help. Her normal nature with a positive attitude wasn't holding up very much anymore and it was sinking again. In just half a day she'd gone from grave, to upbeat, to slipping back into somberness again. Laura's feelings told her this place was worse than bad.

"Let's tell the others," she said. They started to walk back to the house.

A black bird landed at the ground they had stood upon and pecked the grass.

CHAPTER 44

Bored faces waited for Laura and Harry as they walked up to the porch. It was obvious the group hadn't any expectations for their jaunt into the compound. None of them had found anything living on their ventures. They also had dived into their new apparel. Laura had given them the tip on their closets before she set out with Harry. Katie was dressed in a green shirt, blue pants, and white sneakers just like what Laura found in her closet. Strands of her hair were wet. Travis, Rob, and Shawn looked shaved and showered. Their shirts were the same style as Katie's but were dark navy blue in color. Their pants were blue like the women's. Carol and Ashley hadn't washed yet and must have been waiting to do so. Laura so wanted to take a shower. So did Harry. Laura and Harry hadn't been gone that long but the rest had put the time to quick use.

"Hey, guess what?" Laura said. "We found them." She gestured to Harry and he nodded in confirmation. "They were in the corner over there."

Surprise washed over their faces. Rob practically fell off the porch banister and Ashley jumped and did a cartwheel.

"So, they didn't disappear after all," Katie said. She walked down the steps. "But what are they doing over there?"

"Hiding out, we think," Laura answered.

Katie laughed. "Yeah right, that doesn't surprise me. They hate the grey bastards the same as we do."

"But in the corner?" Rob said. There was a puzzled look on his face. For all the bizarre things he'd seen so far this was probably going be another occurrence that made this place stranger or worse.

Harry walked past Laura and out in front of everyone. "We don't know why. We were tossing around some ideas though."

"Why did you say they were hiding?" Carol asked. She was sitting with one leg balanced on the rail and looking like the cover of a housekeeping magazine.

"They weren't making any noise," said Laura. "None at all. Like they're staying quiet on purpose, not to attract attention. And the fact that they all moved to that side. That's what we noticed."

"More like Laura did." Harry stepped forward. "She was pretty fast on that. But like what is typical about this place, we'll have to wait and see."

"So," Rob said. "If they've all moved over there now and they're playing it mute, does that make them paranoid? Or does that make us even more paranoid?" As the words came out of his mouth Rob gave himself the answers to his own questions. They were yes and yes. Paranoia here didn't come without good reason. They had aliens dropping in to watch them on occasion and nowhere to escape. Then throw in that they hadn't fully remembered yet how they all got here in the first place and it was a logical thing to happen. He looked at everyone and decided to answer himself. "Okay, yes and yes. We are the same as the birds."

"Hiding from what?" said Carol.

"Who knows?" Laura shrugged.

"Can't be us," Carol replied.

"We'll have to wait and see what happens," Harry interjected. He didn't want a lot of speculation flying around. "I thought I would ask the Greys about it tonight."

"Suit yourself, Teach," said Rob. He looked at the wall where the Greys always came. "You're becoming best friends with the lollipop men." He nodded to Ashley who cracked a smile in return.

Harry raised an eyebrow to Rob. "It's been useful." His dealings with the aliens had been very helpful so far. Why wasn't this clear to all of them?

"Although, I felt the birds were watching me."

Everyone looked back at Laura.

"Like how do you mean?" said Katie, her eyes narrowing.

Laura stared up at the house and hesitated for a moment. The fake sun was nearing the midway point of their ceiling. "I kept getting that weird feeling from them. Not being just birdlike, but a conscious attention on us for a long time. I'd look up and another one would be fixated on us."

"Weird," said Katie, pivoting a little on her foot. "Maybe they're psycho birds now. But they didn't attack you so that's good."

"Thanks, I'll say," Laura said.

"Yeah, but what made them go there?" Carol's back straightened giving strength to her question. She felt this was really important as they didn't know much.

Katie turned back to her and was about to speak when....

"We're like mice in a lab," Shawn said.

Heads turned toward Shawn who was standing on the side behind everyone. Shawn said very little and when he did it often was a strange summarization of what they were involved in. Everyone was also a little unnerved by it because they shared some belief in what he says.

"Trapped inside at the mercy of our keepers," Shawn continued, his face raining hopelessness.

With that Harry remembered what Laura said to him right before they saw the first bird earlier today: The Greys were going to kill them. He started to wonder if that is the end game for them all and he was keeping himself from seeing that. Was he blinding himself? Harry couldn't let them go down that path together. It would lead them to despair. His mind was stuck. He needed to move forward and change the mentality of their thinking before it was too late. Then he thought of something to say. "Look. We don't know why they all relocated themselves. It's probably because of our artificial sun that we have that they all went to that side of the compound."

"Okay, could be...." Rob said unconvinced, even though the last thing Harry said was a plausible enough reason for the animals' move.

"So, they're alive and they're paranoid," Katie said. She pulled her wavy blonde hair behind her head and tied it in a bun. Rob watched her hair bounce as she moved. He watched right down to her tight butt. She was hot! His eyes did it by making quick glances. Rob didn't want to get caught. Then he sneaked a quick look at Travis and didn't look back. Travis was already staring nails through him.

"It's weird but really no big deal then," said Katie.

"Not yet at least," answered Carol.

"Does anybody else want to take a look?"

"Yeah, I do," Travis said. He'd been listening to this whole exchange about the animals, especially the birds, and he thought it sounded cool. Not to leave out he was ticked at Rob for looking at Katie. Travis started walking in that direction and Katie followed him.

CHAPTER 45

Katie and Travis returned to the house after a little while and confirmed what Laura and Harry had found. Even the part about the watching birds. A few birds seemed very interested in them with their direct stares. Rob and Shawn went out and checked as well. Everyone figured that was quite the negative conversation with Rob complaining and Shawn's depression of being there coming together as one. What they didn't know was their last exploit which had found the black streak on the ground had gone very cooperatively. Carol and Ashley didn't go for Ashley's sake. Their compound was too unpredictable for Carol to feel comfortable away from the house.

The day progressed the same as the others had. Carol and Ashley used the shower and came down to the kitchen dressed in green and blue. Then Harry showered. Afterwards, he talked about what he wanted to ask the aliens later that evening. Travis and Katie hung out on the porch joking and flirting. Travis kept a jealous eye on Rob in case he started to check out his girlfriend again. Rob and Shawn stayed most of the day in the kitchen drinking the strange water and talking sports. Then they went outside for a stroll around the house. Carol and Ashley went outside. Ashley practiced her tumbling. Carol noticed that the strange grass didn't stain the clothing or white sneakers. At least that was one good thing about this place. Laura showered, put on fresh new clothes of green and blue, and felt great after washing away the grime and sweat of the past few days. She felt clean again. Laura couldn't smell herself but she knew any body odor was gone. Everyone's was. That made her laugh on the inside.

Laura walked out onto the porch. To her right were Travis and Katie, Harry was on her left, and down in the yard Carol coached Ashley on somersaults. She walked off the porch but immediately noticed the breeze picking up. And it was picking up fast.

Laura looked to the left side, which they had designated East, and saw what looked like their compound's sky darkening. The fake sun was now far to the other side signaling late afternoon. Long shadows were starting to twist to the east side.

"That's strange," said Laura, hair now blowing in the wind.

"What's strange?" Carol turned toward her, then to the east. The sky was now changing between colors of gray mixed in with some black. It mimicked clouds. But they weren't clouds. "I see what you mean."

The wind picked up even faster and the trees started to rattle. Travis and Katie walked down the porch onto the front steps. Harry leaned against the banister facing east. Ashley leaned against her mom's leg and Carol put her arm on her daughter's shoulder.

There was a rumble. Thunder. Although it wasn't exactly. It sounded reproduced. Hollow.

From the west side of the house Rob and Shawn came around into the front yard.

"Check this out!" Rob yelled. "Now a storm. What'll they think of next?"

"Yeah." Laura looked over her shoulder at him. "And it looks weird."

Their clothes flapped in the wind as it continued to pick up. Everyone's legs stood firm on the ground. Then there was another crack and thunder echoed from wall to wall.

Electric feelings flowed from person to person. Both exciting and scary at the same time. The air was filling up with it. Yet, everyone was both anxious and calm about the storm. The wind's strange effect prevented the flight behavior that people often carry out before a storm. This group stayed put and watched.

There was a flash. Simulated lightning. However, it didn't strike down to the ground in a zigzagged form. It just flashed like a giant camera.

The rat-tat-tat sound of water hitting the leaves started to grow. Down from the ceiling they could see a wall of rain to the east of the compound slowly coming their way. The slapping sound was getting louder. It kept growing until it was at the end of the trees and moved into their yard. The rain tapped down hard on the strange grass.

"I think we better go inside now," Carol said.

Everyone went inside just before the rain started to fall on their footsteps.

CHAPTER 46

The rain poured hard in big drops made more evident by the loud pounding on the roof coinciding with the thumping on the ground outside the house. The noise was disconcerting to some of them. The rain struck the windows with a velocity that should have smashed them but didn't. Some of the drops were the size of golf balls. They would splatter all over and make anyone looking out a window wince with each hit.

Inside everyone behaved like anyone would on any rainy day. They had light inside. All it took was a push of one of those light switches. Everyone ate dinner. The microwavable meals were still tasting good enough. Not that they had much choice but at least they liked their food. The smells of Salisbury steak and Swedish meatballs drifted through the house.

After dinner and clean up everyone gathered in the living room. There wasn't anything else to do. It was a strange living room with no television, plants, or pets running around. The wind whipped around the house surging at times. They could hear the trees bend and shake. Rain would strike the house in waves. The darkness from the storm was like a lamp shade covering the house and blocked the house light from escape. It gave a small feeling of even being trapped inside their house. It was ironic to be more trapped inside of being trapped in general.

The group sat around the room. Carol and Ashley were on one couch. Travis and Katie on the other. The two young adults shared a feeling of belonging to a couch being the only people to have woken up here on one of them in the first place. Laura and Harry sat on the floor.

Laura crossed her legs in front of the fireplace. Harry sat in front of the big window looking west. Rob and Shawn leaned against the walls, Rob in the hallway leading to his bedroom, Shawn by the front door.

Thud, thud, thud. The large rain drops continued to hit the house with a plunk. Together they listened.

"Jeez, don't they know how to do rain?" Rob said. "At any moment I'm expecting one of those pelts to break a window. Then what will we do?"

"It's like they're experimenting with the weather," Laura said. "First a light ceiling. Then a fake sun that rotates. Now an artificial rain storm."

The wind howled outside.

"It's like they're experimenting with a lot of things," Carol chimed in. "We didn't even have any food the first day we were here. Harry had to ask for that." Harry nodded back to her acknowledging his acknowledgement.

"Yeah, it's like they're not quite up to snuff on that," said Travis.

"They make mistakes," Carol continued. "They aren't all perfect like we'd expect them to be."

"We didn't even have new clothing," Laura said. "Like they forgot. Or didn't even think of it. Kitchen table and chairs either. They may be small in importance but still how do you expect people, humans, us, to get by in an observation environment without that stuff?"

"Yeah, and we didn't even have toilet paper at first," Rob snipped. "How'd they miss that?"

"That's because they aren't all perfect like Carol said," Harry added.

"Of all the aliens in the universe, we get captured by the inept ones," said Rob.

Harry continued. "No matter how much more advanced, or Godlike they seem, they are still a living creature in the galaxy. Or universe. Or wherever they come from. They make mistakes."

"Yeah, if we have human error," Katie said, gesturing with her hand. "Then they must have alien error."

Travis nodded. "You're awesome. I love you."

"Thanks, sweetie." Katie smiled. They kissed. Travis peeked at Rob afterwards but he wasn't even watching.

The rain continued.

"The wildlife is limited really when you think about it," Laura continued with her thoughts. They were at the top of her mind right now and she didn't want them to get away. "We didn't have any at first, and I'm thankful that we do now, makes it more like home, but to me the small number makes it seem more inexperienced on their part. Sorta like they just grabbed a bunch of them and put them in a box. And we're in the box."

"Don't you mean a cage?" Shawn said from the front of the room, his voice glum. "We're an experiment."

The group looked at Shawn but not for long. More dread wasn't what anyone wanted to think about now.

"And then they migrated themselves," Harry said.

"To which we don't know why," said Carol.

"Carpetbagger squirrels," laughed Katie.

Everyone smiled. They needed something cheerful.

"Harry, you said they aren't Godlike," said Rob, leaning with his elbow against the wall. He was flipping his ear with his finger. "We sure could use some help from God right now. Think any of that's coming?"

Harry just looked at him. The room was quiet. Thunder boomed over them. There was flashing outside.

"I don't think God has anything to do with this. We just have to hold on."

"Some divine intervention would be nice," Travis said.

"We could use all the help we can get," Katie added.

"I'll say," said Rob. "We need a rescue squad."

"I'm afraid there won't be any help coming," Shawn said.

"No offense, but would you cheer up, man?" Travis gave Shawn a stern look. "Are you trying to bring everyone down or something?"

"It's reality kid."

"I don't care if it's reality. You're starting to piss me off and you're bothering Katie. Knock it off." He started to shuffle off the couch but Katie put her hand on his leg to stop him.

"Okay, just chill out!" Laura yelled. "Travis, you're overreacting." Katie shot Laura a look. Laura ignored it. She thought this conversation was almost getting out of control. Her emotional state was taking a hit every day too, but in the past few hours since the storm started, she'd been able to get one of her core personality traits back to steady herself. That was positive thinking. She needed to spread the word. "Arguing about it isn't going to make this better. We need to stick together. Like a team."

Harry smiled inside. It was good that he wasn't the only one trying to keep this group calm and united. Laura was back.

Carol said, "Why would God do this to us?" This was something that had been bothering her. She was a Christian, as were her children, and it was natural for her to question this in a time of peril. They said their prayers every night yet they were still here in this compound. In this zoo cage. How could good honest people like her and Ashley be forced to be here? In fact, she knew the rest of the group believed in God. How could all of them be here like prisoners? This can't be, but it was.

"I don't think God has anything to do with it," Harry answered.

"Yeah, I don't think so either," Katie agreed. "These are aliens. Why would they have anything to do with God?"

"The stickmen are far from holy," said Travis as he shook his head. "Or why would God put us here? I don't see a connection."

"It's a test," Carol said. She had been thinking hard about this. Very deeply. It was the most logical thing she could come up with in a spiritual sense. She leaned forward on the couch. "They say God tests us all. I think perhaps that is why we're here. We were chosen for a reason."

Nobody answered her right away. No one wanted to offend her because they liked Carol and thought she was very nice and a loving caring mother. Despite everyone's own personal religious beliefs, they thought more in feasible terms.

"This is quite the unusual test," Katie said.

"Yeah, I don't think the old man upstairs would care enough to purposely put us here on his own," Rob added, looking briefly at the ceiling as if looking for heaven.

"Hold on, hold on," said Laura. She had been listening closely and could relate strongly to what Carol was saying and didn't want everyone else to discard her message so easily or quickly. She had thought about these mysteries of life all during her life. Laura wanted to give her some support. "They say that God has a plan for all of us. What if this is part of His plan? Maybe He wants us to experience this for some reason. A reason none of us can understand or know. Or just not know why yet. Maybe it's spiritual growth on our inner side, or experience for ourselves to grow in nature, possibly to be used in the future in our lives. Maybe at some key event. Could be to help or save people. Or just ourselves. We just don't know it yet til it happens and we realize it at that moment."

"No offense, but I think things are a little more practical for us here," Harry said.

"But what if it's not? What if impractical is the way it is? What if that's true?"

"Getting stuck here in a giant simulated human animal cage." Harry shook his head. He didn't buy it. Harry was too much of a textbook teacher. "I don't know if that's what I would credit the Almighty with for secretly teaching us lessons to get experience points in life."

"What if we're not supposed to realize it," said Laura. "Like it's in disguise, misleading, but a master plan is underneath and it's all happening for a reason?"

"Look, Katie and I believed in UFOs and little green men," said Travis. "We knew they existed, and we went looking for them. And we found them. And now we're stuck here."

Katie looked at Travis and laughed a little. "You made it sound like it was so easy. Just go outside and there they are."

Travis half chuckled. "In this case, it was," he answered. "It's happened before. People see UFOs. Just nobody ever believes them. I mean really, how is that God's plan?"

"That it was only for them to experience, and for you to experience," Carol answered.

Ashley was sitting next to her mom but didn't say anything. She had been listening intently and enjoyed the conversation about UFOs. It made her think of the movies. However, she had enough of the lollipop men already and didn't want to play with them again. What she wished for was to be back home playing with her brother in front of the television and watching her favorite movies. She hugged her doll.

"Mommy, I'm bored," said Ashley.

"We all are, honey," Carol answered, even though at this moment she wasn't. For this place's standards, this was one of the best conversations yet. They'd had nothing good to do here other than to talk among themselves. That was good because they did learn about each other each day, but when that is your primary source of entertainment, it can become dull very quick.

One person that wasn't bored at this moment was Shawn. There was a lot of contemplating going on inside his mind and all the voices around him sounded like mush. Nobody could tell because he hadn't said anything for a few minutes since Travis yelled at him, but this was more of a reflection of his inner mood and feelings. Those weren't good. Shawn was gloomy about their predicament. He didn't think they were going to survive trapped in this place. They hadn't seen or heard from any human and appeared to exist to be gawked at by the Greys. There didn't appear to be any way out.

Shawn missed his family badly. At first he couldn't remember his life back home. That seemed to be a result from his ordeal of arriving here. But as the few days had passed, more memories were restored inside his head: his wife Susan, cooking in the kitchen, the smell of spaghetti and garlic bread, and his teenage boys Tom and Trent coming in from playing baseball outside. It all felt so good that he thought he might be worse off remembering what he didn't have now than not being able to remember in the first place. He switched thoughts to the black streak he had found. Had it washed away? And still what was it? Shawn would go back and look for it tomorrow. No matter what anyone said.

Outside the storm rested.

CHAPTER 47

By the time the storm ended the group guessed it was about eight o'clock at night. The artificial storm seemed to roll in, stop over the house, until it eventually quit. They didn't know if it had moved as a simulated storm or was just a giant alien sprinkler system in the ceiling. The mock wind had ceased and there were no more flashes or rumbling noises to distress anyone at sudden moments.

They stepped out onto the porch. It was pitch black out. The watery wall gave off a slight blue glow that could be seen from the house. Water splashed down from the dragon fountain and its statuette was outlined in the dark by the blue glow of the front wall. Rain droplets dripped slowly from the corners of the house and pinged on the ground. Everyone's lungs filled with fresh cool air that could be felt flowing in their blood streams instantly after each breath. Along with the soothing air came a damp feeling that rose from the ground and surrounded the house. Laura walked to the end of the porch and looked about. In a square of light on the ground shining through the windows she could see a few puddles. Still water that rested quietly. She turned and faced the group.

"There are a lot of puddles around," Laura said. "Looks like there's no place for the water to go."

"Yeah, there are a lot of puddles out front, too," Rob answered.

"There's no place for the water to run off into," Harry added. "Looks like they need to work on their drainage system."

"Nice job, Greys," said Rob sarcastically.

"The land is kind of flat around the house." Laura walked over to the rest of them. They were gathered on the front steps. "I guess the ground can't soak it up fast enough."

"Don't they have construction worker aliens?" Travis said. He shrugged. "You know, to work this stuff out."

"On the flip side," Katie punched Travis in the arm jokingly. "They did create the weather."

Travis laughed. "Good point. Not bad for a bunch of Grey balloon-headed sticks. But if it rains too much we might need our own ark."

"Bad enough as it is already," Rob said. "Now we might drown on top of it."

Harry knew they were just talking but he didn't want anyone to seriously think they were at risk of drowning now. "It's not so bad. Remember, this isn't the prairie."

"Looks like you don't get your social moment with the Greys today, Harry," Rob said smiling. He loved giving Harry a hard time about that. "It's so special."

Harry ignored him as usual. Rob was just a smart-ass twentysomething. They thought they owned the world. Anyway, his questions asking why the animals had all gone to the corner would have to wait. The storm had been a refreshing change.

Laura leaned over the porch railing and looked up. She saw some lights sparkling in the sky. It was dotted with small whitish lights spaced unevenly about. There was also a moon. It looked pancaked against the black night. Until now there had always been a black ceiling in their compound. Now there was a night sky. Laura felt a small surge of excitement. "Whoa. It looks like they put a few stars in the sky," she said.

Everyone looked up.

"Cool, Mommy. Look!" Ashley pointed upwards.

No one spoke for a minute. Mouths were silent as their eyes focused on the view.

"I think that's supposed to be our moon from Earth," said Harry.

"Can't tell if that's the Big Dipper or the Little Dipper," said Travis. He was pointing at a certain group of stars on the ceiling. "Kinda looks in between."

"So it's the Middle Dipper," said Katie.

"That's badass, babe," said Travis. He patted her on the butt.

They continued to look up at the ceiling. A few lights were noticeably brighter than the rest.

"Those brighter ones are probably planets," Harry pointed out.

"Yeah, I remember that from astronomy class," Katie said. "What a cool class that was."

"If it is real," Shawn said skeptically. "It all looks fake. How do we know it isn't some celestial sky dome or something? Images projected like a movie."

"We don't, but what does it matter?" Katie asked.

Shawn looked at her. His being stolen away from his life on Earth and put here for their amusement incensed him. "I resent their attempts to placate us like we're children."

"Okay...." Katie said. Her eyebrows rose and she rolled her eyes underneath and looked away.

Laura understood Shawn's point. No matter of changes could deny the fact that they were prisoners here. She also knew what Katie was trying to project in terms of morale. Time for another conversation soother. She looked at Shawn. "I understand both of you. I think the point was that even projected images of a night sky make this place a little more bearable than the enclosed boxed-in feeling I think we were starting to get."

"Or maybe they are real stars and planets?" Travis said. "They just look weird to us. Maybe they have a moon just like ours back on Earth. Maybe it's our first look at their midnight sky. They just opened the ceiling. Maybe it's a sky roof like in stadiums?"

"It's the Alien Dome," Katie laughed.

A few people laughed. All but Shawn and Ashley. Carol noticed her daughter was distracted. She was looking out to the right yard of the house. "Something wrong, honey?"

Ashley shook her head but kept staring. "No, Mommy."

Carol looked out that direction. It was very dark. Night was a heavy blanket lying around them. The tops of trees were faintly outlined from the starlight newly above.

"What is it?"

"Nothing, Mommy." Ashley turned back and smiled at her mom. "Just afraid of the dark, I guess."

"Okay." Carol figured her daughter was wondering about the animals out there. Her daughter was very caring.

Mouths started to yawn and people stretched. Sleepiness started to settle in. Gradually everyone dispersed to their rooms. Laura was the first to bed. As much as she tried to remain positive the feeling of their inevitable end would grow inside her again. Before retiring, Rob and Shawn slammed a few more glasses of the strange water. Travis and Katie giggled their way up the stairs in anticipation of getting naked together. For a moment Rob wished he was with her. Or Laura. Her long legs and curves made his dreams better. On their way back to their rooms, Rob thought about that while Shawn talked about how he missed his wife and kids and wondered how his liquor store was doing. Harry bid everyone a good night and retired to his thoughts. Sometimes they included Carol and Laura. Otherwise he concentrated on how they would get by day to day.

Carol was in her room getting ready for bed when she realized the absence of Ashley. Her daughter had gone to the bathroom but that had been some while ago. Suddenly, she felt alarmed.

"Ashley!" She went into the dark hallway and stood above the stairs. All the lights were out and everyone was retired to their rooms. She turned an ear to the stairway and listened. Nobody answered.

Carol didn't want to disturb anyone in their rooms but where was her daughter? Quickly, she went downstairs. A few steps echoed a hollow creak under her feet. She got to the bottom and turned to the living room.

There she was. Her daughter was looking out the window in the same direction as earlier.

"Ashley, come to bed." She turned and went back up.

"Coming, Mother." Ashley followed upstairs.

CHAPTER 48

Sleep roamed restlessly around the room and over the bed. Inside that sleep, lying hidden, was the nightmare. It rested itself in Shawn's unconscious. Lying in stealth. Looming for a time to come alive. Waiting for a time to repeat the night before. The minutes ticked into hours. It awoke. From somewhere in his head it spread out infecting his dreams. He saw the hovering light close in on him. There were inflated Grey heads watching him with the black eyes. A taller one wearing yellow stood behind them. His stare burned sometimes. A pulsing sound vibrated the room. He was trapped on a metallic table. Naked. Arms and legs fastened straight by some invisible force. His mouth couldn't touch a scream. He couldn't even yell.

Every dream that ended rolled into a new one. The next dream was the same as the last. Trapped. Powerless. Exposed.

Inside his mind he felt someone speak to him. It was them. He didn't listen. Didn't want to hear. The hovering light was a tube. It started to hum. The bottom opened and it turned a reddish color. They watched him. Each dream. The invasion of his body began.

He woke.

Gasped deeply.

CHAPTER 49

The morning rose but the fake sun didn't. Outside it was still dark and dreary. The watery wall still circulated beyond. It had a small glow to it under the dark sky. A constant reminder that they couldn't get out.

Laura was in the kitchen. Carol and Ashley were too. Together they sat at the kitchen table and began to eat. Every minute they looked out the window. Perhaps hoping to feel at home again.

The pain in Laura's stomach sliced her again. It did so every morning. She thought what Katie had felt the day before was the same thing. A sharp prick the size of a nickel on the bottom of her stomach. She looked across the table at Carol and Ashley. They were eating eggs and sausage meals. Carol was careful not to make any mess, always wiping her mouth. Ashley's hair kept hanging down into her eggs. Laura hadn't mentioned it yet but was curious if Carol had been having the same pains.

"Have you had any stomach pains in the morning?" Laura asked. She took her first drink of the morning. Their strange tasting water was so good.

Carol looked up at Laura from her plastic box. She chewed for a few moments, looked out the window for a second, and then back at Laura and swallowed. "Yes, I have. It's kind of a sharp pain. I feel it in at the bottom of my stomach. So does Ashley." She nodded to her daughter, who kept eating, swinging her legs underneath the chair.

"Okay, because I do too. Every morning. It's quick. Like a stabbing feeling. Real painful. Sometimes I lean over a little bit from it. The pain comes back again the next day. I never have it again later in the day though. Not after breakfast."

Carol took in what Laura said for a minute. "I noticed it's only in the morning. Ash?" She looked at her daughter. "Have you had any of those stomach pains lately?"

Ashley nodded, yolk running down her face. "I didn't want to tell you. It hurt, but it's better now, Mommy." She smiled and took a drink of water.

Carol looked back at Laura. "Maybe the others have it, too?"

"We'll have to ask," Laura agreed. Her stomach felt better now.

Harry came down the stairs. He smiled at the girls, went straight to the fridge and drank down a glass of water, and then to the breakfast cupboard. Within seconds the microwave was cooking his breakfast. An oatmeal smell filled the kitchen.

Travis and Katie came down next. Each drank a glass of water and they peered out the windows and frowned in disappointment. Next there was some chatter from the back of the house. Rob and Shawn emerged from the hallway, yawning and scratching like they were at home. Everyone seemingly was wearing the same clothing as the night before. However, all their uniforms looked the same so it was hard to tell. The kitchen felt crowded.

Rob was rubbing his neck. He looked at Shawn. "Hey, did you have any strange dreams last night?"

Shawn looked at Rob. His mind didn't want to go there. He'd had enough. Finally, he grunted, uncertain.

To look at them was to see their hair matted. Laura laughed. "Hey, you guys redesigned bed head."

The two of them looked at her but neither cared enough to answer. Katie smiled at Laura in approval of her joke. Travis chuckled as well. Harry was done at the microwave so Rob drank some water and took his turn heating some breakfast. Shawn stared across the kitchen out the window. As he did Laura thought she saw him grimace in pain but only for a brief second.

"Doesn't look like our weather got any better overnight," Katie said.

"Nope," Laura answered, taking her last bite. "Still like an ugly rainy day out there."

"I wanna check something," Katie said. She opened the door and stepped onto the porch. Travis followed her. She had a towel with her and playfully snapped it back at Travis. He jumped and smiled. His girlfriend was awesome!

It was wet outside. Dampness was strong in the air. The temperature felt the same as it always did, around seventy degrees. That's perfect as far as anyone was concerned. It also suggested that their atmosphere was constantly regulated and done very well.

"The thermostat here is kept the same," said Katie. "It never seems to waver."

"That's one thing they do well, I'll say," Travis said.

"Alien technology at its best," Katie said. She walked down the porch steps and looked around on the ground.

Travis gave a perplexed look. He knew Katie so well that he could usually know what she was thinking. But not this time. She knelt down. Finally, he asked, "What are you doing?"

"Looking for worms."

"Why?"

"Cause, I want to go feed the birds." Katie shrugged. "Besides, what else is there to do?"

"Okay." Travis stepped down in the yard and looked around. No birds graced the compound. Nothing ran either. "They all must still be hanging out in their hideaway corner."

Behind them the front door opened and Laura, Harry, Carol and Ashley came out onto the porch. Rob and Shawn remained inside eating and drinking and discussing heavy metal music.

Katie had plucked a few worms from the strange ground and held them in the towel in her hand. She stood up and looked at the four puzzled faces watching her from the porch. "I want to go see the birds and feed them. Anyone want to come?"

"I do! I do!" Ashley held her hand up and looked at her mom.

"I guess it'd be all right," Carol said hesitantly.

"I'm in," Laura said. "I wanna go back over there."

"Me, too," said Harry, walking down the steps.

"You wanna go, Carol?" asked Katie. "No offense, but you don't get out much."

Carol thought about it. Mostly she thought of Ashley. What if something happened to her and she wasn't there? She would never forgive herself. "Okay, I'm going."

"Better let the guys know," said Laura. She turned and shouted into the house. Something indeterminable was yelled back.

"Wait!" yelled Ashley. She ran into the house to the kitchen table where Rob and Shawn were sitting. She put her doll on the table. "Molly is tired and wants to take a nap. Would you two watch her while we go look for the animals?"

Rob looked across the table at Shawn and he returned the look to Rob. They both smiled.

"Sure, kid. We can do that," said Rob.

"Yea!" said Ashley. She pushed Molly up on the table between them and ran back outside. As she ran out the door she heard Rob say, "Molly, are you a football or baseball fan? Do you like to shoot pool?"

Katie and Travis led the way down into the clearing.

Katie walked gingerly and cupped the worms softly in the towel. She was afraid of crushing them and kept her attention on her grip which was hard to do as Travis walked along beside her cracking jokes. It wasn't long and she was laughing with him. Ashley skipped along next to her mother and started talking about Kenny. Carol felt guilty for not thinking about him more but there was something about this place that blocked so much of their memories. Whenever they remembered things about their lives back home or the last moments before they got here, the memories would drift away again. What they did know was they had been abducted and put here in this zoo. Laura and Harry remained quiet for the most part. A few causal things were said between them but mostly they walked along looking for birds, rabbits, or squirrels that weren't to be seen. The consensus among them was their animal neighbors were staying in the corner of the compound.

"Looks like we're always gonna have to go to them," Laura said. "They stay in that corner. And that's a weird thing. They all stay there. But why?"

Harry shrugged. He didn't know yet.

As they approached the start of the hill, Travis turned around and looked back towards the house. There were some lightning flashes in the far end of the enclosure, but no storm. The morning had been very overcast and bleak like when a storm had ceased but still lingered. Now at the far side, the dark sky was dissipating, and their fake sun was casting sunlight again. Yet lightning flashed and seemed to be doing so in a jerky unnatural way.

"I get the feeling they're still messing with the weather," Travis said. Everyone stopped and turned back. They saw a zigzagged flash that seemed to dance across the ground behind the trees. "Looks like we spoke too soon about our alien weathermen. The weather Greys."

"I think their weather machine is broken," Harry said.

What wasn't said but felt by all, was that if there was something going on with their artificial weather, this might be a problem in the future. The unpredictability of the unnatural lightning for one thing. It was scary as it seemed uncontrolled. They didn't need any more problems.

Puddles of water lay sporadically on the ground. Reflected in their liquid faces were the trees standing near them. When a slight wind blew, they would ripple in pattern.

They walked over the hill and through the rows of trees. Laura started to think that a person could get lost in a forest like this. The trees and grass were kind of like a preserve inside this structure. A preserve which they were inside and part of the wildlife. That they were the same as the birds and squirrels. She shuddered for a second and her morale plummeted. When were they going to get out of here? Were they even going to get out of here? When were the Greys going to come next? She decided not to think about it as it brought her down too much. Laura looked at the trees.

Harry looked straight forward as he walked. An uncomfortable feeling dwelled inside him. It just didn't feel right. He didn't know why. They didn't see any animals yet so that might be giving him a feeling of isolation. However, it was the same yesterday, and he hadn't seen them until they went far enough to the corner of the compound. Maybe it was just the fact that he didn't get to speak to the Greys the night before due to the storm? In a strange way, he had begun to feel connected to them. That he could ask the Greys for help and they listened gave him a feeling of security. A feeling of not being so alone. Harry reasoned that must be it and continued walking.

Carol felt good because she was with her daughter. The ever nurturing and protecting mother that every day she strived to be. The fact made more difficult because she couldn't be with her son Kenny. She couldn't remember him for long because every time she thought of him his memory would slip through her mental grasp. Every time she thought of him Kenny would stay past the edge of remembrance and remain in the world of the forgotten. It frustrated her because she knew something that she loved and cared for was somewhere but beyond her reach. Carol thought it had something to do with this place although not sure how yet. She looked down at Ashley, who was smiling in enjoyment of this playful walk, and that made her feel better. Guiltily, her thoughts of Kenny sank away, as they had every day. Carol was back in the present. The now that included her daughter.

Ashley thought this was fun. We're going to feed the birds. This trip was like the ones she and her brother would take in the woods behind their house. The adventures they would have playing games like hide and seek and pirates of the forest. Ball tag was a favorite too. There were so many places to hide outside in the backyard. Sometimes she would sneak around to the house and get something to drink while her brother was still out looking for her. That was always funny. She never told him that. Ashley wished she had some lemonade now. It was fun to play outside with Kenny but then the glow balls started to come. At least there weren't any here yet. The big fakers. She continued to skip along staying close to her mother.

Katie and Travis still led the way. They traded more jokes but Katie was more serious than usual. She carried the worms carefully, and if distracted might forget herself and squeeze a little too hard, and squish them. She opened the towel to check on them, and they were there, pink and wiggly. Travis thought they were disgusting yet his girlfriend didn't. How strange?

Katie closed the towel. She thought about how distant the past seemed. Since they'd been here she and Travis had remained close. That was a big help to have her boyfriend here is this strange place to help her feel comfort and strength. Even with the other six strangers, now becoming friends in a sense, she wasn't alone as long as Travis was here. The aliens appeared to be trying to make their strange new home more like their real home, back on Earth, but it didn't help. Katie struggled with her memory of what happened before they got here. She remembered they always wanted to see a UFO and aliens. Wanted to get it on video and blow the lid off it worldwide. However, after this experience she regretted it and wished she could take it all back. She blamed this desire for having put her in the position to have been taken by the aliens. She knew this much had happened but couldn't remember the details. Katie also remembered she was in a local college, and her all-important cell phone which she, or anybody, didn't have anymore. All that, mixed in with their abduction, was the most she could recollect. She couldn't even remember her family. Something blocked the rest of her mind. She didn't know what that might be.

Travis shared the same beliefs that his girlfriend did. They had discussed it among themselves often since arriving here. It was incredibly ironic that their young lifelong quest to capture little green men landed them here in this prison. This animal cage. If he could take it back, he would. The old adage was true: Be careful what you wish for. He would be from now on.

Travis trekked along next to Katie. Her hair bounced along looking pretty. He was very happy to be with her. Especially, that if he had to go through being trapped here, he was doing it with her. Or was it the opposite? That if she was trapped as a prisoner, he was there to accompany her. Either way it was the same to him. What was also the same for him, as the rest of the group, was he couldn't put his finger on events prior to waking up. There was the video camera, his cell phone, a giant bright light, and then he was here. Every time he racked his brain to remember it wouldn't connect. Travis knew he had a family but he could only remember his dad. An invisible wall stood vast between his memory and four days before.

They stopped. Everyone behind held up abruptly.

At the base of a tree ahead, a small dark shape the size of a hand lay on the ground. It didn't move.

"What's that?" Katie asked.

"I don't know." Travis squinted. "Let's move closer." He inched forward.

It was feathery. A bird. And it was dead. Lying on its back, legs stretched out fully extended. Travis knelt down but kept his distance a few feet. Everyone gathered around behind him. There was something strange about the body. The beak was open. The eyes were … not there. It was hollow!

"Holy crap, what happened to it?" Katie asked.

"I don't know," Travis answered. He looked along the ground for a stick to poke it with but there wasn't any.

"Why's it stretched out like that?" Laura asked.

"It might be rigor mortis but that's not like any I've ever seen," said Harry.

Laura resigned herself in agreement and went down on one knee. "I guess."

Everyone was huddled together peering at it with contorted faces of question.

"It's dead," said Katie. "Do I get any style points for stating the obvious?" She meant it as a half-hearted joke.

"With me you do," Travis answered. They smiled and bumped fists.

A faint but rancid smell was coming off the body. Drifting slowly. It made their noses wince.

Carol got down on her hands and knees and moved to the side to get a different angle. She was bobbing her head up and down, positioning herself, like she was a camera. "It looks like you can look right down inside of it," she said. "I don't want to get too close but it looks empty."

Nobody wanted to get any closer. The recoil people get from germs and disease, that people feel are invisibly coming at them upon seeing something dead, was holding them back.

Travis looked at Carol. "A dead lifeless bird. And I mean lifeless like nothing inside of it. No guts. No heart." He said to her with question in doubt. "What the hell is that?"

"I don't know," said Carol, shaking her head. She looked in the tree above but only saw the branches and leaves extending out. Ashley hopped over and knelt next to her, mimicking her mom. She put her hand on her chin in a look of concentration.

Nobody touched it, but upon careful inspection, there wasn't much to inspect. No blood surrounded the body. There didn't appear to be any liquid or secretion of any kind. The body didn't have any visual scars or cuts. There wasn't anything on the ground around it. Just the bird.

"It seems like just a dried-up body," Harry said. "Looks like it might have fallen here. From a branch." He looked up at the tree.

"Or from the sky," Travis said. "Or anywhere. Heck, who knows around here."

"Maybe it happened in the storm?" Katie said.

"Yeah, good point," Travis said.

"Maybe," said Harry unconvinced. He wasn't sure of anything. The fact that the animals had moved to the corner on their own accord was strange enough. Now they found a dead one. And strangely dead. This would surely lead to something else. Something that probably wasn't good for them.

"How do you think this happened?" Laura asked. She was staring hard at the bird. Trying to look inside. Trying to look inside its mouth. Trying to look through the empty eye sockets. The inside was as dark as the outside.

"I don't know," Harry answered.

Laura rested back on her heels and took a deep breath without opening her mouth. She saw something near another tree. It too was black and about the size of her hand. She stood up and pointed. "I think there's another one."

Laura led the way and the rest followed her. They approached it slowly but clearly they could see it was another bird. The same as the first one they found. Rigid. Looking up. Beak open. Rotting.

They came up to stand next to it. This time nobody retracted as they had before. The discovery of the first one had seemingly made them immune to the sight already. The smell was also there but not too strong.

"Do we even bother asking?" asked Katie rhetorically.

"I wonder if this is a pattern," said Laura, but she knew it was.

"Mommy, look." Ashley pointed toward some other trees.

In the path's direction they were headed, a couple more animals lay on the ground. Although, now there were also a few larger ones. Together they approached and saw that mixed in with a few birds, were a couple squirrels and rabbits. They were in the same condition as the birds. Bodies stiff. All dead.

"What is this? What the heck's going on?" Travis said.

Katie dropped the towel and the worms fell out and jiggled around.

"What's the matter, babe?" Travis asked.

"Look," she pointed forward.

The breeze blew along in a long drag and the trees waved back and forth.

The group made their way ahead. The putrid smell grew on their senses as they approached. Eyes perplexed, as much as their senses, on alert. All over the ground were dozens of dead animals. Birds, squirrels, and rabbits. There wasn't one that flew, ran, or hopped. Bodies were spread out on their backs that looked like they had fallen out of the sky. Legs stiff and pointing up. All expressionless. Mouths open, holding invisible screams.

"It's like the souls were sucked out of them," Katie said.

They dispersed about, picking their next step carefully, everyone mindful not to touch or kick anything. One dead rabbit lay belly up in a puddle. The water caressed it. There were no visible attack or puncture wounds on any of the animals.

"What the heck is this?" Laura said. She put her hands on her hips as if she was making a stand.

"I don't know. This is weird," said Harry.

"This is fucked up," Travis said.

Ashley thought it smelled vaguely familiar. It unsettled her. "Eww, smells like garbage!" She pinched her nose.

"Whatever it is, it isn't good," said Carol. She looked at Ashley. "Don't touch anything, honey!" Ashley nodded in return.

"Jeez, they're all dead," said Laura. "Overnight. Just like the birds got plucked out of the air. And the squirrels. And rabbits. Like they got yanked out of the trees and on the ground. Just zapped or something. Did anyone hear anything last night?"

Everyone shook their heads no.

"It'd be nice if there were some branches so we could poke them," Travis said. "Move them around."

"Let's get some," Harry said. Travis agreed. They went over to a tree, Harry got on Travis's shoulders, and grabbed a low hanging branch that wasn't very thick. He pulled and twisted but it wouldn't break off easily. The only noise came from the leaves whisking as they shook the branch.

It was still relatively dark in this forest corner of the compound. The sky was still covered with clouds overhead and they were under the trees. Laura looked back the way they came but didn't see much light coming their way. At least not anytime soon. This part of the compound had the look of a storm before it happens.

It was quiet except for an occasional breeze that ringed in people's ears and Harry and Travis's branch breaking. Harry was constantly telling Travis to hold him up when he lost his balance and they wobbled around. "Don't drop me," Harry said a lot. "I'm not," was Travis's reply as he staggered about. Ashley thought they looked like clowns at the circus and couldn't help but laugh a little. She pulled on her mom's sleeve but Carol shrugged off the sentiment. This was very serious and she gave her daughter a look to convey this. There were a bunch of dead animals around them and that wasn't good.

At the far edge of the scene Katie saw the watery wall. She knew they were in the far corner of the compound. She looked around and her eyes caught a bird, squirrel, and a rabbit lying on the ground seemingly in a triangle. The bodies were bookended by two dark puddles. She thought it was a strange looking coincidence for them to have fallen in that way. *Just strange luck*, she figured.

A cracking sound rang out and Harry broke off a branch that fell down. Travis lowered Harry down and he jumped off his shoulders. The branch was still attached to the tree so they both started kicking at it to break it loose. After a few kicks it was free, and they pulled it loose from its bark skin, that seemed to not want to let go.

Harry picked it up like a spear and looked at it. "This was more difficult than I would have thought but the trees aren't the same as the trees on Earth. These seem a little synthetic in a way."

Travis rubbed it too. "It does seem different. Almost rubbery. I guess I'm not surprised. Everything else here seems to be artificial."

Harry went to the nearest animal, a dead rabbit, and poked it with the branch. Nothing. Next he used the branch to push it. The body rolled over onto its other side but was stopped by its rigid legs. The face was frozen in a what looked like a scream.

"I don't know what to say," Harry said. "It's dead."

"Yeah, but their bodies don't have anything left inside," said Travis. "They're empty."

They looked around and didn't see any hanging in the trees.

"Obviously, no more are falling now, if they fell," Harry said. "Whatever happened, it was during the night."

"Is that all of them, do you think?" Laura said walking up.

"It sure looks that way," Katie answered. She was standing away next to the farthest of the animals.

"I suppose there could be some others that made it off to other parts of the area," said Harry.

"Or escaped," Travis added, his eyes shifting between Harry and Katie. She was standing a little too far away for his comfort so he was keeping a watch on her. This place was potentially really dangerous and that risk was growing fast inside him.

Carol had shared that feeling for days now, ever since they mentally violated her and her body. She pulled Ashley next to her. Keeping Ashley within arm's reach made her feel safer. Her daughter's attitude had taken a quick change in the last minute since the guys broke that branch off. Upon seeing the scene with all the bodies spread about, Ashley's initial feelings had changed about taking a fun trip to feed the birds. Very bad! She looked up at her mom.

"Mommy, it looks like a battlefield."

"It could be, Ash," her Mom replied, still looking at the sight. "All of them dead. And we're inside with them."

"What do you mean?" asked Travis. He gave her an uncomfortable look.

"I'm making a point that we need to look at. These animals are all dead. Somehow, or from something. We might be next."

Laura, Harry, Katie and Travis all shared quick glances. Inside those glances were angst and warning which were ever growing within the group. The strangers. The friends. The prisoners.

"Whoa, wait a minute," Harry said. "We don't know what caused this. It could be a virus or something...." Harry stopped on his own words.

"Either way, we're in it," Carol said.

"It doesn't look like a virus," Laura said. "It looks like something you can't even say. I don't think there's a word for it."

"I do," said Carol. "Death."

Katie was being quiet about this and listening to the others talk. She was looking at the group and observing everyone standing in the middle of the scene. It was a mixture of confusion and the unknown. To look around was taking in a lot. A lot of life that no longer was so. She felt sad along with the growing apprehension inside her. Sad that these animals were apparently killed. Maybe they had been hunted? Katie didn't know. However, if they were all gone what did that leave? That left them! Although, to this day nothing had threatened them. Nothing had even remotely been dangerous to them inside here. Just the Greys, who were their captors but hadn't been violent yet. However, based on the mental scans they had done on them days before, they all knew they were capable of some evil as well.

Katie looked again at the animal triangle. She frowned. Something didn't look the same. One of the puddles wasn't where she remembered. It appeared to have moved closer. She blinked hard. Her eyes must be playing tricks on her.

Her attention was drawn back by an argument breaking out. Carol was going at it with Travis and Harry. Laura was trying to moderate. "Quit with the doomsday scenario!" Travis yelled. "Don't yell at my mommy!" Ashley shouted. "I'm not yelling at her!" Travis shouted back. Carol looked down at her and realized she needed to stay calm for her daughter.

"Let's be quiet," Laura said. "We don't know if anything else is out here."

"Don't you ever stop?" Travis said harshly. He was still upset, and Laura's team unity speeches were starting to get real old to him.

"There could be something else here," Laura answered harshly, her lips barely separated when she spoke. Her eyes were burning. What didn't they understand about this? She didn't like being spoken to that way. Especially before they die.

Travis saw the anger in her eyes and that resonated. It crept deep into his consciousness. He thought for a moment and had to admit to himself that she made a good point. If there was something around them they didn't want to attract it. "We need to get back," he said. "Do we take any of these animals back with us?"

Harry raised an eyebrow and looked at him. "No. I don't think we should. Do you, or anybody, want to carry one?"

The consensus was very quiet but a resounding no. But overall what was going through everyone's minds was what do they do now? What does this incident mean? What was going to happen to them? No one spoke. Carol's face was red. She was still angry. This was mixed with the fear growing inside her. Ashley was standing still, loyal to her mother. Laura took deep breaths to calm down. She was afraid animosity was starting to fester within the group. Animosity starting from their imprisonment here. Animosity from their helplessness. Laura thought they would fall apart soon and she couldn't do anything about it. She must regain herself and get control back. Harry was turning around as if he was looking for something. He didn't even know for sure what he expected to see but he didn't find it. Probably something that would make everything better but it wasn't to be found. Travis had been starting to lose his self-control too. He needed his rock. He looked at Katie in a silent invitation for her thoughts.

"That's one good thing you can say about this place. We don't have any insects or they'd be buzzing around here like crazy," Katie said. She saw they were all upset, especially her boyfriend, and wanted to set a different course of thinking among them.

Travis smiled. He could always depend on her. She was awesome!

"Okay, everyone relax," Harry said. He stepped out from the group so he could see everyone. His own little soapbox. "Remember, we're all friends here and we're gonna need each other. Let's get going, back to the house, and don't touch anything. Besides, it stinks around here."

That agreed with everyone. They all felt they'd been there long enough already. There was a feeling among them that they were leaving a crime scene.

The group started back to the house. They carefully walked through the bodies, picking their spots to step, and careful not to lose one's balance. Harry led the way in self-praise that he was once again the strongest one and voice of reason. He rapped his stick on the ground like a warrior walking on the hunt. Although in the back of his mind this might be more of a retreat. Laura, still flowing with negative thoughts inside, didn't care to comment. She was wrestling hard to control emotions and using her inner chi, concentrating her energy of life power, to regain her focus. Carol was calming down but she was on protective mother alert. There were weird things going on and they were in the zone of whatever it was. And so was Ashley. Carol was tremendously troubled by this. Travis started to feel guilty for arguing with Laura and Carol, especially when they agree that there might be trouble lurking for them, and yet from his standpoint he'd been unreasonable and argumentative. He would try for more self-restraint from now on. Travis walked over to Katie. It felt better to be next to her.

Katie started walking but quickly looked back over her shoulder. She blinked hard again. That puddle looked closer to her now. Her eyes were definitely playing tricks on her.

CHAPTER 50

Rob looked up from the kitchen table and out the window and saw the group coming over the hill. He noticed they were walking fast and some of them even broke into a light jog.

"Hey, they're back," he spoke to Shawn sitting across from him.

Shawn turned in his chair and looked out the window. They had been bored waiting for their return. They even started to regret a little not going with them. However, they had been remembering more about their past lives before they got here. Rob had been thinking about how he missed sports, chasing women, shooting pool, and drinking beer. Shawn had been spacing off thinking about his family, baseball, the family liquor store, and movies he'd like to see again. He squinted as he watched them come closer to the house.

Rob had a better view of them from his angle and he could see them all. The fake sun had broken out and cast a nice midmorning light across the compound. The light cast on their faces revealed looks of uneasiness and apprehension. He didn't think they looked right. "They look rattled."

"How can you tell?" Shawn looked at him.

"Just something. Look at their faces. Especially Laura. She looks disturbed."

"Oh." Shawn turned around again. The returning group walked onto the porch and he got a better look at them. "Yeah, something isn't right. They don't look all cheery."

The six came inside and went into the living room. Rob and Shawn watched them and looked at each other. Ashley came into the kitchen, grabbed her doll off the table, and went back into the living room. Rob and Shawn saw that she looked scared. "Okay...." said Rob. He and Shawn pushed their chairs back and went into the living room. Everyone was sitting on the sofas except for Harry who was staring out the window. Nobody said anything but they did look up at them.

"What's the matter?" asked Rob. "What happened? You all look so weird."

"We found them," said Laura. "They're dead."

"What?"

"All of them."

"Dead? How?"

"They're just lying on the ground."

"From what?"

"There's nothing inside of them," Katie said.

"Huh?" Rob looked at Shawn, who didn't know what they meant either.

"We found the carcasses of animals," Katie proclaimed.

"Like animal skins?"

"Their insides were gone, dude," said Travis.

Rob grimaced. "Like the bodies were empty?"

"Yeah, they were hollowed out."

"Hollow. How?"

"We don't know," Harry said turning around. "That's how we found them. The bodies were stiff. Arms and legs pointing upwards towards the ceiling, or sky, I mean."

Rob stared funnily at Harry. "Jeez, this place gets weirder and weirder."

"Yeah, but we got a problem," Shawn spoke. His mind was thinking back again to the black streak he had found. "What did they die from?"

Harry felt alarmed again. They were at that point in which panic might set in. If there's something that did this, they're vulnerable to it. He better stop it quick. "It's okay. We haven't seen anything out of the ordinary that would suggest there is some danger. It's probably something with them. I think they were some sort of fake artificial ani-mals anyway. Just like this place, and our new sky, and weather system." Harry smiled, hoping that would misdirect them.

Shawn thought his black streak was out of the ordinary, very strange, but not dangerous.

"I don't feel comfortable," said Carol. "It's not safe."

"Stop it," Harry said strongly. "I'll ask them...." His voice trailed off. Through the front living room window he saw the light peel back again on the ever-flowing watery wall. There was a flash and the window in the wall rolled back and revealed three tall adult Greys, surrounded by smaller Greys. All extremely thin with big heads and black eyes. More Grey children. They all were watching the house.

"Uh-oh," Harry muttered. He got down on the floor. "We have company."

"What?" said Laura.

Harry waved everyone to get down. Rob and Shawn dropped down. The rest got off the couch and stayed still. Everyone was looking at Harry with questions on their faces. He crawled up below the front window. Slowly, he looked up and peeked out the window. He quickly ducked below it again. Harry turned to everyone. "They're out there again. The Greys. With the little ones."

"Kid aliens," said Katie.

"Great," Travis said sarcastically.

Rob crawled over to the window and sneaked a look. He dropped down and faced everyone. "Those things are out there again and they brought their kindergarten class with them. We're the freak show for them."

"Great," Travis said with more sarcasm. "How nice they're on a field trip."

Harry peered out the window again. "It looks like they're waiting for something and I think that something is us."

"I don't want to go out there," Carol said.

"Me neither, I hate the lollipop men," Ashley said, shaking her head.

"Yeah, no kidding," Laura said. "What are we gonna do?"

"Get pointed at," said Shawn. "Humiliated."

"I'm surprised they don't throw us peanuts," said Rob.

Come out of the house.

"What was that?" Laura asked. She was very alarmed.

"I don't wanna play this game anymore," Carol said. Her voice was edgy. "They get into our minds. Show up and watch us like show and tell. Then we find all the birds, and such, dead for no apparent reason. Strangely dead on top of that. Now they want us to come out and play. Uh-uh." She was shaking her head quickly.

Come out of the house.

Everyone heard it. Actually, it was more of a feeling. Something that sounded off in their minds. In their consciousness. They knew what it was. The Greys were summoning them.

"We need to get away from this," said Laura.

"Yeah, you won't have an argument there," said Travis. "But how? Where can we go?"

"Don't go out there," Katie said. "Stay inside. That'll give them the hint."

"I don't know if that will work," said Harry. He and Rob were both next to each other leaning up against the front wall. Neither of them wanted to look again. "The way things go here, I don't think we have a choice in the matter."

Come out of the house.

"I don't wanna go, Mommy," said Ashley. She grabbed her mom.

"We won't, honey," Carol hugged her close.

"Wish we had some weapons," Rob said.

Come out!

The voice was stronger this time. They could feel it. More stern. Like going from a needle to a hammer.

"I think they're getting angry," Laura said.

Moments went by. Everyone stayed still as if they were being hunted.

NOW!

Everyone grabbed their heads in anguish. A sharp pain passed through their bodies and cut their minds. After a few seconds, they felt better. The sting receded and they could think clearly again. They exchanged distressed looks which sent a message among them all that they were powerless. And that they better not disobey.

FASTER!

Again they were hit! Like a sword, it split their minds in two. Everyone doubled over in pain. Slowly, it waned again.

"I don't think I can take much more of this," Carol said, her voice mixed with sadness and hysteria.

"We better go," said Harry. He got up and started for the door.

"But what's going to happen outside?" Shawn asked, crawling out of Harry's way.

Harry stopped, hand on the door handle. "What's going to happen inside if we don't?"

"We can't hide!" Carol yelled and put her arms on Ashley. "We're their pets."

Harry looked at her. His thoughts told him that all his communication with the Greys hadn't made any ground work at all. That maybe all along they were just humoring him and putting up with his requests, until they were finished with them. For whatever purposes that might be. "I see your point."

"We better go outside now or they're going to kill us," Katie said.

"They're going to kill us anyway," said Laura following her to the door.

Together they filed out onto the porch looking like survivors of a natural disaster. Their faces resigned to their fate without any hope. Forced to do something not of their will but of something else's wishes. To go out and be the main event for some sort of spectacle. They were live entertainment.

The Greys watched them. The Yellow stood on the left again. The Red stood on the right. The Female stood in the middle. Her golden locks a magnet for the eyes. This was as much a shocking sight as it was pretty. She did not appear to have breasts. Light from somewhere reflected off the star emblem on her bright green tunic. The child Greys still didn't wear anything. At first, no Grey moved. They just stared. Then like before, they turned, but this time to the Female. She spoke to the little ones. It was done in a way that she didn't move her mouth but they knew she was doing it. A moment passed and the child Greys turned around and faced the house again. Black eyes watching. They all pointed.

CHAPTER 51

The bright light closed the wall and the Greys were gone. They were invisible again to the company of eight who were left to wonder what goes on behind the ever-flowing wall. The group was left to ponder what the aliens were doing in regards to them without their being able to see. Without their knowing what their real purpose was for inside this compound. Inside the animal cage, if that was what it was. Were they watching them? Were they testing them? Were they experimenting on them? That last question resonated deep inside their invading dreams. The dreams that started the last few nights. Dreams nobody liked. Dreams raiding their sleep.

A minute passed and the group relaxed. Arms hung down by the sides of their bodies. The rigid tension in their bodies went slack and they let their guard down. It was a relief to their bodies, but not to their minds, as that couldn't help make their morale better. Their spirits sank down into their own pit resting in the underground of their consciousness.

"It's humiliating," said Katie.

"No shit," said Rob. He gave her a glance and looked down. "Being forced to come outside against our will and be looked at. Mocked at. Like some attraction in a carnival."

"I guess it's like field trips for their little Greys," said Laura. "They come and watch us to see us in a supposed natural habitat."

"Yeah, and if we don't come out, they make us," Carol said.

"Oh shit, I wonder what that textbook is like," said Travis. He put his hand up in front as if holding a book. "Here are the people of Earth. They're called Earthlings."

"Knock it off, stop it!" Carol yelled. "I don't think it's funny."

Travis kept reading from his hand, mumbling something in a smart-ass way. He didn't care anymore. Didn't care if anyone was angry with him, except for Katie. After this last encounter, he was tired of caring.

Carol stared at him with wide white-burning eyes that could set a town on fire. To the group she might be losing it. To Carol they all were monkeys in a cage.

"All right, all right," Katie said walking up to Travis. "Let's chill." She pulled his hand down to stop the imaginary book reading. He shot her a quick glance of annoyance that surprised her but he quickly recovered and smiled at her. Travis was surprised at himself. For a brief second he had been upset with Katie for forcing his hand down. He had never done that before and felt guilty. It was this place at fault!

Rob looked hard at Harry. "Looks like your friends sure are doing a number on us now, man."

"They aren't my friends," Harry replied. He felt partly offended. "And can you blame me for trying?"

"We're their show and tell." Rob kept at it.

"Jeez, we have enough problems, we don't need this fighting," Laura interjected. She looked strictly at Rob. "He did a good thing, Rob. He asked the aliens for things we needed and we got them."

"Yeah, I guess," Rob snorted. "The stickmen. Heck, there's even a chick stickman. A stickchick. How weird is that?" His last comment was rhetorical but he was upset and needed to vent it out. Rob didn't like Harry's chatting with the Greys for a couple reasons. He thought it gave Harry an unfair advantage in this prison that they were inside. Perhaps if the Greys decided to kill them all Harry might be spared. The other reason is he thought Harry enjoyed his little ritual with them too much. And this place wasn't to be enjoyed.

"She is freaky," Katie said. "Even the second time."

"Yeah, no shit," Travis said. "My head practically snapped backwards the first time I saw her two days ago."

"Their creepy alien kids."

"They might hear you," Carol said strongly. Her face was stone.

Everyone stopped and took in her meaning.

"Or scan you," added Harry.

After a moment Laura said, "Let's go inside. I think we need to get away from this for a while. I need a beer." She was the first to the door.

They went inside. All except for Shawn. His eyes moved from left to right as he watched them go inside while trying to remain inconspicuous as possible standing over to the side. He didn't need to get away. Shawn was going back out. He wanted to see the black streak on the ground again. The black mark that in a way he thought was his. It belonged to him. He found it. The thing meant something to him but he didn't know what yet. Shawn wanted to go investigate it. He wanted to see it again. That is if it was still there a day later. A day after their night of stormy weather.

Shawn watched the back of Rob disappear into the house and the screen door gently close with a metallic clang. He quietly shuffled across the porch, down the steps, and across the front yard. He looked back to see if anyone noticed but didn't see anybody. Nobody shouted out at him either. With the coast clear, he quickly scampered to the forested area in front of him. At least a forest by this place's criteria. A forest absent of animals scurrying about, or plants, and flowers giving off their beautiful smells. Being overweight his potbelly bounced up and down, he started to sweat, so he quickly settled into an easy walk. He felt better when he was out of the clearing of the front yard and had the cover of the trees to hide him as he went on his little quest. If they realized he was gone, it would be too late for any of them to stop him from doing what he wanted to do, because he knew they wouldn't want him to venture out. They would say it was too dangerous. Shawn knew there was truth to this but he needed to see his discovery again. With any luck, he would return before they noticed he was ever gone.

Shawn strolled among the trees always looking for anything unexpected. Everything looked the same as he remembered. The trees were tall and shook with leaves of a strangely green color. The trunks were covered in a bark skin that seemed artificial too. That was another thing the group had come to find, that everything inside this place seemed manufactured. Shawn felt something bad was going to happen. That's the way it seemed to be going with the dead animals and being paraded around like a circus act.

The breeze comfortably made its way through the trees and helped calm the adrenaline he was feeling by sneaking off on his own personal exploration. Shawn hadn't felt a surge like this since he skipped class in high school and outran the monitors patrolling the parking lots. It was darker and shady under the tarp of the tree cover. The light from the fake sun shined down in shafts of white light that found holes in the foliage above.

Shawn stopped. He recognized the strange zigzagged pattern on the tree to his right. This was the place. A rush of excitement shot through his body. The black streak was gone from the ground. It had probably washed away in the rain. Shawn walked over to where it had been and knelt and examined the spot. The grass looked the same as everywhere around him. Daringly, he waved his hand over where he remembered it lying on the ground. There was no residue of the stain left behind. Shadows lay about from the canopy of branches high above. Some looked as if to be hiding behind other shadows. However, there was still enough light for Shawn to see clearly. He felt the ground but it was the same weird grass that covered the compound. There was no trace of the black remains. It was gone.

Then his nose picked something up. A growing smell that wasn't there before but now was noticeable as if it just arrived. Shawn looked around, in front and back of him, and among the trees but didn't see or hear anything. The smell was getting a little more dense and unpleasant.

Shawn waited. His nose twisted. It seemed to get closer. There was a familiarity to it and his memory started racing to remember. Shawn stood up and took a couple steps back. He inhaled a few breaths to clear his lungs. He felt better but only momentarily as the odor made its way up to his nose again. Now it was more intense. The daggers of stench jabbed at him and he recognized it as the smell from the black streak. Albeit unsure, he thought it was a smell he'd smelled days ago exploring in the trees. Shawn scowled. He turned in all directions but didn't see anything around him. Nothing was on the ground. No black streaks. No animals alive or dead. He didn't see anything in the trees either. The shadows lengthened as the midday sun was on the farther side of the compound. They surrounded him and seemed to stretch out along the ground and reach for his feet. Frustration was starting to swell up inside him because the smell was coming from somewhere and he couldn't find it. And Shawn was starting to get nervy.

The breeze returned around the trees and shifted along the ground blowing little waves in the grass. It provided some relief to Shawn's senses as the stench was whisked away, but only for the moment, and it returned as quickly as it had gone. And it smelled closer.

Shawn reeled and started walking back to the house. His pace quickened. Step by step. Faster and faster. Now all he could think about was how much he wanted to get out of there. About how much he regretted going back out to look for it. Sneaking out of the house like he did when he was a little kid. Like his kids did when they were younger. Going back out alone. Without telling anyone where he would be. Of course, that had been on purpose, because they would have stopped him if they knew he was heading out and prevented him from rediscovering his find. But now he didn't think that had been the right thing to do. It was a mistake. The ownership he felt for the black stain had driven him out there. Pulled him from the house and his companions. Out alone isolated among the trees. Into the strange rotten smell that he couldn't get away from. Like it was following him. His nose inhaled it deeply and blew it out again in rejection.

Shawn stopped walking. He was standing in some sunlight now. The light gleamed on his skin. As he turned around the hairs on his body bristled in alarm. He saw nothing there except grass, trees, and shadows swaying about. The wind blew and the leaves chattered. The stench remained. Ruining life.

All Shawn owned out here was his shadow.

He wheeled around and continued onto the house. His nose was repelled as it breathed in and was relieved as it breathed out. Step after step. The smell permeated. With each stride, it was there. With him. Moving as he did.

Shawn stopped. Sweat flowed out from the pores in his skin. An invisible hand of fright grabbed his heart. Again, he turned around but didn't see anything but his sense of smell was on full blast. Shawn whipped back around again. Still nothing but the smell remained. The stink seemed to be coming just over his shoulders. He squeezed his fists until they were pale white and then released his rising fear. Something was here. Shawn didn't know what to do. He turned again and again in all directions. Everywhere he turned it smelled behind him. Avoiding his every move. Finally, he faced forward again. He wiped the sweat from his face and his eyes focused on the house between the trees. He was almost home.

Shawn started to run.

A brushing feeling gently touched the back of his neck. The feeling reminded him of when the edge of a newspaper quivered against his skin from a blowing fan.

CHAPTER 52

Laura sat looking out the window and tracing imaginary figure eights on the kitchen table. She was trying to think of what they could do. How could they get out of this? What will happen the next time the Greys beckon them with their minds?

Ashley skipped into the kitchen, got a glass of water, and skipped back to the living room where she was dancing and playing doll with her mom. Carol was distraught and trying to forget about the morning's events through directing all her attention to Ashley. This wasn't hard for her because since being there she had been on full-time protective mother alert. However, she was having difficulty concentrating on their dancing games that Ashley would perform, and she would be the judge. The desperate situation they were all in affected her and kept setting her mind adrift. Ashley had to constantly remind her to pay attention to her when she was dancing.

Katie and Travis had gone upstairs to their bedroom. Laura heard the door shut so they wanted some privacy. However, this time it probably wasn't for fooling around but to get away from the mental stress caused by the Greys, mind control, and dead animals that had their bodies hollowed out inside.

The guys had all gone to their rooms too. No noise came from them.

Laura thought about their confines. The Greys had wanted them put there in a natural environment just like life back home on Earth. It was pretty evident that they weren't on their home planet anymore. They did provide them with food and their strange-tasting water.

They were given necessities for the bathroom like soap, towels, and toilet paper to their gratification. Then finally they were given new clothing and shoes to wear. But the thing about it was that except for their strange tasting water, the Greys didn't have it prepared and ready for them when they got here. They had to ask for it all. This struck Laura like it was their first time abducting humans and they were inexperienced at it. The aliens had the big picture covered but overlooked the little stuff.

The depressing feeling of being under constant watch, or surveillance, by the Greys returned. It smothered the group's optimism like a blanket over a flame. They had blocked it out at times, only to have it reinforced with another visit in a humiliating way that deprived them of their self-respect as individuals, and as civilized evolved human beings. The visits were chipping away at them and making the group feel a little subhuman.

The lights went out, the refrigerator stopped humming, and the microwave went dark.

"Aw, what now?" Carol complained.

Laura looked out the window but it was black outside. They were completely covered in a blanket of darkness. There was no fake sun. The only thing she could see was a faint blue glow from the watery wall across the yard.

"What the heck is going on!" Rob yelled as he stomped out of his room into the kitchen. "I hate this place!"

"I don't know," Laura answered. "It appears to be some sort of power outage."

"No shit!" Rob yelled.

Laura held back her anger caused by his response. She needed to keep her cool.

"Can't see anything outside," Carol said from the other room. "It's like a city-wide power outage, but it's this zoo."

It was pitch black inside too. Laura couldn't see Carol or Ashley. She couldn't see Rob either and he was in the room with her.

"Anybody know what's going on?" said Harry from the top of the stairs.

"Not exactly," said Laura. She pushed her chair back and carefully walked to the bottom of the stairs. "It's completely dark outside so it looks like a complete power outage."

"The stupid aliens forgot to pay their electric bill," Rob shouted up the stairs.

"Maybe they operate on a grid too and it blew fuses or something?" Laura said up to Harry.

"I suppose," answered Harry. "Or giant solar panel grid, or plasma, or alien green technology crap that I'm sure they developed. Who knows? Maybe there was a solar eclipse or something."

"So what are we going to do?" asked Laura.

"Not much we can do," Carol said. She was now standing at the edge of the kitchen. Ashley was next to her.

"At least the aliens can't see us. I'm going back to bed," Harry said. They heard his door close a moment later.

Another moment of silence passed between them as they were waiting for something to happen.

Finally, Laura spoke. "Well, I guess that sums it up. Any ideas? Any eureka moments for us here?" Her last question carried a hint of sarcasm but it was more of a reflection on their situation than anything.

"Yeah, I guess we'll retire," Carol said. She looked down at Ashley. "What do you say, hon?"

"Sure, Mom," Ashley said. "Just no glow balls."

"I guess we have no choice," Laura said. "The boring gets more boring."

"It's about all we can do right now," Rob said and he turned. He stopped when closing his door and looked at Shawn's room. Shawn hadn't come out. Rob shrugged and closed his door.

CHAPTER 53

The next morning Laura's eyes opened and immediately looked at the window. There was light leaking out from behind the curtains. The power inside the compound was back on. Relief expelled from her as she let out a long breath of air. *Perhaps a little bit of normality has returned to our lives for this day*, she thought.

Her stomach interrupted the pleasantry with a sharp sting that made her wince.

Laura got out of bed and changed into a fresh pair of clothing and her bright white running shoes. After carefully opening her door and seeing that the coast was clear, she defeated her paranoia and went downstairs to the kitchen. Everything was the same as she remembered it the day before. Apparently, nothing had changed because of the power failure and that was a good thing.

She got a glass of water from the globe in the fridge and leaned over the kitchen table to look outside. Everything looked the same in front of the house as well.

Footsteps on the stairs grew louder behind her as Travis and Katie came downstairs followed by Harry. As if on cue they heard Rob's door open and he joined them in the kitchen.

Immediately, all of them got their own glasses of water and drank them down. That made Laura curious.

"Were all of you that thirsty?"

Everyone nodded and drank more.

"Do any of you have a sharp pain in your stomach every morning?"

Everyone nodded.

"Since the day I woke up here," said Travis.

"Me too," Katie said.

"Nasty little stomach pain if you ask me," said Rob. He drank some more.

"I don't know what it could be," Harry said. His glass tinged as he tapped his finger against it. "I supposed it could be a bug of some sort. A virus. Or maybe bacteria."

"That we all have?" Katie questioned.

"Sure, I guess," Harry said. "It seems perfectly plausible for us to have caught the same thing. We're all in here together."

"Great, on top of it all we're in one giant Petri dish," Travis pooh-poohed.

"Wait a second. I noticed that it seems to go away after I drink the water," said Laura. She waved her empty glass. "Did any of you?"

"Yeah, I guess," said Katie uncertainly. "That's why we're down here drinking it. Although, I never looked at it like that. I just thought I was naturally dehydrated in the morning."

"I did," Carol said from the stairwell.

Everyone turned and looked at her in surprise. She was good at moving around quietly.

"Or at least I'd started to wonder," Carol continued.

"We!" Ashley said next to her.

"Yes, we did, honey," said Carol. "Laura and I talked about this yesterday. We'd kinda been noticing it the last couple of mornings. It's just like Laura said, we'd wake up, thirsty, and have a stinging sensation in our stomachs, but after some water we never thought of it again."

"Exactly," Laura said. "As soon as I had a cup it was gone. And I don't think it will be back til tomorrow morning again."

"So what you're saying is that the water somehow squelches the stomach pain?" Katie asked.

"Uh-huh," Laura nodded.

"Okay, sounds good," said Katie. "But what is causing the pains? Is it some sort of alien morning sickness?"

"That's why I said bacteria or something," Harry said, feeling they needed to listen to him more. He had been correct so many times already about this place.

"I don't know," said Laura. "That's a good possibility but--"

"I don't think it's related to anything like that," Carol cut her off. "I think it's something they did to us."

"How so?" Harry asked. *There she goes again on a crazy tangent*, he thought.

"Like when they took us," Carol continued. "Abducted us. They did stuff to us. Don't you all remember this? Before we got here. Before they put us here."

Everyone remained quiet for a few seconds that felt like minutes. Their silence was born from disbelief that was mixed equally with the belief that it was true.

"Experiments they did on us," Carol said, her voice sounding unbalanced. Almost as if the words she was saying were carrying her over into a deranged state. "I've been having these nightmares. So has Ash. Have you been having them? Any of you?"

Their faces shifted and exchanged glances. Nobody wanted to look each other in the eye or get caught doing so.

Finally, Laura spoke. "Yeah, I've had them."

Everyone looked at her now. The sound of her voice serving as an invitation to look without revealing in their own eyes that they all had them.

"They're horrible," Laura said. "It's like you're hospitalized but they do things to you. Inside you."

"Me too," Katie said quickly afterward. She shivered as she talked. "Travis and I just thought it had happened to us so we didn't want to say anything."

"That is true," Travis said, nodding in agreement.

"Yeah, there are bright lights above you," Katie continued. "And you're on this table. And this thing comes down from the ceiling."

"What about the other guys?" said Laura.

Harry was quiet but he knew it was true. He'd been having them every night. "Yes. A surgical instrument comes down and does *surgeries* to you. And they stand along the cold metallic table that you're on and all watch you. The little grey bastards."

"See what I mean," Carol said. "We're all having them."

"That doesn't prove anything," said Rob. Deep inside he knew it was true but his masculinity wouldn't allow him to succumb to this. It wouldn't allow him to admit that he couldn't protect himself. That he was powerless when this had happened. "We're all just hallucinating. How do you know it's not something they put in the water? Like some drug or something to make us think this way?"

"Cause it's true! That's how we know." Carol's voice was teetering on the edge of rationality becoming unhinged. Yet, what she was saying made sense to everyone. Even to Rob.

"Do you think that's it then?" asked Katie. "We're dreaming distant memories in our subconscious. True memories. The memories of what happened to us before we got here. After all, none of us can really re-member what happened to us to get here in the first place. And the pain we have in our stomachs is from whatever they did to us when they took us. It's like a scar in our stomachs."

"And when we drink the water it goes away," Laura added. "Could this be the reason our memories go away, too?"

"How's that?" Rob asked.

"There's something in the water."

"It does have that strange taste after all," said Travis. "Maybe that's it."

"Could be," said Carol. "But as long as you all know what it is and what has happened. I'm not crazy!"

"Yeah, but if the water also erases the memories, then how come we're remembering the nightmares now?" Rob said. He wasn't ready to relinquish control of the definition of what had happened to them over to Carol and Laura yet.

"That's a good question," said Laura, and she thought for a moment. "I think it's because our memories are stronger now and it's all coming back to us. They're getting too strong to be held back from our conscious remembering. Too strong for the water to suppress them. Perhaps even because we've been here long enough now that we've adapted to this place."

The group was quiet while looking at each other in silent agreement. It all made sense.

"That sounds logical," Harry said. "That certainly explains a few things. But what all did they doctor on us, we don't know. Possibly cut something out of us. Or implanted something in us."

"Or implanted something in our stomachs," said Katie. The beliefs she held before being in this compound flooded to the forefront of her mind.

"We don't know yet."

"Maybe we shouldn't know, dude," Travis said.

"I hate 'em!" said Carol. "They're animals to do that to us."

"I agree," said Rob.

"The stomach pain is some result of their experiments on us," Harry said. "It seems that, other than being the most important thing to drink, the water is some sort of control mechanism on all of us. On us animals in the cage."

"And we can't do anything about it," Rob said.

"Once we drink it we're okay painwise," said Harry. "Same with the nightmares of experimentation. We're not supposed to remember. We drink the water and they get buried away. Masked inside our subconscious."

"So what if we quit drinking the water?" Rob asked.

"Get dehydrated," Harry answered with a smile. He knew that wasn't the answer Rob wanted. "And I imagine your stomach will hurt all day til you drink some."

"But the good news is we don't have to worry about that anymore," Laura said. "Drink all you want. We're all starting to remember."

"I don't want to remember," said Ashley. Her cute voice was calming to everyone's nerves. Then someone said....

"Hey, where's Shawn?"

CHAPTER 54

Rob walked back to Shawn's room and the door was closed. He knocked but got no answer. Rob slowly opened the door, his body tense with anticipation for the unknown of what he would see, and peered into the room. The bed was empty and the sheets still messy from the last time Shawn slept there. Clothing hung in the closet. There was no Shawn. Rob walked back into the kitchen.

"He's not in his room," Rob said, concern lining his face. "That's weird. When the power went out yesterday I just assumed he went to his room like the rest of us did."

The lights in the house dimmed momentarily.

"We better look for him," said Harry. His eyes rolled looking at the lights.

They checked all the rooms in the house but didn't find Shawn. They called his name. "Shawn!" Rob's booming voice had a touch of panic in it. An eerie sense that a crime had taken place hung inside the rooms. A few minutes later everyone met back in the kitchen. Their worried faces shared the feeling that something was wrong.

"We'll need to find him," said Harry.

"I'm afraid something happened to him," Laura said. "This isn't right."

"Yeah, no shit," said Rob, as his head hung down. He missed his buddy already.

"Where's Shawn?" Ashley asked quietly, her hands held up to her mouth.

"I don't know, Ash," her mom answered. "But we're gonna find out."

"I hope so," she said. "He's like a giant teddy bear to me."

The power flicked off and on again.

"I see our alien technicians are still having problems," Katie said.

"We might have problems ourselves here looking for Shawn," Harry continued. "Does anyone remember the last time they saw him?"

"On the porch," said Laura. "I'm pretty sure he was. I can't remember now."

"Yeah, he was," said Rob.

"We were all out there after our little show we put on for the aliens," Travis added.

"Mommy, you don't think the lollipop men did something to Shawn, do you?" Ashley said.

"I hope not, doll baby," Carol answered. She patted her daughter's head to try to relax her.

"We better check outside," said Harry.

The group went outside onto the porch. It was the morning hours so their sun was in the east of the compound. Its light shone brightly. On the other side to the west it was still blanketed in darkness from the early morning dawn.

They spread out along the porch looking around the yard about the house. There wasn't any sign of Shawn.

Laura walked to the far left of the porch and looked around the edge of the house. Everything was the same as the day before. The side of the house was still a pleasant white and still gave off a flowery smell although not as strong as before. The yard was that strange green color. The grass spanned into the back up to where the trees marked the end of the yard. The east side trees were tall and elegant.

Laura was stunned by what she saw behind the first row of trees. The Greys were in the compound! Inside with them. They were standing around something large on the ground. She leaned forward over the porch railing and stared harder. The thing on the ground was....

It was Shawn!

"Oh, my God!" she exclaimed.

Everyone turned her way.

Laura pointed to the trees.

The group walked up behind her. There was a collective gasp among them. Shawn lay on his back with his arms rigidly pointing upwards.

"Hey! What happened to Shawn?" said Rob, his voice angry.

Nobody had an answer yet. Everyone just watched. There were four Greys standing on each side around Shawn's body. Two were smaller worker Greys. The other two were the tall ones in charge that wore yellow and red. Their mouths didn't move but they appeared to be having a discussion. It looked even a little like a disagreement or an argument. The Yellow and Red Greys looked down at Shawn and then at each other. They repeated this over and over. Sometimes their arms would point at Shawn. All the while Shawn didn't move.

"What'd they do to him?" Carol said.

"You don't think...." Harry said, casting a look at her.

"The Greys! They're standing around him."

"They're highly civilized," said Harry with frustration. What was it these people didn't understand? "I don't think they would kill him or any of us. They may be our captors but they aren't inhumane murderers."

"They aren't human, Harry," Carol countered. "They're in control. They are capable of doing whatever they want."

Laura had heard enough and put her hands up. "All right, all right! Stop it! You're making it worse."

The sight of the Greys standing over Shawn grabbed their attentions again. The taller Greys continued to discuss. There was no movement from Shawn.

"What's going on?" asked Katie. "Why doesn't Shawn move? Did they seriously do something to him?"

"I don't know babe, but it's weird," Travis said. He put his arm on her shoulder. "All the time we've been standing here he's just lain there."

Laura focused her excellent eyesight on Shawn. She squinted hard and blocked out some of the fake sunlight shining in her eyes. He was stiff as a corpse and she saw that his mouth was wide open. Like all the wildlife they had found the day before.

"He's dead," Laura said.

"Are you sure?" said Harry. "How can you tell?"

"Because he's in that rigor mortis state we found all the animals in. I think what happened to them, happened to Shawn."

Everyone took a good hard look for themselves. Shawn and the Greys weren't too far away for the average eye to see, but all the emotion and disorientation immediately felt by the group had clouded up their thinking. Collectively they looked. There was Shawn, arms bent upwards toward the sky, legs stretched out like sticks, and a frozen look of death on his face.

"Nooo, Mommy," Ashley said. "I don't want Shawn to die."

"Neither did we, honey," said Carol, comforting her with a hug. "Neither did we."

"Those bastards!" Rob said.

The Greys continued to debate, but now they were gesturing and looking in the trees around them.

"Something's not right," Travis said. "Not like before."

"Yeah, it's like they're confused about it," said Katie. "As if they don't have any idea what happened."

"Sure they do," Rob said. "They killed him."

"No, she's right. I've been watching that too," Laura said. She knelt and rested her chin in her hand on the railing. "It's like they're disagreeing on something."

"Yeah, to take credit for a KIA," Rob huffed.

"They're freaky looking savages," Carol said.

"The lollipop men did it," Ashley included. "And they were so nice back home."

"I'm just saying that they didn't do it," said Harry. He felt like he was pleading to them all.

"Maybe they're discussing what happened to Shawn?" said Katie.

"I don't think so," Rob said. "I know they took him, and did something to him, and he's dead. Do you see anything else around?"

"Don't be so quick, Rob," Laura said. "We don't know yet. Look at them. They're not really doing anything."

"Like they say, the guilty always return to the scene of the crime."

Just then Laura noticed on her right that the watery wall was open and the female Grey was standing there. Dressed in green, she was radiant. Her golden hair seemed to reflect the sunlight. Laura wondered what she was doing. What her role in this was. What her role outside in their society might be. To Laura the Female was watching the Greys stand over Shawn's body. Or was she really watching Shawn?

Laura blinked in surprise. For a moment, she thought the Female had looked at her.

"Well, why don't we just go over there and find out for ourselves?" Rob said, and he jumped over the railing down into the yard. He tightened his fists and started walking towards the Greys. As he approached the trees the Red looked at him. Rob's body went stiff. He didn't move.

Don't come over here.

The voice sounded in their minds again. A voice all too familiar to them now. A familiarity that wasn't in friendship.

Stay there.

Laura felt no ambition to leave the porch. She saw a halted Rob standing idly in the yard unable to move, an immobile and probably dead Shawn, and the alien voice was speaking to them in a threatening way. Everyone else must feel the same as she did. Not a word was said and nobody flinched. Carol was petrified and held onto Ashley who clutched her doll. Katie and Travis each stared through wide open eyes. Harry watched the Red hoping all would end quickly.

The Red turned back and proceded to conduct its own business with his group. That creepy feeling given off by the Greys when they pried into their minds faded away to the relief of everyone. It washed over them but left in its wake the nervous feeling that they'd avoided a brush with death.

Rob's body relaxed and he stepped back. At first he didn't know what to do. Seemingly confused, he looked around the yard, at the Greys, and back to the porch several times. Everyone waved for him to come back but nobody dared to say anything. The Greys were still having their discussion and weren't paying them, or Rob, any attention. Rob shook his head clear and slowly walked back onto the porch. He was back with them now and everyone felt good about it.

"Jeez, I don't know what happened," Rob said. "I got up there and it was like a giant invisible wall stopped me. I couldn't move."

Harry shook his head in agreement. "Yeah, they force-fielded your body or something. We saw it all."

"I remember hearing that voice again in my head. It told us to stay over here."

"It did to all of us," Laura said. "Pretty strong this time."

"They send their messages to us telepathically," said Katie. "What's weird is they can control us doing it."

"I still feel pretty weird about it," Rob said. "Can't shake that feeling I get afterwards."

"Yeah, that's how I feel too," said Laura.

"We all get it," Travis added. "I feel like I do after I narrowly miss a car wreck. All shaken and stuff."

"Yeah, I second that," said Katie. "I'm usually in the car with him when that happens."

"Those things," Carol said. "They play with us." Immediately, she flashed a look at the Greys hoping they hadn't heard, or felt, what she said and was relieved to see they didn't. The aliens were still in their conference around Shawn.

The wind picked up and flew along carrying its sense of tranquility to the porch. The trees bent over and the leaves rattled around the house while the coolness of the breeze bristled over the hairs on their skin and their apprehension dissipated away. Collectively, they shared looks with each other.

"That's another thing I noticed," said Katie. "Like you said with the water, whenever the wind comes along it seems to calm me down. Like it's soothing and my fears or extreme emotions go away. That just happened again for me. Did anybody else feel that?"

Everyone shared a silent acknowledgement as the realization of Katie's words set in. She was right. Throughout their time here, when the wind blew along, they all felt a sense of calm come over them. It covered them like a blanket and kept their emotions in check. Especially, their extreme emotions like fear and anger. The emotions that might ignite aggressive or antagonistic behavior smothered by a gentle breeze.

"That's badass, babe," Travis said, and they bumped fists.

"Good point," Rob said.

"It does have a calming effect," Laura said. "Could it be another control mechanism? Like with the water?"

Harry nodded. "Yeah, that's a good possibility. Remember, we don't know for sure if they are control devices, but I will agree that it sure looks that way." He sounded positive but deep down inside he was kicking himself for not realizing this himself. After all, he was the smartest one of them.

"And I can't remember much of the past after the nice wind calms me down," said Laura.

"Yeah," said Katie. "That too."

"That's happened a few times to me," added Harry.

"So it's like the wind makes you forget," said Travis.

Everyone shared nods of agreement.

"Great! They use all the elements to herd us around," said Carol.

Movement beyond the trees caught their eyes. The Greys were searching around the trees nearby. It was clear they were looking for something. The group watched as they searched. The Greys' skinny legs were a strange sight to see. To this day they had stood behind the watery wall or weren't visible from the waist down or were blocked by the medical examination tables in their scary dreams. Their quick-moving legs looked like a perpetual letter X when walking.

Their search lasted a few minutes and they gathered around Shawn's body again. Then his body lifted off the ground. Something was lifting him, but it wasn't visible. The two small Greys took positions on each side of Shawn and walked alongside of him. The Yellow and Red followed behind. Shawn's body floated through the trees and his alien entourage followed alongside. He floated to the hole in the wall where the Female waited. It was difficult for the seven of them to watch Shawn's saddened body with his arms rigidly bent upwards, empty eye sockets, mouth wide open as if he was howling to the sky, and body flat as a board. The Female stepped aside and he floated through the wall to the other side. The worker Greys stepped through followed by the Yellow and Red. Then the wall closed and flowed like it always did.

Sorrow overcame everyone in a big way. Carol, Ashley, Laura and Katie started to cry. Harry, Travis, and Rob mourned in their guy way, alone with their own individual thoughts. Especially Rob, who leaned against the support beam of the porch. Shawn had been a friend to him. They both shared the downstairs like it was in his college days and had shared many discussions about life. Whatever in the world had happened to Shawn, he didn't deserve it. He was a loving and caring husband and father and certainly didn't deserve to die. And not in the mysterious and apparent horrible way that he had.

"Bastards. I can't believe they killed Shawn," said Rob.

CHAPTER 55

The day returned to a semi-feeling of normality, but the absence of Shawn hung in the air. The unanswered question of what happened to Shawn was a huge void in everyone's mind and would probably continue to linger on like a sickness. For how long was yet unknown.

The women had stopped crying and collected themselves along with the men and they went inside the house. This helped as the house served to put a barrier between them and what had happened outside even though they were only a small distance away. Mostly everyone sat around and had small conversations but nothing was deep in thought. The fake sun outside passed over the house as the day grew long. The light winds blew nicely and gave an appearance and feeling of being back home on a beautiful summer afternoon. The house often creaked and groaned when the gusts were stronger than normal.

They ate their meals throughout the day. Some ambled out onto the porch but didn't stay long as the memory of what had transpired was too much to bear. Everyone wanted to get away from that and not be reminded of it.

The Greys never showed the rest of the day. Everybody was in silent agreement that the Greys were responsible for Shawn's death. They were murderers! Whether it was by accident or a conscious act they were guilty. A few times the question of how Shawn had come to his fate was brought up but those conversations died quickly. What had he been doing out there alone? Had he been out there on his own accord? Nobody knew and everyone was powerless about it anyway. It was assumed the

Greys had used some advanced alien technology on him. The memory of Shawn being *airlifted* out of the compound was too disturbing to relive.

Night came quietly at about a time the group estimated to be eight o'clock in the evening. Harry didn't go out to perform his ritual and speak to the Greys. After today, Harry didn't know how he could bring himself to do that ever again.

Before everyone retired for the night everyone went to Shawn's room. They made up Shawn's bed, folded some of his clothes, and rested them on the bed's edge in a somber tribute to him. This was his funeral. Then they left his room and closed the door.

CHAPTER 56

The night passed uneventfully for the group of sleepers as the previous nights had. It was a quiet night without any storms, and after lying in their beds thinking of the day's past events, everyone eventually slept until the morning. The only interruptions to their slumber were the dreams they shared of experiments the Greys may, or may not have, performed on them after they were taken from Earth. Although, to the group the consensus was that it had happened. The dreams were nightmares. The nightmares were disturbing. All of them went to bed each night hoping they wouldn't have them anymore. However, every night they did and were powerless to stop them.

Laura made her way out of bed and quietly down the stairs to the kitchen as she did every morning. The sharp pain in her stomach stabbed at her so she quickly drank down two glasses of their water. The liquid flowed down her throat and erased the pain as it did each day. She knew that was good for only twenty-four hours but it was the best she could expect.

Laura peeked out the kitchen windows and saw all was the same. The sun was coming up and casting dawn across the compound. The wall was still out in front ever flowing as always. Nothing else moved as there was nothing left to move now except for them.

Carol and Ashley came down the stairs, followed by Harry, and then Katie and Travis. Each holding their stomachs as if they'd eaten something bad the night before. Judging by how Laura had felt this morning, and her companions' faces, the morning pains were getting worse. *We don't need any more problems to add on to everything else,* she thought.

After exchanging morning greetings and everyone had gotten their early dose of water, Laura filled her glass with more water and stepped out onto the porch. She did so carefully, checking on both sides of the porch door and out in the yard before doing so. The wind blew along like every day and sent a refreshing feeling throughout her body.

Behind her she heard beeps and dings from the microwave. There was conversation as they warmed up their breakfasts. Laura was hungry too but wanted to wait until the kitchen wasn't as crowded as it was now. On top of that, she overheard Rob's voice coming in from the back, and he sounded grumpy so she would eat later. She took a sip from her glass and walked to the east side of the porch. The side of the porch that was like a boundary to the unforgivable land. The land that Shawn was found dead in. Yet, it was all the same land. There was no real border between the porch and where Shawn was found. It was all in their minds. And they were trapped inside it.

Laura stopped at the porch railing and took another sip of water. Her fingers let go of the glass. It bounced on the porch floor with its water splashing out. For a moment, she stared out past the trees not moving like a statue. Slowly, she leaned back and rapped on the kitchen window. Inside all conversation stopped. The screen door opened and Rob stuck his head out.

"What?" he said.

Laura pointed east.

The screen door swung open and he stepped onto the porch. The rest followed him outside with curious faces. They all came up behind her.

"What?" Rob asked again. "What is it?"

"Yeah, Laura," said Katie. "What's going on?"

Laura kept pointing and everyone followed her finger to a body lying on the ground underneath a tree near the edge of the wooded area.

It wasn't as large as Shawn's body and it looked grey and black. They realized what it was.

It was a Grey.

"Oh my God, an alien?!" Carol exclaimed. "What the heck is that doing in here?"

"It hasn't moved since I saw it," Laura said.

"Is it dead?" Travis asked.

"I think so."

"It's strangely reminiscent of seeing Shawn yesterday," said Harry.

"Eww, a dead lollipop man," said Ashley.

"It's about time," Rob said with satisfaction.

"Mommy, I've never seen one before," said Ashley, turning to her mom.

"Looks like there's a first time for everything here," said Carol, her eyes never leaving the body.

"Let's find out." Rob heaved himself over the railing and into the yard again. This time he looked both ways, as if he was crossing a busy street, before he proceeded towards the trees.

The six scurried off the porch and around into the yard after Rob.

"Careful, Rob. You know what happened last time," Carol said.

He waved her off. There weren't any Greys around this time to stop him, and from appearances the only Grey in the compound this morning was the one lying in front of him. And that one wasn't moving. As he got closer his pace slowed and the rest caught up with him. They grouped together and slowly approached the body which lay under the first set of trees.

This Grey was medium height, taller than the worker Greys, but not as tall as the Yellow or Red. It was dressed in a black outfit complete with a gold star on the front. Its mouth hung wide open. The body was stiff like the rigid edge of a knife. Its long skinny little arms were bent to the sky. The hard black opaque eyes were missing. Left behind were empty eye sockets cupped into the alien skull. The body was hollowed.

They gathered in a circle around the body.

"Holy shit!" Rob said. "This sucker's dead too."

"Don't get too close to it," Harry ordered.

"Yeah, look at it," said Laura. "Its ugly black eyes are gone. And the body is just a shell. Nothing inside. Just like everything else we've found here."

"Yeah, the same thing happened to Shawn and the animals," Harry said in a subdued tone. "At least what we presume happened to Shawn. We never did get close enough to tell but he looked the same as this."

Rob knelt next to the Grey. He sniffed it and recognition passed over his face. "I know this smell. It's the same nasty smell that the black stain had that Shawn found on the ground a couple days ago. It reeked off the ground. I was with him, remember?"

Everyone nodded in agreement. They could smell it more prominently now. The smell was rising from the body.

"Do you think it's the same thing?" Travis asked, holding his nose.

"Must be," said Rob. "It smells the same."

"I remember the animals stunk like this too," said Travis. He was taking in deep breaths.

"That's for sure," Katie added, softly hitting Travis in the arm. She loved it when he was right although she felt she didn't tell him that enough. Here in this place she certainly would.

During all this, Laura had been thinking. When she and Rob had explored behind the house on their second day there, both had detected a bad stench from somewhere in back. "Rob, do you remember?"

"Remember what?"

"When you and I checked out the back all the way to the wall on our second day here, we smelled something."

Rob hesitated in thought. "Yeah, I do."

Ashley's memories started to stir. Her young mind started to trace back to a few evenings ago. Trace back to her nose and that smell in the hallway.

Ashley let out a gasp.

Everyone heard her and looked at her.

"Mommy." She looked up at her mom. "The smell...."

Carol didn't answer. She just looked at her daughter.

"Mommy, I'm scared," continued Ashley. "It was in the hallway...."

Another cool breeze sent itself through the compound, bringing along its mystic touch, climbing the chattering leaves and the creaking branches. Gone now was their conversation as the breeze swirled around the trees and danced between the members of the group before whisking away pleasantly. It felt good on their skin but this time it didn't have quite the calming affect that it usually carried with it. A few noses twitched as they caught a whiff of something bad. Something a bit more than that emitting from the dead Grey.

"What's going on here?" Carol said. "I mean this is crazy. Shawn dead! Dead animals! And now a dead Grey for Christ's sake! Who's doing it?"

"What's doing it?" Laura said, her face cracking a little bit with fear.

"And what's happening to them? Their insides are gone! How can that happen? Why doesn't anybody say anything about that?"

"Because we don't know," Rob said strongly. "We have no idea what's going on yet."

"We thought the Greys did this to Shawn," Katie said, her eyes shaded with concern. "But now something did this to a Grey."

"Their bodies are sucked out like a straw!" said Carol.

Standing next to her mother, Ashley was feeling like her head was starting to spin. A dead Shawn, a dead alien, dead animals, and nobody knew what was happening. Ashley was really wanting to be home hiding in her closet with her brother Kenny.

Harry started waving his hands. "Okay, so something killed them all. I got it. But don't you think the Greys would know this and would have stopped it? I do. Like their own pest control or something?"

"Look around, dude," said Travis. "Look at what's been going on. It's obvious. There's something here."

"I'll tell the Greys tonight. They'll stop it."

"You believe in them too much."

"They'll know now when they find their dead friend here," said Laura. She was looking around for danger but so far everything was the same. The strange grass was still green and the trees were still pretty.

"And hope they don't blame us," said Carol. "You never know what they'll do."

"Oh, they'll know better," Harry said. "We don't have any way of stopping this. We have no weapons." He was getting more and more worried as this conversation was going on. If they were in danger inside the compound, his belief that the Greys would protect them and have the situation under control, was starting to wear away. A belief made weaker by the dead Grey lying in front of him. And along with that they had no way of protecting themselves.

"So what's doing the killing?" Katie asked. Her arms were held out, fingers extended. She felt they weren't talking about this enough.

"We don't know yet," Laura said. "What we do know is that it does this to whatever it preys on."

"Do we think it's an animal or some kind of alien?" Rob said. "Is it a virus? We know it's not a man."

"But how could this happen to a Grey?" Katie asked. "They're more advanced than us."

"And this Grey looks kind of badass judging by his shirt," said Rob.

"What's with this Grey, anyway?" said Travis. "What's it doing here?" He saw something. Holding his nose, Travis got down on one knee next to the Grey and tugged on the shirt.

"You're the first person to ever touch an alien, Trav," Katie gleamed.

"Thanks, babe," said Travis. He winked at her and continued looking at the Grey's shirt. It was torn. He looked up in the tree above them. Something was waving in the breeze. He pointed to a branch. "Look. It was in the tree. It looks like its shirt got snagged on a branch."

"Oh, you're so good," Katie smiled at Travis. She was proud of her boyfriend.

"Probably got snagged when it fell out," said Harry. "Or when it was attacked."

"So it was sitting in the tree," said Carol.

"Maybe it was hiding," Travis said. "Waiting for something."

"Waiting for it," said Laura. "Whatever it is."

"Maybe that's what it was here for?" Travis said. "To kill whatever it is that's doing this. I think it was like a hit man Grey."

"Oh, an assassin alien!" said Katie.

"Like a big game hunter-type Grey, if they have those," Carol said.

"A Hunter Grey," said Katie.

"Whatever it was," Travis continued. He wanted to finish his thought. "I think it was here to hunt it down."

"And *it* got the Hunter Grey here before the Grey got *it*," said Rob.

"Yes," Travis said.

"That sounds pretty good, kid," Harry said. "We don't know for sure yet but your idea does seem plausible."

"So where's its ray gun," Rob said sarcastically. "We could use it."

"Maybe the Greys don't use anything like that," Laura said, again ignoring Rob's attitude. She realized this was a highly stressful time for all of them.

"But what's that say about the Hunter Grey," Carol said. "Whatever is doing this got him first."

The breeze repeated itself and cut through the air. Soft and yet forceful at the same time. Again, it didn't have the reassuring effect it had in the days before today.

"That's why I say," Carol didn't miss a beat. "What is killing things inside here?"

Harry's mind was turning thoughts over and over inside his head. What would science or logic say? He couldn't conclude exactly but he had some ideas. "I'm not sure yet. I would say it's intelligent but who knows. You don't have to be an intelligent being like us or the Greys to do this. This could be done on instinct. What we do know is that it's a good predator. We don't hear anything at night. None of us have heard anything cry out in the middle of the night, so I think it uses the element of surprise. It either sneaks up on you or ambushes you. One or the other."

"That's very good, Harry," Rob said. "Now can you tell your friends the Greys about it. And oh, by the way, we need some ray guns too."

"Shut up, Rob!" Laura said, she couldn't hold back this time. "Those were excellent points. No matter how much we don't like it, we're here, and something is going on and we need to deal with it."

"I know they were but my point is we're screwed," Rob snarled. "This thing is a killer! My sarcasm is how I deal with it."

"Just chill out!" Katie yelled. She was tired of the bickering. Through their days here, she and Travis had remained collected and had maintained working together as a team. A two-person team albeit but they stuck together. She wanted everyone to do the same. "Look, quit the bitching. Travis and I are still in this together. We're all in this together and need to cooperate. I know I'm not the only one. Laura has been saying the same thing. Remember, a team of seven is stronger than two."

Rob scoffed, even though he knew she was right, and decided to move on quickly. "All right, all right. I hate this place."

"Like we don't?"

"It's okay," Harry said. "Really. We're all stressed. That's understandable considering the circumstances."

"What are we going to do?" asked Carol. Now she was gripping Ashley's shoulders hard enough that her daughter winced.

"Well, let's see...." Harry said, rubbing his chin.

"What are we going to do? What can we do about this?" Carol quickly asked again. She wasn't going to let go. She was scared for herself and more so for her daughter. With each passing day, it was looking more and more like they weren't going to make it out of this place alive. And if they didn't get out of here, they might not live long enough to get to the next day, or day after that. That meant her daughter would never even have a life!

Harry started to speak but no words trickled off his tongue. He didn't have words to say and simply looked back at Carol.

Deep down Laura's resolve was starting to break down again. It seemed to channel down her body, through her legs, and into the ground. She thought they were all going to die and suspected Harry thought the same and that's why he didn't answer Carol. Nobody said anything and stood around in a circle looking at each other in search of answers. The ladies' hair tossed in the wind, and the guys stiffened their shoulders, but never quit looking around their immediate surrounding for something creeping up on them. Nobody knew.

They didn't have many choices or resources at their hands. There was nothing to protect themselves with and they didn't know what was alive inside with them. They were trapped and didn't know if they would get any help from their captors. In fact, the Greys had been more of an oppressing force, not only by putting them here, but with their mind control they had demonstrated on them. After finding the Hunter Grey dead they didn't even know if their captors could even protect themselves. Laura closed her eyes and mentally tapped into her inner chi. She started to focus and told herself.... Be brave.

CHAPTER 57

"Mommy, I want to go back to the house," said Ashley.

"I think we should too," Carol answered.

As if on cue to their words, the front wall flashed and peeled open, revealing the Yellow and Red Greys standing in the entryway. They were surrounded by eight smaller Greys. All seven of them felt the cold stare of the taller Greys' deep black eyes.

Go to the house. You are safe there.

This time they didn't have to be told twice. Everyone started walking back to the house immediately. While constantly glancing at the Greys, the group quickly got back to the house and huddled together on the porch. They wanted to see what the Greys were going to do this time. Especially when the victim was one of them!

The Yellow and Red Greys were led into the compound by a couple smaller Greys. The other Greys were positioned on the sides and in back to form a protective safeguard. Together they walked with vigilance through the trees and stopped at the Hunter Grey that lay on the ground. The tall Greys examined the Hunter Grey and some of the worker Greys kept watch around them. After a minute, the Yellow and Red appeared to assess the situation without any disagreement or discussion like the day before, and were in agreement. What the Greys agreed upon the group could only speculate, but one could assume that both species, human and alien, knew the same thing. That something was inside and killing things. And one of both species had been victims. The Greys weren't invulnerable either.

Something seemed to signal in Laura's mind, and although she wasn't quite sure if it was real or her imagination, she looked over at the entryway and again the female Grey was standing there. She was watching the inquiry of the dead Grey. Her blond hair was glowing behind her green clothing. Over her shoulder Laura noticed that none of her friends were even aware of the Female. They were completely fixated on the Greys and their investigation.

Laura looked back at the Female. She double blinked. Again, she thought the Female was looking at her. Laura blinked again but the Female was back to watching her fellow Greys conduct their inquiry inside the compound. Even though her eyes may have been playing tricks on her, she felt this time it had been for real. This led Laura to wonder why the Female had singled her out. Why would any attention from a superior being be directed at her, a prisoner, inside this human cage?

The Hunter Grey's body rose into the air as if being lifted by an invisible hand. The procession moved to the front wall with the worker Greys on both ends and flanked by the Yellow and Red. To the group on the porch watching them it was like déjà vu from the day before. The Greys walked through the entryway where the Female stood stoic and waited for them. The light flashed and the wall sealed up behind them sending an eerie silence throughout the compound.

On the porch, they didn't move for quite some time after that. Everyone sat in silence. The disregard shown by the Greys towards the group revealed the true distance between them. The distance between captor and prisoner. The truth was they didn't matter.

CHAPTER 58

The early morning sun had risen higher above and the shadows changed their direction and searched for new territory to darken. A quietness was becoming more apparent as if it was rising from the ground underneath them. For the group morale dropped to new levels. Despair was starting to tighten like a giant fist and squeeze any sense of hope out of them. Eyes and mouths drooped as they stared at the porch floor, out at the trees, or at each other. Nobody knew what was going to happen next which led to an obvious question.

"What are we gonna do now?" Katie asked.

"I don't know," answered Harry. He scratched his neck. "Let me think."

A breeze blew along to break up the silence.

"Those Grey bastards are gonna let us die in here," Carol said, no longer worried about what her daughter heard anymore. She felt herself starting to lose control as if her hands were slipping off the steering wheel that kept her steady. "They won't do anything. We need help!"

Harry put his hands up defensively. "Okay, okay, relax. I agree with you, but we don't know that yet about the Greys. It looks like they did try to help us with the Hunter Grey hiding out overnight but it didn't work."

"Hmm, that's comforting," Rob grunted.

"But why didn't it work?" Laura asked. "How could that Hunter Grey get killed? What's in here with us?"

Harry looked at her dead on. "Obviously, we don't know yet."

"Jeez, we assume the Greys put one of their hunters in here to catch this thing and it didn't work." Laura couldn't let this point go. "What is so dangerous that it beat the Grey?"

"Holy crap," Katie said. "If the Greys can't kill this thing, like how the hell are we gonna do it?"

"Look, did anyone see anything yet?" Harry asked. "Did anyone notice something that might indicate a creature or living organism is in here?"

Everyone shrugged and shook their heads except for Rob. "Yeah, Shawn and I did. That black streak smeared on the ground. It was like black tar or oil or something. And it stunk. We never did know what that's from."

Harry smiled. "Good. Anyone else see anything like that?"

Again, everyone shrugged except Rob. "There's that God-awful rotting smell. We've smelled it other times, too."

Everyone was fixated on Rob.

"Shawn had mentioned something about a smell our first day here when we explored in back," Rob continued. He knew he had everyone's attention and he liked that. It made him feel like the man. And he was the man at this very moment and he wanted to drive home the point that the reeking odor was very important. "We also smelled it when we were standing over the dead Grey. Don't know where it came from but it was there."

"Yeah, and it was around all the dead animals too," Katie said grimacing.

"So it's connected with ... death," Laura said.

Ashley was listening to everyone intently. She wanted to remind them about the smell in the hallway the other night but was now too scared to speak.

"Everyone keep your eyes open," said Harry. "Whatever it is, it's here somewhere."

"There's what happened to Shawn, a lot of dead animals, a dead Grey, and the black streak found on the grass," Katie said. "The stick-men better come up with some shit fast."

"We need to come up with some weapons," said Travis.

"Yeah, even if they don't abandon us," Katie added.

"What if they can't kill it?" Travis paused dramatically. "What are we gonna do then?"

"Then they'll just let us rot in here!" Carol said.

It's okay. Everything is fine.

They all knew who it was.

We will protect you. You are safe.

Harry was thrilled with excitement. "See, I told you! They'll handle it."

This time when the voice spoke they didn't submit so easily to its ways. The group had been through too much, especially in the last two days, and it didn't have the same effect. The voice sensed that. It spoke to them again … louder.

We killed it!

The voice echoed inside their heads.

It's dead!

The voice started to take effect.

We killed it!

In a mysterious way, a calmness trickled down onto the porch and seeped into everyone's mind and body. They started to relax. Worry, uncertainty, and fear rushed away in a cluster of colliding emotions. They hadn't forgotten anything that had happened, but the group was washed clean of their anxieties and set to start a new day with a fresh outlook. They started to talk but these conversations were about everyday subjects people discuss back home on Earth. Sports, music, politics, current events, and cultural issues were again at the forefront of their minds. This was easier now knowing that whatever it was that was starting to prey on the living inside their compound had been killed by the Greys.

Laura had blocked out the argument the others were having before the voice had spoken to them. Her mind had been drifting a million miles away with thoughts about home and how they weren't going to live much longer. As her mind wandered she started to relax and the feelings of dread started to float away. Laura started to feel good again. She was sitting up on the railing at the edge of the porch. The wind blew and her hair danced around with it. The idle chatter carried on next to her. Rob's sarcasm rose above Harry's logic, Carol's mothering, Ashley's sweetness, and Katie and Travis's youthful flirtations. She only wanted to keep looking out at the beautiful green trees.

Laura.

Her daydreaming spell was broken.

Laura.

Laura shook her head. All she could see in her mind were dark inverted black eyes, the color green, and long golden hair.

CHAPTER 59

The morning passed into afternoon and along with the arrival of midday the feeling of contentment they had enjoyed started to wither away. Hunger started to fill up the emptiness of their stomachs and boredom took over their attentions. Slowly their conversations stopped and they sat in silence on the porch. The weather started to change and it got dark to their east. The wind picked up and blew more steadily. The artificial weather inside the compound had a way of changing in an unnatural way. It was like the Greys simply threw a switch and turned on a storm. A few in the group turned their faces into the wind. It felt good on their skin even though it dried out their eyes. They blinked a lot, although there wasn't any dust or dirt stirred up and flying about. There was distant thunder and as it rumbled the group's reality settled back in and took root among them. Their morning harmony rolled away with it. The containment message from the Greys had worn off. Now nobody spoke. They were trapped and something in there was killing things.

They entered back into the house and spread out in unison to check around. Laura closed the front door and breathed heavily against it. Rob stayed by the kitchen window looking outside. Harry watched by the front window in the living room and Travis and Katie kept their eyes out the side window of the living room. Carol and Ashley sat quietly on the sofa staring ahead into empty space.

Laura took a moment to block everything out of her mind and search for her inner soul again to remain steady. That was becoming her rock. Her best friend. While doing so she wondered if it had occurred to anyone that whatever was inside the compound might be in the house. Of course, she realized that everything that had happened so far was outside of the house, so it must be their safe haven and she didn't mention it. Ashley did say that she had smelled something a few nights ago. However, nothing happened from it. But what if....

"Do you really think they killed it?" Travis asked, his head turning back and forth from the window to inside. The room felt empty to him now.

"It seemed like it at the time," Harry said. "But I don't know now."

"Are you kidding?" Rob shouted from the kitchen. "No they didn't. They're lying to us."

"I agree," said Laura as she pushed off the door and walked into the living room. "They did it to us again. Like dust in the wind. Whenever it blows, we conform. Made us forget about it for a while and be docile."

Katie got a sneer on her face. "Those big-headed stick bastards! Every time we see something they pull that trick on us and make us all happy."

"It's brainwashing, man!" said Travis, pointing his fist in the air. "It's evil. I hate that crap."

"Of course, they're freaking aliens!" Carol yelled, without moving at all. She and Ashley sat motionless as if their lives depended on it.

"Calm down! Please," said Harry leaning back, his head tilted backwards. The kink in his neck stabbed him as he'd done this a lot with all their bickering. Then again, considering the situation, he knew nothing else could be expected. "Keep your eyes open. And quiet!"

Laughter came from the kitchen. To Rob, what Harry just said sounded silly. He knew they were doomed.

Travis stepped over to the front window and looked out. "Although, we did come out of it faster this time. Got our senses back."

"Back to the world," Katie said.

"They can no longer calm our fears like they could, I guess," said Laura. "I think we're getting immune to it."

"The spell has been broken," joked Katie. She felt it was the least she could do, looking into the face of growing despair, and it helped her keep her emotions calm and steady.

"That's good," said Rob from the kitchen. "No longer being their pets is what I call a good thing."

"We don't even know what we're looking for yet," said Laura. "What is it? An animal? A creature?"

"I'd say an animal," Travis said. "Something alien."

Katie nodded in agreement. "Yeah, something alien. Definitely."

"We don't know yet," said Harry. "It could be anything."

"Why don't you ask your friends, Harry?" Rob's voice soared in from the kitchen. "The friendly neighborhood Greys."

Harry ignored him again. After the last chain of events he didn't feel the Greys were the empathetic hosts that he had started to think they were. He knew the group was more like cattle to the Greys. "That's why I said to pay attention and don't blow anything off."

"But what do you think is out there?" Katie asked.

Harry shrugged. "Maybe it's something else."

"It sucked their bodies dry," said Laura. "And who or what does that?"

"Or maybe it's more than one?" said Travis. "A whole pack of something."

"No!" Ashley said. She was staring straight ahead. "It's not any of that!"

Carol slowly turned and looked at her. "What is it then, Ash? Do you know what it is?"

Ashley shook her head.

"She's a smart little girl," yelled in from the kitchen. "Probably her imagination stirring up in her mind. Kids can figure things out we can't. We have too many years screwing up our minds."

"Thank you for that, Doctor," said Laura sarcastically.

"Honey, have you seen something?" asked Carol.

Ashley shook her head and covered her ears.

The lights flickered and the power went out. They were in a dark house again. However, this time the power didn't go out in the entire compound. Thunder roared to the east and there was flashing outside. The sunlight dimmed to ominous. Another storm was coming in.

"Great, this shit again," Rob said with an angry laugh. "And I'm hungry."

Rain started to pour and everyone sat next to a window. Laura went and sat with Rob in the kitchen. Harry, Travis and Katie stayed put in the living room. Carol rested her head back and stared at the ceiling. Ashley stayed next to her mom. It was time to wait.

But not for Ashley. Inside, her young little mind was in motion. She was deeply processing the images and memories that her unconscious mind was giving to her. Ashley was remembering her big brother Kenny and she missed him. Ever since they'd been in the compound on this planet their memories had been suppressed by some invisible force. Something was keeping their memories vacant like an empty box. It held their prior lives out of reach and they couldn't reach out and cling to them yet. But slowly they started remembering their normal lives on Earth. They remembered more about their loved ones and family. Ashley had remembered with ease the nightly visits that she and Kenny had received from the Greys. She remembered the glow balls they sent to talk and play with them. However, Ashley struggled to remember anything more about her brother and that hurt her inside. That was until now. She had broken through the memory wall. And she felt his touch inside her heart for a split second. She turned to her mom next to her. "Mom, I remember Kenny."

"Yes, I miss him too, sweetie," said Carol. "And I felt he's thinking about us, too."

"How do you know, Mom?"

"Like I said," said Carol. She smiled and brushed her daughter's hair. "I felt it."

Ashley thought momentarily and looked at her mom. "Me too."

For Carol the frustration was over. No longer was she held back from the memories of her son. After that warm touch brushed her soul she could think of him again. Not just as a name but as her son. Her memories weren't complete but were deep enough and getting better fast. Whether it was Kenny peeing in his crib as a toddler, to him throwing a baseball through the living room television, Carol was bringing memories back. A voice inside her said she couldn't even be certain if the touch had been real and not a trick of her imagination, but it felt real enough to her, and she quickly pushed any doubt out of her mind. Carol was sure it came from Kenny and that he was back home thinking of them. It felt too good as it was. It felt like Kenny.

Along with that, the guilt that was swelling inside her receded too. Carol could feel like a good mother again. She knew it wasn't her fault but guilt had festered throughout her being. Each day had passed and without her being able to remember him for long the guilt increased. Often at times, she existed without knowing that she had a son, because of this place. Because of the damn Grey aliens! Now the guilt was leaving her.

Carol and Ashley sat on the sofa and shared this together. While the thunder cracked, and the lightning sliced outside in the pouring rain, they talked about Kenny. They talked about how he liked swords, water pistols, vanilla ice cream, sports, and outer space. Ashley remembered running and chasing after her brother upstairs and downstairs. She could never catch him unless he stubbed his toe. Ashley remembered their football games in the living room. These were more like tackle Ashley games because she was smaller and her brother would always smear her on the floor. Even though she didn't win and it didn't seem fair, she liked it anyway, because she was playing sports with her brother. Carol remembered putting on a monster costume and playing hide and seek with him. However, Kenny was a knight waiting to slay the beast when she did find him, which was usually in his bedroom closet, his favorite hiding place. She also remembered making him his favorite breakfast of pancakes with maple syrup on Saturdays. Her nose could almost smell it now while she and Ashley reminisced. Carol thought about how she often had to play referee between her children and negotiate who got the remote control for the television. It was Kenny for sports and Ashley for her movies. Their eyes met in the darkness of the room and they remembered the last time each saw him and they got scared. What has happened to Kenny back home?

The rest of the group had listened quietly and were touched. They wanted to meet this boy too, and to all it was a shame that this loving mother and her sweet daughter, and sister to Kenny, were trapped here like animals in this alien zoo.

The power flashed on bringing relief with it but only for a moment as it turned off again. The storm raged on outside. Surges of rain pounded the side of the house. Thunder cracked.

"Maybe in this case the angels in heaven really are bowling," Ashley said.

"Maybe so, Ash," her mother answered.

CHAPTER 60

The power failed to stay on a few more times until it finally did about an hour later. Coincidentally, the storm stopped right before the power came on. They didn't know if the two events were related or not. What they did know was they were hungry, so they heated up some meals for dinner and talked about how bored they were. What was shared in silent agreement was that they didn't talk about Greys or dead dried out bodies, although both seemed to hang over everyone's head in quiet dread.

Outside the temperature stayed at its normal seventy degrees. The dark sky cleared out and was replaced by sunlight coming in from the west. Everyone went outside at times to get some fresh air. That's when they noticed another development and that was the disappearance of the worms in the compound. After all the rain, there weren't any worms spread out in the yard. Nobody knew what happened but the group figured it had to do with the death of all the other animals and perhaps they had needed each other to survive in the compound.

By the end of dinner, the group determined the time of day to be around six o'clock in the evening, and it was decided that Harry would do his ritual and go speak to the Greys. It was his idea, and he insisted on it, thinking that it might help them. Harry said that perhaps the Greys would give him some information about what had happened to Shawn and the dead Hunter Grey. More importantly, maybe they would tell him again that they had handled the problem and eliminated the culprit, and they weren't in any danger. Secretly, this was what Harry wanted to hear. The rest weren't as optimistic as Harry, citing that the Greys hadn't communicated to them on any level since Shawn was found. All except for Laura, who kept thinking about the female alien and the sound of her own name resonating inside her head. Laura didn't speak up about it as she didn't want to volunteer this information to anyone yet.

Harry built up his courage and walked out and stood in front of the wall again. It swirled in circles and he spoke to it unsure if there were any aliens on the other side listening to him or not. He asked for information as to what had transpired. He asked what it was that had done this. He asked for help from them. He asked for weapons. He asked if they could go home.

The group was bored with today's ritual and mulled around the house. Mostly they had given up faith in this after the events of the last two days. Rob stayed in his bedroom. Carol and Ashley talked about home. Laura, Katie, and Travis kept an eye on Harry from the kitchen table. Even their attentions wandered as they couldn't hear what was being said. From their view, it was just Harry standing out in the yard holding his arms out. After a few minutes Harry turned and walked back to the house. To no surprise, not a Grey appeared.

As Harry approached the porch he looked at the three of them in the window and smiled. This sparked their interest. Harry came through the front door and into the kitchen brimming with a smile.

"They killed it," said Harry. "They told me so. See, I told you they would."

No one spoke. They exchanged glances around the table. Was this for real?

"They spoke to me out there," said Harry. "It's safe now!"

Laura studied him. He looked overjoyed, even bouncing on the balls of his feet. Harry believed this. "How do you know?"

"Like I told you, they told me."

Laura looked at Katie and Travis whose faces reflected disbelief.

"We rest in peace tonight," Harry said. He bounded up the stairs to his room and they heard the door close with a slam.

They didn't know whether to believe him or not.

"What do you think?" Travis said.

"I don't know," Katie answered. "This place sucks."

"He seemed pretty convinced."

"We all did this before," said Laura. "They plant something in our heads and we follow it. Can't resist it. Remember?"

"Yes, I do," said Katie.

"Then reality sets in after a while and we wake up out of it."

"These crazy stickmen are playing with our minds."

"So we can bank on that being a bunch of bullshit?" said Travis.

Both Laura and Katie nodded.

"But how do you know for sure? Harry's no dummy." Travis didn't want to assume. He wanted to be sure if it was still alive or not.

"He's losing it, babe," said Katie.

"Wait to see when their mind control brainwashing wears off and then see what he thinks," Laura said, pounding the table with her finger. "I think he wanted to hear something from the Greys to reassure himself so he imagined it."

"They hadn't really spoken to him before," Katie added.

"Okay, I just want to know for sure," said Travis. "But it would be totally cool if the stickmen have killed it.

Rob was listening at his door back in the hallway. "Sure," he huffed sarcastically under his breath and closed his door.

Time slipped by and their compound fell into night. The internal weather machine was malfunctioning again. Flashes of lightning were cutting through the night. They were random strikes with no set pattern. It was the second time they had seen this. The wind was holding a steady breeze which added a nice touch to the night.

Carol and Ashley went to bed and Laura, Katie, and Travis sat around the kitchen table talking about life back on Earth. There wasn't anything else to do. The house around them was quiet as if it was asleep. Each time the lightning flashed, their heads turned to look out the kitchen window to catch a glimpse of anything that might be out there, but there was nothing. They did it more on instinct, being drawn to the light, than conscious thinking. Laura kicked off her shoes and socks and slumped in her chair. It felt good to stretch out and let the open air get to her feet. Her red toenail polish had long worn off. Katie leaned on Travis's shoulder and they huddled together in silent comfort with each other. Finally, the three of them decided to retire for the day. Travis and Katie went upstairs, their laughter fading the farther they got until the door of their room closed. Laura went to turn off the kitchen light when she felt a draft of air on her feet. She looked around. The front door was slightly open.

Was the door open before? Did Harry close the door or not when he came inside? She couldn't be sure because he came in so quickly all filled up with excitement. She walked around the center fireplace wall and stared at the door. Lightning flashed outside. Laura looked around the living room and it was empty. Everyone was in their beds asleep. Her hands started to sweat. She thought Harry had closed the door because she would have noticed it open. She was a clean freak and could be anal like that. Or would she have? Slowly, Laura took a step toward the door. Then another step. Another bolt of lightning flashed outside and lit up the open doorway like a neon sign. She thought she saw Ashley on the porch. But her mom was upstairs. Laura knew she was never far from her mother so what would she be doing outside? She moved to the door and took the handle with her hand. A look at the living room windows didn't reveal anything except darkness outside. Carefully, she opened the door, standing rigid for any surprise. It was dark there too. Laura waited. Then lightning flashed to reveal nothing was there. No Ashley. Laura stepped up to the door and pressed her face to the screen.

"Ashley?" she asked. "You there?"

There was no answer. Standing in the doorway she felt the weight of the house press down on her shoulders. Silence crowded up behind her and like an invisible hand began to push her through the door. She opened the screen door and walked out onto the porch. It was very dark except for the light shining from the kitchen and living room windows that cast yellow squares down onto the porch floor and the yard. She could barely see the faint blue glow of their front wall from across the yard. The only sound was the splashing from the dragon fountain.

"Ashley?" she called again.

Lightning flashed in a zigzag pattern and the yard lit up. There might have been something to her left side. Beyond the porch. Something more than a tree. She couldn't be sure. Her mind might be playing tricks.

Laura started to walk down the porch. The door slid off her hand and vibrated with a metallic rattle when it closed. She felt the wood underneath her feet. The breeze blew through her hair and it danced along with it. She reached the end of the porch and looked out. The compound was completely dark from the night. Laura got a sense that she was standing on the edge of a giant bottomless void.

The lightning struck again in the distance and illuminated the ground briefly. Laura saw an empty yard and the trees standing beyond. No Ashley. She realized the little girl wasn't out here and it was only her standing out on the porch. Alone.

Then her nose smelled something. She jerked a little. It was that same nasty smell they had been smelling around the compound. Around everything that was dead.

The stink crawled up her nose. It was permeating from her left but she couldn't see anything around the side of the house because of the darkness. Only the window light fell on the porch behind her. Laura looked up and down trying to look through the dark but she couldn't penetrate the blackness. Lightning flashed again. Laura's head tilted slightly. She thought she saw something black on the side of the house but she wasn't sure. It could be nothing. It was probably nothing. The lightning flashed too quickly to see anything very well. Darkness was back on again and so was the rank smell. It reminded her of back home when farms are fertilized but far worse. She hated this place.

Again, lightning spread its crooked hand across the sky roof and the side of the house was cast in light. It was only for a moment but her eyes focused like binoculars. Laura did see something. She couldn't be sure of exactly what it was but thought it was like a shadow on the side of the house. It was perhaps as long as a man, didn't have any hair, and about an inch thick. She thought it looked like a manta ray or something. It wasn't moving so she couldn't determine what it was. Whatever she saw on the side of the house acted like it was stuck onto it. There hadn't been a long enough period of light to get a good view. Laura knew she would have to wait for another shot of lightning to get a better look at the shadow. But what could it be a shadow of when it's in the dark?

A few seconds ticked by. Then a few more. They felt like minutes. Laura stared at the darkness. Numbness spread up her nose as the smell grew. She waited. She had to see what it was. Their lives might depend on it. Her eyes were trained on the side of the house. A thick wall of darkness blocked her vision. Still she waited. Then another random flash of lightning interrupted the night. Her eyes opened wide. It was gone.

Laura stepped back from the end of the porch. Alarm filled her body. She looked down at her feet and saw she was standing in one of the beams of light from the kitchen window. Quickly, she looked all around her but she was okay. There was nothing on the porch except her. Laura needed to get control of her thoughts for they were scrambling around inside her head. Calmly, she focused and looked out into the yard. The night returned only blackness. She didn't know what to do. Had she really seen something on the side of the house, or was it just a trick of the night playing games on her, and she was seeing things? After a few reflective moments, she was convinced that she needed to know and slid her left foot slowly to the end of the porch. She stepped up with her right foot and peeked around the side of the house. Just then lightning blazed down into the ground and the house was exposed. Laura saw nothing there. The wall of the house was clear. But the smell wasn't. Now it was below the porch rising like smoke from a fire. Now it was underneath her.

It moved!

Panic crawled up her back. She pivoted and ran. Her running feet thumped on the wooden porch floor. She threw open the screen door, its metal creaking like a rusty gate, and bounded inside slamming closed the thick front door. Laura leaned forward, hands pressed against the door.

"What the hell?" said Rob, walking into the living room.

Laura jumped and whipped around to face him.

"What's the matter with you?" asked Rob, with a perplexed look on his face. "Freaking out or something?"

"Shut up! There's something out there," she said. "I saw it!" Laura moved into the kitchen and hunched over the table looking outside the windows.

Rob followed her. "Like what?"

"I don't know exactly. Something dark."

There were footsteps upstairs.

Rob shrugged. "That's not surprising. It's a dark place."

"Dude!" Laura lowered her voice. "Don't be an ass. I mean something dark in color. I saw it on the side of the house. It was like a shadow or something."

Rob's demeanor got serious. "Okay, I'm listening." He knew bad things were going on around them and this might be the crux of it. Rob started looking out the windows too.

Footsteps descended behind them as everyone came down the stairway. Except for Carol and Ashley, who remained at the top of the stairs, much like the first time they had all met on the first day.

Harry was first. "What's going on?" he asked.

"She thinks she saw something outside," Rob said.

"I did see something," said Laura. She looked at them briefly and then back out the windows again. "I saw it during the lightning flashes. I'm sure of it. I smelled it big time too."

Harry saw her body was poised and very tense. He believed her. "What'd you see?"

"Something black. Like a shadow."

"A shadow?" said Katie.

"Yeah, kinda reminded me of a manta ray fish like you see in the ocean. It was on the side of the house." Laura pointed east.

"A devil ray?" Travis said. "Holy shit, those things are badass looking."

"They're scary looking monsters," Ashley said from the top of the stairs.

"What'd it do?" asked Katie as she pushed past Harry at the bottom of the stairs.

"It was just attached there," Laura said looking in every direction of the porch. "Like a sucker on the wall."

"Okay, I believe you," Harry said. He didn't want her to get defensive. "But there's no light outside and the lightning is so quick. Are you absolutely sure and it's not just your eyes playing tricks?"

Everyone knew her answer from the snarling face she gave him.

"Then it wasn't there anymore," Laura said sternly. "It moved because it wasn't on the side of the house anymore. I'm not crazy and I'm not imagining things."

Lightning stabbed the ground in the front yard.

"We know that," Harry said.

Everyone agreed in silence.

"Something is preying on us," Laura said.

"What makes you think that?" asked Travis.

"Because the smell moved underneath me."

As Laura spoke an eeriness crept along with her words throughout the house and into their bodies. They knew they were alone inside the house, within this compound, isolated on a planet they didn't know at all. Nobody felt they would get any help either. Not even from their Grey captors.

"Whatever it is, it hasn't gotten inside here yet," Harry said. "Everything has happened outside."

Ashley clutched her doll to her chest.

"So that's a good thing I'd say," said Rob.

"Obviously," said Laura, with a sting to her voice.

"We need good things," Rob said, ignoring Laura. He hated this place and didn't care anymore to fire back a wise guy comment.

"But this isn't a good thing," Travis said. "A devil ray alien."

"It looked something like that," Laura said. "I don't know what it was for sure."

"We can't let it in!" Carol yelled down from top of the stairs.

"Relax!" Harry yelled. He softened his voice. "It hasn't yet."

Katie cocked her head sideways toward him. "That we know of," she said.

Harry quickly turned to her and spoke calmly. "It hasn't. Look, we're all here. Safe and sound. Remember, the fireplace is sealed and none of the windows open. We're locked up pretty tight inside. Whatever is going on is out there." He pointed to the windows.

Ashley held her doll even tighter. She was really scared. She remembered the smell in the hallway a few nights ago but didn't see anything. Was that the same thing as what Laura saw outside? Ashley didn't know what to say. Everyone was freaking out. Would they be mad at her for smelling it that night like it was her fault? Ashley didn't say anything. She would just tell her doll Molly about it in the morning.

Laura was still peeking out the windows up at the porch and beyond. "It was creepy," she said. "The way the smell seemed to crawl along."

The group spread apart quietly and checked out the windows. Seconds passed into minutes which passed into hours. They all stayed by the windows watching and waiting for anything that might come to kill them. It was suggested to turn off the lights because it left them visible and vulnerable to anyone, or anything, looking inside the house. Eventually they did turn them off but it was very late. They were very tired and everyone was nodding off to sleep. Heads could be heard softly hitting the windows, and walls, drifting in and out of sleep.

They had decided to have lookouts in shifts. Due to the pitch black nature of the night, the focus of their lookout would be on smell, or any suspicious sounds that would clue them to a break in of the house. Those that weren't awake slept on the couches in the living room as it was deemed safer for all to be within close quarters of one another than separated in each bedroom.

The night drifted on.

CHAPTER 61

Lightning's fingers crashed down all around the house. They stuck into the ground while lighting up the inside of the house with short bursts of energy. That was the only source of light for whoever was on lookout, or lying awake, and it provided about two seconds to look at the window and the surroundings of the house. Each flash shined through the windows and onto the walls inside the house like a movie projector. That made it easy for the lookout person to observe the insides of their rooms. As the early morning hours crept by there hadn't been any sightings, noises, or strange smells to announce the presence of something other than them. Laura had still been running on adrenaline so she took the first watch along with Harry. Laura was in the kitchen, Harry was in the living room, and they stared at the windows and waited. Without clocks they didn't know exactly what time it was but after a few hours they woke Carol and Rob who had agreed upon being the relief shift. Katie and Travis were to be last and remained sleeping on the living room couch. Ashley lay in slumber on the other couch where she always slept.

Rob rubbed his eyes, propped a pillow up in the middle of the living room floor, put his hands behind his head, and sat back. Getting too close to the window bothered him. He didn't want anything jumping out at him from the darkness.

Carol went to the kitchen and sat down at the table. She looked straight out the windows but was greeted by nothing except for the darkness. Carol sat staring into the night but it was all the same. Then lightning struck again. The porch lit up and she could see the main girder and the railings. The porch looked clear. She rested her head down in her hands on the table and started to contemplate. Her daughter was always her first thought. So far she was safe. No harm had come to her of any kind. Not like what happened to poor Shawn. What were they going to tell his wife and kids when they got back home? If they even got back to Earth. Carol didn't want to think about it. There was more lightning. She wondered why they didn't stop it. Would the Greys fix it in the morning? Maybe they were sleeping like they were? But they didn't have to stay on guard for anything. The Greys were in control. Carol started to think about the house and the rest of the group. They had held up good so far but their mental strength was running down. Their hope was depleting. Living beings, including an alien Grey, inside with them were dying. And strangely too, like dried prunes. Now Laura thought she saw something on the side of the house. And it had moved.

Carol sat unmoving, her eyes fixated out the windows. She yawned. Her eyelids started to get heavy, her eyes drooped, and her head sagged.

Then she started to dream.

CHAPTER 62

A small finger tapped Carol's shoulder and she jerked awake. She was looking face down at her hands on the kitchen table. Carol lifted her head. The room was very dark. So was outside. Not morning yet. She started to assemble her senses.

"Mom," whispered into her ear.

Carol looked over her shoulder and Ashley was standing there outlined in black. She couldn't see her very well but her presence enough touched Carol.

"Mom."

Carol turned in her chair. Lightning flashed and she saw her daughter's face for an instant, hair curved around in her face, but she wasn't cheerful. "Yes, dear. What's up?"

"Mom, I can't sleep. I feel weird."

"How do you mean?" Carol asked, with some concern but not overly. She figured her daughter was just unsettled by the night.

More lightning flickered outside.

"The house feels weird. This whole place feels weirder than before. And it's not because of the lollipop men. I wanna go home."

"Me too, honey. We will soon." Carol brushed her daughter's hair and leaned forward to give her a kiss.

Flashes of lightning burned the night consecutive times.

Carol was leaning forward and saw a reflection in Ashley's eyes of something dark on the kitchen window. Hairs on the back of her neck rose up as she slowly turned and looked back at the window. She couldn't see anything as blackness engulfed the room. Carol waited. Lightning flashed again. Her eyes widened and her voice caught in her throat. On the window was a black shadowy shape as long as a man. It quickly slid up the window.

Voice released from her throat and Carol screamed!

Everyone snapped awake. The kitchen light went on. Rob had also fallen asleep on his watch but he was the first in the kitchen. In a matter of seconds everyone else converged in the room. Carol was standing back by the kitchen sink. Ashley stood next to her covering her ears with her hands. Her mouth hung open in a silent scream.

"I saw it!" Carol yelled, pointing at the window. "It was there!"

All eyes looked at the window and back at Carol again.

"What did you see?" asked Travis.

"It! Some sort of black thing."

"See!" said Laura, her hands resting on her hips. "I told you all."

"Inside or outside?" Rob asked.

"Outside!" Carol said. She was having trouble calming down.

"Thank God!" Katie said. She couldn't stop staring at the window.

"Just checking," said Rob. That settled his nerves a little that at least it hadn't gotten in the house yet.

Harry was taking it all in. "What did you see exactly?"

Carol looked dead at him. "It was like a shadow or something. As big as a man. And it was fast. It darted upwards."

"Did you notice anything distinguishable about it? Like eyes, arms, wings, fur, or scales? Anything at all?"

"No." Carol shook her head. "Just dark and weird. Like I said it was a dark shape or something. It moved so fast it was like it was never there."

"What?" said Travis. "That's even weirder."

"But I saw it. It's real." She looked at Laura.

"Sounds like you got a better look at it than I did," Laura said.

Harry looked down at Ashley. Her mouth had closed and she took her hands away from her ears. He noticed she looked pretty freaked out. "Did you see it, Ashley?"

She looked up at him. "Yes. For a second and it was gone. I don't like it."

Harry decided there wasn't any need to ask her any more questions. There was something inside the compound with them and it was outside the house and nobody would dare go outside tonight anyway. However, on the positive side now they were starting to get an idea of what it looked like. They needed to make certain of a few things first. "Has anyone opened or seen any open windows in the house?"

Each said no.

"Good," Harry continued. "The house has always been sealed up since we've been here. Can anyone think of any other way that it could get inside other than the front door?"

"I found the front door slightly open earlier tonight," said Laura. "That's how I ended up going outside in the first place. Harry, you might not have shut it all the way when you came in excited about your ritual. We'll have to make sure the door is always closed from now on."

"Good point," said Harry feeling guilty. "Sorry, that might have been my fault. Are there any other ways something could get in?"

There was a moment of silence.

"The fireplace is fake but I'll double check it," said Laura as she whipped around into the living room. "It's closed."

"Good. Anything else?" Harry asked.

"Our garbage disposal under the sink," said Laura. Carol moved to the side and Laura opened the cabinet under the sink. She pulled the small hatch cover over the garbage hole and tightened it up.

"Okay," said Harry. "Is there anything else?"

Again, the group answered no.

"So there's no way that we know of that this shadow thing can get in the house? Are we in agreement?"

Everyone agreed.

There was a flash seen through the kitchen window but it was unlike lightning. This came from the watery front wall. The group looked out the windows but were careful not to get their faces too close to the glass. The wall peeled open and two Greys walked through and into the compound.

"More lollipop men," whispered Ashley.

"I wonder what they're doing," Rob said.

"Maybe they're hunters?" Travis said.

"Maybe...." said Katie.

The Greys split up and went in different directions. One to the left side of the house and the other to the right side. Behind them the doorway opening sealed back up and it was dark again. The two Greys couldn't be seen.

"I think we should turn on all the lights in the house," Carol suggested. She also realized the aliens must not have been sleeping on them after all.

After another quiet moment Laura spoke for everyone. "Sounds like a good idea."

The group turned on all the lights in the house. That provided a comforting feeling that pushed the eeriness of the dark night out of the house and away from them. They huddled together in the living room with a newly found, albeit shaky, strength and confidence that in the light they were safe.

Still nobody dared to go upstairs to sleep.

CHAPTER 63

The Greys moved into position. One went west to the left of the house and hid under a tree. The other walked east to the right of the house and moved within the wall of trees before the start of the hill.

Both waited.

They traded a few telepathic messages but did so sparingly. Their focus was on the immediate surrounding environment of the house, the humans inside, the trees, and the target. The sun they created for the compound would eventually rise in the east. Until then there was only the light protruding from the house as the humans inside had turned all of them on, but the house light wasn't enough to reach the hunter aliens in their hiding positions, and they would have to rely on their own skills and instincts. Their dark thick eyes provided them with exceptional vision in the dark. Unpredictable lightning crashed around the compound and was a big concern for the two Greys. However, they had to hold their ground. It was inside here somewhere.

Time wasn't recognizable. The Hunter Greys didn't move and were poised to attack. The wind blew occasionally and the leaves above and around them rustled. Still they stayed true to their mission. To kill the intruder.

Later in the early morning hours the Grey to the west saw movement to his right. He turned in surprise to see his partner Grey walking across the front yard towards him. There hadn't been any telepathic communication from his partner that he was breaking from the planned assignment. This wasn't procedure. A horrible smell started to drift down from above him and the Grey's reasoning started to scramble. It seemed his partner walked right up to him. In a downward swipe the Grey was gone.

The Grey to the east held his position under the tree. He didn't know his partner's status for they hadn't thought any communication for a time. Nothing had moved. No sounds had been heard. Then to his left side his partner Grey came walking toward him. He sent a questioning thought but didn't get an answer. Then something rancid violated the Grey's senses. His mind twisted. His partner was almost to him. The smell dropped from above. The Grey fell to the ground under it.

CHAPTER 64

Laura's eyes opened to the sight of Rob's sneakers inches away from her nose. If he suddenly jerked or rolled she might be kicked in the face. She was lying on the floor so she sat up to scan the room. Immediately, she felt the kink in her neck from falling asleep in a funny position. Her mind was still foggy and not yet alert but she did start to focus. Everyone was sleeping in the living room. Harry was snoring under the front window leaning up against the wall. Katie was sleeping next to Travis on one couch. Carol and Ashley were on the other couch. Rob was lying on his side asleep snoring in the middle of the floor. All the lights were on in the house that she could see. It was day outside. The fake sun was starting to look more contrived to Laura each day. She didn't know what time of day it might be but it felt later in the morning than usual. Laura's body had the same feeling she got when she slept in the next morning after working the late shift back home. Slowly, Laura stood up.

Rob started to stir. He looked up at her with big bright eyes. Then he leaned up on his elbows and looked around the room. It reminded Laura of how they met there the first day. Rob looked back at Laura and started to speak but she put her finger to her lips to quiet him. Then she gestured to the others in a sign of good faith to let them sleep.

The morning pains shot up their stomachs. Simultaneously their bodies flinched in quick pain. Each of them knew the cure. Laura turned and walked into the kitchen and Rob got up and followed after her. Both poured themselves glasses of water and began to drink.

Laura looked Rob square in the eyes and quietly asked, "So what do you think would happen if we didn't drink this?"

"I think it'd be worse," he answered.

"Would we die?"

Rob answered by returning her look back to her eyes.

They finished their glasses and put them down on the table. In the living room, they heard Harry snort and come awake. He looked befuddled and needed a minute to gain his senses. Consciousness seemed to spread throughout the room as the group on the couches came to life. A very thirsty Ashley bounced off a pillow and hopped into the kitchen. She quickly returned with a glass of water for her and her mother. Carol stretched but sat staring around the room not feeling like getting up yet. Katie and Travis kissed and joked with each other about who had the worse morning breath. Together they went into the kitchen and got some of the strange water from the fridge.

After carefully checking outside, Laura and Rob walked out onto the porch. The screen door closed and rattled. The air felt good deep down in their lungs. The pains in their stomachs had gone away which made this morning much more tolerable. Laura noticed that Rob wasn't being his usual wise-ass self. He was resting against the porch looking down at the ground. To her, he almost looked defeated. Hope wasn't exactly swelling through her veins either.

"The sun inside the compound isn't as far to the left as it would be in early morning," said Laura. "I'd say it must be midmorning."

"Yeah," Rob agreed. "Guess everyone slept longer due to the eventful night."

"I saw it. Whatever it is."

"I believe you," said Rob. "There's something in here. And Carol and the little girl saw it as well. It was like a coming out party."

"I'm afraid it was more like a wake."

Rob looked over his shoulder at her. "Like a shadow?"

"Yes," Laura nodded.

He looked back to the ground. "Can't see it in the dark then."

The screen door opened and Travis and Katie joined them on the porch. Both were smiling. Laura thought about how they enjoyed each other's company and that their relationship had remained pure while they'd been there.

Their smiles disappeared.

Laura followed their eyes to the row of trees on the right side of the house. She tapped Rob on the arm and pointed. He looked and saw lying on the ground between two trees a black and grey body. It was a Hunter Grey. The corpse's arms and legs were stretched out stiff. Surrounding it were the dominate Yellow and Red Greys and eight smaller Greys. The worker Greys stood waiting for their commands.

"Oh, God," Rob said. He stood up straight. "That must be one from last night."

"Where's the other one?" asked Laura. "Weren't there two?"

"I think so," Rob answered. "I bet the other one is toast, too."

The Yellow and Red were facing each other and presumably were in a discussion with their mind communication. Everyone on the porch felt it must have been a highly charged argument as their heads started to hurt. Laura, Rob, Travis, and Katie all grabbed their foreheads. Their faces looked bent from the pain of their headaches. The intense clash between the alien minds was sending out painful brain waves that reached as far away as the house and they were catching the consequences. Invisible pins and needles poked their brains and then finished with a sliding, ripping feeling underneath their skulls. At that point they relaxed as the pain diminished and was gone as quickly as it had settled into their heads. The Yellow and Red stopped their alien discussion and appeared to have come to a decision. However, to the group on the porch a feeling reverberated within them that it was a dubious decision at best and that the Greys were confused and unable to get control of what was killing in the darkness. A fact made the more poignant by another dead Grey.

The Greys turned and instead of going back to the front wall started to walk across the front yard but kept a good distance from the house.

Six of the worker Greys followed along with them in a different formation of two in front, two flank on the sides, and two in back. The Yellow and Red walked in the middle looking like generals surveying the land. Their green manes glistened in the fake sunlight. Behind them to the right of the house the dead Grey rose into the air in the usual procession and floated to the front wall. One worker Grey was in front of the body and the other behind.

On the porch, their senses came back to them all. Their heads cleared of pain as if it never happened. Laura was surprised that she or Rob hadn't seen them when they came outside but their minds had been absorbed with the unrest of the night before. Their thoughts and attention had been taken over by fear, despair, darkness, and the shadow. This morning something new was added to their thoughts and that was another dead Grey.

"God, what was that?" Katie said, shaking her head. "My head started to feel like it was going to cave in like a pop can."

"Mine too, babe," said Travis.

Just then the front door opened and out walked Harry, Carol, and Ashley.

"Holy crap!" said Harry. "Did you guys feel that?"

Everyone nodded.

"What the hell was that?" Harry continued. He looked up and saw all the alien activity out in the yard. "Was that from them?"

"Must have been some mind x-rays or something from the two Master Greys," Laura said. "They seemed to be having an argument. It was pretty intense."

"Yeah, or if we're lucky it was only radiation," Rob said sarcastically.

"Talk about a migraine on steroids," Harry said. He grabbed his head.

"I thought my head was gonna burst," said Ashley. Laura gave her a sad look in return.

"They're monsters," said Carol emotionless.

"Then it stopped," said Harry.

"They quit their spat," Laura said.

"If that's what it was," said Travis. "Kinda looked like they were extremely frustrated, to say the least, and they were letting it rip."

"Like alien road rage," said Katie.

"What was...." Harry stopped as he saw the floating body of the Grey. "Another dead one. Weren't there two last night that we saw?"

"Yeah, that one was dead over there," said Laura, pointing to the where the body had lain. "We didn't notice them right away but they were over there checking it out when we came out on the porch."

"Where's the other one?" asked Harry, his eyes darting back and forth from them to the Greys.

"We were wondering that ourselves," said Rob.

The watery wall opened and the floating dead Grey, along with the two worker Greys, went through it to the other side. Again, waiting there was the Female. She was dressed in green and looking radiant like a goddess. The wall closed.

They watched the Greys arrive at the wooded area on the left and move behind the first row of trees. The Greys disappeared momentarily but then reappeared almost parallel to the porch. They continued in a northern direction and disappeared around the side of the house. The group scrambled down to the side of the porch to watch. Then they saw it. Another Hunter Grey lay across from the back of the house at the base of the first line of trees. It was recognizable with its bodily limbs sticking upwards and a hollowed-out look. They knew what had happened to it. The same as the rest.

From the porch, the Greys could be seen passing between the trees. They moved with a grace about them that made them look like they were walking on water. They moved north and came out from behind the trees and stopped at the body. Again, there appeared to be a discussion but not as heated as the last one. The smaller worker Greys moved into their regular position around the body and waited. The Yellow and Red looked around the land and up in the trees. Clearly, they were looking for something.

"This isn't good," said Travis. "They can't control it."

"Yeah, sure looks that way," said Rob. "And they look clueless about it, too."

"That's three of their Hunter Greys they've put inside here to kill this thing and they've all been killed."

"They're not hitting a good average right now," said Katie.

"I don't think they've encountered this kind of thing before," Laura added.

After a minute, they stopped and seemed in agreement that whatever they were looking for wasn't there. Nobody could tell for sure but they could only guess based on what they witnessed. The body of the dead Grey raised up and quickly in unison they started to march back towards the house and the watery wall.

"Fuck this!" Rob yelled as he flung himself off the porch and charged the Greys. This shocked everyone. He ran at full speed. "Hey! What are you gonna do about this?"

Rob didn't get far. The Red Grey looked at Rob and his body froze suspended in air. He looked like an Olympic hurdler caught in a picture. The Red's fury was felt on the porch in a heated wave of anger that emotionally ignited their brains. The six of them fell backwards grabbing their heads. The Greys continued to walk on without a care in the world. Rob hung in the air caught in the grip of some unseen force. His brain and his bones hurt. The group laid on their backs and rolled onto their sides from the trauma attacking their heads. The alien procession walked past the house at a slow pace to the front wall of the compound. There, without looking back, the Red released Rob from his trap and he fell to the ground. Relief filled his body as pain left him and in its place he was refilled with the joy of returning to normal. Instantly, the group on the porch recovered. The intense hurt in their heads quickly went down to throbbing and then vanished as if it never had been felt.

Everyone on the porch started to stand up. Laura was the first to look at Rob. He was on his knees breathing heavily watching the Greys. He wore hatred on his face.

Each was feeling very rattled. Carol grabbed Ashley and hugged her. Katie and Travis hugged as well. Harry sat down again and leaned on the porch railing. His body ached with the feeling like it'd been run over by a freight train. Laura sat slumped on the side railing and watched the Greys. She asked herself when is this ever going to end?

The wall flashed and peeled back an opening which the Greys went through. If hatred could be drilled from Rob into the back of the Master Greys' heads it surely would be. It was still unknown to the group what was on the other side of the wall.

The Greys disappeared but the Female reappeared and stepped into the opening. In the minds of the group, something had changed. Now they felt dazzled looking at her. There was something different about her. Something not so alien. In a way, she had feminine features. Her blonde hair was special. It glowed with light and attractiveness. Yet, she was a Grey. She had a stick-thin skinny body and large oversized head with those big black emotionless eyes. A Grey.

Laura stared directly at her through the window of the wall. Its water spun and whirled in circles around the doorway which gave the Female the look of being in a time warp. Laura thought the green dress that she wore was pretty and how she would like to have one. She could wear it out on the town on dates and be the most enigmatic woman in any room she was in. The golden star on the dress was an absolute eye catcher. Then Laura realized she was looking at her.

Laura.

She flinched.

Be brave.

The wall's entrance sealed up and gone was the Female behind the waving water. Laura sat still on the porch railing but her inner self was flowing with activity. She knew the Grey was speaking to her but she wondered why. She was just a human being trapped for show inside this place and didn't have any relative importance. Laura also thought it was amazing how the words just appeared in her head. However, it wasn't a word, or the English language, for that matter. She didn't receive it verbally or watch it as the written word with her eyes. It was more of a feeling. A feeling that happened inside her mind. She was sure the Female had communicated with her the day before and today's occurrence made it the second day in a row in which this had happened. Laura thought nobody else had received any communication from the Female. One of her companions could have received a communication but Laura didn't feel that was true. The Female was singling her out. Again, this brought her back to the question of for what purpose?

"Everybody okay?" asked Harry. He stood up and stretched to try to get the aches out. He was answered with some mumbling and grunts.

"Holy shit, what is that?" Katie said. "Some sort of sonic boom to our brains or something? That was worse than the time before."

"That might have been a warning to not let it happen again," said Travis. He was rubbing Katie's back and trying to get himself refocused.

"What do you mean?" Carol asked. "We didn't do anything. He did." She pointed at Rob.

"Exactly," said Travis.

"Speaking of which, we should check and see if he's okay," said Laura. She swung off the porch and down into the yard. First she made a quick glance over her shoulder to the side of the house where she saw the shadow the night before. There was nothing there. Not even a stain. Just a white wall. She turned and walked over to Rob.

Everyone either hopped off the porch or trotted down the porch stairs and followed her out into the yard and gathered around Rob who was standing now. He looked at everyone.

"Those bastards," said Rob.

"Yeah, they aren't the welcome wagon for sure," said Laura.

"Hey, why'd you do that?" Katie asked. She sounded pissed. "That was stupid, man. You know that won't do any good."

"Dude, don't do that again!" Travis added. He sounded more pissed. "Now they're taking it out on us with their mind-probe thing."

Rob glared back at them. "Cause I'm fed up and we need to do something. We're sitting ducks inside here. And those ugly pieces of shit aren't doing anything about it. They can't even protect their own."

A slow breeze drifted past their feet in a soothing motion.

"All right, all right," said Harry. "Here we go again, fighting among ourselves."

"Are you okay?" Laura asked. She was hoping to change the subject and diffuse the situation. "It sure didn't look okay."

Rob nodded. "I got stuck in what felt like an invisible iron hand. They sure have power. But weird, I feel okay now."

"They fried our brains for that," Katie said, not sounding as pissed as before.

"Yeah, dude," said Travis. "I thought my head had been sawed off."

"Rob," Harry said. "We can't have that happen again. Need to stick together on this."

"Don't worry about it now," said Rob, fussing with his clothes. "I see Goldilocks made her return appearance again. She always seems to be hanging out, doesn't she? Always behind that glass waiting for them."

Laura nodded but didn't say anything more. She wasn't going to tell anyone yet about the mind messages. *Be brave* she'd said. Laura knew every ounce of courage she could get would be needed.

"I wonder if she's like a mother or something," Travis said. "Or a nurse."

"I don't think she's a bad alien," Ashley said, her innocent voice sent a calming feeling over the group. She had been very quiet for the last couple days other than talking with her mom and her doll. Her pure voice was refreshing to their souls. "Not like the bad lollipop men that don't care about us."

The wind tapped their attention and started to pick up more and sift through the trees. Everyone had been so focused on the Greys that nobody realized how stale the compound environment had become. Their inside sun was moving along at its normal pace and now shined down on them from an eastern position that would put the time of day at late morning. With the group gathered around in a semicircle, Rob was facing back at them, and he was in a position to see the west side of the compound. He saw that it was getting dark over there.

"Crap, looks like more bizarre weather is on the way," Rob said.

Everyone turned and saw the sky was turning a grayish color mixed with lines of black. A few trees rustled in the wind but there didn't seem to be anything out of order other than the sky. However, where they stood it was basking in sunlight. The humanoid shapes of their bodies were cast in long stretching shadows on the strangely green-colored grass of their home.

"Anyway, they can't control the weather very well but they can control us," Rob sneered.

"Did you all notice something?" Harry asked, his thin hair dancing in the breeze. "When the Greys were in the compound they didn't seem too scared. Like they don't think whatever it is, this shadow thing, is likely to attack them. Sure, it looked like the Greys in control had the worker Greys around them for protection, but could it be they know something we don't? Like this thing only strikes at night?"

"Or in the dark?" Laura said.

"Exactly," Harry said. He looked right at her and their eyes met sharing the same thought.

"Could be," said Laura.

"So you're saying they know they're safe inside here when it's light out?" said Katie.

"Yes," answered Harry. "I think to an extent. They still have those worker Greys surrounding them just in case."

"Yeah, but they aren't the fighters," said Travis. "They aren't the muscle."

"But they're still there to take the attack in case it would happen," said Harry. "They're the victims."

"The sacrificial lambs," Katie said.

"Good planning on their part," said Laura.

"They're monsters and we're gonna die for it," said Carol.

"You'd think the Master Greys could defend themselves though," Laura said. "They seem real powerful. Heck, we've seen that."

"Perhaps, but they don't want to take a chance and get ambushed," said Harry.

"And that is what might have happened to the three dead Greys," Laura said.

"Yeah, but those Greys are like the badass ones," said Travis. "Assassins sent in to hunt it and they got hunted themselves. Holy shit!"

There was a distant rumble of thunder from the west.

"Look!" said Ashley. She pointed behind Rob.

All eyes followed the direction of her finger to where the body of the dead Grey had laid. The same dead Grey lay there again. Motionless.

CHAPTER 65

"What the heck?" said Rob turning around. "Does everyone see that?"

Everyone muttered an agreement but nobody moved as they just stared in surprise. No one knew what to do.

"Why is that there?" asked Travis.

The rustling of the trees in the wind was his answer as nobody spoke.

"What are we supposed to do?" Travis asked.

Thunder crackled in the distant west of the compound.

"There's only one way to find out," Rob spoke up and started to walk towards it. As he did everyone followed behind him and they shared a common feeling of growing nervousness that this wasn't a smart thing to do. The feeling grew more intense the closer they got to the body. The body dressed in black. The body that while in life must have possessed deadly killing skills that a Grey alien would have. That an assassin alien would have. Yet in death this hunter alien was the same as everything else that passed on and no longer lived. Helpless. Lifeless.

The group surrounded the body. After a moment of watching the motionless Grey, Rob stepped forward and kicked at the body. No thud of a body sounded as his foot passed through it like air and he fell back losing his balance momentarily. Rob steadied himself and looked at the surprised faces around him. He stepped up next to the body again. Looking down at it, the body was solid, and he couldn't see the grassy ground underneath. Rob's knee bent back to take another swipe.

It disappeared.

"Holy shit!" Rob yelled.

A collective gasp was made from the group.

"Did you see that?" said Travis. "It's gone!"

"That's not good," said Laura. She started to look around.

"Where'd it go?" Katie asked. "How can it do that?"

"I don't know but it did," said Harry.

"That's just not good," Laura said, but it was more to herself than to anyone else. She was shaking her head.

"Mommy." Ashley looked up at her mom. "Where'd the dead alien go?"

Carol looked down at her daughter. Ashley saw hate crawling over her mother's face. "Probably to hell."

Rob carefully patted his foot around where the body had been. "Nothing here but grass."

"Was it a hallucination?" Katie asked. "Like a mirage or something."

"I guess," said Travis.

Then their noses burned. The smell crept in as if on quiet feet as it rose from the ground and crawled around them. It felt thicker this time.

"That's the smell from the side of the house," said Laura.

"Yeah, and all the dead bodies had it," said Katie.

"You know, the same exact smell came off the black stain that Shawn and I found out there," Rob said as he pointed his finger over to the east.

"Look around," Harry said. "Does anyone see anything?"

Everyone glanced around but there were only trees, grass, and a house to see. The only things that moved were their shadows when they touched and swayed together on the grass when the trees moved in the wind. Nothing else seemed out of place. No one answered Harry's question. Laura was watching Rob who was still standing in the center where the body had been. He sniffed the air for a long time, grimacing as the putridity entered his lungs. She watched his eyes open wide and roll to her right side and focus on Harry. Rob sniffed some more and his head tilted that direction a little. Harry was looking back at him curiously. The educated teacher didn't know what he was sniffing at him for. Neither did the rest of the group as they settled down again and watched Rob watch Harry. Then Harry asked, "What is it?"

"I think the smell is strongest from you," said Rob.

"What?" Harry said. He felt insulted. "What are you talking about? It's all around here."

"It's over by you the most," said Rob.

"Me?" Harry sniffed his arms and shoulders and turned around behind him. He smelled the open air as if something was rising from the ground at his feet. "It smells … close."

Travis stepped over by Harry. He took a whiff of the air and backed away. "Yeah, it's strong around you, man."

"Eww, now it's by you, honey," Katie said, her face wrinkled. "And you don't smell like honey."

Travis turned swiftly around to her. There was surprise mixed with concern written on his face. "What do you mean?"

"I mean just that." Katie leaned forward and recoiled instantly. "I smell it on you more intensely now. Can't you tell?"

"No!" said Travis. He was getting angry.

Laura was watching all of this happen. She saw how in a moment of panic everything among the reasonably tight knit group could break down. And how it would keep breaking down. Things had started down that path.

Harry was looking at Travis with relief as he was glad it wasn't him anymore. Travis and Katie looked at each other in a silent standoff. Rob stepped over next to Travis. He took a big suck of air up through his nostrils. Then he leaned over near Harry and breathed deeply. Then back to Travis and looked him in the eye. The smell from Travis was the same monster that was with Harry. But now it was attached to Travis.

"What? What?" Travis said, his body jerked with agitation and he stepped back. "You don't think it's me, do you?"

"No, honey," said Katie. She had to calm him down. She stepped forward to him and touched his face in a reassuring way. "We just noticed it was strong around you now."

Travis looked deep into her eyes and relaxed.

"Yeah, man. It's cool," said Rob. "Just relax."

Travis shot him a look. "You relax, man! We're gonna die here."

Katie squeezed Travis's arm and he looked at her. She wanted to get him refocused and not directing his anger towards Rob. Through her hand she felt his arm muscles soften and she stepped back and gave him a smile. However, she didn't see her boyfriend return the smile. Worry was on his face. Her head turned cockeyed in question and now Travis moved closer and smelled her. He withdrew as if in pain. Travis sniffed himself doing a comparison test. He looked at his girlfriend. Then he smiled as to not alarm her and spoke. "Honey, I don't want you to be alarmed but now you smell like I did."

Katie looked down at herself. She looked at her arms, her legs, at her feet, and at the ground around her. Her hands ran through her hair like she was giving herself a shampoo. There was nothing. Only that penetrating sickly smell that was now emanating from her. It made her nauseated. And scared.

She looked up at Travis, turned to Rob, over to Harry, back around at Laura, Carol and Ashley. She opened up her hands and asked, "Why me?"

"Why anyone?" Rob answered blankly. By now he didn't care anymore and felt everyone should be ready for the worse. The only thing he felt was the need to survive. "We're all getting a dose of it."

"This place is hell!" Carol said.

"What's going on? Make it stop!" said little Ashley. Her mom gripped her shoulders with a hard squeeze. She and her mom were watching from the side. For Ashley, this was a nightmare. She recognized the smell. A smell she knew had been in the house nights before. A smell that kept coming for them. All her new friends were in danger, an alien dead body disappeared, and the mysterious rancid smell was moving from person to person in their direction. Her young eyes could see the panic hatch in each person when the smell latched onto them. Her young ears could hear their fear. Her mind knew that nothing could protect them. Not even her mom.

A strong breeze blew through the compound and wrestled the trees out of their laziness. The leaves chattered high above the group in what sounded like a conversation in their own language, and the shadows on the ground danced around underneath the seven of them before returning to their resting places hiding from the midday sun.

Katie went relaxed. The fear was gone as she didn't feel the smell on her now. The relief on her face was reflected back by Travis who smiled at her. His girlfriend was normal again. Rob slowly stepped forward, watched her carefully, and smelled her. Katie looked at him harshly. "Stop smelling me!"

"Just checking," Rob said.

Travis shoved him. "Hey man, back off!"

Rob fell back but caught his balance quickly. He shrugged his shoulders around to simulate shaking it off. Rob didn't care.

Laura felt it rise from behind. The smell was on her back. Slowly, she turned around but didn't see anything. The smell ripped her nose. It was atrocious and made her stomach sick. Laura glanced at Carol and Ashley and they saw her horror. Her hands started to shake. "It's on me now."

Rob, Katie, and Travis turned to her, their own hostilities forgotten.

"It's on me," said Laura. "I don't know what to do."

"There's nothing on you," Rob said. "I can't see anything on any of you."

"But it's here, I smell it," said Laura. She was starting to unravel a little bit. "It's on me." The same encounter she had in the darkness the night before was happening all over again. And she felt it touching her.

"Stand still," Rob said. He took a few steps towards her and peeked around at her back. She was standing straight as if on a high wire act. Rob didn't see anything there but his nose burned from the smell. He grimaced and started to cough.

"What?" Laura said, as she turned her back to him. "What do you see?"

Rob stopped coughing and cleared his singeing throat. He felt thirst start to build up inside him. "Nothing." Rob coughed again. "That's just it. There's nothing on your back."

Another breeze shot along suddenly and trees tossed around and shadows on the ground stirred about in menacing shapes all over the yard.

"What is it...." said Laura, but the panic in her voice switched off. She looked at Rob and breathed in. "Now you have it."

Rob heard the words but they mixed in with the rising stink that now surrounded him. He looked on each side of him even though he knew there wouldn't be anything to see. Rob took in the open air, and as with the others, it was coming from behind him. Slowly, with his head looking over his shoulder, he turned around in a circle. The smell was there. It was next to him. "I don't see a thing but it's here. How do I get rid of it?"

Harry had been standing back shocked by what he'd been watching. An invisible terrible odor was passing from person to person and they didn't know what it was or how it was doing it. "Whatever it is, this smell, it's moving among us. It's gone from each one of us except for Carol and Ashley."

"It's like it's stalking us," said Katie.

"Yeah, but like how can a rank smell stalk people?" Travis said. "It's an odor, man!"

"Yeah, yeah, but what about me?" asked Rob. "I've still got it. Get rid of it!"

Nobody knew what to say next. They didn't know how. They didn't even know what it was. They couldn't see anything. There was nothing to grab and pull or throw off him.

"Maybe it's a figment of our imagination," Katie suggested. "Like mass hysteria from this place."

"Are you kidding me?" Rob said to her with a nasty glare. "Does your nose smell hysterical?"

"I don't know then!" Katie yelled back. "But it's not getting any better!"

Carol and Ashley were abhorred watching from the side of the group. The putrid smell was attaching itself like a leech to them and causing confusion and fear. It was making its way down the line in their direction. Carol couldn't let it get to her or her daughter. Ashley felt so freaked out that her young mind quit thinking and went into shut down. Carol slowly took a step back, as she didn't want to bring on any attention from the group, or the smell, and she pulled Ashley with her.

"It stinks!" Rob yelled. He started to walk around grabbing at his back and arms as if trying to pull something off him. To the rest it looked like he was pulling an invisible blanket or coat off but couldn't quite get it. Rob was getting more frustrated as he turned in circles. Everyone backed away from him when he stepped in their direction like he was contagious. "Shit! Shit! Shit!"

Carol and Ashley were meticulous in their retreat, slowly inching away step by step, and remaining almost anonymous over to the side. They backed up under a shaded tree.

Turning wildly in disarray Rob lost his balance and slammed into Harry, whose foot planted into the ground and he buckled over, and they fell down together amidst screams of anger. Harry sat up and kicked out at Rob who rolled on the ground out of his reach and sat up on his knees looking confused. What his face didn't reveal anymore was panic or anger. He sniffed himself and looked up. "Hey, I think it's gone."

"No, it's not."

Everyone looked at Harry.

"It's on me again," Harry said, his face decayed to looking grim.

"What the hell is going on?" Laura said.

Under the tree Carol and Ashley's noses sensed something. It was coming.

Harry stood up. Everyone moved away from him like he was infected with a plague.

"What?" Harry said. "You act like I'm a disease. It's not my fault!" Harry took a step toward them but they all stepped back. Harry got angrier. "It was on you all too. You all had it! Don't treat me this way. I don't deserve this after everything I've done for you."

"What are you talking about?" Travis said. He pulled Katie around behind him. "What did you do?"

Harry took another step forward, this time toward Travis. "I'm the one that talks to the Greys. I'm the one that got us food and clothing. My ritual did that."

"Why don't you all just chill out!" said Laura. "Harry, stay where you are."

Harry gave her a desperate look. "I don't know what's happening but the smell is killing me and it's not my fault. I want it off." Harry took another step.

"Don't move Harry!" yelled Rob. "Nobody else wants it."

In the next second, Harry's only thought was that he didn't want to be the victim and to give it away from him to someone else. "Neither do I!" He lunged at Rob but missed as Rob jumped around to the other side and started to hop looking like a boxer. Laura, Travis, and Katie moved away into the backyard. Harry turned around and faced them. His back was to the house and frustration was boiling up inside him. He smelled himself again. When finished, he fell to his knees and started to dry heave.

Laura watched Harry with a mixture of fear and sadness. Fear of what was mysteriously among them and how powerless they were to stop it. Her sadness came from watching a very intelligent man, who was thorough and good at analyzing their situation, and coming to conclusions as to how they should try to solve their problems, struggle like this. She also felt fear and sadness because they had no control or power inside the compound and were basically at the mercy of their captors the Greys.

Careful Laura.

Laura froze. The voice again....

The growing storm in the west rumbled louder and lightning started to flash. The wind picked up a faster speed and started to blow in from a westerly direction.

The darkness of the shadows moved in a silent wave across Carol's back. Then the smell slithered behind Ashley. It grew and flowed into their noses. Although it was different this time. First it was rotten decay as it drifted up and touched their senses. Ashley pinched her nose closed. However, then it seemed to peel open and it had a syrupy bite to it. Carol felt dizzy for a moment and caught her balance before she fell. Ashley's face was in a scowl and didn't notice her mom. Ashley was still like a statue. Carol regained herself, cleared her head, and started to think about escaping. Then the sweet flavor rolled over and up came the putrid underbelly smell that had plagued them for days. It shot a bolt of nausea throughout their bodies. Carol turned around like the others had done but there was nothing except for the stench. She glanced at Ashley who looked up at her but wasn't moving. Carol turned around and watched the other companions. Her ears quit listening so she couldn't hear what they were saying but her eyes saw them in a silent contest with Harry. Carol felt surrounded. It was in front of them tormenting their companions and now it was behind them. What she didn't know was how it was in two places at one time.

Ashley broke free and ran towards the house.

"No!" yelled Carol, and she ran after her.

Everyone except Harry, who remained hunched over, waiting to jump on someone, saw Ashley dash through the backyard. They watched her run around the deck towards the west side with her mother struggling to follow her. In the background behind the running girl were dark clouds rolling up and flashes coming their way.

"Ashley, stop!" Carol yelled.

Ashley may or may not have heard her mother. Her little legs were running as fast as they could away from the bad stuff. She was scared and wanted safety. And that meant inside the house. Closer and closer the safety of the house came to her. From behind she heard her mom's cries for her. The shouts weren't getting farther away so she knew her mom was chasing after her. Ashley felt she was right on her heels just like running in the yard back home. She heard the rumbling thunder of the coming storm. The lightning flashed its dance but that's not what scared her. What scared little Ashley was back there among the trees with the rest of them, and she was getting away. Faster and faster her feet hit the ground. Ashley was almost home. Except as she turned the corner around the side of the house her nose told her something that she didn't want to believe. The smell was with her.

CHAPTER 66

Harry saw his chance to get rid of this thing and he pounced. Blaming Rob for the smell's attachment onto him and moving with surprising strength, he tackled Rob. Down they went in a heap and Harry ended up on top of a surprised Rob. Harry tried to stand up to run but Rob grabbed his shirt and pulled him back down to him.

Laura, Travis, and Katie turned around and watched with shock as the two scuffled and swore at each other. Laura couldn't believe what was happening. For all they had endured the group had remained tight and in control. Now they were crumbling by the minute.

Harry started swinging his fists. Using both legs, Rob kicked him off. Harry landed with a thud a few feet away. Rob got up and stared at Harry. His body was enraged, half in shock, the other half in anger.

"Let's get outta here," said Travis. He turned, nudged Katie in his direction, and they ran toward the house.

Laura didn't know what to do. The two guys were fighting. Now Travis and Katie left her. That smell was somewhere lurking around. Her head felt like it was spinning back and forth. Laura turned and on her athletic legs sprinted through the yard and she caught up to Travis and Katie as they rounded the side of the house.

Carol was standing near the front of the house holding Ashley by the arms and scolding her for running off. Ashley was crying.

"But it won't go away, Mom," said Ashley.

"Yes, it will, Ashley." Carol wanted to calm her down but she didn't know what to say. "We gotta stick together."

Laura, Travis, and Katie approached them cautiously and stopped a few feet away.

"Why'd she take off?" asked Travis, directing his question at the mom.

Carol looked up at him with an unbalanced glare in her eyes. She looked like two people in one body. It gave Travis the chills. "She did because the smell came up behind us. It's on her now!"

"Behind you?" said Katie.

"Yes! Can't you smell it?"

The three of them smelled the air. Laura's nose was stabbed with the rancid smell. But after a second it developed into what reminded her of maple syrup on pancakes. Then after another second passed, the putridity was back again. Katie and Travis shared looks of disgust. Katie was wrinkling her nose. Travis was looking around at the trees.

"This is different," Laura said. "It's got a sweetness to it."

"Yeah, no kidding!" Carol said.

"But not for long," Katie added. "Then it's back like a sewer."

"It's never going away," said Carol. Her voice was really uneven.

"I don't understand how it was behind you when it was hanging onto us," said Laura.

"I know...." Carol's voice trailed off.

CHAPTER 67

Rob wanted to get away but his senses stopped him. The smell climbed over his shoulders and into his face. His stomach surged to puke but only bile spilled forth. Harry had done what he had wanted to do and that was to give it to someone else. The stench ripped his nose. He looked at Harry who was sniffing himself with satisfaction and a smile crossed his lips. Then he sensed Rob's angry stare on him and his smile disappeared. Harry looked up. Rob watched Harry's face turn white and Rob knew he had him. He was going to give it right back to Harry. Then his right nostril flinched sharply and Rob looked at his own shadow falling away from his right arm. The smell seemed particularly strong there.

Harry dashed away with amazing speed that left Rob stunned as he watched. Harry ran towards the house. Harry's lungs heaved inside his chest as he breathed oxygen and it sucked into his blood stream. He was going for the safety of their house. Rob ran after him. Even though Harry had a big head start on him he thought he could close the distance. Faster he ran but Harry was just as quick. The distance to the house was closing but Rob couldn't gain any ground. He thought it was his own inadequacy that kept him back. That he wasn't a good runner anymore. He was about thirty years younger and was far back trailing an older man. How could this be, he asked himself?

This was simply because Harry was being driven by madness. He wanted to get away from whatever it was that was prowling around. He hated the smell more than anything in the world. Harry needed one thing. To get away.

Harry ran up onto the porch, threw the screen door open, and slammed into the front door. He pulled at the door but didn't turn the knob so the door banged in the frame. The rest of the group over to the side of the house looked around startled at the sudden disturbance. Ashley quit crying and Carol stopped saying her mixture of punishment and reassurance to her daughter. Travis, Katie, and Laura stood speechless as nobody knew what was happening.

Then Rob came around the front of the house yelling at Harry who finally opened the door and ran into the house. The door closed as Rob tried to enter the house and it knocked him down onto the porch. He got up cursing, pushed the door open, and went inside.

To Laura's eyes she saw more chaos spreading among them all. Then her eyes were blinded momentarily as the compound's fake sun broke free over the top of the house casting sunlight down and shifting the shadowy shade caused by the side of the house. She shielded her eyes in time to see Rob through the window running up the stairs after Harry.

Rob ran up the stairs. Each step echoed through the kitchen to the upstairs. He heard Harry's bedroom door slam closed as he reached the top. Rob turned and ran down the right corridor and heard the door lock as he reached it. He grabbed the handle anyway but it held firm.

"Harry! You bastard! Let me in there!" Rob started hitting the door. "You've given me this thing and I'm gonna give it back to you."

Inside his room Harry was pacing back and forth. He kept looking at the door waiting for Rob to cave it in and come in after him. Worse yet, he would get the rancid stench back. What was he going to do?

The pounding on the door continued.

"Open up this door you asshole! Or I'll get you tomorrow." Rob was feeling very empowered through his anger. "You'll have to come out of your room tomorrow!"

Downstairs the door opened and Laura, Travis, Katie, Carol and Ashley came inside. The pounding and yelling rained down from upstairs. Then it stopped. For a moment, there was brief silence but then there were footsteps and Rob came down the stairs. He stopped at the bottom and looked at them. No lights were on inside the house so it was a little dark but everyone took a step back from him anyway as they could see the anger that raged in his eyes.

"What are you looking at?" Rob waited but they only stared at him. "That asshole stuck it back onto me!" Then his nose sniffed something. He turned all around and looked back at the group. "You stink too, but it's different. It's sweet."

"We know!" Carol yelled.

Rob ignored her and walked through the kitchen and back to his room. They heard his door slam shut. To Laura this whole scene was starting to be a little reminiscent of a broken home but with dire impending consequences that were waiting on the horizon.

Rob pulled his shirt off and threw it on the floor before walking around his room in circles. He was punching his hand with his fist and his anger poured out of him with sweat. Rob pulled off the rest of his clothes and went over to the closet and threw them on the closet floor. Then he continued to pace around his room. He was breathing heavily. In and out pockets of air flowed from within him. However, after sucking in more breaths of air he stopped. The smell wasn't on him. Rob could smell it, but it wasn't as prevalent, like on top of him anymore. It still existed somewhere, and he didn't know where, but no longer did he feel it wrapped over him like a heavy thick blanket on a hot summer day. He relaxed.

Rob wanted to clean off. He thought taking a shower might wash away the lingering terrible smell that was haunting them. That seemed to be following them. Moving between them in their circle.

He grabbed his towel from the closet and went to the bathroom closing his door behind him. If Rob had peeked back into his room he may have seen a shadowy movement inside his closet.

CHAPTER 68

Laura pressed on the kitchen switch and light filled throughout the room. Travis did the same in the living room and the darkness inside was chased away. But that wasn't all that was chased away. A few moments passed by and each of them was lost in their own thoughts deep inside their minds. All were silent. All were tired. All realized that the syrupy smell wasn't there anymore.

Laura spoke first. "Hey, it's gone!"

Katie sniffed the air and slugged Travis in the arm. "Yeah! It is."

Travis breathed in. "Cool! No more stink."

Laura thought about how this was the first positive thing that had happened to them all day. She sat up on the counter and stretched out her legs. Her muscles and bones felt better immediately. Her stomach growled loudly. She planned to eat soon.

Katie and Travis were smiling and gave each other fist bumps.

"Mommy, did you hear that?" Ashley was playing with her hair in her mouth. "The smell is gone. I can tell."

Carol just stood there.

The stress, which was colored with fear, had taken a negative toll on their minds and bodies. Their minds felt assaulted while their bodies ached from head to toe. All they wanted to do was rest.

Travis walked into the kitchen and got a drink of the strange water and sat down at the kitchen table. Katie sat down next to him and drank from his glass too. She figured they share the same germs anyway so what does it matter? Both Travis and Katie stretched their legs out under the table and rested their heads on the back of their chairs. Travis had a pinching feeling in his lower back and this helped relieve it. Katie's feet were sore so she kicked off her shoes and stretched out her toes.

Carol sat down at the end of the table. Ashley placed her doll on the table edge facing the window and hopped up on her mom's lap. Together they stared out the window. Ashley was swinging her legs wishing she was back home with her brother and even the glow balls. She wished she was back in her yard playing games and waiting for her friends to come over. Ashley imagined how fun it was to run inside and raid the freezer for popsicles and ice cream.

Carol's thoughts were far from the innocent fun people enjoy in their youth. She hated them. The funny looking Grey lollipop-headed aliens. Their captors. They brought her and her daughter here to this prison place. The aliens took her and her little girl away from home. Away from their lives. Away from Kenny. Away from family and friends. And they didn't even ask them. They didn't care. These thoughts were a burning sensation inside the core of her brain. Just sitting there exhausting mental fumes. Carol thought about how you can't do that to people. You can't just steal people's lives and use them for your own. That's criminal. Worse, it's evil!

The storm outside was getting closer. The thunder was starting to sound like it was next door to their house. The winds were blowing at a faster rate and could be heard beating the sides of the house.

Carol's eyes didn't leave the window. She was looking where the Greys enter through the watery wall and into the compound.

"Well, it seems like we're not leaving the house again for the day," Laura said.

"Unless the Greys tell us to," said Katie. "Or make us."

"Oh, God. Let's hope not." Laura went into the living room. "I think I'm gonna make camp in here."

"We too," said Katie. She and Travis followed Laura.

"Mommy, are we going into the living room, too?" said Ashley.

Carol didn't move.

CHAPTER 69

Rob walked into his room with a white towel wrapped around him feeling refreshed all over. He looked out the window at the ongoing row of trees standing tall over the never-ending sea of grass on the land. Rob didn't see anything move that was alive. The only movement he saw was the storm winds blowing hard causing the trees to sway back and forth. The fake sun was now on the other side casting a shadow of the house on the yard in front of him, but that seemed to be shrinking fast as the approaching storm closed in over the house.

Rob dropped the window curtain and walked back to the closet and stopped. The smell hit his face. It was coming from his closet. His nose hurt. Rob looked down at his clothes on the floor. They have the smell. He thought he would have to find a way to wash his clothes or burn them tomorrow.

He slid some of the clothes hangers to the side and hung his towel up on the bar to dry. Rob was trying not to breathe. He picked out a dark blue shirt and blue pants, not hard being they all looked the same, and began to turn away.

His eye caught something. There was a bulge in the towel. He turned his head. It was gone now. Rob blinked. Did he really see that? Or was it just his imagination? The towel was hanging down straight as a board. He looked at it some more but didn't see anything. Holding his breath, he walked over to his bed, got dressed, and went and opened his door to peek into the hallway. He heard some idle chatter from the living room so he knew they were probably going to stay there for the night like they had done the night before. Rob didn't want to spend the night in a room with anyone else. He felt safer shut away in his own room tonight. Rob thought of Harry and snorted his distrust of the guy. At the same time Rob felt glad to have time now to cool his anger down overnight. He closed the door.

A loud crack of thunder surprised him and he jumped a little. It's not like a man such as him to be startled from the weather but this time he was. That must be from all the distress that he and everyone else had been going through. Especially losing a friend and nice guy like Shawn who was killed in some mysterious way. The feelings of being trapped like an animal, of being isolated inside without any resources or anyone to help, and constant fear grabbing at them each day was now starting to become too much to bear. The knowing that something was wrong and that death might be imminent was a sharp knife edge that would cut into the forefront of his mind and Rob would constantly have to turn away and push it back into his subconscious. This defeated the spirit. And it was worse now that something seemed to be prowling around them.

Rob lay down on his bed and stared at the ceiling listening to the wind outside and the thunder boom and the house rattle. He drifted off to sleep.

CHAPTER 70

The night crept by and there was movement inside the closet. Like a shadow it came out into the room. With no sound, it meticulously moved with a slither to the bed. There was no way to see it as it blended perfectly into the darkness of the room. A room in a dark house engulfed by a storm outside.

Up it rose at the foot of the bed. There it waited and watched its snoring prey. It watched its victim deep in slumber, chest breathing up and down, and completely oblivious to what was about to happen. Exposed and alone.

The shadow entered the bed for its kill. There was no hesitation this time. Without a sound, it attacked with sharp quickness and covered the victim's body. It swallowed its victim's face. Immediately a rhythmic sound started to pulsate. The body underneath it struggled and shook. The victim tried to fight back. The shadow continued. It sucked. The victim underneath thrashed about unable to scream out the horror it was living as it was smothered by the shape. The rhythmic kill continued as the shadowy creature sucked and pumped the life out of its victim's mouth. Its prey struggled and thrashed about to no avail. Its death was done already. The body went limp. Arms and legs fell lifeless by its side. Like a shadow it moved silently off the bed and left the room sliding under the closed door. It left behind a dried out hollow shape of a man.

CHAPTER 71

Ashley awoke with a start. Her eyes took a minute to focus. Perhaps because the dream she had been having seemed so real. A horrible dream at that. There had been a big bright light that she was blinded by. Then she felt as if she was flying in slow motion. It wasn't a normal sensation of flight, but more of a feeling of being lifted up, and carried along like an invisible hand holding her up. Then the scene changed completely and she was running in a maze. The maze was made of glass and was completely white in color. Something was chasing her but she didn't know what it was. Run and run Ashley did but she couldn't get away from it. Down each corridor she went until it led to another one and she ran down the next passageway. Each series of hallways led to a choice of two other directions to go and Ashley would choose the next corridor to test her fate. Eventually, she fell exhausted to the floor. She knew the chase was still on. Ashley crawled and crawled as fast as she could, hand over hand, knee and foot over each other, but it wasn't good enough. It was still there behind her. She would turn and look but she couldn't see it. She couldn't see it ever. But it was still there following her. It was after her.

That is when she came awake. Ashley stared forward with a crooked view of the living room. After a bit, she realized she was lying on the sofa with her doll at the back wall next to her mother. Her mom was sound asleep breathing in a slow but steady rate. In the dim light, Ashley could see that sometimes her mom's mouth would flinch and her eyes would dart around behind closed eyelids during her sleep.

Ashley wondered if her mom had nightmares about the maze like she did.

The time was somewhere in the middle of the night but she didn't know exactly when. They could never tell for sure without having any clocks in the house. That was something the Greys had inconsiderately forgotten to give them. They had basically guessed on the time of day during their days here based on where the fake sun was in the sky.

Ashley rolled over onto her stomach and looked around the room. The living room light wasn't working correctly from the storm again knocking out their power hours before. Occasionally it would flicker on but go off a moment later. The sliver of light inside the room was bending around both sides of the fireplace and coming in from the kitchen. The room wasn't entirely lit but there was just enough to make out how it looked even though it was dark for the most part. She saw that Laura was sleeping in the middle of the floor with her head propped up on two pillows. Travis had fallen asleep under the front window of the living room and Katie was sleeping beneath the side window. They had taken watch to start the night but to no real surprise had fallen asleep. It was difficult not to. The day had been very stressful and everyone in the group felt weakened because of it. Even a young healthy girl like her.

Ashley's mouth was dry. Her lips felt like dry paste. She was trying to decide whether to get a drink of water or not. Of course, that meant getting up from the comfort of lying on the sofa and walking into the kitchen to get it. That would require some work. Little seven-year-old girls deserve to be lazy too. It's part of their job. She thought if little kids were meant to work at a young age they would have been born as grown-ups. At this point she might usually get a pudding pop if they had any here but that would also mean getting up and going to the refrigerator. For now, she'll be thirsty.

The storm outside had mostly passed. There were no disturbing rumbles of thunder or flashes of lightning. Only an impassive but steady pouring of rain tickled and tapped the roof and the porch ceiling outside the house.

She smacked her lips and decided to get a drink of water. She hung her leg over the side of the sofa to get up.

Ashley stopped.

Her nose started burning. The smell was here. And it was growing. She knew it must be getting closer. Ashley shot a quick glance at her mom but she was sound asleep. She looked over at Laura, Travis, and Katie but they were all in slumber. Then she looked at the hall leading back to Rob's room. It was coming from back there. And moving this way. She grasped her doll and held it tightly. The smell grew quickly until it was next to the end of the sofa. Ashley didn't move. Fear held her pinned down. The smell continued and then her eyes saw it. Like a wave in the darkness something moved through the room. Her eyes blinked in disbelief. Ashley couldn't tell for sure if she'd seen something or not. It was hard to tell in the darkness. She tried to follow it but didn't see it now. The dark of the room hid it away again. Ashley couldn't be sure if it was her imagination or not. The smell seemed to have moved away and was closer to the front door but her nose still burned. She watched. There was a small pyramid of light by the front door coming from the kitchen. She saw nothing. The room was still darkened. Frightened, Ashley watched patiently. She wanted to run to her room and lock the door but couldn't. Indecision crossed her young mind. What was that? Did she really see something?

Then Ashley saw movement and she knew her answer. Something went out under the door. She stared in disbelief but knew it was real. But to her eyes it was something unreal and had never been seen before. A silent alarm went off inside of her and chills ran down throughout her body from head to toe. Death had passed through the room and it looked like a living shadow.

CHAPTER 72

The morning came and Carol stirred awake. Her mouth opened in a yawn and she stared at the ceiling. For an instant, she felt back home again in the country. That didn't last for long. The sleepy fog of her mind cleared and her memory started to take over from the dreamful state she had been inside minutes before. Reality came to the front of her consciousness and she knew where she was. Like a thick black curtain falling down to cover a window, Carol's deep-seated hatred set down upon her and scorn for their captors flowed through her blood again. Hate started to boil inside her. Hate for the Greys. Hate for this place. Hate for putting them there in the place where they were going to die.

Carol moved her arm a little and it brushed up against someone. She turned to her side. It was her daughter. Ashley was sitting next to her on the end of the sofa but she didn't speak. She didn't even move. Ashley was just staring at the front door. Her doll lay in her hands that were cupped on her lap.

"Ashley," Carol whispered.

She didn't answer. She didn't even turn around.

"What's the matter? Are you okay?"

Like a statue, Ashley kept staring at the door.

"Hey, answer me." Carol sat up and grabbed her arm.

Ashley turned and looked at her mom. Carol saw emptiness in her eyes. Ashley wasn't all there. Carol looked harder and saw that it wasn't emptiness, but that she was scared.

Ashley spoke. "I saw it."

Carol hesitated. "Saw what?"

"It."

"What do you mean?"

"The shadow."

"What shadow?" Carol didn't want to believe.

"It's a shadow, Mommy. That's what's been following us."

Carol just looked back at her. She didn't know what to say. Her daughter described what she had seen on the window the day before. Gone for the moment was her never ending abhorrence for the Greys. There was something new to add to her growing insanity. What was her daughter talking about? Was her daughter imagining things?

From the other side of the room came a voice. "What's a shadow?" Travis was slouching against the wall.

"Yeah, we've been listening to you," Katie said. She was lying on the floor watching them. "Did you say you saw a shadow?"

Ashley turned back around. "Yes."

"That's what Laura and Carol said yesterday," Katie said to Travis. He nodded in agreement.

"Wait, wait, wait." Laura sat up and rested on her elbow. She knew where this was going. It was what she and Carol had seen. "You saw a shadow? Where did you see this shadow?"

"Yes, I did. It moved through the room in the middle of the night and I saw it disappear under the front door." She pointed to the door.

Travis, Katie, and Laura sat up straight quickly and looked at the door. Travis shuffled on his hands over to the side of the room next to Katie. Laura did a crab walk over to the side sofa. Their stomachs jabbed at them as if vying for their attention which wasn't to be had right now. All three stared at the door for a long moment.

"It's hard to see," Ashley continued. "You kind of see it but you don't. But it was here."

Carol released her grip on Ashley's arm. Carol was silent as she didn't know what to make of this yet. Travis and Katie kept exchanging glances with each other, at Ashley, and the front door.

"Ashley, no offense but...." Katie said as she leaned forward from across the room. "How do you really know you saw it? You didn't dream it, did you?"

"No."

"It was dark in the room, right?" Travis said. "Are you sure it just wasn't the storm and the kitchen light playing tricks?"

Ashley shook her head.

"How do you know for sure?"

"Because of the smell."

Travis, Katie, Laura, and Carol's faces went white like ghosts. That was enough evidence for them to hear. The sense of security they all felt inside the house was gone as well. Ever since they'd been trapped here in this human zoo there had always been one place they were safe and almost unaffected by what was going on outside. The house. Now that was violated. If it could get inside, which it already had, then they were vulnerable. They were defenseless.

Ashley was back to staring at the front door again. This was unnerving to her mother. Carol thought Ashley seemed a little possessed now. Like she was taken over by an alien spirit. As she sat there, unmoving, eyes fixed straight ahead, Ashley looked like a doll you'd find in a kid's playroom.

"How did it move?" Travis asked.

"It just drifted, or flowed along." Ashley's eyes never left the door. "It kind of like faded in and out."

"Where'd it come from?" Katie asked.

"Back there." Ashley pointed down the hall. "From back where Rob's room is."

A surge of panic spread throughout the room and triggered everyone's own internal alarm. There was danger for Rob.

Travis was the first one up. He bolted from the floor and down the hall. Katie and Laura followed him. Ashley casually watched them disappear into the back. Travis got to Rob's door but it was closed. Katie and Laura came up behind him. Back in the living room Ashley went back to watching the front door. Carol sat up on the sofa. She was next to her daughter but felt a million miles away. There was a change with Ashley and her mother sensed it.

Ashley turned and looked at her mother. "I'm scared."

In back Travis started knocking on the door. "Hey, Rob. You there, man? You up yet? C'mon out if you are." There was no answer from Rob. Travis looked at Katie and she nodded in agreement. They would have to go inside and risk the anger of Rob if he was okay. However, at this point his anger would be a good thing as it meant everything was the same as before.

Travis turned the knob and pushed the door open. It didn't make a sound as it opened to reveal the room. The silence seemed to grow louder with each passing second. Staying back a little, Travis and the women peeked cautiously around the edge of the doorway and saw nothing out of place. The light wasn't on; the room was dim. The curtains covered the windows but some light sneaked around the edges. The closet doors were open. There was a bed and Rob was on it.

"Hey, Rob, you awake?" Travis asked.

Rob didn't stir.

Travis took one look at Katie and stepped into the room. He looked around carefully but it seemed empty except for Rob. Katie and Laura came into the room behind him. Travis walked up to the bed and stopped. His mouth dropped.

Katie saw her boyfriend's face and hesitated. She knew something was very bad. Her eyes trailed downward to the bed. "Oh, my God," she said and buckled over in disgust.

Laura was more calm and approached on the left side of the bed. As she did she looked at Rob lying there. He looked the same as everything else that had died. His body was on its back and very rigid. His arms were stretched up and out to the sides. On his face, he wore the horrified frozen look of a man screaming in agony. His mouth was wide open and his eyes were two empty holes below his forehead. The smell of death rose off him like a horrible perfume.

"It must be the death pose," Laura said. Nobody answered her but she didn't care. She might not have heard them if they had. Laura's thoughts were that it had happened again. Another killing. And it was one of them. Their second death. But this time it was inside the house with them. Laura could see it all enfolding now. A chaotic web was being cast around them. Its smelly web of black death silk cast itself now within their house. Inside their home. Inside the place they retreated to and knew they were safe. Their one-time sanctuary. Now it was no more. Their sanctuary was cracked.

"It's inside," said Travis. Suddenly, he was panicked and checked under the bed. He stood up and walked over to the closet and looked around inside. "I don't see anything."

"Maybe not," said Laura. "Remember, Ashley saw it leave the house. I don't smell it. The only smell I get is coming off Rob's body. Do you smell it anywhere else?"

Travis hesitated a moment. "No."

"Okay, so we don't know exactly what is doing this or how," said Laura. "But it's godly awful."

Katie straighten herself. "What the fuck are we gonna do?"

"We have to find a way to kill it for when it attacks again," Laura said.

"How?" Katie said. "We don't have any weapons. We have no way to defend ourselves."

"I know but we have to find a way. This shadow is hunting us."

From the doorway came an edgy voice. "And it will kill us all." Carol was standing there.

They all looked at her. To everyone she seemed to be spiraling downward into a tornado of craziness. From the look on her face to the deranged flavor in the tone of her voice. Carol turned and went back to the living room.

The three of them shared some looks and invisible thoughts about what they were going to do next.

"Man, she's losing it," Katie said.

"Gonna have to watch her," Travis added.

"I have a question," said Katie. "What happens when the shadow comes back?"

"We need a plan," said Laura. "I think we better go back to the living room and get everyone together. And we should wake Harry up if he isn't already."

"What about the body?" asked Katie.

"Leave it," said Travis. "For now."

CHAPTER 73

The three went back to the living room. Ashley hadn't moved from the sofa. She was still staring at the front door. Carol was in the kitchen drinking water but came into the living room with the arrival of the rest of the group.

Laura looked out the windows before turning around and facing the group. Everyone was looking at her. There were footsteps on the stairs. Harry was coming down holding his stomach. While they waited for him a pain shot through Laura's stomach causing her to grimace. The morning sickness of this place struck again. She straightened up a moment later when it eased and she arched her back. She didn't want anyone else to see her in pain.

Harry got to the bottom of the stairs. Looking paranoid, he quickly glanced around the rooms. He was obviously on the lookout for Rob.

"It's okay, Harry," Laura said. "We have something to tell you."

Harry stepped into the room and read their faces. He knew it was bad. "What?"

"Found Rob this morning in his bed," Katie said. "He was killed overnight."

"Yeah, man," Travis said. "Life sucked out of him."

"The same as all the others," Laura added.

Harry didn't say a word. His educated brain was already processing the situation. Another one of them killed. This time in the house. They were vulnerable. He knew they were in serious trouble.

"And we're next," said Carol as she walked by him and sat on the sofa next to Ashley.

Harry noticed Ashley's firm stare. He could feel it brushing by him and crashing into the front door. She hadn't noticed him yet. To Harry she looked as if she was on the sofa in a trance.

"We're in danger," said Laura. "Our intruder came inside, or got inside, somehow, and killed Rob. Probably in his sleep. We found him in his bed. He's back there if you want to see him."

Harry nodded his head in understanding.

"We've got to find a way to stop it," Laura continued. "Or better yet, kill it. We aren't getting help from the almighty Greys. Our loving captors." Her last two comments were filled with sarcasm. She was starting to feel as if they were just thrown into the lions' den and left to fend for themselves.

Harry looked back at Ashley. "What's she staring at?"

"She saw it," said Carol from the sofa.

"She saw it?" asked Harry.

"Yes!" Carol said. Her voice was angry. "She saw what's been stalking us. The killer."

Harry pondered for a second. He looked back at Ashley. She looked up at him.

"It came through the room last night," said Ashley. "I was awake."

"What is it?" Harry said. He scratched his face as if to hide how interested he was to hear the answer.

"Like a shadow," Ashley whispered.

Harry mused over it. A shadow? That's like what Laura and Carol had said they saw the day before. He was expecting to hear something like an animal or a lizard. Then again, those were Earthly creatures from the human world, and what they were used to in their own world. They weren't on Earth anymore. This was a different world and they weren't among anything here that was human except for what was left of them. Harry hadn't expected this. "So what is the shadow?"

"It was hard to see," said Ashley. She stared back at the front door. "It was dark in the room. It moved funny. Like it faded in and out. It was a shadow."

"So nobody else saw it?" Harry was looking everyone over.

They all answered no.

"We need some sort of weapons, man," said Travis.

"Like what?" said Katie. "We don't have anything."

"What about ripping apart some of the house?" Travis said. He walked over to the fireplace and started to feel around it. "There must be something we can use. I don't wanna die here."

"Nobody does, hon," said Katie. There was a tone of sympathy underlying her voice. She wanted her boyfriend to remain calm and not to go off on his own tangent. Katie wanted him to know they were all united together.

"What about getting some branches to stab with?" said Travis.

"That's no good," said Harry. "We can't cut the branches. Remember how hard it was to get that one branch off?"

"What about the posts in the handrail of the stairs?" said Travis. "We could kick some of those out."

"They're too skinny to be effective weapons," said Harry. "Besides, they might break in half as we kicked them loose."

"What about the chairs and tables we have here?" asked Travis.

"Those are made of a strange plastic," said Laura. "I don't know how we could even use them."

"Okay, then we have those electric razors," continued Travis.

"But those aren't any good unless we're fighting in the bathrooms," said Katie "Ha ha...." She finished that thought off with a sarcastic laugh.

"We need something," exclaimed Travis.

"It doesn't matter. You're still gonna die here," Carol said emotionlessly.

"Shut up would you!" Katie turned to her and yelled. "You make everything worse with that shit."

"It's the truth. You have to face it," answered Carol. Her voice was flat.

Katie didn't know what to say next because she knew it wouldn't do any good. Carol was lost. So much for unity she reasoned, but she thought she should still say something and not let Carol's gloomy words hang in the air. She lowered her voice. "There has to be a way. We have no choice."

"Yeah, we have to start looking around for something we can defend ourselves with," Harry agreed. He already had an idea bouncing around in his head that abhorred him.

"We don't even know what will work either," said Katie. "Need to make it a good one."

"Is there a way to just prevent it from getting to us?" Travis said. "Like other than staying awake at night in the living room? With the lights on. Which is lame."

"We don't even know what it is really," said Katie. "Or how to find it."

"We don't have to find it. It will find us," said Laura.

Harry thought now it's even worse. This shadow can barely be seen and it can come and go as it wants with stealth. They don't have any weapons. They needed outside help. "I can go out and do the ritual again and talk to the Greys. I haven't done it for a while. They have the power. We need their help."

"Do you really think they care enough to help?" said Travis. He sat down on the fireplace ledge and looked at Katie. He needed something positive to lay his eyes on. "They don't give a shit about us."

"What other choices do we have?" Harry was starting to get a little frustrated. He felt they needed to start following his lead. They were in desperation and he had a plan to get them out. Harry thought he'd guided them in the beginning, and now it was time to make it to the end, but they had to trust him. "We don't have anything to stop it. The Greys surely will have ways to deal with this."

"Sure, they'll help," Carol said sarcastically. "They probably put it inside with us."

Laura turned to Carol. "I don't believe that. They wouldn't want their stars harmed. They want to show us to their little Grey kids on their field trips."

Carol only stared at Laura in return.

"I'll start preparations," Harry said, with some relief now. He was glad they were behind him in speaking to the Greys. He could save them. Although, a small little sliver of guilt was growing in the back of his mind too. The guilt was his relief that he wouldn't have any confrontations with Rob after what happened the day before and last night. He told himself it wasn't true but he knew it was. Harry was relieved Rob was dead otherwise he thought Rob would have killed him.

Ashley continued to stare at the front door. It was an unnerving feeling that was starting to spread around the room. For everyone Ashley was a breath of fresh air. Her youthful innocence made them all feel good. Especially in a trapped place like this. She reminded them all of home. Of when they were that young themselves. When they had no worries or fears unlike now. Of a time when they could laugh, play, and start learning things in the great big world they were going to grow up in. However, now it seemed like a switch had been turned. And Ashley had been switched off from that. That she was now turned and filled with fear and danger. Her youth stolen away. Now she was scarred mentally the same as the rest of them.

Quietly everyone looked at Ashley who was in the same position as when they woke up. She hadn't moved all morning. Ashley sat straight up. Her eyes were wide open, legs together, hands cupped with her doll in her lap. Her mother was getting really worried about her.

"What's the matter?" Carol asked.

"I'm waiting," Ashley said.

"Waiting for what, doll baby?"

"I'm waiting for it to come back."

CHAPTER 74

They all drank their fill of the strange water to hydrate and stop the morning stomach pains they all endured. Everyone microwaved their breakfasts. Carol brought an egg breakfast to Ashley and put it down on the table in front of her. The hot smells of eggs and sausage drifted up and tantalized her. To her mother's relief she broke her stare of the front door and began to eat. However, she always kept her eyes on the door while she chewed.

When all were finished Laura, Harry, Travis, and Katie went out onto the porch. They were skeptical of the safety in doing this but for an unknown reason each felt it was safe at the time. They checked to make sure it was safe around the front and the sides of the house but it was clear. The nasty smell which accompanied their shadowy intruder wasn't around. The weather outside was sunny and there was now no wind. Each knew that could change at any moment as the weather inside their compound was becoming more unpredictable each day.

"Another strange day," said Travis. "Starts out normal and then gets weird."

Almost as if on cue there was a sudden shot of thunder and lightning and it turned black in the east. Then it slowly rolled over to a grayish color and turned sunny again. To the group on the porch it was unsettling.

"More to come we see," Katie said.

"And it's even more chaotic each time," said Laura.

Harry was rubbing his chin already analyzing it. "I think they've lost control of the weather machine."

"They forgot that nobody controls the weather," said Laura. "Not even on their planet."

"It's looking like dangerous this time," Travis said.

There was another blast of dark weather but this time closer to the house. Then it slowly faded away and there was complete sunshine again.

Harry turned to the group. "I better get out there then before it gets worse." He jumped down the stairs and started walking to the ritual spot where he had spoken to the aliens. Another loud flash of stormy weather surged in the east. It made Harry duck down as if something was thrown at him and he had to get out of the way. Harry felt more uncomfortable with each step he took. He was exposed out in the open with the shadow creature somewhere inside. He was walking up to the watery wall to ask for help, or more like for mercy, from their callous captors, and now there was a threat of weather that could potentially kill him. Harry kept looking between the wall in front of him and over his shoulder to the east. Paranoia fueled his growing fear that each second might be his last. That each step was the one step before his very last step. That the end was coming. Finally, he reached the spot of the ritual. Harry started to calm down but then another deafening crash of weather exploded. He cringed and grabbed his ears. It sounded like a bomb had exploded inside the compound. Now the wind started to blow. Its invisible fingers tickled his skin. Harry started to relax. He stood up and opened his arms. It was time to start.

"Oh, great ones of power," said Harry. He knew as stupid as that sounded that flattery and worship might appeal to the Greys' egos. Harry felt as if he was a Mayan priest praying to the gods on top of a pyramid in Central America. "We need your help please. Something is hunting us. It's like a shadow and moves...."

A light sliced the wall and it peeled open revealing the viewing room they had seen too many times already. There stood about twenty small Greys accompanied by the adult Yellow Grey and Red Grey standing behind. The blonde female Grey stood in the middle. Her green uniform and gold star shone brightly.

Harry watched them and didn't say a word. He didn't move. They were looking at him. The spidery tingly feeling crawled up and down his body. It came from their deep black eyes. Their soulless eyes.

At once all the small Greys pointed at him. Harry was shocked. The Greys were laughing at him. They thought it was funny as this silly human tried to communicate with them and ask for help. He couldn't hear it but he knew it. He felt it down to his bones. And Harry did have a soul inside of him. His soul felt violated.

Harry looked at their tiny fingers. He saw them focused on him. Small grey twigs that even he could snap if he got his hands on them. Harry knew he was the goat. The goat in a cage in the zoo. He turned and walked back to the house humiliated.

CHAPTER 75

On the porch Laura's jaw had dropped. Harry looked like a small mouse standing in front of a giant elephant. He looked small and weak. The Grey children had debased a respectable and wise man. They embarrassed Harry like he wasn't even a man. Laughing at him like he was a subhuman. Mocking him like he was a lowly animal. But then to them he was just an animal. He was an animal, as they all were, in their zoo.

There was a stoned look in Harry's eyes as he came walking up and onto the porch. He was speechless. Harry felt hope now had flown out the door. They were trapped inside with nobody to help but themselves. They were going to die.

"Those bastards," said Katie.

"Dude, we're screwed anyway," Travis said.

"We need to make some changes," said Laura. "We need to come up with something quick before it comes back ... tonight."

Harry looked up at her. "I have an idea for weapons."

CHAPTER 76

Harry's idea repulsed him. He thought of it earlier when they told him Rob was dead. Rob's body was still back in his room lying there possessed by rigor mortis. It was strange that the Greys hadn't come into the compound and taken him out like they did with Shawn and the dead Hunter Greys. But now they were more desperate with the Greys' apathy for them. His gross idea would make any person sicken immediately. He had hoped he wouldn't have to confront it but now the situation dictated so.

"We can use Rob's bones for weapons," Harry said. "Like spears. Or something to stab with."

There was no immediate answer. The idea was so absurd nobody thought he was serious. Although, clearly by the look on his face, he was.

"Are you serious?" Katie asked. There was a ghastly look on her face. "If you are, that is so nasty."

"Talk about walking over a dead man's grave," Travis said.

Laura stayed quiet. Harry's idea shocked her at first but now she was thinking about it.

"How else are we going to survive?" asked Harry. "We don't have anything to fight with."

"Take the bones out of his body?" Katie asked. "How are we going to do that?"

Silence was drawn in and out with each breath among them while they watched for Harry to respond. He was thinking hard about how to word his answer because he didn't want to shock them. He needed them to help him, and have the confidence to perform what he had in mind, but every way his thoughts went was a bad way to say what they had to do. Eventually, he couldn't wait anymore. "We'll have to cut his bones out."

No one answered. They stared at him with disgust mixed with disbelief on their faces. Harry watched them all waiting for an answer. He didn't think it was going over too well but that didn't matter because they had to do it. Then the three of them started to look at each other as if measuring what the overall feeling of the group was going to be. Collectively, they were horrified.

"You've got to be kidding, but you aren't," Katie said. "Cut him out? Tear him limb from limb?"

"With respect of course," said Harry.

"Dude, that's barbaric!" Travis said. "No way, man."

"Look we have to!" Harry knew he had to get demanding with them. "This is our lives I'm talking about and some of you will need to get past the unpleasantness of what we have to do."

Laura was thinking hard and trying to process. The thought alone of ripping out the bones in Rob's body was grotesque enough, but now she was watching the chaos from this place build slowly, and it involved an act she never in her lifetime thought she would have to live through. However, a strange realization was taking place for her. There wasn't much choice. They had nothing. The fight to survive meant they would have to go to extreme measures. They were in danger. Something was preying on them. They were defenseless and desperate for anything to help. They needed weapons. They needed some sort of security. By doing this it could be accomplished. Laura changed her mind on Harry's suggestion.

"I think we should do it," Laura said, which got strange looks from Katie and Travis. "If we don't we're doing nothing. We need to survive."

Harry was quick to move on that. "See, Laura knows. We have to do this."

Katie and Travis looked at each other. They were scanning the other's face trying to read what the other would decide on. "What do you think, babe?" Travis said.

"I don't know," said Katie. "It's really sick. That was a guy we knew. Now to chop him up? That's a hard thing to swallow."

"Do you want to live or die?" Harry said.

"I'm with him," said Laura. "We've gotta do it. And quickly."

Travis turned to them more convinced now. "Okay, but how are we gonna do it?"

Harry had been contemplating that for a while. "We'll use the kitchen knives and the rocks from the fountain." He pointed outside to the stones that made up the base of the fountain. "They're loose, not held together, and they'll be easy to grab."

"Those knives are so dull," Travis said. "They'll never work."

"The Greys weren't gonna let us have real knives," said Katie.

"The rocks are the key," said Harry. "Lots of them are shaped like a cutting tool. We'll break some of them to get edges. The knives can be secondary. We'll have to cut and slice away to get down to the bones. Then we'll break them off." He looked around to judge how they were taking this and continued. "After we get the strongest bones, like the leg bones, we'll sharpen them down with more rocks to get some sharp edges. That ought to get us some stabbing weapons."

Everyone took in his plan and thought it over. It sounded like it would work.

"I'm in," Katie said. She nudged Travis in the side with her elbow.

Travis looked at her and then at Harry. "Me too."

"For survival," Katie said.

"For survival," the other three agreed.

CHAPTER 77

The weather clapped above the house and a loud bang of thunder echoed throughout the compound. It was clear the weather inside was malfunctioning again or perhaps just getting out of control. Streams of lightning shot down into the yard around the house causing the four of them on the porch to pull back up against the porch wall. Now the threat of being struck by lightning was another risk they had to be careful of.

They needed to get some of the rocks from the fountain so they waited a few minutes. They all sat in a squat position, Harry on the left, Laura in the middle, and Katie and Travis on her right. Another boom of thunder sounded and lightning flashed. Laura started to count. When she counted to about thirty seconds another clap of thunder and lightning occurred. She started her count over. Harry, Katie, and Travis listened to her pretty voice say the numbers. Harry thought about how math was the universal language and here they are lost in the universe listening to math as it's dictated in their own Earthly understanding. When Laura got to thirty-two the weather struck again. She repeated the process. Katie and Travis held hands. Harry looked at the trees to the east watching for anything. This time when Laura counted to twenty-seven the weather bellowed again.

"Okay, it seems to be going off about every half minute," Laura said.

"Weird, cuz it wasn't earlier when Harry was out there doing his ritual," said Katie. She looked at Harry. "Valiant try by the way."

Harry nodded in thanks but he knew it had been a humiliating waste of time.

"I know," Laura answered. "But for some reason it's doing it now and that's a good thing. Maybe something in its technology clicked in that self regulates it or something."

There was another bang of weather above them and a stream of lightning struck right next to the fountain. It left a burning smell in the air. They all stared at the spot on the ground where it had hit.

"Oh my, that was hot!" Travis said.

Laura knew that didn't make what she was going to say next any easier. "We have to run out there and get some of the rocks for Harry's plan. The weather seems to be flashing around every thirty seconds. We'll go in teams. Me and Harry first and then you two go. Okay?"

Everyone agreed.

"Now we'll use the time in between lightning strikes to do it," Laura continued. "But before we do this why don't we have an idea of what rocks to grab. Let's study them from here so we can make a direct run and grab at what we need."

They all agreed to that too. Laura had some good ideas. Another blast occurred and everyone jumped back. Immediately, they began to study the circle of rocks. A few minutes passed, as did a few more shouts from above of thunder and lightning, and then it was time to do it. From the porch, each had identified some stones they wanted to grab. These rocks weren't square in shape but more triangular and would provide an edge for cutting. More thunder and lightning blasted the area. Laura and Harry got ready to run out to the fountain. Hunched down on the porch they looked like two sprinters waiting for the gun to sound and the race to begin. They waited.

The weather roared and flashed. Laura and Harry waited a few seconds to make sure it was safe. Then they sprinted. There was a thick smell of burned electricity in the air that singed their nose hairs. A feeling of approaching death hovered over them while they were exposed out from underneath the shelter of the house. *The thunder will sound our last moment alive within thirty seconds*, they thought.

Their feet thudded to a halt on the strange grass as they got to the fountain. Quickly, they picked up four rocks each. The rocks were about the size of bricks.

"We've got about fifteen seconds," Laura said. She had been counting the time in her head. "We gotta move."

"Amen to that," Harry said as he turned back to the house. As he did his foot slid out from underneath him. He stumbled and dropped one of his rocks. Laura turned and tripped on it sending her sprawling and her rocks flying forward. One rock hit her in the chin.

"Oh God, I'm sorry," said Harry desperately. He was half crawling to pick up the fallen rocks and trying to help her up.

"C'mon, never mind!" Laura yelled. "We have to go. Got about ten seconds left."

Katie and Travis were screaming encouragement from the porch.

Laura gathered up her rocks. Blood was dripping from her chin. Her knees felt scuffed from her fall. Harry was sprinting away from her with a limp in his left leg. *About five seconds left,* she thought. Laura's legs burst forth with strength. *All those years on a treadmill,* she thought, *helped.* She ran to the house in a straight line to the porch. She saw Harry get to the porch and drop his rocks. Katie and Travis were shouting to hurry. Two seconds … one second … Laura bounded on the porch and threw her rocks. Katie and Travis jumped to one side. Harry was on the other side. Laura's right leg landed on the porch and she slammed up against the front wall of the house. Just then the thunder pounded and a streak of lightning grazed the front yard. Its brightness was like the sun and they shielded their eyes to not go blind. Then it was over. A burning smell was strong and floating in the air. Laura pushed herself up and sat against the wall. Katie and Travis rushed over to her.

"Are you okay?" asked Katie.

Laura smiled back. "That was close."

"That was hard core, Laura," Travis said. He liked the adrenaline of the close call even though he knew he shouldn't.

Harry was breathing rapidly and staring at Laura. He was thinking that was very close and that they almost died. That she almost got fried because of his mistake. Because of his clumsiness. Guilt of what could have happened was filling up his head. Harry was looking at her feeling not as relieved as he thought he should but felt more like he'd just had a brush with death and lived for another day.

"Okay, that's done," said Laura, but she knew they had more to do. "Let's check out what we got and see if these will do the trick."

They had eight rocks and put them in a line on the porch floor.

"They look good," Laura said.

Harry snapped out of his funk and kneeled next to her. "They're wedges. We can use those to slam down and break and cut. They seem to have sharp enough edges. Good job." He patted Laura on the shoulder.

"You helped," Laura replied. "You almost got cooked with me."

There was another crack of thunder and lightning struck down into the fountain itself. The dragon split apart and rocks shot out in an explosion.

"Uh, do we really have to go out there and get any more rocks?" Katie said. "Are these enough?"

"Yeah, no shit," Travis said. "Holy crap, that blast was wicked."

Laura completely understood what they meant. She was looking over the rocks laid out in front of her. Some blood dripped from the cut on her chin and splattered onto the rocks. Using her shirt, she wiped it off, hoping that wasn't a sign of things to come. Laura looked up at Harry. "What do you think?"

Harry was looking them over too. They had chosen well. All eight of them had sharp edges. "We can try it with these. If we need any more, we know where to get them."

"Good, I love the Fourth of July and all," Katie said. "But next time let's go rock collecting on a lightning-free day."

"Let's start," Laura said. It made her feel better that they were being proactive for the first time. Until now they had been completely helpless. Now they might muster up some of their own help.

They went into the house.

All the while something was prowling around in the shadows of the trees.

CHAPTER 78

Carol was sitting next to Ashley on the sofa where they had been all morning. Carol was feeling concerned about her daughter's reclusive behavior. Ashley wasn't talking and was obsessed with watching the front door. Carol had been asking her little questions any mother would ask, but her daughter only mumbled and shrugged her shoulders in return. Ashley was twirling her thumbs on her lap when the four of them came in from outside and entered the living room. Both Carol and Ashley looked up at them with curious faces. Outside another boom of thunder sounded off and lightning hit the ground somewhere. This time it wasn't directly over the house.

"We've got a plan," Laura said. "We're gonna use the bones in Rob's body and sharpen them down." She hoped that didn't sound too blunt.

"What?" said Carol. Her eyes changed from concerned mother to disbelieving.

"Yeah, we're doing it," said Katie.

"We'll make them into weapons," Laura said nodding up and down. She wanted Carol to be on board with this. "It's all we got."

"How?"

"By using these rocks from the fountain and the kitchen knives," said Laura. Each of them was carrying two rocks and she showed them hers.

Carol stared at the rocks, at them, and then at Ashley who now was looking at Laura. Carol smiled. "Good. If it kills that shadow thing, I'm in. And if it kills the Grey bastards, that's payback."

"Okay," Laura nodded. She wasn't sure how to take the unhinged tone in her voice. It was as if Carol got a thrill from the idea of killing a Grey. Laura couldn't blame her as she and the rest of the group had dwelling inside of them deep-seated hate for the Greys. It was they who took them from Earth like animals and put them here. It was they who put their lives in danger inside this compound where something was stalking and preying on them. It was they that seemed unwilling to help them. That was all natural in the human psyche. However, what worried Laura was what if Carol's growing hate for the Greys and continuing state of mental decline would turn on them?

There was bright light outside the windows and this time farther to the west the thunder roared again.

CHAPTER 79

They moved into phase two of their weapons plan which was the actual surgery. They tore up some of their shirts and pants and tied them around their noses and mouths to serve as facemasks. Harry and Laura went into Rob's room and put the rocks on each side of the bed. Katie and Travis got the kitchen knives and joined them in Rob's room. Carol stayed with Ashley who was again watching the front door.

Rob's body was petrified stiff. The smell wasn't your typical dead body smell resembling rotten eggs or rotten meat. It was the same rotten smell on everything found dead inside the compound. It was something alien.

They walked into the room and took positions around the bed. Every one of them felt queasy inside. This was something unprecedented in each of their lives. There was a dead body in front of them. A dead body that had been a live person with thoughts, dreams, wishes, and feelings the day before. They were standing next to him as he lay cold and lifeless. Now they were going to desecrate his body for his bones.

Harry grabbed a rock shaped with a sharp wedge. He looked it over and determined it was like a stone knife. Rigor mortis was completely set in on Rob's body as it was close to twelve hours since he was killed. The exact time of his death they had no way of knowing, but he had been killed sometime during the night, and it was now close to midday on the day after. Harry decided to start with the left arm. He wanted to see if it would work first before trying to break the stronger leg bones like the femur and the tibia. He stood next to the bed and decided to strike at the scapula where it fits into the shoulder. Harry lifted his rock high above his head and looked at the three of them as if waiting for permission. All three nodded slightly.

Harry saw Carol in the doorway.

"Do it!" Carol said strongly.

Harry slammed down hard. There was a crunch but no blood spurted out. He moved the rock around and started to grind it as if trying to cut through the last piece of gristle on a steak. He chopped at the arm a few times, cutting skin, muscle, and tissue, until he knew it was severed. Next he used the rock to drag the arm apart from the body. He looked up at Laura who was across from him. She raised her rock up and brought it down on the shoulder. There a was disgusting cracking sound and the body rocked a bit. No blood spattered onto her either. Laura wasn't sure if she had broken it entirely free or not. She slammed her rock down on the bone again and again. Her hands were getting sore and cut from the rigidness of the rock. Laura chopped a few more times and it came free. Like Harry, she used her stone to pull the arm away from the body.

"There's no blood," Laura said, looking up at Harry.

"No, there isn't," answered Harry. "Like all the other bodies it appears that our shadow creature sucks all the liquids and juices out of its prey. Appears to suck the blood out, too."

"I thought he had rigor mortis?" asked Katie. "Because of how stiff he is."

"So did I at first, but this is a different kind of rigor mortis," said Harry. To the other three Harry looked like a doctor in an operating room. The rock he held in front of him was like his scalpel. "An alien rigor mortis caused by the shadow creature's attack. There's no liquid or gases left in the body to cause a human reaction. This is alien for sure."

They heard the rumbling of thunder outside and it sounded closer to the house than the last time.

"I don't know what's going on outside now but we better hurry," said Harry. He looked at Travis next to him. "Your turn. Bring it down hard."

Travis stepped forward and leaned against the side of the bed. He looked down at Rob. His eyes scanned the body down to the leg in front of him. He focused in on the upper thigh, the femur, and began to build up his strength which had gotten weaker living in this place.

"Hold on," said Harry. "Take off the pants. Don't wanna have to cut through them too."

Travis knew he was right. He put his rock down and took hold of Rob's pants. This grossed him out as Travis was very uncomfortable about this. No guy wants to pull off another guy's pants. Travis thought about how the women in the room might find this silly and ridiculous. However, he knew it was just a thing that only a man would understand. He hesitated.

"I can help you," Katie said. She thought that might speed him up.

"No, no, babe," Travis said. "It's barbaric, but I got it." He told himself to get over it quick and that this was for survival. He tugged on Rob's pants. They didn't budge so he pulled harder. They slid off over the dead man's knees and Travis pulled them down to the ankles. Travis thought, *thank God, Rob had underwear on.* Travis picked up his rock and stood back over the hip where the femur was connected. He raised his rock, sucked in all the air he could breathe, and swung the rock down and yelled. A loud crack broke out through the room. Everyone looked. The leg looked badly damaged. Travis brought his rock up and came down hard again. It crashed into the bone and severed it loose. He dropped his rock on the bed and stepped back and sighed. "I don't want to have to do that ever again."

"Good job, partner, but you still have more leg to break," Harry said as he leaned over to inspect the break. "But now you gotta do the knee."

Travis looked at him sideways. He wished he was home texting on his cell phone.

Next it was Katie's turn. She got close to the bed, lifted her hands above her head, and froze. She couldn't do it. Everyone was watching and waited. She still couldn't do it. The pressure started to build upon her. Katie knew all she had to do was bring it down on the hip.

"I'll do it for ya, babe," Travis offered.

"No, I can do it," Katie said instantly. She wanted to do it. She had to do it. If not for them, but more for herself. They were all in this together and she was going to pull her load too. The pressure was mounting. *It is for survival*, she told herself. Katie smashed her rock down into the leg and heard something snap hard. She looked down and saw a direct hit. She had done it. The bone didn't look dislodged yet so Katie smashed it a few more times. Splinters of rock peeled and shattered off causing everyone to blink their eyes. After a few hits the leg bobbed up and was loose.

Harry was pleased. "We have more to do. The arms and legs have been broken off but now we have to sever those too. That'll give us eight bones to work with. We'll use the knives and rocks to peel off and clean the skin off the bones." Harry looked around at the disgusted faces of the others looking down at the body and at him. "Then we'll use the other rocks to sand those bones down to a fine point for striking."

Working as a team they broke the arms and legs into separate bones. The cracking sound made them wince at first but after several breaks they were getting used to it. There was a unique kind of disconnect that came with doing the necessary actions to survive. A disconnect that clicked in with each of them the further they got along with what they were trying to do and accomplish. A disconnect that pushed aside the normal obstructions in everyday life and opened the doors for motivation to overcome and achieve what needed to be done. It was driven by why they were doing it. Each of them knew it was to try and help ensure their survival.

Next came the awful experience of cutting off the skin, muscle, ligaments, and membranes from the bones. It was a daunting task but made easier by the fact that all the liquids were gone from the body from the shadow creature's attack. No blood or fluids spilled out onto the bed or onto their hands. However, the body hadn't started to decompose very much yet as it was inside the house, away from the light of the fake sun, and in the carefully regulated temperature of seventy-degree weather of the compound. Strangely, there had been no greenhouse effect inside the house and it had remained comfortable during their time here. The bacteria in Rob's body were no doubt starting to break down his body's insides but the smell wasn't as bad yet as it would ordinarily be in most cases. Harry thought some of the bacteria had gone along with the bodily fluids when they had been sucked out of Rob's body when he was killed. Although, the smell was growing. The four of them worked hard as fast as they could. They cut and scrubbed. They cut and cleaned. Then they had eight bones ready to be sharpened off to a point for stabbing weapons.

Thunder rolled over the top of the house and the lights went out again. In the living room Ashley and Carol heard frustration expressed through cussing from the back of the house. It was dark inside the house, but outside there was still daylight, and some of it trickled through the windows and cast yellowish squares on the floors. However, most of the room, and especially in the corners, was dark. Ashley continued to watch the door but on the edges of her eyes she saw things move in the corners of the room. They moved but didn't go anywhere. They rose into the air or snaked along the floor but Ashley kept her eyes on the door. She knew they really weren't doing that. It was just her mind playing tricks on herself. Carol waited, sitting next to her, and her mom didn't say anything. There was nothing there, Ashley knew.

In the back the four amateur surgeons waited. Each held a knife, rock, or one of the bones from Rob's body in their hands. Quietly, they waited in the dark before they continued. There were bones to sharpen.

Moments of blackness quietly hung in the air before they were brushed away when the lights came on again. Not one of them knew if the Greys fixed it for them like a utility company, if the compound had a backup power supply, or if the power just came on again by itself. Regardless, their power was back and lights filled the house.

Ashley's eyes froze on the floor by the door. She thought she saw something. A shadow, but she couldn't be sure. She blinked. It had seemed to remain on the floor after the light came back on but now it was gone. Driven by fear, Ashley started to bounce her foot up and down. It was coming back again.

In Rob's room, Harry scraped on a humerus bone with a rock and the other three followed his example. The rocks dug into their hands as they worked. Little jagged edges rubbed hard on their skin. It reminded Travis of sandpapering wood back on Earth with his dad in their garage. Each brush made a rock on bone sound and made them cringe at times the way fingernails scraping across a chalkboard can do. However, they continued to sharpen the bones to a point. Muffled breathing exhaled through their make-do face masks of ripped clothing which were drenched with sweat that streaked down their faces. Laura's face mask was also stained with dry blood from her chin. The chipping away of bone was the only other sound in the room. They continued until finally each of them had finished shaving two bones each into a sharp pointy edge. Together they shared glances to reaffirm they were finished and had done the right thing.

"Let's go," said Harry.

They turned and went to the living room with their bone spears in hand.

CHAPTER 80

They entered the living room and stood in front of the fireplace. Immediately, Carol was staring at the bones in their hands. The pointed ends looked sharp enough to poke out her eyes from across the room. Ashley slowly looked their way, her eyes not wanting to leave the front door, and settled on the newly made weapons. She looked up at Laura standing there tall, pretty with long hair, a fit body, and now loaded with a sharp weapon for fighting. Laura looked like a superhero.

"Here's what we did and here's what we got," Harry said. He held out his bone spear and carefully moved it around to show it off. It wasn't very big. In fact, none of them were very long. They were more like bone knives.

"It won't do any good," Carol said, her voice unwavering. She had been thinking about their chances. "We're just the lambs in the pasture. Those bones aren't enough."

"Well, at least it's something!" snapped Katie, who was tired of Carol's negativity even though she, and everyone, knew it was spouting out of some growing insanity inside of her.

"I appreciate the sentiment," Carol said almost in a whisper. Her eyes had a glazed look over them.

Travis put his arm around Katie. Harry felt offended as he was trying to help save them. Laura looked at Carol, then down at Ashley, and thought they better move on from this right away. "So what do we do now?" She walked over and looked out the living room windows. "Just wait?"

"I don't see what else we can do," answered Harry.

"I'm good with that," Travis said. He gave Carol a nasty look and went over to the side window and looked out. "Remember, it's not like we want to have to use these bone weapons. We don't want it to come back, you know."

"It will," Ashley said. Everyone stopped and looked at her. She was staring at the front door again. "It already has but now it's gone again. It likes the darkness."

Nobody knew what she meant exactly but they understood the general theme from the seven-year-old. Nothing was said but their eyes traded glances with each other.

"Anyway, let's hole up and get ready for tonight," Harry said. "We don't know what to expect."

Everyone agreed.

"I also think we should get our rocks from Rob's room, and get a few more from the fountain outside, and stash some in here. We can possibly use those as weapons too."

Again, everyone agreed.

"Hey, I wanted to ask everyone something," Harry said. "Has anyone else noticed that the Greys didn't come in and ceremoniously take Rob's body away?"

There was a quick moment of silence.

"Maybe they didn't realize he'd been killed," suggested Laura.

"They sure seem to be all-knowing," Travis said. "But they aren't."

"Yeah," Katie agreed. "Or they don't pay attention to our house much. Hell, we didn't even have food at first."

"Who cares?" Carol said. "Don't want them in here anyway."

"Just food for thought," said Harry.

There was another pause of silence, then Travis spoke. "You know, except for earlier today when Harry went out there, the Greys haven't been coming around us very much. Only to pick up their dead."

"Yeah, and to get Shawn, but good point," Harry said.

"Good one, babe," Katie smiled at Travis. "Maybe there's something to it."

"They didn't even bother coming for Rob," said Laura. She felt a little sick. Even though she had been liking him less as the days had gone by, he had been the first person she'd known here, and she felt a bond with him for that reason. They had awakened next to each other alive inside here. Now he wasn't alive anymore. "Unless they didn't know he was dead."

"Who knows?" said Katie, shrugging her shoulders.

"Yeah, but how wouldn't they?" Travis asked. "They have higher intelligence. Look at their super big heads."

"Guess they don't know everything," said Laura. "They're cold like ice."

"You don't think they *actually* care, do you?" Carol spat from the couch. "And what if they did know that Rob was dead, do you think anything would change? To them we aren't even humans."

Laura looked at Carol but made sure to keep an even voice. "I'm just saying that despite their superior knowledge of things like space travel and what seems to be some sort of telepathy. And judging by the messages I've gotten...."

"Messages?" asked Harry.

"What are you talking about?" Katie followed.

Laura hesitated and chose her next words carefully. She didn't want to share that she'd received a couple messages from the female Grey. Laura wasn't even sure of it yet herself. "You know, the messages we've gotten like when they ordered us to come out of the house."

They all nodded in understanding.

"I mean that we think about them in ways that we humans think and keep putting our own mindset on them in trying to figure them out. What I mean to say is they probably have a completely different culture, and mental psyche, and wouldn't think or see things the way we do. We keep thinking they would know that Rob was dead. Maybe not. He wasn't out in the open. Maybe they have a completely different focus right now on whatever they're doing and wouldn't even bother to take Rob's body like we would expect them to. Just because they took Shawn's body and their own kind, those killer type Greys, doesn't mean they would come in here and take Rob. We think of them in our terms so we think they're all intelligent and when we don't see something that we expect immediately think that something is up or wrong. I'm not saying this is why. I'm just throwing this out there as a possibility. Just like I'm throwing out the possibility that they aren't all godlike as we think and expect them to be."

Everyone contemplated her point. Outside the thunder blasted again as a reminder of the weather situation.

"So let's not read too much into that yet," Harry said. He lifted his eyebrow to Laura waiting for her approval of what he said.

Laura nodded back. "There also could be a real serious reason, unrelated to what I just said, as to why they haven't come inside the house. I'm only saying for us not to panic. We need to stay collected."

"Word on that," Travis said.

CHAPTER 81

The afternoon was replaced by evening with the oncoming night looming in the distance. The thunder and lightning continued to sound irregularly but clearly were slowing down and not as frequent as earlier in the day. There was sunlight inside the compound but it looked faded like it would at dusk back on Earth. The group stacked a pile of sharp rocks from Rob's room and the fountain, in the corner of the living room in case they were needed to fight with in desperation. Everyone ate dinner and began to get settled in for a long night of waiting on alert.

The Greys hadn't appeared or visited them today. Laura was on the porch enjoying a peaceful moment to herself. A nice moment away from the disgusting operation on Rob's body back in his room. Away from Carol's increasing psychosis that was slowly pulling her away from reality. She held a bone spear in her right hand and was watching alertly for any strange movement around her or in the yard that might be the shadow moving in, but she was more trusting of her sense of smell now as the creature emitted a foul decay.

A pleasant breeze blew along and it felt good on her face. Laura thought about all they had been through and now where they were. They were trapped alone and needing to fight for their lives. Her thoughts were interrupted by the metal squeak of the screen door opening, and Harry walked onto the porch.

"Anything?" he asked.

"No."

"I'm gonna scoop up the rest of Rob's body parts in the bed sheet, tie it up, and lay it out there in front of the wall door for them to take."

Laura felt nauseated. Harry could tell from the look on her face.

"Sorry, just wanted you to know," he continued.

Laura swallowed. "That's okay. Thanks for the warning." She didn't sound very thankful.

Harry went back inside and back to Rob's room.

Laura continued to stare ahead. She looked at the quiet fountain and where the rocks had been blown apart by the lightning. No more water poured from the fountain. The wind blew nicely.

Laura.

She snapped alert. The voice was inside her head again. Talking to her mind. Laura knew who it was from.

You must protect yourself. It's trying to kill all of you.

Laura didn't look around the compound. She didn't need to. Her eyes focused on the doorway area of the watery wall.

Stay strong. Protect yourself. Be brave.

Laura squeezed her bone spear tightly as a rush of strength flowed through her body. *We can do this*, she thought. *It's not a choice. It's something we must do.*

She turned and looked back through the screen door into the living room. There Ashley was sleeping on the couch with her mother holding her. Travis and Katie were sitting at the kitchen table discussing people they knew. Harry came out from the back of the house holding a white sheet wrapped up like a bag. He stepped out onto the porch and pulled it up over his shoulder.

"It's heavier than I thought," he said. Harry wasn't a big guy by any means and the rib cage, hips, shoulders, hands, feet, and skull were making this more difficult than he had expected. "I had to use both sheets."

Laura made a grimace and didn't answer. She could see what must be bones protruding out and forming a jagged pattern in the cloth. Laura turned around. The wind still blew along nicely yet had shifted its direction. But she sensed there was something not so nice riding along inside it.

Harry went down the porch stairway, careful not to let the bag swing around, and come off his shoulder.

"What about the shadowy thing out there?" Laura yelled.

"Screw it," Harry answered. He started across the front yard towards the front wall. There was still a nice wind about. But Laura was getting itchy about something yet unknown. Travis and Katie came onto the porch and stretched.

Nobody saw the black shape watching them.

CHAPTER 82

Ashley dreamed absolute. Her mind was finally at ease after a terrifying night and day of watching and waiting for the return of the shadow creature. It rested tranquilly and began to organize itself putting everything back into the order of a young mind. Her mom drifted in and out of her dreams. She was followed by her friends Casey and Elizabeth. Next were dancing lessons, popsicles from the freezer, and the rare visit from her dad. But something was missing.

Ashley looked down at her bare feet and wiggled her toes. She was standing on a white glass floor. Ashley looked around and she was in a white corridor again surrounded in silvery light. There appeared to be no ceiling, only the light above her. It was quiet. Not even a whisper or a drop of water. All quiet like her house in the morning. She would get up before anyone else and go down to watch television. Then her mom would wake up, come downstairs, and make breakfast. Something was missing ... her brother. Kenny.

From behind there was a presence. She moved away. It came closer. Ashley looked behind her but didn't see anything. But it was there. Invisible. She needed to get away. Needed to run. Ashley looked ahead down the corridor and saw Kenny at the end of it beckoning her to run to him. She started to run. The presence followed after her. She looked over her shoulder but couldn't see anything other than silvery white light. Ashley ran faster. Kenny waved her on towards him. He disappeared around the corner. She ran after and turned down the way he'd gone. Kenny was running ahead of her. She couldn't catch up as he was always faster than she was. The presence was still behind her. Kenny ran down another passage. Ashley struggled to keep up. Her little legs would move faster if they could. Kenny turned into another passage. Ashley followed. Her lungs breathed a steady flow of oxygen. There was never an end. Each corridor led to another one that lead to another one. She cried out to Kenny but he didn't answer. He kept on running. Ashley turned into another passage he'd run into and stopped suddenly. It was a dead end.

"Kenny. Kenny. Where are you?"

He wasn't there. The presence was coming around the last turn towards her.

Ashley woke up on the couch in the living room. Her mother was resting next to her. There was no maze, no Kenny, and no presence after her. But it had seemed so real.

CHAPTER 83

Ashley sat up on the couch. She looked at her mom next to her who returned her look but didn't say anything. Carol felt powerless and had given up hope. Ashley could see the back of Laura on the porch through the screen door. Laura's brown hair was blowing in the wind. Ashley stood up and walked to the front living room window. She pretended to comb her doll's hair. Outside it was dusk and the light was fading. However, in the compound's typical weird way it was dark and fading from the west and not the east.

"Mommy, the sun's weird again. Night is coming from the other side now."

"That's good, honey," Carol said, sounding disinterested. She was thinking of the coming dread of what might happen overnight from the killer shadow. Carol looked up at the ceiling. "Maybe this screwed up place has a change of orbit or something. Like if Earth changed direction. How ridiculous it is."

"It...." Ashley turned around to her mom but something caught her eye from the side of the house. She looked through the window of the living room at the hill in the distance. A smile crossed her face. "Kenny!"

Her mom looked at her quickly. "What?"

"It's Kenny! He's here! Up on the hill." She dropped her doll and ran out the front door. The door squeaked fast and slammed shut.

"Ashley, where are you going!?" screamed Carol, as she sprang off the couch after her.

Laura turned on her heels as the door swung open and Ashley ran on the porch. Each step of her little feet made a pounding sound on the wood. Katie and Travis stared at her in surprise as she jumped off the porch and ran into the yard. Carol frantically followed her daughter onto the porch, pushed Laura out of the way, and ran to the end of the porch. Laura caught herself on the porch railing.

"Ashley! Come back here!"

Ashley was almost at the first row of trees when she turned around and pointed. "It's Kenny, Mom! He's over there. Look!"

Carol didn't see Kenny. She didn't see any people at all. "What are you talking about? There's nothing out there."

Everyone on the porch looked but nobody saw anything but the hill, trees, and the fast fading light. It was getting dark outside.

"Yes, he is Mommy! It's Kenny. Yea!" Ashley ran through the first row of trees into the clearing beyond.

"Jesus. Come back here!" Carol yelled. She climbed over the railing and dropped down on the side of the porch and raced after her.

Laura was dumbstruck and didn't move. She was confused because nobody was out there. Travis and Katie ran to the edge of the porch. Laura followed them.

"Hey, are you crazy? That shadow creature is out there!" Travis yelled. He turned to Katie. "I can't believe this. That shadow thing is somewhere out there."

"Oh my God," Katie answered.

"And I don't see anyone out there," said Laura. "Did you hear what she said? Something about Kenny was on the hill."

"Whaaat? That's crazy," Katie said. "I know she misses her brother and all but still he's not out there."

They watched Carol run through the trees and into the small field. Ashley was a small shape moving ahead of her.

"They don't have any weapons," said Travis. "Not even one of our bone spears. Just the little girl and her going-senile mom."

"I'll go," Laura said. She clutched her bone spear tightly and lifted herself over the railing into the yard. She ran after them to catch up.

Travis looked at Katie. He didn't know if he should follow or not but he did know he wouldn't feel very good about himself if he stayed on the porch like a chicken. "We have to help."

"I know," she responded.

Together they climbed over the railing with their bone spears and ran in pursuit.

CHAPTER 84

Harry heard the commotion coming from the house behind him and turned around. He saw Carol running from the house into the trees. *She must be running after someone,* he reasoned. Probably her daughter. Only the little girl could bring that kind of passion to her mother. He saw Laura, Travis, and Katie on the porch. Then Laura jumped off the porch and ran past the trees. A moment later Travis and Katie did the same. What is going on? Harry was standing at his ritual site so he tossed the bag with Rob's body remains down onto the ground. It landed with a sound of bones rattling.

Harry didn't think anyone leaving the house at the onset of nightfall was a good idea. Something major must have happened. That also left the house open and vulnerable without anyone there. He ran back to the house. The bag lay on the ground as a sad reminder of Rob's life.

CHAPTER 85

Ashley ran as fast as she could. At the bottom of the hill she stopped to catch her breath. From behind she heard her mother calling for her.

"C'mon, Mommy! He's up here." Ashley started up the hill. Her feet dug in hard to help her climb.

Carol wasn't far behind and reached the hill bottom moments later. She was winded and didn't bother to cry out to her daughter. Carol rested for a second and heard Laura, Travis, and Katie running up behind her.

"What the hell's going on?" Laura shouted as she ran up to the hill. Travis and Katie pulled up next to her.

Carol took a final deep breath. "Ashley thinks she saw her brother up on the hill. I have to get her." She started to climb the hill. The others followed her.

Ashley was at the hilltop. There was no Kenny. Only the trees lining away to the west under a canopy of setting darkness. She looked around the surrounding trees. "Kenny? Kenny?" Her brother didn't answer. He wasn't there. Her feelings felt hurt. She had longed to see her brother again, and she had, but now he was gone.

Carol got to the top of the hill. She grabbed Ashley. "Don't *ever* do that again."

"Mommy, Kenny's not here."

"Of course not." Carol was holding her anger inside. The fear she had of her daughter being killed here kept pushing it upwards. Her fear and anger together were a knot swelling in her throat.

"But I saw him."

Laura, Travis, and Katie arrived at the top.

"No, you didn't," Carol said firmly. "That was your imagination. What you saw was your mind playing tricks on you."

"Maybe he went that way into the trees," Ashley said, pointing toward the trees.

The others saw that was the same direction they had found all the dead animals days before. A collective chill passed throughout their bodies.

"Kenny was never here," said Carol. "And we're not going anywhere other than back to the house."

It was dark. Complete nightfall was minutes away. Only a small radiance of light could be detected by the naked eye. The trees were black trunks against a dark background. It was reminiscent to them of being on summer vacation as a kid and having to get home for bed after dusk. Laura thought she might hear her mother call her name at any moment. For Travis, it was his father. To Katie it could have been either of her parents. Ashley didn't have to imagine. Her mom was here now and angry with her.

"It's so weird out here with no life," Katie said.

"Yeah, no kidding," said Travis. "You'd think we'd be used to it by now."

"It's cause we're away from the house," Laura said. "Out here. Exposed."

"We can see the top of the house from here," said Katie. The house looked like a black pointed triangle in the dark. Glimpses of the house lights could be seen through the trees.

"We better get back quickly," said Laura.

"Can't complain on that," added Travis.

"Carol. Ashley." Laura spoke with gentleness. She didn't want to rock Carol's current rational behavior into the world of irrational. "C'mon, were going."

Carol didn't look at her. She was staring at her daughter's face. She was unwilling to let go of her daughter's attention after running off. The other three waited for her to respond. Finally, she said, "Okay."

Laura thought that was creepy. She turned to start down the hill.

"Wait a second," said Travis.

Laura stopped. Everyone now looked at him.

"What?" asked Katie.

"Do you see something?" He pointed back into the trees. Everyone followed.

"See what?" Katie said.

He took a step forward in front of them and crouched down using his bone spear for balance. "What is that?"

"What's what, Travis?" Katie was already frustrated.

Travis pointed again and tilted his head. He was trying to focus his eyes on something he wasn't sure was there or not. "Look down that row of trees. Do you see it? I'm pretty sure it moved."

Everyone was looking that way, squinting against the darkness. A small distance away there looked to be a shape on the ground next to a tree. It was too dark to tell for sure. Night was upon them and their eyes seem to be passing in and out of focus. The shape was there one moment and gone the next. Then it was there again. Not moving.

"Kinda," said Katie slowly. "I'm not so sure I do though."

"Me either," said Travis, now doubting himself.

"I see something, I think," said Laura, her voice tapering off into uncertainty.

Carol and Ashley saw it but didn't say anything. They watched.

"What is that?" Travis repeated. "I think something's there."

"Yeah, I do," Katie said. "But then I don't. It's like...."

Everyone blinked. It was closer now. It had moved. But nobody saw it move.

"Holy shit," said Travis. "I think it moved."

"Me too," said Katie.

"It did move," said Laura. She was staring at it but still wasn't sure if she saw something. It seemed to not completely be there. Her eyes saw it one moment and then didn't the next. She knew it had to be the darkness causing this.

"Hey, do you two see this?" Katie directed it at Carol and Ashley.

Ashley nodded back at Katie. "Uh huh." Carol was unmoving. She looked like a protective statue on Ashley's back.

Without realizing how, the shape was closer now. It had covered half the distance and was only a couple of trees away.

"Oh Jesus, it moved again," Katie said. She backed up to the edge of the hill. "It's even closer now."

Travis backed up next to her. "Yeah, I think so too." He held his bone spear out in front of him in a protective position. Katie and Laura did the same. They looked like jousters.

Carol, with her hand on Ashley's shoulder, slowly stepped away. Without taking her eyes off the shape she walked her daughter back next to the other three.

Then it wasn't there anymore. Only the darkening shadows of the night were left. And fear took root with them.

Laura knew she had good eyesight and she was trying to watch the shape closely. This was made more difficult by the fact that it seemed to merge in and out of the night. Still Laura trusted herself to see through the darkness and see if there was something there hiding in the dark. She thought the shape was alive and moving. Her mind said it was real but her body didn't. Yet, she was still standing there as were her companions. Laura's mind started to contemplate that for a second. Why were they still standing there? Why were they leaving themselves exposed to danger? She knew why. It was because despite their increasing alarm they weren't convinced yet that what was in the dark was real. The shape blended in with the night too well.

They watched.

"I've lost it," Travis said. "Does anyone see it?"

Nobody answered. They waited. The night was too still. Too quiet. Nothing moved. Nothing made a sound.

A syrupy smell reached out from the night and tickled their noses. It masked what came next. The rancid smell of death had found them again. They smelled it creeping forward. It was coming right up to them.

"Oh my God! It's the shadow killer!"

"Run!"

CHAPTER 86

Harry stopped in front of the steps of the house and caught his breath. He was looking west to see where his companions had gone but it was difficult to see. The fake sun had almost set itself. Dusk was close to falling completely into night and the row of trees that lined the side of the house blocked his view of what was beyond. The light from inside the house cast through the windows, onto the porch, and overlapped onto the ground. They looked like rectangles a couple feet wide on the strange grass.

Harry listened intently but didn't hear anything. The strange absence of the sounds of the natural world inside the compound always emphasized how unnatural the place was.

The weather was behaving better now. The lightning wasn't blasting uncontrolled and the thunder was quiet. Inside it was a nice seventy degrees in temperature. Harry thought that perhaps the Greys had finally gotten a hold on their weather creation. Yet, despite the seemingly docile climate, he couldn't hear anyone.

Harry was going to shout for them but caught his words at the tip of his tongue on a second thought. He didn't want to attract attention to himself standing there alone in front of their empty house. Harry thought they might not hear him anyway and it would be a waste of energy. His mind took him back over to in front of the watery wall to where he had left the remains of Rob's body. The Greys hadn't appeared yet to take them. Harry wondered if the Greys considered the leftovers of Rob too far beneath them and wouldn't take them anyway. Maybe it's not part of their alien culture to do that? However, they took the other dead bodies victimized by the shadow creature. His nose brought his thoughts back to in front of him. He smelled something. Behind him. Getting stronger. Hideous. He knew what it was. It was ungodly.

Slowly, Harry turned around expecting something to jump out at him but nothing did. He looked into darkness. The trees could barely be made out off in the distance. The smell was in front of him. Harry remembered that it seemed to move around without being seen in the shade. Quickly, he stepped into one of the squares of light on the ground from the house. He looked down at his feet to check that he was standing squarely in the middle of the light. His alien issued sneakers were bright from the window light. One shoelace had come undone but he didn't dare bend down to tie it. He looked around again. His ears listened hard to the night.

The smell was in front of him now and moved around to his right. Harry focused his eyes to try to see better. He looked at the ground and in the air but still didn't see anything. The destroyed dragon statuette stood in back as if afraid to help him. The night started to spin around him even though it looked all the same. His eyes were blinking rapidly to clear out any faulty night vision he might have. His heartbeat started to pound inside his chest. It was in front of him again and moving. Harry felt it was stalking him like a tiger tracks its prey. His body locked into a crouched stance looking much like a shortstop would. He brought his hands up in front of him holding his bone spear in a defensive position. Harry was getting ready for the attack. He couldn't imagine how Rob and Shawn must have felt moments before their deaths. Moments before the shadow stalker, this demon in the night, sucked their life's essence out of them. A shiver went up and down his back. Now it was there for *his* turn.

From over the hill past the trees he heard someone scream. He needed to move! Harry dashed up the porch stairs. He crashed into the door trying to open it. As he gripped the handle the grotesque smell behind him moved closer. Adrenaline rushed through his veins. He flung the door open, bounded into the living room, turned on the balls of his feet and slammed the main door shut. The house was quiet. The lights in the living room and kitchen provided a reassuring feeling but only for a split second. His nose could smell it through the door. He backed into the living room and raised his bone spear above his head ready to fight. Harry wondered what the shadow was. Was it closer to a lizard, a mammal, or a bird? It wasn't like anything he had ever heard of being on Earth. However, it was a killer all the same and Harry wasn't going to let it get away. He was going to strike it.

The power flickered. *Not now*, he thought. The lights stayed on. Harry clutched his bone spear tightly. It was coming for him. The power flickered again and the rooms went black. Harry's fear factor heightened and streamed through his veins. He was trapped in the dark at its mercy.

Harry lowered the sharp point of his bone spear into a position like if he was spearing fish. He couldn't see anything but if it came up in front of him he could stab downward at it. Harry waited. The silence grew louder in a way that caused his ears to ring. He thought if the shadow didn't get him maybe the looming quiet would. Then his nose quivered. The smell was inside the house.

The lights flickered on. Quickly, he raised his bone spear expecting it to be in front of him about to pounce but it wasn't. Only the floor lay in front of him. Harry looked around the room at the walls, up at the ceiling, but he didn't see it. There were only the two sofas, a table, and himself in the room. The fireplace was empty. He looked down the hallway leading to the back of the house but didn't see anything there either. Harry hadn't moved from the stance he had taken but he knew it was somewhere. The rancid stench was alive inside the house.

Holding tightly to his bone spear, he checked the stairs but they were empty. No lights were on upstairs. Just darkness waited at the top. He walked slowly into the kitchen but didn't see anything. It wasn't under the table, around the chairs, or on the counters. He checked around the refrigerator but saw nothing. Harry walked over to the front door and touched it. He didn't know why he did but it felt better to do so. Harry could still smell it. The foul odor was here.

Then his eyes looked into the living room. For an instant, he thought he saw it near the edge of the sofa. He blinked again and it wasn't there. Harry's mind started to race. What should he do? He wasn't sure what he'd seen and thought it was his imagination. However, he knew it was here somewhere and he didn't want to die. Then his educated mind concluded his answer. He'd go up the stairs and wait for it to come up. It wouldn't be able to sneak up on him that way. And he could kill it!

Harry climbed the stairs backwards. Slowly, he went step by step backing upwards. He carefully felt each step before he placed the weight of his foot down as to not lose his balance and fall. The lights dimmed a little. Harry held his breath. The foul stench was existing strong inside the house. Almost as if it was moving around. His foot reached the top step and he stopped. Harry's body went cold. He felt a presence behind him. That rancid smell approached his back. Harry turned and looked into the darkened hall as the lights flickered and the house went black.

From out of the darkness it attacked! It seized upon Harry and covered his face and body knocking him backwards. He didn't even have time to scream. Harry slid down the stairs making hollow thumping sounds from each step. The bone spear flew somewhere down into the kitchen and rattled around. His shoulder crashed into a handrail post and lodged his body halfway down the stairwell. The shadow engulfed him. A rhythmic sound pulsated its crime. Harry struggled underneath but to no avail. The shadow performed its kill in rhythm and sucked Harry's life out of him. His arms and legs shuddered before his body stopped. He went limp. The darkness of the powerless house hid the evil that had taken place. The shadow moved silently down the stairs and escaped under the front door. Behind on the stairs lay another empty corpse of a man.

CHAPTER 87

Laura was running down the hill in front. She could hear the pounding footsteps of the others behind her. Laura had been extra careful going down the hill and didn't fall. She gripped her bone spear tightly in her hand. Laura landed at the bottom of the hill with a thud and sprinted off. She thought to stop and wait for the others to catch up but her body didn't obey that thinking. It was time to flee. She wanted to get away from the shadow creature. She didn't want to be its victim and die a horrible death.

Now Laura was sprinting across the grass and could see the light from the house between the spaces in the line of trees. The shadow creature was somewhere after her. She could feel it as if it was right behind her. Close enough to be riding on her back. From behind she heard a yell and a body tumbling down the hill. There were some words exchanged between Travis and Katie and then she got the sense they weren't trailing behind her anymore. She kept running even as guilt flooded her consciousness and told her to go back.

CHAPTER 88

Carol stumbled on the hill and fell, taking Ashley with her. They landed hard on their backs and rolled to the bottom. Carol's back flattened like a board and was a bit numb. Carol smelled the rancid syrupy odor coming downward on the hill. She got up on one knee and remembered her daughter. "Ashley!"

"I'm right here, Mom!" Ashley grabbed her mom's arm in an attempt to lift her up. "We gotta run!"

Together they stood up and ran and crashed into Travis and Katie.

"Fuck!" yelled Travis as he went sprawling on the strange grass. His rib cage pounded the ground and he rolled over his bone spear.

"Shit!" Katie yelled as she fell backwards onto her butt and her bone spear smacked her in the face. Her tailbone ached and her face stung. She looked over at Carol and Ashley and up at the hill. She could smell it there. It was coming. "We gotta go!"

"Let's go, Mommy!" Ashley pulled her mom's arm to get her to stand.

Carol pushed herself up and started to run. Ashley was alongside of her. "Everyone run!"

Travis stood and helped Katie back up on her feet. Their noses flared with putrid pain. Together they ran for the house.

CHAPTER 89

Laura stopped at the trees and looked back. In the fading light, she couldn't see much except for darkness. She looked back at the house to judge the distance and was shocked. The house was gone. There were no lights. Laura focused her eyes again. She knew it was there because the house couldn't have just left the compound. She watched in that direction. As she did the surroundings of the night seemed to close in around her. Laura started to feel smothered and wrapped up in darkness. She continued to stare in the direction of the house and its dark outline started to take shape. A black shape within blackness. Panic filled her body. She knew the power had gone out again and this was the worst time for it.

Her ears caught some voices in the distance. They were coming. She felt better as her guilt subsided a little bit. However, Laura was disappointed in herself. She had let fear step on a core characteristic of herself as a human being and that was to always do the right thing and to go back and help. But she had run instead. Laura would have to live with that. She breathed in and caught her breath. She listened and could hear them coming towards her now escaping in the dark shades of night.

CHAPTER 90

Travis felt slow. He dug his feet into the ground to try to run faster but he felt flat-footed. With each driving step, he couldn't get away fast enough. Katie was right next to him keeping up. That never happened before. The truth was he was at his fastest speed. However, doubt was telling his mind it wasn't.

Katie raced along next to her boyfriend. She knew if she could stay with him they would get away. She stumbled but caught her balance and tore forward. Her head was swinging from side to side. She wanted to get away.

Travis heard her trip and reached out to grab her but he missed. His sudden rush of alarm was relieved when she stayed up and continued to run next to him. He looked over his shoulder but couldn't see anything. But he could smell it from somewhere behind. It was following.

Katie knew Travis was next to her and it made her feel some comfort in all of this. It was a small amount of comfort scattered about inside fear and danger. Carol and Ashley were a few feet in front of them. She didn't want to trip them up but she couldn't stop her momentum. The shadow was chasing them. The foul odor was coming from behind and she felt it was reaching out for her. With every step she took, it was always behind her like a coat covering her back.

In the darkening chaos, Travis stepped on the back of Carol's leg and they went down again. Elbows and knees scraped the ground and grunts and swearing sounded out. Katie slammed into Ashley knocking her to the ground. She heard Travis and Carol yelling at each other and Ashley was starting to cry next to her. Frantically, she sat up and was facing back toward the hill from where they had come.

Katie looked into the darkness and saw something moving towards her.

CHAPTER 91

Laura ran for the house. Her body surged with adrenaline and sweat poured from out of it. She stopped in front of the house and looked back for her friends. She heard them in the distance. However, the night around her remained still.

She smelled something. It came from the porch. Like a crooked old finger, it extended out and picked at her nose. Her eyes led as she slowly turned back to face the porch. But there was no light and she couldn't see anything. Her body started to shake. Laura knew it only existed when the shadow was near. It was the smell of death.

Laura stared at the house for a moment that felt ten times longer than it was. Her feet were planted flat on the ground and she couldn't move even though her brain was telling her to do so. Laura didn't even raise her bone spear in defense. She waited for the shadow to get her in the dark.

Then it was gone.

CHAPTER 92

"It's here! Move!" Katie yelled. Fear sprung her forward pulling Ashley along with her. Just turning away from the dark shape coming forth set her free.

Travis was bounding away next to her shouting encouragement to Carol to run faster which she was. She was in good shape and a healthy mother in her forties but it wasn't simple words that were driving her. It was driven from her increasing loss of sanity from this place. Driven from her and her daughter being trapped like animals. Her rising insanity made her run. It was her fuel.

They ran through the row of the trees at the edge of the yard. Small branches snapped in their faces like whips stinging and cutting at their skin. They burst through and ahead was the house but no one could see it very well because there were no lights. They ran forward knowing it was there by its black shape in the night.

Laura stood shivering in fear. She could have been dead. Where did it go? Was it still there? From over on her left she heard fast footsteps loudly running up to the house. She wasn't alone now. Laura didn't smell it anymore. The rotten smell had disappeared but she wondered how it could have been in two places at the same time. And worse, what had it been doing at their house?

Laura heard the others run up behind her. She turned to warn them. "Stop!"

Travis was first to arrive at the porch. "What?" He knelt over to rest and catch his breath.

"Don't go in the house!"

"What are you talking about?"

"It's coming!" Carol screamed as she and the others ran up behind Laura.

Katie stopped to rest next to Travis. Carol grabbed Ashley and pulled her close to her. Ashley started to cry again. Everyone was breathing heavily.

"I smelled it on the porch!" said Laura.

Nobody said anything except for Ashley who cried louder. Everyone stared at Laura's silhouette in the night. It was nearly pitch black and they could barely see the faces of each other. The compound was a world of darkness.

"What?" said Travis. "There's no way!"

"I got here and I smelled it," said Laura.

"How?" said Katie with disbelief. "It's chasing behind us."

"It moved past me. Then it was gone. I don't know where it is now."

"How was it at the house and up on the hill chasing us at the same time?"

"There must be two of them," said Laura.

"Jesus," Katie swore. "What was it doing?"

"Hunting," Laura replied.

"Oh shit!" said Katie. "What do we do?"

"Damn!" said Travis. "And the lights are out in the house."

"Must have been another power outage, thanks to the aliens," said Katie.

Laura's fingers were twitching. "We won't be able to protect ourselves."

"Like I said, it's coming!" Carol said insanely.

"We have to go inside," Katie said. "It's right behind us."

Ashley continued to cry.

"If we go inside we're boxed in with nowhere to go," said Laura.

"Well, we won't survive out here either, you stupid...." said Carol.

Laura looked at Carol and spoke firmly. "We're not trapped outside, Carol."

No one spoke except for the wind that finally gusted along making their hot and sweaty faces feel refreshingly cool for a moment.

Then Carol started. "Oh God! Oh God! We're gonna die!"

And the smell approached from behind. Its syrupy stench announced its arrival. Everyone turned and looked into the side yard but it was too dark to see anything. A giant sheet of blackness blocked their eyes but it was out there. Somewhere. And then it started moving. They smelled it over by the fountain. The shadow creature was stalking them.

Ashley screamed and ran onto the porch.

"Ashley!" Carol yelled and chased after her. Everyone followed quickly. The loud stomps from their feet echoed rapidly off the porch ceiling. The front door was ripped open, almost pulled off its hinges, and they pushed into the house. Travis slammed the door shut behind them. It was completely dark inside. Laura and Katie felt around in the darkness looking for the light switches. Carol pulled Ashley close to her and backed up until she felt the bottom of the stairs against her feet. Travis brought his bone spear up over his head. It was too dark to see anything but he was ready to strike.

"I found a switch but it's not working," Laura yelled from the back of the house. "There's no power!"

Katie was flicking a switch in the kitchen. "Nothing here either. We're screwed!"

The smell was closer now.

Laura walked back into the living room and stood there. She looked at the windows and saw a world of black covering them inside the house. Her nose twitched. The rancid stench was spreading into the rooms. Inside her mind Laura started to pray.

The power hummed back to life and the house filled with light. The group felt saved. They had hope they would live again. That was shattered when Ashley screamed.

Everyone gathered at the bottom of the stairs. They saw Harry stuck in the railing halfway up the stairs, his drained body motionless on the steps. Arms stiff pointing upwards. Harry's face frozen in a lifeless stare.

The smell at the front door disappeared back into the night. Laura, Travis, Katie, Carol and Ashley all traded looks of horror with each other. Another one of them was dead. The shadow had killed again.

CHAPTER 93

The group was in shock and despair crept in with a bang on them. They had lost three human beings, people of flesh and blood that they knew, to a stealthy killer that moved camouflaged in the night. There was no help in sight. Their keepers, the Greys, didn't care.

They huddled in the light of the living room throughout the night scared and on guard. They switched off in shifts as they had the night before. Two at a time were on watch so they could watch each other in case one of them fell asleep. But in truth everyone nodded off to sleep at one time or another. The dire situation and the body's need to recover with rest were too much for them to resist at times. However, nothing came for them during the night. At least not that they were aware of. Perhaps it was all the downstairs lights being on that cast out a shield of protection. Or maybe it was simply that the shadow creatures didn't need to hunt or kill any more for that night. Surely, the shadows would be back.

They left Harry's body where it was, stuck in the posts of the stairway, as a temporary grave until morning. There had been a short discussion about what to do with his body and the decision was to put him outside in the morning for the Greys to pick up. That was if they would even do so because lately the Greys had been absent in the mortuary business as well.

Then the fake sun rose and morning came.

Laura was on the last night shift with Carol who had fallen asleep next to her daughter but Laura didn't care. She was wide awake from a mixture of scared alertness and meditation. Laura thought they had to reach out and try the aliens again. She knew it was the female Grey with the blonde hair that had communicated with her by sending her mental messages. That is where Laura would go.

Everyone awoke as it slowly got brighter outside in the compound. Nobody was very rested which was evident by the dark rings around the eyes of their haggard faces. Ashley kept her head buried in her hands. Carol tried to soothe her daughter's fears by rubbing her daughter's back. Travis and Katie shared a morning kiss before going into the kitchen and having their morning drink. They both grabbed their stomachs and bent over in pain when walking. Laura waited a minute before following their lead and getting her morning fix as well. She knew the morning pains started when she moved around and got up in the morning. That seemed evident with Travis and Katie too. Carol and Ashley were still on the sofa and hadn't gotten up yet so they showed no signs of stomach pains. She would watch them closely when they did get up. To Laura the question remained of what was causing their morning sickness.

Travis and Katie came back into the living room, looked out the windows, and sat down under them. They leaned back against the wall, shoulder to shoulder, and began to wait. Everyone was quiet. Ashley finally looked up through her fingers and started to watch the front door again. Her mom stared blankly at Laura. Hatred seemed to pass across her face although Laura wondered if it was directed just as much toward her and the group as it was the Greys. Carol seemed to be like a cornered animal now. Laura finished her water and sat down next to the fireplace.

Paranoia started to seep in and infest them all. When would the shadows come back? How would they come back to prey? Which one of the five of them would die today?

"I'm going to go ahead with the ritual that Harry used to do," said Laura.

The room was quiet.

"I'm going to continue it on and try to talk to them."

"What good will that do?" sneered Carol. "They don't care!"

Laura looked at her but didn't say anything right away. She wanted to keep this calm and not let it get out of control. "You're right, they don't care. But we're being hunted and killed."

"And they haven't done a thing to help us." Carol grit her teeth.

"Hold on," Katie said. "They did send in those specialized Greys."

"Lot of good that did us," Travis said as he looked at Katie. "They got killed."

"Then they tried but it turns out they can't help us!" Carol yelled.

"They should be able to," said Katie. She didn't want to drop the point. "They're aliens. They're far more advanced. You know they can do something."

"I think they're at a loss of what to do," said Travis. "Then again we haven't seen them for two days."

"They just don't care," said Carol.

"I think there might be a way," said Laura. She wanted to tell about the female Grey but was too scared to say she had gotten communication from her. They might take it the wrong way that she had been hiding it. Especially Carol. "I have to try."

Katie looked at Laura. "Do you think they will really even listen?"

"Yes, I'm optimistic."

"Good luck with your new friends," scoffed Carol.

"Something else I noticed." Laura ignored Carol again. She was too far lost for her to consider. "It looks like the shadows are going after the males, too. Or at least it seems that way. It could also be that they were just alone at the opportune time, but what I know is that three of the men are gone, and Travis, you're left."

"Oh God," Katie was panicked. She grabbed Travis's arm.

Travis looked at Laura contemplating what she said and nodded. "Yeah, you're right. Or it's a coincidence, but it doesn't look likely."

"We don't know that for sure yet." Katie didn't want to believe it. She didn't want to lose her boyfriend. She loved him. "Harry, Rob, and Shawn were alone when it got them. This backs up why the thing struck and killed them before us."

"I don't think that's it, babe," Travis looked solemnly at Katie.

"Maybe they're just opportunistic," Katie was starting to plead selfishly just as much for herself. She couldn't lose her boyfriend or be alone.

"They're hunting out the males. Looks like the laws of our jungles apply out in space, too."

Laura wanted everyone to refocus. "Okay, but no matter whether someone is being targeted or not, they're after us all anyway, moving around the way they do. Have you realized that? Like when we were in the backyard and it was jumping around from person to person?"

"Yeah, I guess," said Katie.

"Makes sense," Travis agreed.

Carol looked unemotionally at the youngsters and then back at Laura. Her head turned robotically as if on a swivel. Ashley was listening intently to Laura while biting on her nails.

"It jumps around in the dark. Like it moves in our shadows," said Laura.

"Figure it was waiting for Harry then in the dark," said Travis.

"Yeah. It could have even tracked him by staying in his shadows. Remember how close we could smell it but couldn't see it?"

"Heck yeah," said Katie. "It's disgusting. And you can't get away from it. Like it stays with you."

"Right. Unless you can tag onto somebody else basically." Laura paused to look out the window. Something had caught her eye but it was nothing and she continued. "I think that is what Harry was doing when he was jumping on Rob. I don't think he knew exactly why it worked, and he was panicking, but he wanted it off him so badly that he realized if he got close to somebody else it would attach to that person. That happened to be Rob."

"Right, good points," said Travis. "Sure seems that way now that you say it."

"What happened to Harry anyway?" asked Katie. "We haven't talked about it yet. Or do we want to?"

"Don't know. We left. He went out and dropped off the rest of Rob's body," Laura said. She hesitated at how gross that was. "And he was alone. We took off to that hill and it must have got him when we were at the hill, obviously."

"Ashley, what did you see?"

"Don't ask her," Carol said protectively. She thought her daughter had been through enough already and she was afraid they would blame her for what happened to Harry. That they would blame her for the lollipop men. Carol wasn't going to allow it.

Laura knew this would be difficult. She had to work around a very protective mother who was getting close to being beyond reason. "We need to know."

"What difference does it make? He's dead!"

"Shut up!" Laura lost her temper momentarily but regained herself. She needed the girl to trust her. "Ashley, we need to know. It might help us live."

Ashley puckered her lips. She knew everyone's eyes were on her. "I saw my brother Kenny. He was up on the hill running around. We used to play all kinds of hide and seek games." She looked at her mother for her approval. "I saw him, Mommy. I did, honest."

Carol squeezed Ashley's arm gently. "I know you did, doll baby." She spoke with a tender tone that sounded almost foreign to the others. Gone was the cracking hostility that she had grown into.

"So you saw your brother?" said Laura. "Days ago we saw that dead Grey dressed in black in the backyard and when we went to it the body disappeared. It's like something is playing with our minds. Could this be the same thing? Like an illusion?"

Carol grabbed Ashley's shoulders protectively. "If she saw her brother she saw him."

"I don't doubt that she saw him but he wasn't there," Laura said calmly.

"My little girl wouldn't lie," said Carol. The growl was back in her voice.

"We know that," said Laura. "It's a trick by someone. By something."

They all shared glances among themselves in understanding. Even Carol seemed to come together, her fall from normality briefly halted, and she rose into comprehension with what Laura said about their situation.

"Be careful what you see then," said Travis.

"Yeah, it might not be real," Katie said. "And stick together, too."

"I agree," said Laura. "Nobody goes anywhere alone. At least not at night."

Everyone agreed.

"I need to put Harry's body out into the yard," said Laura. "See if they come and take him. Anyone want to help me with the awful task of getting him down off the stairs?"

"We will," said Travis. He and Katie went to help Laura.

The three of them unpinned Harry from the railing on the stairway and wrapped him up in a sheet from his bed. They carried the body out into the front yard where the ritual always took place and left it there tied up next to the smelly bag that contained Rob's body parts. Each carried their bone spear in case of attack.

They walked back to the house and kicked out the broken supports in the railing. A few of them had sharp points so they decided to use those as weapons and put those in the living room. All five of them gathered in the kitchen, warmed up their breakfasts, and ate without much conversation.

The Greys did come out from behind the watery wall and took the body of Harry. They did so in the same matter as with the other bodies both human and Grey. That gave each of the group a small, but short-lived, feeling of satisfaction that the unfeeling Greys did honor Harry, one of their own, in life and death. They also took the bag that contained Rob's body and disappeared behind the wall again as if they'd never been there.

But they had been there and Laura was going to go and try to speak to them. She waited until after lunch time and headed out in the afternoon.

She walked cautiously with her bone spear ready in anticipation of the unexpected. Laura didn't know if the Greys would stop her and hold her body in suspension like they had done to Rob. Or if the shadow creature would start to stalk her now that she was out in the open. However, with each step she took, neither of these possibilities transpired. Her body didn't get trapped in an invisible vice grip and the rotten smell of the shadow didn't make itself known. Laura felt relieved as she got to the ritual spot and looked at the wall. It moved beautifully with its waters flowing in and out of itself. She thought it was hard to believe that the cold and ruthless Greys were on the other side. Perhaps they were on the other side and laughing at her. Laughing at the puny human. Laughing at the fool. Laura shrugged the thought of that off. She had no choice and it was a decision she had made. She would reach out. And she would do it to one specific Grey.

"Oh, Lady Grey," Laura started. She was thinking of the Female. The one they called Goldilocks. She was imagining the strange blonde hair the alien had and focused on that. Laura tried to feel the same feeling as she had when the Female had communicated to her before. She wanted to establish a connection link to the Grey. Laura wanted their minds to be on line together. "Female Grey…." She tried again but stopped because it sounded really stupid to her. There was a way to do it and that was just to think it. To feel it. Laura started to pull her emotions into herself and focus them on the Female. She roped in her feelings and held them down inside. Laura had one goal and that was to direct her concentration at the Female. With a deep breath, her eyes closed and her body relaxed. Her breathing became tranquil. Effortlessly, she sent her mind towards the Female. And it didn't take long for an answer.

I'm here Laura.

Laura felt relieved. The Female had responded. There was a chance for them after all. She needed to feel her own thoughts and let them pour out of her. She concentrated hard and pulled herself down within herself. Her body tensed for a moment and let herself go. "We need help."

You've been strong and brave Laura.

The Female was a soothing influence on Laura and her fears immediately started to calm. Desperation started to fade away. The Female was communicating not by language but through feelings. She tapped into Laura's emotions. The thoughts she felt zipped into her mind with astonishing speed. Yet they arrived with incredible ease that she understood what they meant.

"Something is inside here hunting and killing us," said Laura.

Don't give up Laura.

"Can you help us?"

Come with me.

There was a bright flash that made Laura look away and the wall opened. After a few seconds, she looked back. There stood the Female.

CHAPTER 94

The rest had grouped on the porch to watch. Their feelings ranged from hope and desperation to a big waste of time. That was until the wall opened and revealed the Female. Goldilocks as they called her. They watched Laura drop her bone spear and walk through the bright opening and the wall sealed up behind her. She was gone.

CHAPTER 95

Laura looked at the Female. The light behind her cast a halo effect up on her hair and around her head. Her inverted black eyes were like dark leaves on her oversized head. They didn't cut into Laura like the eyes of the Yellow and Red did. The Female's eyes were different. Laura felt humanity in them.

She stepped forward and walked through the opening in the wall and felt no pain as she did. The Female stood next to her and watched her. Laura looked at the Female and stepped back. The strangeness of seeing up close the Female's oversized head, strange eyes, and blonde hair made her gasp a little but she quickly recovered and remained still. She looked back into the compound at the house with everyone watching on the porch. It felt reminiscent of leaving home for the first time when she went off to college and her family waved good-bye to her. Laura became sad.

I'll show you something Laura.

She snapped back to the Female. The large black eyes didn't blink or move but Laura knew they were full of life inside. No threatening feelings penetrated her and she wasn't scared. In fact, there was more of a maternal protectiveness that resonated from the Grey that seemed out of place in this world, but she felt it none the same.

"Okay," Laura answered. She didn't know what to say and she was in the Grey's control.

Follow.

Laura moved up next to the Female, who turned gracefully, and they started walking. She made a mental note to herself that they were going in an eastern direction in accordance with the inside of the compound. They walked inside an invisible bubble that appeared and disappeared with each step they took. The bubble had a ten-foot radius around them. Laura couldn't tell what it was made of because it appeared to flow along coming right out of the air. Looking up and down at it she became very curious. The Female sensed this.

It's a protective orb to shield you from dangers in the air while you are out of your natural environment.

Laura nodded in understanding. She didn't know what to say. She didn't know what they were doing yet or what was going to happen. If it wasn't for the calm nature she felt from the Female, she would be terrified. Laura wondered if the Grey could read her mind, or feel her emotions, and did she even need to speak in verbal communication at all? The Female felt this too.

You can interconnect with me however you'd like Laura.

"Okay," Laura said again, still unsure what to say. It was unsettling how she would think naturally and in return get replies inside her head as if they were having a conversation. Laura thought about how unfair it was because she didn't get a chance to retract or rethink her own thoughts before the Female would know what she was thinking. Laura didn't get to keep her own personal thoughts to herself. It was like an invasion of her mental privacy. What worried her the most was she didn't want to think anything bad about the Female that would offend her. The Grey wasn't hostile and appeared to want to help. Their first ally here on this planet and they needed her.

"Where are we?" Laura spoke naturally.

You're on a planet called Elesterra. It is in the constellation Sagittarius X and is more than 120 light years away from your planet. Both are unknown to Earth because they're hidden in clouds of cosmic dust.

That sounds so far away, thought Laura. Then a feeling of humor drifted into her body that she knew came from the Female. The Grey understood.

"If you don't mind my asking, are you called...." She wasn't sure how to phrase her question.

You would call us Elesterrians.

That makes sense, thought Laura. Again, another feeling of humor drifted into her body.

"Okay, I have another question," said Laura. They walked together down a corridor that emitted a bright whitish light. The bubble orb moved along with them before vanishing again in a rotating pattern. "Why are we here?"

To be seen and observed by our populace and our children.

"That's what we call a zoo back on Earth."

Yes. This place has species from other planets and galaxies too.

Laura knew where this was going so she spoke carefully. "We as individuals didn't want to come here. We've been taken away against our will. That's called kidnapping back on Earth. And three of us have died now."

I know.

Laura felt remorse flow into her body from the Female.

And I feel great regret with pain for this. This hasn't happened for many planet rotations.

"What are those?"

When a planet completes its travel around its orbit. Aren't those what you call a calendar year?

"Oh yes," Laura nodded. "That must be your Grey lingo."

Lingo? Do you mean some form of communication?

"Yes." The protective bubble materialized and disappeared into thin air again as Laura walked next to the Grey. The corridor was starting to feel more like a tunnel and now glassy windows appeared on both sides of her. "What is your name?"

We don't have names in the way that you do. We just know and feel each other as individuals. Let me see if I can show you.

Laura felt a strong feeling grow inside her. It started from within her body and warmly spread out inside her. She wasn't scared. Laura knew it was the Female communicating over to her. It was like the Female's mark. She didn't exactly know how to interpret it other than this was in a sense the Female's name. Not done with language but done with feelings.

You can call me Goldilocks if you like.

Laura felt embarrassment. The Female's ability to read her mind was incredible. The Grey knew about the nickname they assigned to her from an old fable and that was something Laura wished she hadn't found out. Especially since it was Laura who first said it. On the positive side, she didn't seem offended by it. Laura thought maybe their alien race didn't take offense to things said or done. In fact, the feeling came to her that the Female liked the name. The Female's ability to feel and read everything about them was starting to overwhelm her. She needed to find a way within herself to deal with it because as a living being it made her feel naked.

"What does the symbol mean on your uniform?" Laura asked.

This represents our sun.

"Oh, I see."

They approached the first window on the right. The window was as tall as she was and it flowed in the same liquidly way the wall of their compound did yet she could see through it. They stopped. Laura looked inside and saw an enclosed area but this was different from hers. The ground, the sky, and what were small mountains in the back were all blue. There was something falling inside the area too. Laura stared at it hard. It was blue snow coming down softly. *How pretty*, she thought. Then in back something caught her attention. Something about the size of a small dog with some sort of fin on the back of it was moving up and down. It raised up, moved a few feet, and settled down again. It camou-flaged perfectly into the blue snowy ground with its fin sticking straight up. The natural environment kept it hidden behind a blue blanket of falling snow. Laura saw another one move to her left. And then a couple more behind them. There was a whole herd of the them inside moving around.

Ice creatures from a bluish moon of a large gaseous planet. They use their fin to detect food while staying protected down in the frozen ground.

They walked to the next window this time on the left side. Laura looked inside to a flat world of grayish and blackish terrain that looked very dry. The sky was very dark. There was ash all over and fumes of gas were puffing out of geysers. Giant flat squares slowly walked on the ground. They were dirty gray in color and had four legs on each corner that bent with several joints as they walked. They looked like walking solar panels.

Silicon. Born of a unique world of depleting oxygen. Where life evolved from the chemistry on what would be an unfriendly planet for you Laura.

To Laura they were computers that were alive. Then all at once they all fell flat into the ground and became part of the rocky landscape. Over on the left, another square tilted itself up, and fell sideways into a flat side of a big rock. It was like something had sounded an alarm that only they sensed. They blended in identically with the land.

Laura and the Female moved on.

"How long do they all stay here? Do they ever leave?"

Some do. Depends on the species.

"What about us? Do we get to go?" Laura felt sharp guilt from the Female.

It's undetermined. Your group is one of our special attractions.

Laura knew it was just like they had feared. They were pieces of meat to them.

You're amazing with your wide range of abilities. Many of them yet to come into existence.

They arrived at another compound area but it was dark inside except for fast blinking lights that were zipping around very quickly. Other lights were stationary in the air and blinked but weren't moving. Laura couldn't see any structure inside because the lights didn't illuminate enough to reveal the topography. They blinked on and off like fireflies but were bigger like the size of baseballs.

They are living proton lights. Watch.

Laura watched closely for a minute but nothing happened. She was about to question the Female when in back a giant light the size of a beanbag chair flashed. Laura stepped back in surprise from the size of it. The light flashed again more quickly this time and continued to do so. It reminded Laura of a huge strobe light. As it continued to flash the surrounding terrain became slightly visible and she saw some shafts sticking up from the ground that looked like trees. The smaller proton lights were darting around but were landing on these shafts. Laura now saw that the stationary ones were sitting on the shafts, blinking, and then took off and flew around themselves. The huge strobe light in the middle continued to shine.

That's the mother in the middle flashing her communication to the flock.

"On Earth we call that a queen bee."

They continued down the passageway. Laura noticed the Female never walked ahead or behind her. She was always even with her.

Next they came to another window. Inside was a world full of reddish mud. Dispersed around the area were reddish hills that were as tall as a house. It reminded Laura of the images of Mars she'd seen on television sent back from the NASA rovers on the planet. They didn't stop to watch for animals living inside and the Female offered no explanation.

They walked to the next room where she saw a brown rocky landscape with bright red circles on the ground spaced evenly apart. Laura looked and didn't see anything else except for two moons in the sky that cast white light across the enclosure. They were on opposite sides of the sky.

Those are two of their moons for that planet's environment.

Laura kept watching the red circles because she knew they meant something. Perhaps they were some sort of anthill. She looked from circle to circle and then something moved. A neck raised out of the ground and a head popped out from the end. It was bright red like the circles on the ground. Another neck rose out of the closest circle to it and slowly a head emerged. The necks dangled across from each other, rising up and down, and moving in circular patterns. They continued to dance for a few seconds longer and then the first one attacked. Quickly it reached out and bit the other, let go, and disappeared back into its hole in the ground. The other neck swayed back and forth in the air and dropped on the rocky floor.

Its bite is deadly and they compete against each other as you just saw. It attacks. Then it retreats to avoid any danger and then will go back to get its prey.

"It eats its own?"

Yes. Is that any different than life on your planet?

Laura knew what the Female meant. "No. We have that too. And in more ways than just eating."

It's part of the nature of the universe to compete. Not just human nature.

"Alien cannibalism. Survival of the fittest, I guess."

Yes. And the universe is aware of its lethality. This animal is bright red because of how dangerous and poisonous it is. It even has a red warning sign on the ground around the hole it lives in.

Laura understood. She knew of frogs in Central and South America that were red to announce to predators that they're poisonous. So why wouldn't some of the same survival tactics exist elsewhere in the universe? It seemed natural to her.

A flying brown creature flew in and took Laura by surprise. It was two feet long and had eight red wings that were also two feet in length. Laura wondered if the wings were poisonous too. The creature landed on the dead neck-creature and started to dig into its skin. The flying creature had one big eye like a Cyclops and didn't appear to be affected by the poisonous red skin. The flier continued to dig unaware that the other neck-creature was coming out of its hole again. Slowly it raised up, dangling itself in the air. The bright red was apparent like a bright flare to Laura. Its head popped out of the end and it started to make circles. The flier fluttered its wings, busy going about its work. Then the circling neck-creature struck down and bit the flier. It turned sharply and its wings slashed out at the neck-creature but it missed. The neck-creature retreated down into the ground. The brown flier lifted into the air and swooped over the neck-creature's hole but missed as it was too late. The flying creature continued to soar up but then it stalled in the air and fell down crashing on brown rock. It lay there dead. Slowly, the bright red neck revealed itself again out of its hole and dangled in the air again, before circling down and biting into the body of the flier. It avoided the red wings and was careful not to touch them. In the light reflecting off the moons down into the enclosure, Laura watched the neck creature start to eat.

CHAPTER 96

All the events Laura had witnessed were a lot for her to process. They were in a zoo with alien life from other planets and put there for entertainment and scientific reasons. They were like a science project. Or like Shawn had said, they were animals in a zoo.

The Female wasn't hostile and was very friendly. Laura didn't get any feeling of malice from her at all. In fact, the Female seemed to want to help and was reaching out to her. She was being shown a tour of the facilities and allowed to witness alien life within the zoo. Laura thought that might make her the first human in history to have seen these other alien life forms. That would be true unless they weren't the first to be taken here. She wondered if this had been going on for hundreds of years. However, more importantly she needed to know how they could get back home to Earth. That and what was the shadow thing that had been preying on them? What could they do to kill it? Would the Female help? Laura needed to ask more questions. She needed information.

"That's quite a sequence of events," Laura started. "Clever, the neck animal killed off its competition and used it for bait to lure in some prey. Very impressive."

Yes. We have this happening all over the zoo as you call it. Life forms from other worlds carrying out their natural existence here for our species to see.

"And to educate your children."

Yes. But they aren't children like your species or the life on planet Earth.

Laura noticed for the first time the Female called Earth by its name.

I should explain. We recreate ourselves by copying from what already exists. We're duplicates.

"You're clones?"

Yes. If that is what your Earth description is for it. Over millions of planet rotations we have evolved past family. As we evolved we moved beyond the universal nature of instinctive reproduction and heredity to a scientific overall approach of continuing and preserving our species. A decision was made to let science take control with our created technology to genetically make our species for the future without creating any errors. It was also believed that we had created this technology therefore it was created by something of nature. A nature created by and existing in the universe and therefore it was natural to use within the existing laws of the universe. That is the first principle of theory in our culture for our species.

"I see." To Laura that sounded like the Ten Commandments or the United States Constitution. She wasn't surprised that the Greys would have a basis of belief in which they lived their society but now it was laid out in front of her. To the Greys, if nature created them, then it was justified to use whatever they invented in any way they deemed fit, because it was being done in the name of universal nature by beings made by the universe. There was no scientific ethics debate within the Greys like there is on Earth about these issues. It was like the Greys' moral clause.

But what's happened is that over millions of planet rotations of duplicating ourselves we're beginning to think we've lost our nature. We don't seem to have what you call feelings anymore. Through the constant recreating of our species emotions have been lost. We've also lost basic skills of survival and existence that we had possessed millions of planet rotations ago and now we rely too much on our own created technology.

"Right, I understand." Laura was thrilled the Female was opening up like this. She could feel it coming from her with each thought placed inside her head. "Like you're too much of a clone or a robot now. You don't feel like a Grey anymore. On Earth, we would say you've lost your humanity."

We got away from that and we miss that. That's why I'm part human. I'm one of a few who were created using an ingredient of biological genetic material taken from people from your planet on other expeditions to Earth. That is why I feel for humans and understand you. I care for you and want to help. That is why I've been watching your area and have reached out to you. I chose you because you're a very good person Laura. We need more of that in the universe. There is too much bad out in the universe. There are good and beautiful places too. But we need more living beings like yourself populating the amazing universe.

The feeling of empathy from the Female tingled throughout Laura's body. She didn't know what to do. "You're what we call a hybrid."

Of course my blonde human hair distinguishes me from my fellow Greys.

"You're awesome!"

They are still deciding whether to continue with the humanizing of some of our kind or not. It is an incredible monumental decision for our civilization and the direction of our species.

"I can understand that."

Naturally you can. You're human. But I know you have other questions such as when you and your group of cohabitants can go home? Or what is the alien being that is killing you?

"Yes." Laura didn't know where to start. "When do we get to go home? That thing is some sort of shadow creature and it's killing us."

First I don't know when you can return to Earth. The Masters wear the colors of Yellow and Red. They planned to keep you for a long time. At least for several planet rotations.

"The Yellow and Red Grey seem very negative in this universe."

I feel bad for the indifference from the Yellow and Red towards you and your cohabitants. They are a product of our high evolution with lost emotions. They are very highly advanced and very powerful with their mental evolution. And very dangerous.

"What is the shadow creature that's killing us?"

The name is the Illucii. We don't know where it comes from but it has been rumored to have been discovered on other planets. Life forms have been found void of liquid. Empty. It nourishes itself from the juices that flow inside of life.

"The Illucii. It smells really bad."

Yes.

"Pretty sure there are two of them. There's a sweeter syrupy smell with one of them."

That's the female.

"That's how we know when it's around but we never know until it's too late and it's among us. It stays hidden."

Yes. It hides in dark places. Like your shadow.

Laura remembered two days before when the Illucii were jumping among them in the backyard.

Yes. It was them.

"It must have evolved that way. Like it has its own built-in camouflage."

It is also very flexible. It can move in ways that your species and mine can't.

Laura stood remembering for a moment. There was that one night she thought she saw Ashley out on the porch. Then there was the time they saw the dead Hunter Grey on the ground and it disappeared. And last night little Ashley thought she saw her brother up on the hill but he wasn't there. People were seeing things.

It's intelligent. The Illucii can project images into the minds of other beings.

"So it's not just an animal. It has evolved telepathy like you have."

Yes. From whatever way and whatever planet it was born on it has developed powers of the mind of its own kind.

"The Illucii was using its mind power on us as bait, to lure us out, so it could prey on us."

Yes. I scanned your mind to trace for evidence after the bodies of your co-habitants were found and I believe the Illucii has done that.

Laura thought about what the Female had just communicated. The Illucii can leave a mark on your mind? That was too scary. What else could it do to her? Could it scar her, or any of them, for life?

That's unconfirmed.

Laura looked back at the deep dark eyes. She had almost forgotten that the Female could feel her thoughts. That too was a little unnerving. "Can it read our minds like you can?"

That's unconfirmed.

Laura knew they needed to kill it. "The Yellow and Red are very powerful but they haven't helped us at all."

They are very powerful and I feel very sad for the deaths of your fellow species.

"It's like they'll allow us, their special attraction, to die."

Come.

They walked further down the passageway. The wall on both sides shined its bright whitish light upon the orb around them. The orb materialized in its rotating pattern as if laying down a path for them to walk on. They continued until they reached the next windows. The Female signaled toward the swirling window on the right. Laura looked inside and saw a moist swampy environment. There was a green substance everywhere that reminded her of algae. It was even spreading onto the translucent window that she was looking through. The Yellow and Red Greys were inside standing over a body of some kind. A few small worker Greys were rushing around them performing their work functions. Laura saw a yellow and green striped creature that was round like a small coffee table. There were what looked like foot-long fingers outlining the end of the body. She couldn't be sure if those were actual fingers but they looked like support limbs of some kind to move around on. The finger legs were sticking straight upwards. To Laura it looked like a giant yellow and green dandelion, without the stem, turned over on its back. The body looked to be in a phase of rigor mortis like the bodies in her compound. The Yellow and Red looked as cold as they had when Shawn was found.

It's loose in the zoo.

"You seem surprised. You didn't expect this could happen, did you?"

No. It was considered that our knowledge and technology were ahead of any mistakes of this kind.

"The most highly developed technology can't stop everything. There are always going to be mistakes or consequences whether unintended or unforeseen."

True. Another fact of the universe.

"Do you know how it got loose in the zoo?"

It can survive in many different environments.

"Do you know how it got here?"

It was hidden and came in on one of our ships. We found a black substance that it leaves. It's also been found elsewhere in the zoo.

"Like a stowaway," Laura said. She felt a warm feeling of agreement from the Female.

It's stealthy.

"How can we kill it?"

I'm working on that. The Masters won't want their prize damaged. They will help.

"What if they don't?"

If they don't I will get permission to help myself.

Laura knew they operated under a chain of command like people on Earth did. Or at least there was a pecking order of sort. Laura knew she and her cohabitants were at the bottom and needed to get home to where that wasn't so anymore. As long as they were on Elesterra they were like insects to be squashed. "What's your plan?" Laura felt the serious gaze from the Female's black eyes grip her mind like a vice.

You'll have to find the Illucii. See it. Concentrate on it. On both Illucii. And after you do that we can send in our Hunters to kill them. They will use their mind strike to kill it from within. We can project and control a wave of energy called a mind strike from our minds. We all of our species have the capability of it but they are trained in it.

"I see." Laura was nodding her head in approval. Then she got worried expecting the worst. "What if they fail?"

Then I will myself.

A feeling flowed into Laura that told her the Female was more powerful than the Hunter Greys, but they were the soldiers of their race, and this was their job. "Okay, so when the Illucii come to kill us I'll do that. I have to basically be the bait. Can any of us do this and concentrate on them?"

Yes. We can channel through any of your minds and navigate to the Illucii. We've had difficulty locating them because of how stealthy they are. This way by seeing them through your minds we can then track a position on them and go in and eliminate them.

It sounded very risky to Laura but it was more than they had before to hope for. They had a chance. She allowed some feelings of appreciation to convey to the Female and in return received a mutual feeling that was understood.

Time is done. Let you return now.

As they turned to walk back through the passageway curiosity got the best of Laura and she took a quick look through the window on the other side. Her eyes were captured by what she saw. Inside it was grassy, much like Earth, and a hairy humanoid animal with four legs was kneeling on the ground. It was covered in dark brown hair and was looking around for something. The animal patted its head a lot. After a few moments, it started to walk on all fours. It wobbled from side to side.

We need to go Laura.

An invisible force nudged her to start walking back the way they came.

"What was that animal?"

Something from the past.

Laura felt it was something more.

CHAPTER 97

They got back to the compound and Laura turned and faced the Female. The watery wall was bubbling next to her but she could see the house and trees inside. The invisible orb materialized and disappeared again one final time on her tour of the zoo. Laura knew that even though she couldn't see the bubble that she had been kept safe inside it. The Female stood looking directly into her with those black inverted eyes.

"Okay, I've got the plan."

Good Laura.

Laura wanted to ask about the morning pains. "We get pains in our stomach every morning. And then they go away after we drink the water from the globe inside our refrigerator. Do you know why?"

There was more sorrow from the Female. Then it turned to guilt.

I'm sorry to tell you that we made that. It's a side effect from the tests we performed on all of you when you were brought on the ship when they took you from Earth. There were numerous tests run on you that included taking some biological specimens which cause the morning pains after a night of rest. The water cures them for a day. The Masters realized it also served to control the inhabitants of the zoo. It's a control factor.

"Will it ever go away?" Laura didn't want it anymore.

We think it should over time but it could be native to this compound. In a way I think the stomach pains are attracted to our technology and the closer you are to it the worse it gets. I don't think it would be as severe back on Earth.

Laura felt more distress upon feeling the Female's answer. She didn't want to live the rest of her life with these stomach pains. Especially after they gave them to her and to her group of companions. This was even more reason she wanted so badly to get back to Earth. Her body felt the Female empathize back to her in return.

"We call that morning sickness but for a different reason." Laura wanted to put a happier spin on it. "But usually for a much more celebrated reason."

Again, the Female felt understanding.

You may have noticed that the wind inside your area has a strange effect on you and your companions. That's because it's special and designed to calm your feelings and anxieties. To make you passive.

"To make us docile like pets."

I'm sorry Laura. The water and wind are control factors used throughout the zoo. It's what the Masters do. They don't have the understanding of a deep and good person like you.

"Thank you." Laura didn't know what else to say. The Female was very gracious to her.

Laura saw that inside the compound it looked a little dark again like an internal storm was starting. "What's up with the crazy weather? It keeps changing and acting erratic. Lightning flashing all over the place."

A feeling of acknowledged embarrassment passed over her.

We've had some problems. Our weather machine was created to imitate your home planet's environment to make it as real as possible. This was done for us and for you.

Laura said, "But the nights are dark. Except for the fake moon and stars that were put up on our ceiling."

We can change that. We can open the sky for you at night but not during the day because of the planet's atmosphere.

"Uh-oh, what's wrong with the planet?"

We can't do that during the day because the atmosphere is too dangerous. There was an accident years ago that had a distinct effect on the planet. This planet has two suns and during the day it's too hot and there's too much ultraviolet radiation that fills the atmosphere. The planet's outer layer isn't as strong anymore and can't withstand the double dose of rays from both stars.

Laura only had to think the next question and the Female responded.

Our power systems exploded years ago from a big blast of gamma rays that hit the planet and disrupted the protective shield from radiation. It cut slices in the atmosphere.

"I thought you all could control that with your advanced technology."

Proves that technology can't solve everything. The universe is too big and powerful to be controlled by technology created by life existing within the universe.

"But you're still here on this planet?"

That is also because of our advancements. We've had to adapt and build a more underground existence since then. We have survived and will.

"Do you know how the accident happened?"

We don't know where the gamma ray burst originated from. It slammed into the planet suddenly. There is more to it than that on our end though. We were advancing too fast and it got out of control. When we used our systems to protect us and the planet it made everything worse.

That confirmed a belief that Laura had thought for years about her own humankind so she wanted to share it. "I think we on Earth have been evolving in those regards too quickly as well. I think it's okay to have it. Just important not to get too far ahead of ourselves. I call it a microwave society." Laura felt agreement from the Female.

"Unfortunately, I think there's no way to stop it. Once things start rolling along they can't be stopped sometimes."

Until THIS happens.

Laura took the Female's point to heart.

Time for you to go. And remember.

"Kill the shadow."

Be brave.

"I am."

CHAPTER 98

When Laura got back to the house everyone looked inquisitively at her. A few of them were happy and greeted her with smiles except for Carol whose face showed contempt. Laura decided she would avoid her as much as possible.

Laura had picked up her bone spear at the ritual point and carried it with her as a sense of empowerment. The spear was now a symbol of strength to her. It was a symbol that they had a fighting chance now to kill the Illucii that was hunting them. To hold it gave her confidence even when her mind didn't believe the Female's plan would work. Not at least without losing a few more of their lives.

"I've got a lot to tell you," said Laura.

"Are you one of them now?" Carol asked sarcastically.

Laura ignored her. "We need to go inside and I'll explain."

Everyone followed her into the house and they sat around the living room. The fake thunder started to roll again in the east and the wind began to blow against the house as another storm was starting to grow. Laura told them about the empathy the Female had for them and about how the Female was part human DNA. She told them about intricate workings of the zoo and what she had seen on her tour of it. To a few of them it was much like sitting around a camp fire at night telling ghost stories. Laura described in the best detail what she could remember. They were amazed at the discovery of other alien life forms and what they were like and how they had behaved. The fact that they were light years away from Earth gave them a creepy feeling of isolation and made them feel more alone than at any other point while being there. She told them about the Greys' weather machine and its malfunctions inside the compound. She also told them about the disaster that happened to the planet's atmosphere from the gamma ray burst. Then Laura slowly got into the more difficult details of what she had learned and explained about the stomach pains and what they were. She also told them about their drinking water, and the blowing wind inside their compound, and their functions of being control factors used on them. This had a dehumanizing effect on everyone. Finally, Laura told them about the Illucii. She hadn't wanted to scare the group so she waited until last before revealing what was hunting them. Morale wasn't helped by the fact that little was known about the Illucii. Laura did explain that the Illucii stalked its victims by hiding in the shadows of its prey. After all that had sunk in Laura explained the Female's plan to the group. They responded with empty stares.

"So now we're bait?" Travis asked, a hint of anger in his voice.

Laura shrugged. "I don't know what else to say. That's her plan. And they can kill it."

"So we have to let it in here and attack us for them to kill it?" Katie asked. She didn't believe in the plan. "We're dead."

"We're not letting it attack us because it's going to attack us anyway." Laura wanted to direct the way they thought of the plan. "It's coming for us. It's feeding on us."

Travis snorted. "That's great."

"Hey, what the heck?" said Katie. "We're dead anyway so what choice do we have?"

"It doesn't matter who it is that the mind strike goes through, so we have to work together. It can be any of us. She said they can zero in on it through our minds and pinpoint it if we concentrate and focus on it."

"Like we're the GPS," Travis said. "Terrific."

Ashley was sitting with her doll at her mom's feet and chewing on her hair. She was listening as intently as any of the adults were. She looked up at her mom. "Mommy, are the lollipop men really gonna help?"

Carol didn't look down at her. She kept watching Laura. "Those bastards want us to die for them."

Everyone looked at her but nothing was said. Ashley was staring up at her mom but her mother didn't acknowledge her so she looked at Laura. In those blue eyes, Laura saw sadness for the first time, and she knew Ashley thought her mother wasn't her mom anymore.

The thunder cracked outside and the wind blew a steady serenade as rain started to fall. It darkened more in the compound like any summer's day would in the Midwest with an approaching storm.

"More alien weather," Katie said. "Stupid weather machine."

"Yeah, trying to control weather," said Travis. "Not gonna happen."

Laura didn't want to lose focus. "Okay, so we know the drill, right?"

Everyone except Carol nodded.

"There isn't anything we can do until the Illucii come back for us. In the meantime, stay alert, and look out for any signs of it. Especially for that smell."

"Yuck, it stinks," Ashley said.

"Hell yeah, it does," said Travis. He held out his fist to her and Ashley did a little fist bump with him.

"We don't know when it's gonna come either," said Katie.

"No. We don't," said Laura. "But it will."

"That's for sure," said Carol. She sounded detached like she was in a different place than they were.

CHAPTER 99

Everyone went about what had become the usual routine. They sat around looking out the windows to keep alert for the nasty smell of an approaching shadow creature. They ate dinner and everyone settled back in the living room and kitchen. Again, there were nervous faces that looked out the windows in anticipation of the Illucii.

An hour passed into the evening, the light of the fake sun outside started to fade, and everyone felt comfortable enough to take some showers and get the sticky dirty feeling off their bodies. Carol and Ashley were the first to clean up. Carol didn't look any more settled when she came down afterwards. Her face still possessed its hateful stare. A stare that if looks could kill would destroy the Greys at first sight.

Travis and Katie were next. Their love making made their shower longer than normal. They realized that this could be the last time they had a chance to be together romantically. That this could be their last night alive.

Laura was last to go. She wanted to shower and change quickly to be downstairs before nightfall. She finished drinking a glass of water in the kitchen and set it in the sink. The kitchen light was on but it began to flicker. Laura looked at it. That isn't what they needed now, one less room of light. The light seemed to be all that protected them at night. It stopped flickering and she watched it for a minute to assure herself that it was okay and went upstairs.

Near the top there was a tingling sensation on her right leg above the ankle. She scratched it and proceeded into her room and collected some soap and a pair of towels, put fresh clothes on her bed, and went to the bathroom. Laura stepped into the bath tub and felt instantly refreshed as the water shot down from the shower and ran along her body. She lathered up with her soap and ran it over her shoulders, along her arms, around her breasts, the rest of her body, and let the water carry suds down her legs. The water trickled through her toes and gurgled down the drain. She smelled the soap and took in its fresh scent as artificial as it was. For manufacturing products from Earth to make it seem more like their home, Laura thought the Greys hadn't done half bad with the soap. Her mind drifted some more. Laura thought about how she would love to sleep in her own bed again but she didn't mean her bed on Earth. She meant her bed here in her room in this house. That was strange to her. She washed and rinsed her hair. The water dripped down into her eyes and into her mouth. Laura spit it out softly and she started to forget the peril that she and her companions were in. The stream of water rained from above and Laura leaned down to wash her legs. She stopped. Just above her ankle where she had felt the itch on the stairs there was a purple scratch on her skin. It was about as long has her finger. Then it disappeared and her skin was pale white again. She thought that was strange. She was sure that she'd seen a purple mark on her leg. Laura examined both her legs but didn't see anything else. She stayed bent over in the shower, water bouncing off her back, watching her ankle but nothing happened. After a minute, she decided everything was okay and to chalk it up as her imagination due to the stress of their dire predicament, which wasn't a surprise around this place. Especially after the night before when Ashley thought she'd seen her brother running around outside. How that was possible had been standing on the edge of her mind bugging her all day until the Female had explained about how the Illucii use their mental powers to make other beings see things that aren't there. It must have been them.

With one final look at her legs she ended her shower and toweled off. Water continued to drip on her hair from the shower above. Laura stepped away and the water continued to slowly fall and land with a soft thud on the bath tub floor. She wrapped her towel around herself and bundled her hair up in a fresh towel. She opened the door and peeked out to see that she was alone. More importantly there was no smell from an Illucii. Quickly, she went to her room.

Laura changed into her new clothes, hung her towels up to dry in her room, and went down the stairs. As she descended the stairs the tingling sensation was back on her leg.

CHAPTER 100

They sat in the living room and waited. The light outside faded away and the night shuffled in and took root. So did the ever-growing agony of waiting for something to happen. They rested themselves in the living room with two of them on watch at a time. The living room light was working well but the kitchen light would flicker occasionally. With each flicker the tension in the room grew a little more right along with the wait. The wait for what the night would bring. The wait for the shadow creatures to come.

Nobody could bring themselves to sleep yet. Laura took first watch with Carol. Ashley stayed by her mother's side. Travis sat next to Katie by the fireplace. Everyone remained quiet, listened, and most importantly smelled. Their attentions focused outside of the room. Right now, they were in their safe zone of the living room. However, what they feared was outside of that and they didn't want it to be breached.

As if they shared the same mind, Travis and Katie both looked up and saw something through the side window. Travis got up, took a few steps forward, and peered further out. Katie got up and came up behind him. Laura couldn't imagine what it could be. She glanced over at Carol whose hateful face was one of puzzlement. However, Ashley didn't move. She hated the hill now where she had seen Kenny the day before.

"Hey," Travis broke the silence. "The stars are out."

Ashley's mood changed instantly and she jumped off the sofa. She ran to the window and pointed outward. "Mommy, just like home."

Carol's face turned back into a scowl. "Sure. Those bastards."

That reminded Laura about what the Female had said. "Oh, I forgot. The Female had told me they would open up the ceiling, like a sky roof, for us."

"But only at night because of the atmosphere, right?" said Travis. "We don't wanna be cooked."

"Right."

Katie was curious. "Let's go outside on the porch and see it better."

Laura hesitated. "You think that's a good idea?"

"It's the best thing I've seen since I've been trapped here." She slapped Travis on the butt. "You coming, babe?"

"I'm not letting you go out alone," said Travis. He looked at Laura unconvinced. "Just keep your nose alert for that smell."

"Our noses." Katie wheeled around, grabbed her bone spear, and cautiously opened the front door. Travis was behind her. After a few seconds, she deemed it safe. Holding their bone spears, they stepped onto the porch.

"Can I go, Mommy?" asked Ashley.

"No," Carol answered sternly.

Laura didn't want to get in the middle of it, so with her bone spear in hand, she walked to the front door. It was slightly open from Katie and Travis going outside. She waited.

"But I wanna see the stars. They're outside seeing them. Why can't I?"

Carol gave her a blank stare. "No."

Laura breathed deeply and didn't smell any trace of the Illucii. She turned around to Carol. "It's not really my business but I don't smell the shadow creatures. I think it's safe right now. We'll be careful. Just saying...."

Carol's blank stare turned scornful. "No."

Laura took a second look at Ashley and went out on the porch.

Ashley looked out the window again and then back to her mother.

"Bad things out there, doll baby."

CHAPTER 101

Laura stood on the porch and watched. It was serene. The compound was quiet. A nice summery breeze ruffled her hair and the leaves chattered softly in the trees. Katie and Travis stood at the rail on the west end of the porch. Laura didn't smell any hint of the Illucii so she walked to the end and joined them.

Laura rested her hands on the porch rail, and after a glimpse at the side of the house to make sure it was clear, leaned out and looked above. What she saw was beautiful. The night was decorated with waves of light from stars that littered the sky. Two moons hung brightly. The one on the left was bigger, orange in color, and the other moon was gray. Behind the moons there was a comet soaring between them: a snowball scraping across their picturesque sky. They walked to the other side of the porch. There they saw more beautiful stars and a gaseous cloud with many colors high in the sky.

"Wow," said Katie. "Wonder what that could be."

"Probably some new stars forming," whispered Laura.

"Looks like a bunch of diamonds on a necklace out in space."

They kept watching. A slow gust of wind blew over them. Nobody detected any smell from the Illucii yet. Everything seemed good.

"That cloud is cool but I think I like the other side better," said Travis. He went back to the other side and the women followed him. They all saw Ashley in the window looking at them.

They stood and stared at the stars. For each of them it brought back childhood memories of doing the same thing on warm summer nights.

Wondering what was out there. Wondering if anyone else was out there. Or if anyone was watching them back.

Travis saw something among a cluster of stars. He pointed farther west. "Look at that group of stars. See what it looks like?"

Laura and Katie looked but didn't see what he meant.

"Just above those trees over the horizon."

They kept looking. Laura focused her concentration and saw a strange patch of stars. As she continued watching she saw what he meant. A constellation of stars grouped together looked like a human skull.

"Oh God," said Laura. "It looks like a skull."

Katie agreed. "Holy shit. I see it now."

"That's what I thought," said Travis. "Talk about an omen."

"Death's on our doorstep," said Katie.

"It seems like an evil reminder," Travis said.

As if laced with thorns, it crept into their noses. The rank stench wasn't strong yet but they smelled it just the same. The Illucii were coming.

"Quick, inside," Laura said calmly.

"No arguments there," said Travis.

They rushed into the house. Travis locked the door, even though it wouldn't do any good, but it made them feel better. The kitchen light flickered a couple times as they took positions in the living room with their bone spears ready.

"What happened? What happened?" asked Ashley. She jumped onto the sofa next to her mother.

"We smelled it," Katie said. She was almost in a runner's stance on the floor.

"It wasn't real close but it was close enough," said Laura.

"Yeah, and that's too close," said Travis.

Carol had her bone spear now. "I'll kill them." That made the rest of the group glad she was there. Carol's deteriorating sanity would make her rage a good weapon.

They waited. First it was minutes and those turned into hours. The Illucii didn't attack. During the night, they thought it was smelled from the front door at different times but nothing happened. They couldn't be sure if they had smelled it or not. No smells. No shadows. No Illucii. The wait continued.

CHAPTER 102

Morning came quietly and a tired group of people stirred to life. Travis and Katie had the last watch of the night. Katie had fallen asleep on the floor. Travis was barely awake resting against the wall next to her. His head bobbed up and down as he slid in and out of sleep, lightly bumping the wall behind him, producing a soft knocking sound in the tranquility. Laura was slumped over on the sofa while Carol and Ashley slept in their spot on the back sofa. Travis's head tilted and his body started to slide on the wall. He jerked back up and this time broke out of sleep. Travis looked around the room wide-eyed in brief panic but settled down upon seeing everything was as it had been the night before. He sniffed the air and it was clean. No Illucii.

His bone spear lay on the floor next to him where it had fallen overnight. The end of it rested loosely in the relaxed grip of his hand. Travis peered over his shoulder out through the window. It was sunny like any summer morning in the Midwest back on Earth. He leaned on his bone spear for support and got up and immediately his stomach stung him a sharp pain. Every morning they all suffered from the morning sickness. Travis couldn't wait to get away from it. He knelt next to his girlfriend and gently woke her. Katie's eyes opened and after a big yawn she smiled up at him. "I'm getting some water," Travis said. He went into the kitchen.

Katie sat up, stretched out her arms and legs, and stood up unsteadily before gaining control of her balance. She softly shook Laura awake who had been lying asleep on the side sofa. When Laura looked at her,

Katie gestured over at Carol. "No way," Katie whispered and went into the kitchen.

Laura looked over at Carol and Ashley who were sound asleep and decided to leave them alone because she too didn't want to deal with Carol who was starting to scare them. Laura sat up, and like a gun with a bullet, her stomach shot pain through her body. She breathed deeply to settle herself down. As she continued to breathe, her thoughts started to replay yesterday's events, especially the tour of the zoo she'd been taken on. In a way, it was like a dream. They were trapped on a planet far from home in mortal danger, their fate hanging in the balance, and with a risky plan in which they were the bait to bring out and expose the killers in the open. This all felt like a five-thousand-pound weight resting on her shoulders. She thought by the end of the day it would drag her down into the underground.

Her thoughts stopped as Laura's leg twitched with an itch. For a moment, she thought a centipede might be crawling up her leg and she slapped at it. The itch stopped. Just like the night before, she thought it was her imagination. Then it started again. And it got worse. Laura thought it was strange because there were no insects in the compound so she pulled her pant leg up. She recoiled in horror! Two black and purple lines started above her ankle and ran halfway up her leg. They crossed in the middle. She didn't touch it and pulled her pants back down over her leg. It twitched again. Her brain started to race. What is it? What was she going to do? She couldn't let the rest of them know or she'd be outcast. Like a disease. They might even kill her.

"Something the matter?" Travis was standing by the door drinking his water.

"No," she quickly answered. "Nothing at all."

"Okay." Travis had noticed on Laura's face that she looked scared.

Katie came into the room behind him with her glass in hand. "I feel better now."

"Good deal," said Travis. "Let's check out the porch."

They put their glasses down on the ledge by the fireplace and went outside.

Laura looked down at her leg. She grabbed the pant leg but held off her internal urge to pull it up again. It scared her too much to see it. What if it was worse?

"I saw that."

The voice came from the sofa. Laura glanced to her left. Carol's eyes were wide open watching Laura.

"I saw you see your leg."

Laura stared back. She didn't know what to say. She was caught. Her leg twitched again. She better say something. Carol was waiting. "I bruised it. Two nights ago, when we were running. I fell on a rock." Laura immediately wanted to kick herself. There weren't any rocks inside the compound.

"Ohhh," Carol's voice rang out with disbelief.

Laura knew she better leave to change the subject and got up and headed to the kitchen.

"What's black and purple and is hidden all over?" said Carol.

Laura stopped. She looked at her.

"Laura's leg."

Laura's back shivered and the panic of truth started to swell up in her neck. There *is* something on her leg! Her stomach ached again. She needed to get a drink of that special water and quickly went into the kitchen and started to drink.

Carol sat up but didn't get up off the sofa. She brushed her daughter's hair and stared through the living room and out the front window. Carol knew they would all end up dead and it was only a matter of time before the shadows came for them. She was waiting.

In the kitchen, Laura finished off her second glass of water and her stomach felt better, but her anxiety told her she had to get out of the house. She went into the living room, and without looking at Carol, grabbed her bone spear and joined Katie and Travis on the porch.

From the sofa Carol watched the three of them talk though the window. She brushed Ashley's hair again. Ashley lay next to her reliving her maze dream each time her eyes blinked.

CHAPTER 103

On the porch Katie and Travis laughed when they could but were too tired and depressed and mostly talked about random thoughts. Laura joined them.

"So what do you think?" asked Travis. "They didn't come and get us last night."

"Yeah, it's weird," Laura answered.

"It's like they're waiting or something," said Katie.

"Or maybe they aren't hungry yet."

Katie shivered. "That sounds so gross when you put it that way."

"Sorry," said Laura. "It's just something I've been wondering about."

Travis pointed his thumb discreetly at the living room window. "Carol hasn't left the sofa. Like a bird of prey waiting for a mouse. She's crazy."

"Getting crazier," added Katie.

Laura flinched. Her leg felt very uncomfortable. The young couple noticed.

"What was that?" asked Travis.

"You okay?" Katie asked.

"Oh yeah, it's nothing," Laura answered. She couldn't let them know about her leg. She was worried about Carol, but after hearing them talk about how crazy she was, Laura could decry her as insane and out of control if she said anything. "We can't relax at all. The shadows are out there."

Everyone agreed. For the next hour, the three of them talked about how they missed their lives back home on Earth. They missed family, friends, and enjoying the regular things that people do and experiences that are easily taken for granted.

It was turning out to be the nicest day inside the compound. The sun was out, the trees and grass reflected the light beautifully, and a cool refreshing breeze was blowing around. The morning became a tranquil moment for the three survivors.

The door swung open and Ashley jumped out onto the porch. Her face was full of smiles. "Hi!" she said. Her sweet voice oozed naïve optimism. Laura admired how the young mind of a girl could be upbeat and positive after being trapped in this place day after day. She reasoned it might be something that gets turned off inside an adult's mind that has amassed a lifetime of experiences and responsibilities to care about.

"Hey sis, what's up?" said Laura. She was glad Ashley had joined them.

"I wanna dance."

"Okay." Laura looked around the yard and she didn't see anything that was dangerous. However, truth was in the air. She inhaled, sucked it into her lungs, and didn't smell the Illucii. "I guess that'd be okay as long as we're here."

"Is your mom okay with that?" Katie asked. She was expecting Carol to come crashing through the door any minute.

Ashley shrugged her little shoulders. "I don't know. Mommy's talking to herself so I came out. I want to see the sunshine."

Laura felt relieved that Carol wasn't coming out but didn't know if that was a good thing or not. She didn't feel comfortable with Carol around and now Carol might be talking to herself, and who knows what that meant or what it might lead to.

"And dance," said Ashley.

Travis looked out into the yard because he wasn't sure that it was okay. Laura didn't seem too worried. He glanced at Katie but she was watching Carol inside the house through the window. Travis didn't want to alert her in any way that might entice her to come outside so he looked away. *Keep her inside*, he thought.

Ashley was waiting. "Better check the roof," he said. Travis walked past them onto the steps and looked above. He smelled the air but it wasn't grotesque. Slowly, Travis continued down a step at a time and stepped out into the yard. He scanned the porch top with his eyes but didn't see anything. Nothing rancid. No black shapes. It seemed safe. He smiled at the girls. "Looks good."

"Yea!" said Ashley. She jumped off the porch and started doing a dance in the yard.

Travis stepped back onto the porch.

"You're so brave," said Katie.

"Thanks, hon," said Travis. He kissed her.

Laura didn't feel any better. The inevitable fight for their lives with the shadows weighed on her immensely. The Illucii would come for their kill. Her leg jabbed at her again and it felt worse than before. The thing growing on her leg horrified her. What was it and how did she get it? She had to keep it together and control her breathing. Her mental toughness squeezed hard to hold her away from falling into panic.

Ashley started doing somersaults again in the yard. Over and over she went like a wheel rolling out of control. Then she would spin around in circles like when she was in dance class. Travis and Katie started to talk among themselves but absent were the giggles that these two young lovers would share. Throughout their time in this depressing place, they had managed to cling to each other for support and needed to keep doing so. As Ashley danced around her movements caught Laura's eyes. At first it didn't seem like a bad idea, but watching Ashley now made her start to reconsider and think that it wasn't good, and it might attract the attention of the Illucii. She nudged Katie. "I thought of something. Do you think this might be a red alert for the shadows?"

Katie and Travis looked at Ashley. Neither answered.

"Or does it even matter anymore?" said Laura.

Travis walked to the edge of the porch and turned back to them. "I guess not. We are the chickens in the pot."

Katie made a face at that. "We can keep an eye on her. And noses. We're right here anyway."

"Yes," said Laura. "We can't go anywhere."

A light flashed and each knew what it was. Ashley stopped in the yard.

"When's it going to end?" said Katie.

The watery wall split open and a class of Grey children were watching them. The Yellow and Red stood in the middle of them like field marshals commanding their troops. The Female was in back behind the children. The feeling of a mass of eyes watching them overtook them on the porch.

"Fuck this!" Travis grabbed his bone spear, jumped off the porch, and hurled it at the wall. It soared high in the air and arced downwards looking like a perfect hurl by an Olympic javelin thrower. None of the Greys moved. They stood like rigid statues. The bone spear flew down and before it reached the Greys it struck something unseen. The spear ricocheted away. It dropped to the ground, bounced around, and rolled harmlessly away.

Pain cut through Travis and he bent over in anguish. Everyone knew where it had come from. The Yellow and Red distributed psychic punishment for an example as much as it was for control. Travis went down on one knee but the Greys pulled him up into a standing position. Next the energy came over Katie, Laura, and Ashley. Their bodies started to burn from inside. The fear of death took root.

Then the screen door opened and Carol screamed out in hatred. It was an ear-piercing scream but nobody could move to cover their ears. "Don't touch my girl!" Carol commanded. The group felt their bodies relax as the Yellow and Red released their mental grip and they were freed. The Red shot a mind strike and it slammed into Carol. Her scream curled off as she was knocked backwards into the house.

Laura was petrified and she didn't know what to do. The look in Katie's eyes reflected that she felt the same. Travis was too fixated on the Greys to turn around and stared at the wall not daring to move. Even Ashley was too scared to call out to her mother and cried believing her mother was dead. Laura looked at the Female but she was motionless like a statue. There wouldn't be any help from her and Laura thought it wouldn't be fair to expect any.

In the opening a small Grey standing in front lifted its hand and pointed a finger at the house. Then pointed down at them. The group knew they were the subject of a discussion. That they were being explained. A few more Grey children pointed at them. And more Grey children after that until they all were pointing at them. Then the opening in the wall closed and they were gone.

A big gust of wind blew around them.

"Just when you think it couldn't get worse," Katie said. "Those assholes come back."

Finally, Travis turned around and faced his girlfriend. "No shit."

"Mommy!" Ashley screamed and ran inside the house.

Laura felt shaken and her fingers were tingling. She watched Travis and Katie hug. The screen door banged shut behind Ashley after she went inside. Laura wanted to help and so she followed inside the house. Carol was sitting up on the floor of the living room with Ashley next to her. Carol looked at her. On instinct, Laura stepped back because she remembered Carol knew about her leg.

"Are you okay?" asked Laura.

"No, my brain hurts," Carol growled. "I'll kill them." She looked down and rubbed the temples on her forehead with her fingers. Her eyes squinted back up at Laura. "How's your leg?"

Ashley looked at Laura. "What's wrong with your leg? Are you hurt?"

Laura didn't want to talk about it. "Nothing," she said and walked into the kitchen. She poured herself a glass of water from the refrigerator, drank it down, and went out on the porch again. Travis and Katie were leaning against the rail.

"How's psycho doing?" asked Travis.

"She said her head hurts," answered Laura.

"You know, in a way, she might have saved us," said Katie.

"She's still off her rocker," said Travis with disgust. "Crazy like a loon."

"I know but...." Katie hesitated. "Can we count on her to help us?"

"Who knows?"

"She took quite a mind strike from the Red," said Laura.

"Yeah, it was wicked," said Katie.

"We'll have to watch her," said Travis.

"Maybe her brain is scarred now," said Laura.

"Again," said Travis. "Who knows?"

Katie glanced over her shoulder at the wall. "Being treated like an animal is so degrading."

"That's no shit."

"And being hunted like food by the shadows."

"It sure is."

The wind slowly blew again, sifting through the picturesque morning, and making it feel like the perfect picture that it really wasn't.

"They'll come tonight," said Laura.

Everyone looked out into the yard.

CHAPTER 104

The evening came after a slow day that was punctuated with a late afternoon rain storm. The power in the house fluctuated on and off at times. The changing internal weather inside the compound was a daily event and they had stayed sheltered inside the house.

Laura walked onto the porch that creaked with each footstep. A mist was starting to develop and drift along the ground. Rain water dripped from the ends of the roof. It was warmer than usual and she felt some sweat on her forehead. Her nose didn't smell the Illucii but she didn't feel any safer either. Laura looked around the yard but she couldn't see the watery wall that stayed hidden behind the rising mist that was getting thicker. She also couldn't see the bluish glow that the wall emitted. The trees were disappearing in the mist and looked like floating circles in the air. She wondered if the Greys were watching them right now. Were they watching her now on the porch? Maybe they were keeping an eye on them to protect them? She wanted to believe that but couldn't convince herself of it. More likely they were simply observing them.

For Laura, it was the calm before the storm. They had all spent the day waiting for the night to come. For the time, they expected the shadows to come. Her leg jabbed at her again but now it felt worse than before. She moved to the end of the porch and pulled her pant leg up.

Her breath left her body.

It was hideous now. The mark on her leg was a swirling shape of black and purple colors. It was a rash unlike any she had seen before. She didn't know what to do.

The door spring creaked and Travis and Katie came onto the porch. Laura straightened up.

"What's the matter?" asked Katie, sensing that something was wrong.

"Oh, nothing," said Laura. "Just checking the air." She hoped that would fly.

Travis was looking at her funny out of the corner of his eyes.

"It looks weird out," said Katie. "Where'd the mist come from?"

"That's what we don't need," said Travis. "Makes it harder to see."

Laura looked around. "We just need our noses this time."

There was a distant rumble and thunder reverberated in the east beyond the mist. Lightning flashed on both sides of the house.

"We better get inside," said Laura.

"Yeah, really," said Katie. "The weather thing is starting again."

Travis agreed. "I don't even think they care."

"Maybe the radiation from the outside atmosphere causes the mechanical problem," said Laura.

"Whatever it is, we don't want to get hit by it," said Travis. He switched hands with his bone spear that he had retrieved and looked deep into Katie's eyes. "You ready, babe?"

She met his stare. "I guess. Ready to get it over with. The never-ending sense of oncoming dread."

With some final glances out in the yard, Laura, Katie, and Travis went inside the house. Carol was sitting on the sofa with a blank stare on her face. Her bone spear rested against her leg. Nobody was sure if she would use it or not unless it was to protect her daughter. In that case, they knew she would. Ashley was sitting next to her. She looked at Laura with a scared face. "When the shadows are here will the lollipop men come?"

Laura hesitated. "Let's pray."

They all sat in the living room and began the wait. About an hour passed by that felt more like hours. Outside more thunder rumbled and jagged lightning flashes illuminated the mist making the night come alive. It was a laser light show beyond the windows. Laura's leg was itching badly with a gross feeling like it was moving on her. But she couldn't touch it because everyone would see her. When there was no thunder, a deathly quiet hung inside the house. Everyone shared blank stares on their faces.

A few more hours passed and something caught Laura's eye in the window. She looked hard and couldn't believe her eyes. It was her mom! She was on the porch. Laura knew it was impossible. Her mom was dressed in a yellow shirt and had her brown hat with a brim to shade the sun. What was her mother doing here? Did the Greys take her too? But there was no sun. Why would she be wearing a hat? Her mother called her name and disappeared. Laura stood up.

A hand touched her knee and she looked down at Ashley's face peering up at her. "Where are you going?" she asked.

Laura cleared her head. "I don't know. I saw my mother."

"What?" said Travis, who was sitting against the fireplace. "Your mother's not here."

"I know it doesn't make sense but I swear I saw her." She quickly sat down feeling confused. But she knew what her eyes had seen. How would her mom be here?

"Where did you see her?" asked Katie. She was sitting next to Travis. "On the porch."

With a big step Katie eased into the center of the room and carefully looked out the window. "I don't see anyone." Thunder cracked and she sat down in a hurry.

The lights dimmed momentarily. Again, Laura leaned over the sofa edge and looked out the front window. Lightning flashed close to the house. Her mom wasn't there. It must have been her imagination. She sat down and gripped her bone spear tightly. Laura continued to think. How could her mom be here? She started to slide her hands up and down her bone spear and it made a whisking sound. And then she knew.... It was the Illucii. Laura was immediately upset with herself. How could she have been so stupid?

The Illucii had started their hunt. ,

Carol was staring straight out the front window when a head popped up from below the windowsill. Two familiar blue eyes looked into the room at her. It was her son Kenny. Here. On this planet. Inside the zoo with them. He smiled at her and ducked down below the window. "Kenny!"

Everyone looked at Carol.

Ashley tugged on her mom's sleeve. "Where, Mommy?"

"Stay here, doll baby," said Carol. She stood up with her bone spear and started walking to the front door. Travis and Katie stood up and blocked her way. They held their bone spears at waist level. "Get out of my way!"

"It's the Illucii!" Laura shouted.

"You can't go out there," Travis said sternly. "Nobody else is here except us."

Carol grit her teeth. "Move."

"Your son isn't out there. Sit down and chill out."

"Move."

"It's the Illucii!" yelled Laura.

"Yeah, please sit down, Carol," Katie begged. "Don't do anything that gets us killed."

"Move!" Carol ordered.

"It's the Illucii!" Laura yelled again.

"My son is out there and I'm going to get him and save him."

Travis was becoming angrier by the second. "Look lady. Sit down! You're becoming an obstacle to saving our lives." There was a menacing tone to what he said.

Laura intervened. "He's not out there, Carol."

Carol stared at Laura. "I saw him!"

"It's the shadow creatures. They're playing mind games to trick us. They use our memories to bait us," said Laura.

"Please sit down, Carol," said Katie.

Travis and Katie held their bone spears firmly.

"I'm sorry but your son isn't out there," said Laura. "It's them!"

Travis jabbed his spear at Carol. "Get back, bitch!"

Carol held her spear up defensively by reflex.

Laura saw things were about to get out of control. "Everyone take it easy. We have to stick together."

Carol looked at her and spoke sharply. "Would you shut up with that stuff."

"No," Laura was getting angry. "We gotta fight to survive! And we gotta plan!"

"It's not gonna work." Carol's voice was rough like a rusty nail. "We're dead already." She turned back to Travis and Katie. "Move."

"No!" said Travis.

"If you keep me from my son I'll kill you!"

Laura intervened. "Your son is safe back on Earth. He isn't here."

Carol turned to Laura. Her face was white with anger. "Okay, leg woman."

"Mommy, Mommy," said Ashley. "He wasn't there when I saw him either. Remember?"

Carol stopped. Her daughter's words seem to click inside her. Carefully, her senses reorganized themselves away from Carol's hatred for the Greys and this situation they had put them in. They matched together and her wits got rational. She looked at the window again. Kenny wasn't on the porch. He wasn't even here. She was seeing things. Carol dropped the bone spear in one hand and turned to Ashley. "You're right, doll baby. Wishful thinking, I guess."

The kitchen light started to flicker giving the kitchen a bouncing light effect.

Katie thought she felt a tap on her shoulder but she wasn't sure. She turned around but nobody was there. Katie told herself that of course there wouldn't be. Everyone is right here inside the room but it had felt so real. She knew better than to check but decided to look anyway. With her bone spear poised to strike, she took a step around the fireplace, and peeked into the kitchen. In the sputtering light, there wasn't anyone there. Just the kitchen table and the chairs. Katie stepped into the kitchen.

"Katie," said Travis.

"One second, babe," said Katie. For some reason, she felt compelled to go in there. Katie stepped further into the kitchen, her bone spear ready for attack.

Travis looked at Laura with worry. He didn't know what Katie was doing. Travis took a step and looked around the fireplace after her.

Katie stopped in the kitchen. Nothing else was there. But there was something on the rail of the porch. Something out there was reflecting the kitchen light back through the window. Katie couldn't tell what it was other than it was small. She took a step toward the front door.

"Hey, where are you going?" asked Travis.

Laura saw her too. "No! Don't go outside!"

Katie turned around. "There's something on the porch. It's metallic I think. Maybe it could help?" She turned and grabbed the door handle.

Travis grabbed her by the back of her shirt. "No!"

"Ouch!" Katie whipped around and pushed his hand away. "That hurt."

"What are you doing?" said Travis. He got close to her face. "You can't go outside. The shadows are out there."

Ashley sat down on the sofa and started to cry. Carol sat next to her and tried to calm her down.

Katie bit her lip in frustration. "Maybe it's a gun or something. I just wanna take a peek."

"No," said Travis firmly. "I can't let you."

"There's nothing out there," said Laura. "It's the Illucii playing tricks."

Katie looked back into the kitchen and it was there now on the kitchen table. The light flickered but she could see it was a cell phone. "There it is. It's a cell phone." She started into the kitchen but Travis grabbed her arm. She turned around with anger on her face. "Let go. It's just a cell phone."

"Babe," said Travis. He looked at the table and didn't see anything. Travis was surprised she was behaving this way. He loosened his grip on her arm. "I'm not losing my girlfriend to this place if I can help it. There's no cell phone on the table."

"Yes, there is. It's right there." She motioned to the kitchen.

Travis looked again and shook his head. "No, there isn't." He wanted to get this through to her.

"It's right there," she said. "Don't you see it?"

Laura was looking at the table too but it was empty. She felt really distraught by what was happening. Despite that they knew the Illucii had the ability to make them see things, why were they still being fooled and believing what they saw? Then she knew for sure. The Illucii's mind power was so strong that the Illucii could change their reality. Laura knew they had to fight back.

"Katie, it's them!" Laura exclaimed. "The shadows. Playing mind games! That's why I thought I saw my mom."

Katie looked at her inquisitively. "So they're fucking with us?"

"Of course, they are," said Travis. Now he had her coming back to reality. "Why would our cell phones be here and why would they be of any use to us here? We can't call anyone."

Katie didn't answer. She looked back at the table and didn't see the cell phone now.

"It's just to get you curious enough to go outside," said Laura. "The same with me and Carol. This is a highly intelligent species."

Nobody said anything. Everyone was weary of this constant battle inside the zoo.

"They have incredible mind power," Laura continued. "Their mind games are so strong that they still convince us that what we are seeing is real. Their illusions can override our knowledge of what is real and what isn't real."

"Those bastards were playing tricks on me," said Carol coarsely. She was holding Ashley who had stopped crying. "And I won't let them win."

Travis was watching this unfold in front of him. He was the man. He was with a bunch of females, including the love of his life, that ranged from seven-years-old to middle-aged mother. He was afraid they were going mad by starting to have illusions about home. And borrowing from Laura, they needed to keep together, and stick to their plan. It was the only plan they had but if they deviated from it they were surely going to die.

Katie's shoulders sagged. "I'm so stupid," she said chastising herself. She gripped her bone spear hard. "How could I fall for it and not believe you?"

Thunder crackled outside that cut the silence.

"Where are the lollipop men?" said Ashley.

The lights went out.

The house plunged into darkness. Nobody moved. In their minds, everything stopped. It was quiet save for the distant rumbling of thunder that rolled across the sky above the house. No one spoke. Everyone listened for what was coming next. Laura could see Travis and Katie outlined against the fireplace. Lightning shot down to the ground casting Laura as a silhouette against the window. Carol knew that Ashley was next to her.

"What...." Katie started.

Travis hushed her. He touched her with his hands to stay put. Nothing happened except for some thunder that growled and echoed off into the distance. They looked out the windows. More lightning flickered illuminating the mist surrounding the house. They were left listening to the darkness of the night. To each of their senses, the room was getting darker by the second. A cold visual of lifelessness growing and taking root around them. A visual that cast out feeling by covering over its surroundings. The blackness of the room crept in on them from all directions and ate at their last sense of security. It was a giant shroud moving in to cover the dead.

Laura felt a tingling in her mind as if someone was in her head. It lasted only for a moment and was gone. The Female had been there waiting for the shadows to come.

A rush of wind outside made the front door quiver in the door frame. Still they waited. Everyone gripped their bone spears tightly. Carol adjusted her position and sat back in a rigid stance. Ashley hugged her doll while looking around at the sofa for something that wasn't there yet. Travis and Katie stayed focused on the window behind Laura. There was nothing but mist floating outside. Laura watched the front window but for her there was only mist to see. She took a step toward the window.

The smell appeared to come from their left. Slowly, it sneaked into the house, spreading outward. The stench was looking for them. The Illucii were prowling around outside.

Laura strained her eyes in the darkness to see anything but she knew it was to no good. The shadows were the darkness. They were perfect copies of it. They moved around inside of it and hid inside the shadows of their prey. They were the perfect stealth killer.

Travis grabbed Katie by the arm and positioned himself in front of her by pulling her behind him. They didn't think it was inside yet but the rank was getting stronger. Lightning flashed outside and in that second Laura tried to see on the porch but the light was gone too fast. She could only see the basic outline of the railing and porch posts but nothing else except for floating mist.

The blackness in the room collaborated with the rank odor to conspire in a suffocating way as if they had concocted a secret deal together to snuff them out. But it wasn't only their senses it was crushing but their optimism that they would survive. Moving in to flatten their hope of living.

Ashley started to think about what if a shadow sneaked up behind her and her mom on the sofa. Just like her cat would do to her back home. The shadow would get them in the darkness for sure. Her back felt cold. Her body started to shake. Then next to her, she sensed her mom get up, and walk to the front door and go out onto the porch. Ashley didn't know why her mom would do that. Her mom wouldn't leave her. She would never do that. She hopped off the sofa, felt her way around the table, and stood somewhere between Travis, Katie, and Laura who were very quiet. She looked back at the edge of the sofa where her mom had been sitting but didn't see her there. Ashley turned around again. Why'd her mom leave her? Thunder cracked loudly above breaking the silence, and the lightning flashed, and through the window she saw that her mom was on the porch. "Mommy!" She dashed to the front door, flung it open, and ran out after her.

CHAPTER 105

Carol was still sitting next to her daughter when she heard a sliding sound on the table. It scared her more, afraid that a shadow was in front of her little girl, and about to pounce. On instinct, she reached out next to her for Ashley but she wasn't there. Thunder and lightning crashed outside and she saw her daughter suddenly burst out of the room. "Ashley! No!" She jumped from the sofa and slammed into Katie and Travis. All three of them went sprawling on the floor with their bone spears rattling against the walls.

To Laura, all she heard was shouting and a crash of people falling hard to the ground. One of the bone spears made a cracking sound as it flew up against the window. Startled, Laura dropped her bone spear. "What's going on?" She cried in desperation.

Carol scampered over Katie and Travis. She grabbed her bone spear and burst through the front door. "Ashley!"

CHAPTER 106

Ashley was out on the porch but her mom wasn't. The stench was worse outside. She didn't even care because she wanted to find her mom so bad. "Mommy?" Ashley took a few steps. "Mommy? Where are you?" Inside she heard a loud noise of some kind and Laura shout something.

"Ashley!" Carol rushed onto the porch.

"Mommy." Ashley turned around smiling.

"What are you doing running out here?" Carol was furious.

The smell was strong outside.

"I followed you, Mommy. But how did you get back inside?"

Carol paused. She didn't know what her daughter was talking about. "I didn't go outside. What are you talking about?"

The smell was close by.

"Yeah, you did, Mommy. I watched you."

Carol took a step forward. "I did not. We need to go inside now!" Her nose was burning. Carol looked around but it was too dark to see anything. The mist blocked most of the light that reflected down through the open sky roof from the planet's moons. Carol realized that she had been so alarmed about Ashley and caught up in her own anger that Ashley had run outside, that they were now trapped in a vulnerable position on the porch. Defenseless. Her hands gripped her bone spear. She was ready to thrust it.

More thunder roared across the compound and lightning flashed carving itself into the ground. It served to light up the yard for a second. In that moment Carol saw her daughter's beautiful innocent eyes looking at her. And in that moment, Ashley could see the anger in her mother's eyes turn instantly to love and adoration for her. Then it was dark again.

The smell was there.

"Mommy," Ashley whispered. "Now would be a good time for the lollipop men to come."

The power came back on and the house filled with light. Beams of light spilled out onto the porch and Carol and Ashley could see again. Carol looked at Ashley but she was staring at something behind her mother. Ashley looked at her mom strangely.

"Mommy, you have two shadows."

"Huh." Carol turned around but only saw her shadow expanding away from her on the porch. "No, I don't, baby. I have only one."

"When the lights came on I saw one jump into the other."

Carol grabbed Ashley and pulled her back against the window. She looked hard and her eyes went white. Her shadow was darker than usual. A quick glance at Ashley's shadow and she knew she was right. They didn't know what to do so they stared at her shadow. The porch shook under their feet from a low boom of thunder that rolled overhead but Carol didn't move and neither did her shadow. From their left the wind stirred up and blew a fast blast of the nasty odor into their faces. Carol felt nauseous and began to gag. Ashley covered her nose. However, they didn't turn away. Their eyes kept fixated on her shadow. Kept their eyes staring down at something that was there. Something hidden that didn't attack yet. They watched something, which if they moved, might provoke it to attack. And as long as they didn't move, it didn't move. This was almost a game. A game at a standstill. They kept watching it. And it kept watching them. They stared. A dark wave shifted its position inside it. They knew it was there.

Carol raised her bone spear and screamed. "Die!" She lunged forward stabbing into her shadow. The sound of bone scraped on the wood porch as something dark quickly moved off the porch into the protection of the night. It was moving. Their noses detected the smell. It came around to the other side but stayed just on the edge of the house light. They could see it. They could see movements that were lost going between the light and the darkness.

The shadow quickly shot up and landed on top of the porch. Carol jerked in reaction by holding her spear up to block. "Oh, my God. It's on top!" Her breathing was fast and she was starting to pant.

"We need to go inside Ashley!" Carol yelled. "Now!"

Ashley wanted to run but was too scared. She pinned herself up against the window. Carol was surveying the ends of the porch roof. She bobbed and weaved looking all over for it and felt desperate. Just knowing it was up on top of them somewhere freaked her out even more and the air was leaving her lungs faster.

"Ashley! Run! Inside!"

Another night breeze blew from east to west and they lost the scent of the shadow's location. Carol and Ashley froze. It whipped under the porch roof and quickly crawled across the ceiling.

Ashley screamed! Carol turned and stabbed upwards at it. She started swinging away but it stayed out of reach. Ashley thought she saw three deep purplish eyes on it. In a moment with her mother flailing about, they looked to come together as one, and then become three again. It grossed her out.

"Die! Die!" Carol was ignited with rage and stabbing like crazy to kill it. The only thing in life right now that she ever wanted was to save her daughter.

Then out of the darkness Hunter Greys came onto the porch. Carol was so lost in her attack that she turned and stabbed one of them with her bone spear. In response, it shot a mind strike at her that threw her back against the house. She hit it with a thud.

The Hunter Grey in the middle tried to focus in on the Illucii but it was jumping all around on the porch ceiling. It was a shadow of endless movement. The Hunter wanted to zero in on it to deliver a killer blow but due to the shadow's quickness could only send mind strikes to hurt it and slow it down. They had to kill it.

CHAPTER 107

In the darkness of the room things had happened quickly. Katie and Travis lay spread out on the floor after Carol had run through them. Their bodies ached from the collision. Their eyes strained to see in the black void around them. However, their noses detected danger, and the syrupy smell grew worse inside the house. And closer.

Laura felt around in the dark for her bone spear. She had to find it! Her hand touched something smooth. That's it! She grabbed it and stood up. Laura clutched her bone spear aggressively and sniffed the air trying to locate where the smell was coming from. Somewhere in the dark, Katie and Travis were cussing and scrambling to get up. Laura focused towards the open door. It was coming from that direction and it was inside. "Get away from the door!"

Katie was standing up and Travis was in front of her, bone spears in hand. Darkness stood in their way but they smelled it like a force in their face. They stepped back into the center of the room. Travis held his bone spear level to strike and walked backwards. He knew when the attack came it would be too late to defend himself but he would try anyway and hope. Katie was stepping back behind him. She felt the presence of Laura behind her, across her back, and she felt sandwiched in. The smell was moving closer.

The lights came on. Everything looked the same to them inside the room as before the lights had gone out but the front door was open. The screen door was closed. The dark fireplace rested cold in the middle wall. They could see that Carol and Ashley were on the porch pressed up against the front window. They couldn't see the shadow but sensed it was inside. They could feel its presence. The smell hung in the air. It was in the room somewhere.

"Remember when it jumped around between us?" Travis said.

"Yeah, like it moved around in our shadows," added Katie.

"Spread out," said Travis.

Slowly, the three of them moved apart from each other, looking at the floor underneath their feet. They turned around to see their own shadows, which clung to their bodies, scared at what they would find. Outside on the porch a fight was going on and each of them could hear it. However, their lives at this moment were inside. Their lives were inside with a killer, and as they turned in circles looking for it, nothing could be seen. But it was here.

Travis stabbed his shadow. His bone spear thudded against the carpeted floor. He looked at Katie and Laura with a crazed look in his eyes. He stabbed at Katie's shadow. She jumped back in alarm expecting the Illucii to spring out and attack her. But it didn't. Next he turned to Laura. Travis knew it was there. He brought his bone spear down hard and the end broke off with a cracking sound. Nothing was there but a tear in the carpet. Katie stepped back toward the fireplace.

Next to her, the darkened fireplace moved.

CHAPTER 108

The Hunter Grey sent a spread of mind strikes in the direction of the Illucii. One of the strikes slammed into it and it flew back against the porch ceiling. The shadow shook it off, its eyes rotated in a circle, and launched back at the lead Hunter Grey. In a microsecond, the Hunter focused and shot a strike directly into the attacking creature, knocking it to the side of the porch. Another Hunter Grey, blocking the end of the porch, zapped it with a mind strike. The Illucii flipped in the air, released a black discharge of an oily substance that splattered onto the porch floor, and smacked into the wall. Instantly, the Illucii slithered up the wall and started to dance on the porch ceiling.

Carol was lying on the porch floor in a daze watching the fight go on. Her head scorched with pain from the strike she'd been hit with. Her head tilted over and she saw the Hunter Grey that she had stabbed lay dying on the floor. It had a bluish blood flowing out of its wound where she had stabbed it. Another Hunter was standing over it and appeared to be applying some healing process which Carol couldn't see but she could feel.

Between throbs of pain inside her skull, her eyes rotated up at the ceiling, and saw the shadowy creature staying elusive. It was hiding the best that it could in the darkest area of the porch. Above her. She looked back down at the lead Hunter that was almost in front of her. The Hunter was taller standing so much closer. Carol's head continued to hurt and her senses were blurry. She thought she heard a scream from inside the house but couldn't be sure. The lights inside the house flickered again.

She saw the light bounce off the deep inverted holes of the Hunter's eyes. The thunder roared and the lightning flashed around them. It made her head throb even more. The Hunter Grey working on the injured Hunter had pulled him off the porch, down into the yard, and was still attempting to administer some unseen help to him. Another Hunter Grey had come out of the darkness in replacement and got into position on the porch.

The lead Hunter was trying to box in the Illucii with systematic strikes shot up to cut off each route of escape. The lead Hunter was getting ready to deliver the final blow.

Then the shadow creature fell and landed on the floor of the porch. It lay motionless.

CHAPTER 109

Katie screamed!

"It's there! The fireplace! I saw it move!" Her heart jumped up into her throat and she took a step back. But only a step. Her feet stopped. Something told her it was too late for help and that she couldn't get away. That she was caught. To simply give up. Katie's movement froze. Her brain sent impulses to move but she didn't. Katie couldn't believe that, and her mind wrestled with itself. She struggled with mind and body and backed away another step. But that grip of despair was still holding her. Again, she thought it was hopeless. To simply accept her fate. The desperation she felt knotted in her mind squeezed tightly and out shot her own rejection to dying. Why? Why would she accept being caught and killed? Why should she accept dying? Like an animal. She wasn't dead yet and could stop it before it happened. Katie wouldn't accept it, and she wouldn't be caught. Now her eyes focused on the fireplace with a vision that meshed into a kind of tunnel vision that faded away on the edges. The fireplace looked empty. The rank smell penetrated her senses. She stared harder. But it wasn't empty. Ripples stirred in the unlit fireplace. The darkness was moving. She had to make her feet move away.

The lights flickered.

It jumped. Laura and Travis saw the tail end of a quick movement that seemed to blend in with Katie.

"Katie!" yelled Travis. He took a step forward expecting her to fall over from an attack. However, she didn't. She looked pale white.

Katie had seen a form leap toward her within the blinking light. Now she couldn't see it. But she could smell it coming up from beneath her. She knew it was between her legs. Katie looked down. Nestled between her feet was her own shadow. It was beneath her. The lights flickered again and partially faded, sending the room into semidarkness, just as the thunder rolled in unison with the lightning flashing outside. She freaked and raised her bone spear up and stabbed down hard on the floor. There was movement underneath her and the shadow went up her back. A reeking rush filled her senses with a prickly feeling up her spine. Two arms materialized out from it, grabbed her by the shoulder, pulled her back, casting a shadow downward away from the thud of the bone spear as it struck the floor. Katie screamed again! The force of the attack knocked her off balance and she dropped her bone spear. The creature was on her back and she wanted it off. Katie started to whip around in circles to try and throw it from her shadow. She was yelling in fear. Faster she turned. The lights in the room continued to flicker.

Travis was in a riding horse stance with his broken bone spear ready to strike. But he didn't. He didn't know what to do. His girlfriend was under attack but it was happening too quickly and he couldn't see the Illucii very well. The sounds of her torment hurt him to the breaking point and he thrust his spear forward and stabbed. He missed. He got her instead.

Katie shrieked in pain and fell back over the table.

CHAPTER 110

The dead Illucii lay on the porch floor. The lead Hunter Grey stared at it but hesitated. He looked at the Hunters on both sides of him and they stepped in closer. The Hunter was unsure of just what happened but he didn't want to wait for a surprise. He focused hard and sent a sharp mind strike into the form on the floor.

Carol watched. The mind strikes couldn't be seen, but they could be felt, and she knew it was a powerful one from the pressure she felt push up on her face. However, it was hard to determine if it had an effect. The Illucii lay there. The Hunter stepped closer.

Carol was watching the dead Illucii carefully. It was close to her. Too close. She slid herself away closer to the front door. Ashley was standing quietly next to her. Carol reached out for her, but Ashley stepped back and didn't express any emotion. With one look at her daughter she knew Ashley was traumatized. Her eyes were ghosts.

Carol looked back to her right at the Illucii on the floor. Behind her inside the house a tumult had developed, and she heard a female scream, but she kept herself alert to the threat at her arm's length. The Hunters moved in a little closer. The left one was directly in front of her now. They were watching it intensely. She looked at the shadow again. The creature lay flat. However, something was different. The smell was a nasty sting in her nose but it wasn't coming from next to her. Something wasn't right. Carol knew the smell wasn't coming from the shadowy body next to her. It was coming down from above her. She looked up. The lights were now flickering inside the house and it cast shadows across the ceiling. The shadows leaped around the ceiling with each flicker. Except for one that stayed the same. Carol watched it between the seconds of darkness and light. She knew it wasn't a cast off from the light. The creature that lay dead next to her was an illusion. The creature was still on the ceiling.

"It's up there!" Carol pointed at the ceiling and screamed.

The Hunters looked above. On the ceiling the shadow creature was moving toward the end of the porch to get away.

"Kill it!" Carol yelled! Then she looked in horror at the front door. Ashley was gone!

"Ashley!" She grabbed her spear, got up, and ran into the house. "No!"

CHAPTER 111

In the flickering light, Laura watched her friend Katie in horror. The deadly shadow creature was on her like a cape. It could kill her at any moment and she was fighting desperately for her life. Katie's screams of desperation cut into her own soul and Laura started to cry internally for her. Then in Travis's attempt in vain to save her he wounded her. Katie fell flat on the table on her back. She grabbed her right side where she was bleeding below her rib cage. Travis yelled out in anger and frustration at himself.

As the light inside the room faded in and out, something moved from underneath Katie. It moved in front of Laura. She looked down and the shadowy form slid along the floor and rose up in front of her. She froze at the sight of it. The syrupy stench of it was unbearable and she wanted to puke. The Illucii looked her in the face. Its purple eyes shifted. There was something of a mouth but it was hard for her to tell other than that it looked empty. The light kept flickering inside as if she was in an old movie projection theater. Laura needed to strike it but the bizarre sight of it a foot away from her face held her tightly. She thought she was dead.

Suddenly, the shadow dropped down and lingered around her right leg. It slid back from her a little. Again, it raised up and looked Laura in the face but backed away some more.

Ashley burst through the front door and ran up the stairs. The creature turned and quickly went up the stairs after her.

CHAPTER 112

The Hunter Greys were quick. The lead Hunter primed his mind ready to attack. The Hunter on the porch end shot up a blocking strike that cut off the Illucii's escape and forced it back into the middle of the ceiling. The Hunter on the other side stepped in where Carol had been and sent up his own strike that prevented escape on the other flank. The Illucii exuded more rank smell and it poured out of it now. It was pulsating. The lead Hunter blasted the creature with a killer strike. The shadow shook violently, drooped, and fell. Its body made barely a noise as it landed on the porch.

CHAPTER 113

Laura was stationary at first. Carol burst through the front door. She looked over at Laura with eyes ablaze with anger. Then she yelled her daughter's name and ran up the stairs in pursuit. Katie was on the table moaning in pain and Travis was standing over her apologizing. He turned and looked at Laura with desperation on his face.

"Help her!" said Laura. She didn't know how badly Katie was hurt but he needed to help her.

He looked at Katie and back at Laura. Guilt was flooding his body. "I didn't mean to hurt her."

"She knows that Travis, just help her!"

"Okay," Travis said breathlessly. He turned back to Katie who was holding her wound and cussing to help relieve the pain.

Shooting pain climbed Laura's leg and made her cringe. She went down on her left knee to relieve the pressure on her other leg. Again, she grabbed her pant leg but stopped herself from pulling it up and seeing the black and purple mark. Right now, Laura couldn't bear to see it on her body.

She looked out the front window and saw some Hunter Greys. Laura looked back to Katie and Travis. Katie was still lying with her back on the table groaning loudly. Travis was standing over her applying pressure to the wound and apologizing more.

"It went upstairs," gasped Laura. "So did Ashley and Carol. I'm going!" She stood back up and ran to the bottom of the stairs. She looked out the front door and didn't see the Female in the yard. Laura searched her own mind for a connection with the Female but she didn't find it. Where was the Female? Wasn't she going to help them? Her mental search was cut in half when she heard Carol yell from upstairs. Laura turned back to the staircase and looked upwards.

CHAPTER 114

"Ashley!"

Carol was at the top of the stairs. Her feet had slammed down in panic on each step as loud as the thunder outside. It was dark at the top and Ashley didn't answer her. To Carol the upstairs rested in darkness and seemed to grow like a giant umbrella unfolding to cover the staircase as she got to the top. Carol stepped on the top step and stopped. She looked to her left. The door to her bedroom was closed but there was a blinking slim beam of light coming from the crack below the door. Inside the room and between claps of thunder, she heard sniffling.

"Ashley!" She grabbed the door handle and pushed the door open. Ashley stood rigidly in the flickering light at the foot of the bed. She looked at her mom with wet shiny eyes and sniffled her sadness again. "I hoped to keep it out Mommy, but it's in here."

Then the repugnant syrupy smell took root and filled up the room. Carol gripped her bone spear tightly. "Where is it?" She turned to the closet.

"Mommy, it's not there."

Carol looked back to Ashley. The flickering light made it hard for her to get a good focus on the room. However, she was in survival mode and it was driving her to fight. Her heart pounded like it was going to escape out of her chest. Where was the shadow? Again, she looked at Ashley.

Ashley's eyes looked down to the foot of the bed next to her feet. Carol followed her daughter's eyes. The bed sheets hung down over the end but didn't touch the floor. The darkened space under the bed rested there. She realized the creature was behind her daughter.

"Get away!" She grabbed her daughter by the arm as the light blinked off and she pulled Ashley behind her. The light flashed on again, and something was attached to Ashley, stretching from under the bed to her back. It recoiled back under the bed. Carol yelled and stabbed underneath the bed. The light dimmed into black again. The Illucii sprang out and spun around her spear. Carol couldn't see the shadow when it ripped into her face.

CHAPTER 115

The blinking lights from the kitchen on the right and the living room on the left, provided a shakiness to the staircase. Laura felt vertigo play with her senses. She knew it was only an illusion, that there was no time to waste, and convinced herself that she needed to press on. The thunder was rumbling outside. Slowly, she started to climb. Each step was taken in darkness or in light and she carefully climbed the stairs. Laura gripped her bone spear tensely ready for any attack.

The lights flashed off and on and appeared to be timing itself to do so with each step she took. Laura stared ahead of her. The upstairs was darkness waiting for her arrival, but not before laughing at her, and mocking her on her climb. Each flutter of light allowed her to see momentarily and get a glimpse at the top before stealing away her vision again.

Laura watched carefully. She was ready for the creature knowing it would fly out to kill her. She was close to the top and her right leg burned with each step. The house went dark again. She waited. There was a loud thump upstairs. She listened. The rancid smell wasn't as powerful as it had been down in the living room so Laura reasoned the Illucii must not be at the top of the stairs. But it was somewhere. Again, she started to climb to the top but it was dark and she stumbled to her knee with a thud. Laura froze. Nothing happened. The house was black. She listened harder. Then her eyes saw some brightness from one of the rooms upstairs and the kitchen light shined on again. The power was back but for how long she didn't know. Still she waited.

Another boom of thunder sounded and trailed off into human crying. It was Ashley. Quickly, Laura stepped to the top. The bedroom door to her left was open and the light was on. From where she stood the bed inside the room was visible. Ashley was crying in the room but she couldn't see her yet. She checked the hallway quickly. Her bedroom door was open to her right but the light was off. The bathroom in front of her was open but dark as well. There wasn't anything on the banister and the hallways seemed clear. However, it was dark and she wouldn't see the shadow anyway. Her nose was her radar now searching for the nasty smell. It wasn't out in the hallway with her. For it was in the room with Ashley.

Laura turned and went into the room.

Carol's body lay on the floor motionless. The white sneakers of her feet pointed toward the ceiling. Laura got chills down her back when she looked at Carol's face. She was hollowed out.

Ashley was on her knees next to her mom crying. Her hands rested on her legs and she looked up at Laura. Tears streaked down her cheeks. Laura hated the Illucii even more now. For the pain it had caused them. Hunting them. Killing them. Using them. And hurting Ashley by taking her mother away from her. She had to kill it.

"Ashley, where is it?"

The light faded into black again. Ashley's crying filled the silence of the room. "Ashley...." Laura stopped. The rancid smell of the alien creature flowed over her. It was in the room but she couldn't see anything. She got into a fighting stance with her bone spear ready to fight when attacked. Deep down she knew it would be too late because she would never see it coming in the dark. Silently, she prayed for the light to come back on. The lightning continued to flash outside and illuminate the bedroom windows as flashing squares. She might have seen something but she was in darkness again. The smell started to tear at her and decay her nose. She snorted to blow the penetrating smell back out her nostrils and shake it off but to no avail. Her nose burned. It was getting closer. Then the lights came on.

To Laura, the room looked the same. She looked at Ashley, Carol's body, at the bed, up at the ceiling, the walls, behind the door, in the corners to both sides of her, and back at Ashley again. She didn't see it. The stench was an invisible blanket overwhelming her face. It burned through to her ears. The light wavered again. Laura saw something move around the edges of Carol's body. She gripped her bone spear tightly and raised it high to stab downwards. Ashley was still looking at her with crying eyes. For a split second, she wondered why it wasn't attacking Ashley, but she already knew. The shadow didn't strike in the light. It liked to stay hidden in the dark.

The light faded out and came on again in a sporadic pattern. She blinked twice. It was gone. Where was it? She couldn't see well in the flashing light. And it was here. So close. Laura began to feel panic inside. "Ashley! Did you see it?"

Ashley was still looking at Laura. The flashing light in the room made it hard to see, but Laura's sense of smell was still good, and she had smelled the putrid creature suddenly move by her a moment ago in the darkness. Where was it?

Ashley had been kneeling next to her mom's body sobbing since before Laura came into the room. Her seven-year-old heart had given up. Her mom was gone. They were going to die. She looked at her mom again and felt her heart sink deeper. Ashley looked up at Laura. In between the blinking lights she saw it move on the wall. It moved to the next wall. Up onto the ceiling. Coming on top of Laura.

Laura saw Ashley's eyes and at that moment she knew it was too late. The dark presence closed in on her back. It was behind her. Laura felt a tingling in her mind. As if someone was in her head. Laura knew the Female had checked into her mind. Her heart beat like a drum in her chest. Adrenaline surged throughout her body. She turned around quickly. The shadow sprung at her like a dart. With a scream, Laura swung her bone spear in an arcing motion, and spun around and fell backwards into the corner of the room. She still gripped her spear and scrambled to get up expecting to be attacked. To her surprise, she wasn't.

She looked at the floor, back up at the ceiling, and at the walls and didn't see it. Where was it? The only thing different in the room was that Ashley had moved. She was now standing motionless, on the other side of the room, away from her mother's body. Ashley was pale white with fear.

Laura brought her bone spear up in a defensive position and something wet and sticky dripped onto her hand. She looked at it. There was a silvery black substance on her hand. It was thin like water. She flicked it off the ends of her fingers.

Ashley was staring at her. Laura found it disturbing. She continued on. They needed to find the creature and get out of the room. Laura reached out for her. "Ashley...."

Something moved on Ashley's back. Laura took a step to the right. There was a secret in her shadow. An ooze of silvery black was rolling downward behind Ashley. It was blood.

The Illucii was there!

The Female connected into Laura's brain and Laura felt a surge of thought so much more powerful than anything she could have imagined. It contained a wealth of knowledge that she couldn't have dreamed of living in the realm of Earth. All the vast years of universal existence within the Female's genes coursed through Laura. A surge of power projected itself from her mind and shot into the Illucii hiding in Ashley's shadow. The force from it knocked Ashley down to the floor. The Female's mind strike roasted the shadowy creature. It pulsated and poured out its pungent smell faster and faster. Laura was frozen as it happened. The Female had locked into her and she was a conduit for the elimination. Next she surged the killing blow. Laura felt it flow through her mind. The Female's mind strike finished it off and the once living shadow flopped quietly to the floor never to move again.

CHAPTER 116

In the blinking lights, Travis had forgotten how many times he apologized to Katie. There were no words to describe how upset he felt for injuring his girlfriend. She was rightfully angry at him and he understood that but it had been an accident. He was trying to save her life! And perhaps by misfiring, and stabbing her instead, he'd saved her after all. Travis needed her to know this. However, he was having trouble conveying that to her through the wall of pain that she was dealing with by fuming back at him. Travis continued to try.

Katie sat up and exhaled deeply. Her eyes looked up at him. He felt his heart stop. This was the worst moment of his life. She hated him.

"Ow! My side is killing me."

"I'm so sorry, honey." Travis got down on one knee in front or her. "I didn't mean it. I was trying to stab the--"

"Okay. Okay. I know. I know," Katie said. She gestured to him to calm down. "My side hurts like a bitch."

"Apply pressure. We'll have to bandage it up."

"Except we don't have any bandages."

Travis thought about that for a moment. "Yeah, that sucks. We'll have to ask the Greys. They wouldn't want you to die."

Katie looked up from her wound. "You sure? They didn't seem to care til recently. Like tonight."

Travis nodded. He couldn't think of anything to say. All his words were swallowed up by guilt.

"Babe, I still love you. Even though you stabbed me," said Katie. She smiled.

A feeling of incredible relief filled Travis throughout his body. He hugged her.

"Ow!" she said. "My side."

Travis started apologizing again.

"Hey, wait," Katie interrupted him. She hastily looked around the room. "Where is it? What happened to it?"

Travis thought for a second. Then his eyes exploded. "It went upstairs!"

"Where's Laura?"

"She did too! Went chasing after it. She said Carol and Ashley were also upstairs."

"Holy shit! What was that about? We gotta get up there." She tried to move but grabbed her side in pain.

"C'mon," said Travis. "I'm not leaving you down here alone. That creature will come up from behind and get you." He grabbed her hand and pulled her to the stairs. The house lights continued to fade out and come on again. Both saw some Hunter Greys on the porch through the front window.

"Must have been a fight outside," Katie remarked.

"Yeah," said Travis. "While we were fighting inside."

They stopped at the bottom of the stairs. They looked up but didn't see anyone. A breeze grabbed their attention through the open front door and refreshed their faces. Thunder roared above to remind them of its presence and lightning flashed in sequence while the mist glowed in the dark. They could sense movement on the porch which they knew were the Hunters.

Travis was about to yell up the stairs when something outside caught his own eyes. Behind the mist a tall shape came forth. More lightning flashed around the house and he and Katie saw the Female step into the yard. Her blonde mane flashed in the dark. Katie squeezed his hand. The Female was here.

CHAPTER 117

Laura grabbed Ashley and hugged her. Ashley hugged her back in sheer joy that she was saved and still alive. They stood up and cautiously began to exit the room. Laura shielded Ashley from looking at her mother and both kept their eyes on the dead Illucii. Its flat body lay there on the floor. Its rank odor still rose into the air. Despite its death they didn't know if that was real or not. They couldn't trust it. The creature was very sneaky. In fact, they didn't know what life was like in the compound without its prowling threat hanging over them, and seemingly waiting for them around any corner. To their relief it never moved and Laura and Ashley got to the top of the stairs.

"That mind blast from the Female really did the trick," said Laura.

"She's the best lollipop girl in the whole world," said Ashley.

They descended the stairs and joined Travis and Katie at the bottom. Immediately, Laura saw the Female outside in the yard. Ashley saw her too. They knew for sure that the Female had been true to her word.

CHAPTER 118

The morning came nicely. The four survivors slept in the living room with the lights on, not feeling comfortable to sleep separated in their rooms yet, and so soon after the trauma they had endured. Before they fell asleep they had discussed what all had taken place the night before. The fight with the Illucii upstairs, the mind strike that was funneled through Laura's mind, and the death of Carol. The Hunters had inspected the house for any more danger and ruled the house was now safe. While doing that, they cleaned up the two dead bodies of the Illucii. They also had the funeral procession for Carol. The group kept Ashley back from it as her mother's body floated out the house. She cried more and it broke all their hearts. It affected the feelings of the Female too. Ashley, as well as the others, received a feeling of sadness from her.

Laura was the first to wake. She lay on the back sofa. Immediately, she thought about the horrible thing on her leg but felt no pain. The Greys had given her some sort of medication the night before to curb its pain. For that Laura was very thankful. She didn't dare look at it yet in case it had gotten even worse.

Ashley stirred next to her in a sad image of what used to be her and her mother sleeping together. Travis and Katie slept on the other sofa, shoulder to shoulder, heads softly resting against each other in slumber. Laura ran her hand through Ashley's hair, and nicely patted her on the head, to convey a gentleness to the girl who had been through so much. She felt so sorry for Ashley. Felt it was cruel that this sweet girl had to live through this experience and worse of all lose her mother. It was a wicked twist in the road of life that fate had thrown in front of this poor girl. Ashley mumbled something in her sleep and settled again. Laura thought someone was going to have to watch over her. Then Laura's thoughts turned to her mother. Despite how crazy Carol had started to become, Laura thought about how much of a good mother she was, and how honorable she had been. Carol never left her daughter's side and protected Ashley during her time here. Even gave her life to save her daughter.

Laura looked around the room. The sunlight was starting to light up the compound casting it as a beautiful day. The bone spears were resting against the sofas because nobody felt safe enough to give them up yet. She slid off the sofa carefully to not wake Ashley who rolled onto her back where Laura had just been sitting. Her stomach gave her another dose of morning pain so she went to the refrigerator and drank a glass of water. Immediately, her stomach felt better. She sat at the kitchen table and watched the wind blow the trees around in harmony.

Katie woke. Her eyes opened into the brightening room. She stretched out her legs and rubbed the sleep out of her eyes. It felt refreshing to be relaxed for the first time since being here, but the relentless danger they had been through hadn't exited her life yet. She reasoned that maybe it never would anyway.

Katie moved and felt a painful sting from the wound on her right side. She rubbed it lightly and her side felt better. The healing treatment administered by the Grey Doctors the night before had been excellent. She didn't know what all they had done but she was already healing fast. But of course, she knew it would be. It was otherworldly.

Her big lug of a boyfriend was asleep next to her with his head resting on her shoulder. Travis had been so sweet throughout the night with his incessant apologizing for stabbing her when he tried to save her from the Illucii. She felt she hadn't appreciated his efforts at the time but that was because she'd been in pain. Katie loved that he was protecting her, and now after it was over, thought he was more wonderful than before in doing so. She thought he just needed to work on his aim some more.

Katie didn't want to wake him but when she moved her shoulder Travis's head fell down her arm and he came awake. He looked up at her and smiled. Travis was thrilled that his girlfriend was alive and that he was alive with her. Especially after his mistake of stabbing her. Guilt still hung heavily on his heart and probably always would.

They kissed and Katie got up and went to the kitchen. After sharing a smile with Laura, she came back with three glasses of water, put one down on the table next to Ashley, handed one to Travis, and she and her boyfriend drank their morning sickness away.

While Katie walked over to the front window, Travis glanced over at Ashley lying on the sofa and saw her eyes were open. She was awake. He filled with empathy for her and left her alone to lie there with her thoughts. Travis didn't know what he could say to make her feel better anyway. He walked over to Katie.

"Someone will have to take care of her," whispered Travis.

Katie nodded. "We will."

The morning passed by calmly and the group embraced the tranquility of the moment. It was by no means paradise but it was the closest thing to it since living here. No storms passed through from their inside weather. There were no pungent smells from the Illucii. The only shadows they saw were from the swaying of the trees in a vivid scenic day. It would still take a while for the group to adjust but they were slowly getting better.

They ate their lunches, spent some time on the porch, and by early afternoon had settled down lazily around the house. Nobody felt comfortable to venture out into the yard. Travis and Katie were sitting at the kitchen table. Ashley sat on the living room floor with her doll and looked out the window to the west.

Laura decided to get some air and went outside and leaned on the porch railing. The breeze blew her hair around in tangles and she brushed it out with her fingers. Then there was a flash from the watery wall and the doorway opened and the Female stepped through the wall. The light behind silhouetted her body as if she had come from another dimension. In a way, Laura thought she had. The Female gracefully walked through the yard toward the house giving her a walking-on-water effect. Her mane of hair waved in the wind giving her a nice human touch. The Female walked up to the house and stood in front of the porch. Laura felt a warm friendly emotion come over her body. Inside the kitchen, Travis and Katie were staring out the window in amazement. They walked onto the porch and stood behind Laura. Ashley followed them out on the porch too. They hadn't been this close to her before. The three of them had never seen Goldilocks face to face.

You did very well Laura.

"Thanks."

I was in your mind all along but didn't want to make my presence known in case the Illucii might detect me. The plan went well.

"We lost one."

I'm sorry about the mother.

Sadness flowed among them from the Female.

"So are we."

She was brave.

"We call that the human spirit."

It's the nature of the universe.

Travis, Katie, and Ashley, standing behind Laura, felt the messages from the Female too.

You're not out of danger yet. We believe the Illucii didn't attack you because of the virus on your leg. It didn't want to ingest that.

The others behind Laura all exchanged glances of surprise. None of them had known about the virus.

"So in a weird way it saved my life?"

Yes. From the Illucii. We need to address what's on your leg now.

"What is on my leg?"

It's a virus caused by the gamma rays left over in the atmosphere. To the best of our knowledge you were exposed to it when I gave you a tour of the zoo.

"But we were in that bubble."

Yes. Something went wrong. It wasn't meant to happen. I'm very sorry for this.

Laura felt sympathy fill her from the Female. The group could feel it too. "I understand," said Laura.

We believe the best course of action is to return you to your home planet.

Everyone was stunned.

The virus feeds off the other gamma rays in the atmosphere. That's how it stays strong. Separating you from the gamma rays' pollution will essentially cut off its life source of survival and the virus should die on your leg and you will be safe. It saddens me to say this. You will have to go. I will miss you.

Laura was elated! She was getting out of this place. The Female sensed it.

It was difficult but I got the Masters to agree. They realized this was the only way.

Laura knew that meant the Yellow and the Red.

"When?"

Now.

Laura was shocked! This was over. Excitement surged through her body. Travis and Katie's mouths dropped and they looked at each other. Ashley hugged Laura. She rubbed the top of Ashley's head.

"How?"

We'll leave in one of our specialized spaceships. This one is different from the medical exploratory ship that you were on before. This one is shaped with different dimensions for faster speed. We'll travel through a passageway of wormholes. There is one we have connected to your planet. The Earth.

Laura looked down and contemplated everything. She'd been here with strangers and many who had died. They were now her friends. Her survivor friends. They'd been through a lot together and did it primarily on their own. Her eyes started to water from a rush of emotions that ran through her. They ranged from sadness to happiness and she didn't know how to process it. She turned and looked at Travis, Katie, Ashley, and then back to the Female. "What about my friends?"

Disappointment flowed into their bodies from the Female.

I'm sorry but the Masters won't allow it.

"Will they get to go home?"

There was more disappointment.

I don't know that answer. But I will be here.

Before anyone could object, the wind blew, and mixed with a gentle mind strike from the Female, whipped around to create a sense of calm and passiveness among them.

Travis and Katie held hands.

"I'm gonna miss you, Laura," said Ashley. She started to cry.

"I'll miss you, too." Laura hugged her.

Time to go.

Laura turned and hugged Katie and Travis. "We've been through a lot together," she said. "I'll contact your family and let them know you're okay."

"Don't let anyone forget us," said Katie.

"They'll never believe you," said Travis.

"Please try," said Katie. "Remember the stuff we told you that only our families would know. They'll know it's us and believe you then."

"I will," said Laura. "They will know."

"God," said Travis. "I hope so."

Ashley held up her doll to Laura. "Please take Molly back with you. She has been through a lot and wants to go home."

Laura cupped Ashley's hands and held them. "Are you sure?" To Laura this represented something more than a little girl giving up her favorite toy. It was Ashley maturing a bit. She had been through so much already and was moving beyond the behavior of a normal seven-year-old. Laura thought that was too much too fast and that Ashley would need the doll with her here in the zoo. "But I think you should keep Molly. She needs you. Molly will continue to be your friend here."

Ashley thought about it. She smiled and hugged Molly. Then she hugged Laura again who hugged her back.

Time to go.

"Bye."

"Bye," Travis and Katie said.

Ashley hugged Laura one more time before Laura turned and followed the Female through the yard. Right before they stepped through the opening in the wall, Laura took a final look back at the house and her friends that she wouldn't see again. Tears streaked down her cheeks. She missed them already and hoped that never seeing them again wouldn't come to be. However, Laura also had feelings of guilt. She felt bad that they were kept back trapped on this planet and she got to leave. Yet, she couldn't deny that within herself she was incredibly happy to be going. It made her feel bad because it was selfish to feel that way and at the same time Laura knew it was also natural for her to have these feelings. Any person would. Any human would. It's a human survival instinct and a person does have the right to self-preservation. She still felt bad just the same. It was a form of survivor's guilt. A survivor's guilt for living through the horror of the compound. Laura took in the final scene for her own memory. The house. The yard. The trees. And her three remaining friends.

Ashley stood between Travis and Katie who had their arms around her. They looked like a modern day young family. Travis and Katie were her parents now. They waved to Laura.

Laura gave a final wave good-bye and stepped through the watery wall and out of the compound.

CHAPTER 119

Life in the compound had changed into a mundane boring pace. The days went by lazily with no major events except for more humiliating visits by the Grey Masters and the Grey children. The wall would open with a flash and they would go out on the porch and stand around. The Grey children would point at them. Their fingers were like little mental prods on their brains. Then the Grey exploratory class would go away, the wall would seal up, and life would resume to normal. Travis, Katie, and Ashley had determined that compared to being hunted and killed by shadowy alien creatures that it wasn't so bad in that regard. After the passing of time the three remaining survivors became immune to it. They even started to joke about it and would show some bizarre behavior like jumping and hopping around, or acting out scenes from movies, to entertain the Grey children on their visits. They had no idea what the Greys thought in return. They never communicated with them and only pointed their skinny little fingers. As days turned into weeks the three of them didn't care anymore.

They had started to exercise by doing push-ups, sit-ups, and jogging to keep in shape. Most of this was done to fight off boredom and have something to do. Interestingly, nobody had gained weight, which led them to believe that their fake food was absent of much fat or excessive calorie intake. The Greys kept them well supplied with food. They even created some new drinks for them like an artificial coffee and orange juice. Ashley was really happy about the fake orange juice and grew to like it more than the real thing.

Travis and Katie invented some games with Ashley to play. Some of them were competitive with a lot of running and others were just to make their minds think harder. They also took on the serious roles of being teachers for Ashley and did their best to teach her in school subjects such as English and Math. Originally, they had no supplies, but after asking the Greys they were provided with some artificial paper and pencils to help them teach. The controlled weather of the compound still provided some excitement from time to time. Storms would roll in periodically and lightning would still go crazy at times. One day their house was struck and the Greys had to come and do house repair. However, the weather was doing better inside which meant the Greys had managed to control it better.

Days passed by and they couldn't remember how long it had been since the fight to survive against the Illucii. A strong bond had developed between Travis, Katie, and Ashley. They took long walks in the compound among the trees behaving more and more like a family. All they had was each other.

One evening when the sky was golden with a sunset they all gathered out on the porch to enjoy the evening. The wind blew slightly and brushed the hairs of their skin. Travis and Katie sat on the front steps laughing about the television shows they liked to watch. Ashley walked over to the end of the porch and stared out west at the setting sun. In an hour, the roof of the compound would open and it would be replaced by the stars and moons of this planet. The wind ruffled her hair and she looked at the trees. Suddenly, Ashley thought she smelled the rank smell and it was gone. Then the leaves of the trees chattered as the breeze blew a little harder and hidden inside the wind Ashley thought she heard her mother's voice call her name.

CHAPTER 120

The Triangle spacecraft came out of its wormhole on the dark side of the Earth that faced away from the sun. It traveled in the void of space for a while towards the planet until it started passing satellites and other space debris before the craft disappeared. It reappeared over the Pacific Ocean, having used a dimensional jump to avoid the entry into Earth's atmosphere, and headed in a northeastern direction. The night was clear and the full moon hung in the sky casting white light across this side of the world. The craft shifted west, avoiding a typhoon, and banked over some tropical islands, heading towards the West Coast of the United States. It traveled silently over some boats and up the coast line, staying perfectly hidden in the night, before it crossed over land in California and headed east.

Deep inside the mountain bunker of NORAD in Colorado, the United States Air Force was already on high alert, and tracking the unidentified moving object. US Air Force personnel sat in front of their controls with blinking lights monitoring the skies above the Northern Hemisphere. The Air Force commander gave the order to scramble the fighters.

Engines blasted fire and two F-22 Raptors soared into the night sky in pursuit of the moving object. They dipped to the right, turned south, cranked up to over 2,000 miles an hour and headed straight on an intercept course at Mach 2 speed.

The craft continued to silently move east passing over highways and small towns that slept quietly in the night. It flew over a campground with burning fires and campers who never suspected a thing. For them it was a beautiful summer night under the stars. Then the jets roared high above and the campers looked up in awe for planes that were already gone. Only the distant echo of their engines shook the night air.

The Triangle craft kept on a steady course at a moderate speed. The Raptors followed from high above to observe the flying object. The moon assisted the fighters by casting its light down over the land and making it easier for the pilots to see that it was a perfectly shaped triad with a sleek surface. It left no contrail behind it. They identified the object as the same craft that had been tracked many times before.

The Raptors descended and flew up behind and locked in on it for a missile launch. The first pilot was in communication with his control and the green light was given to shoot it down. The first Raptor locked on with its weapon's system. The Triangle went faster. The pilot's thumb moved to press down on the fire button.

The Triangle disappeared.

The pilot didn't fire. Both fighters kept their course. The Triangle reappeared on their left in the north. The fighters turned left and locked on. In a blink the Triangle disappeared again. The Raptors stayed steady and waited. A few seconds ticked by. Then the Triangle reappeared on their right to the south. The fighters flew back to the right and the first fighter quickly locked on and fired. The missile streaked toward the craft with a burning tail that curved behind it like a snake. Moonlight glistened off the Triangle as it held its course. The missile shot to destroy the alien spacecraft hit nothing but empty air. The Triangle had vanished again. The pilot communicated back to his command what was happening. His commander issued orders to make sure to shoot it down.

The fighters waited. It wasn't long and the Triangle popped up in front of them. The second Raptor on the right fired. Its missile burst forth like a blazing comet and contained a hunger to destroy the alien craft. Closer and closer it got before the missile cut through air where the alien craft had been seconds before and missed. Its rocket tail could be seen flying off into the night. The Triangle materialized to their north again. Immediately the Raptor on the left fired. The missile barreled down at the craft. Both pilots hoped the quick attack would catch it vulnerable. They watched it tear a path towards the Triangle and just when there should have been an explosion there wasn't. The missile was a fading smear of fire in the night sky going away from them. The Triangle had evaded their attacks again in what was like an aerial sidestep. An airborne move that was done with as much ease as it was done safely. The pilots had no explanation for what they just saw.

The Triangle was above them on the horizon now. Then it was below them. And it bounced between their south and north again. It was jumping around. The fighters held their course waiting to get another lock on it but the alien craft was too fast. Then the command sent orders to stand down and return to base. The Raptors turned around and flew off into the night.

The Triangle stopped jumping and proceeded east on its original course.

Across the military command frequencies, a new command was issued.

"Mars five. Mars five. Initiate."

CHAPTER 121

A sonic boom shook the night sky of the Midwest and a black plane flew east at five times the speed of sound. The USAF Mars Fighter engine thrust with a systematic rumbling pulse that gave the plane a sound as if it was breathing. Some families in towns far below stirred awake in their beds, thinking they were experiencing an earthquake, by the slight rattling of the windows in their houses. Left behind in its wake, was a silvery ring-shaped contrail, that could be seen in the moonlight. The Mars was triangular and thin for aerodynamic maximum performance in hypersonic flight. It possessed twin tails on both wings and sliced through the atmosphere with very limited air resistance. To one observer on the ground, who thought he saw it pass in front of the moon, while walking his dog: It looked like a black wedge in the night.

At Mach 5 speed the Mars flew straight up on the Triangle from behind, slowed down, and locked in its own laser system. The pilot already had the go-ahead from his command. There was a boom and the Mars's electrolaser shot a plasma beam at the Triangle. The laser splintered the air around it, superheated the atmosphere to form a tunnel for the beam to shoot through, and hiss down to destroy the alien craft. It only took a second....

And in the next second the plasma laser pierced through the open air and didn't hit a thing. The Triangle had vanished into thin air again. It reappeared next to the Mars on its right side. The pilot arced his plane to his left, flew north but turned west, and came back around behind the alien craft. The Triangle didn't change its course. It didn't vary its speed. The pilot locked in the laser system and again a plasma laser tore off in the night. Before the pilot could see the laser miss he could see that the Triangle was gone.

The pilot wasn't frustrated for he, and the Air Force, had expected this. The pilot radioed in to command what had transpired and what his next course of action would be. On the screen in front of him he saw the Triangle was now directly behind his plane. Instantly, he yanked the plane's joystick and flew in a southerly direction to his right, releasing the rumbling pulse of the Mars that reverberated over the sky, and the black wedge circled around to flank the alien spacecraft. Again, the triangular alien craft didn't counter in any way the Mars's movements.

The pilot flew up on it and this time he had a different strategy. Through all this they had kept on an easterly course. The alien craft obviously had a destination. He was going to fire a spread of lasers and try to catch it when it reappeared again. The Triangle might come back into one of the lasers. The pilot had noticed some passenger jetliners flying in their airspace, but at different altitudes, and he didn't want to risk shooting one of them down. He brought the Mars around and up behind the Triangle. Instead of locking on with his laser guidance system, he fired an array of lasers spanning the horizon, laying out a net of plasma to catch the alien craft. As expected the Triangle vanished. What wasn't expected was that it didn't rematerialize. The lasers shot off into the night sky but there was no Triangle. It didn't come back. The pilot looked as his instruments. They talked back to him but not with a location on the alien craft. He used his keen vision to look for it in the night sky but didn't see it. He could feel tension start to build up inside him. He kept the black wedge flying east across the Great Plains.

Then the target appeared on his screen in front of him. The pilot looked up through the Mars's cockpit glass. The Triangle was above him. The pilot swallowed hard. Then the Triangle disappeared and appeared miles ahead. Vanished. Reappeared even farther ahead. The

Triangle disappeared out of sight. The pilot radioed back to command and they told him to return to base. The Mars reversed its course and with a boom was gone over the night sky.

CHAPTER 122

The Triangle's dimensional jump was too advanced for human technology. It was a technology the Greys' science had long ago developed. They had created the ability to disappear from one dimension into another and then reappear again. The Greys used their dimensional jump to stay one step ahead of humans on Earth.

CHAPTER 123

The Triangular craft quietly flew in low over the trees and stopped above the front yard of a house. Laura's parents' house. The house she grew up in. The place where the Greys had taken Laura. The Triangle hummed and three lights shown around a bluish white light on the bottom of the ship. A beam of light shot down to the ground from underneath the center of the craft. Laura was in the light. The light stopped, the Triangle went dark, and quietly drifted off to the south under the cover of night.

Laura remained.

Laura stood in her yard struggling to comprehend where she was. And then she knew. She was back where it had all begun. Where they had first stolen her. Laura took a step but staggered and went down to one knee. She hadn't been on Earth for a while and needed to adjust to its gravity. *This will probably take some time*, she thought.

Laura pulled her pant leg up and already the black and purple virus was starting to dissipate and her leg was turning white again. She felt dazed but that made her feel better already.

Laura heard a squeaking noise. She stood up and looked at the house. Nobody was home. The noise triggered her memories of growing up. The chair on the porch was rocking back and forth. She knew the energy from the craft had caused it to rock. The squeaking started to slow and then stopped altogether. She was home.

Laura looked around. It was a cool summer night with a clear sky and all the stars were out showing off how pretty they were. She took an extra look at them knowing she'd been out there. Finally, a peaceful wind blew along and the trees danced a little within it. That was more magic that added to the serene night that it was.

Laura took one more look around and began to walk to the house. As she stepped onto the porch, Laura stopped. In the back of her mind, she felt someone speak to her. Three words.

Laura. Be brave.

The End

Made in the USA
Lexington, KY
10 June 2018